FRANK  BEEN MORE UNIMPRESSED ... SIGHT OF ... E DOOR.

Mos ... g resemblance to a weasel some joker shoved ... ie was trying to cultivate a mustache, but his five o'clock shadow ... ck enough that it throttled any attempt at more refined facial hair. He didn't look great, either. Dark circles bruised the undersides of his brown eyes. Moss started when he took Frank in, as though he was surprised to see him.

Moss was the source of that nervous gasoline scent, and close up it caught more like the wrong side of a bender. Whatever dime-store cologne he'd sloshed over the sweat was losing the fight. That nervousness poked the wolf. The little man smelled like *prey*.

PRAISE FOR MOONLIGHT SPECIAL

Everything in *Moonlight Special* is delivered with the force of a prizefighter's haymaker, down to the last line. // Robinson takes us nose first into the scents and smells of the City of Devils, all the grit and grime, the nightclub's swirling smoke, orange blossoms in the hills outside of town, now and then a hint of boudoir. And blood. — A. J. Sikes, author of the *Redemption* trilogy

Robinson's writing is // elegantly grim and moody, sexy and inviting, rich and edgy. Naturally, I can't top his own wording: "honey drizzled on barbed wire." Fine-tuned, not a word wasted, until every moment, every understated look, every word, and most importantly, every character *bleeds*. // Justin Robinson is a master class writer that's as skilled as he is imaginative and soulful, making him the perfect storyteller. — Julie Hutchings, author of *The Harpy* trilogy and the *Vampires of Fate* series

PRAISE FOR *UNWITCH HUNT*

With this fun fantasy, Robinson expands the world of his *City of Devils* series... // Robinson leavens the mystery with a lot of humor // and a charming heroine. This adventure is sure to delight with its embrace of being oneself whether others accept it or not. — *Publishers Weekly*

Justin Robinson has yet again sent one sailing out of the park, over the stands, and somewhere into the neighboring county. — A. J. Sikes, author of the *Redemption* trilogy

PRAISE FOR *A STITCH IN CRIME*

Robinson's tale is a treasure trove of monstrous delights and, despite Jane's gruesome origins, she proves an endearing lead. With its heady blend of noir and campy horror, this rollicking adventure doesn't disappoint. — *Publishers Weekly*

PRAISE FOR *WOLFMAN CONFIDENTIAL*

Robinson's writing is a delightful cross between H.P. Lovecraft and Raymond Chandler, and it revels in its oddities and dark tones. His eye for detail and entertaining side characters (a cornucopia of monsters that have overrun L.A. and often speak in tongue-in-cheek one-liners) create a delightfully rich atmosphere that the reader can plunge into. — *Publishers Weekly*

PRAISE FOR *FIFTY FEET OF TROUBLE*

Once again, Justin Robinson provides an engaging and entertaining romp through the world of noir Los Angeles post-monster war. He's hilarious, his characters are endearing and boy, can he weave a mystery. — Ashley Perkins, *Game Vortexer*

PRAISE FOR CITY OF DEVILS

Robinson crafts a uniquely interesting world that is sure to please horror, science fiction, and mystery fans alike. — *Minneapolis Books Examiner*

MOONLIGHT SPECIAL

JUSTIN ROBINSON

Candlemark & Gleam

For information, address
Candlemark & Gleam LLC
38 Rice St. #2, Cambridge, MA 02140
eloi@candlemarkandgleam.com

Library of Congress Cataloging-in-Publication Data
In Progress

ISBNs: 978-1-952456-22-0 (paperback), 978-1-952456-23-7 (ebook)

Cover art and design by Athena Andreadis and Kate Sullivan

Editor: Athena Andreadis

www.candlemarkandgleam.com

For the Owl and the Turtle

ONE

The viscous puddle in the middle of the Persian rug used to be a gremlin. To the casual eye, say that of a patrol wolf on his first day in uniform, it might look like the remnants of a late-night meal of raw possum that a drunken ogre had upchucked on the way to the commode. It did have a half-digested look about it, with the green and yellow fluids caking on the threads of the rug and the bones gone all rubbery. Detective Frank Wolfman had seen more than one gremlin buy it this way, so he knew what he was taking in even before the fresh-faced kid who looked like he hadn't seen his first full moon told Frank where the ghoul shat in the graveyard.

"Name's..." The kid paused. Frank didn't blame him. Of all the hinky handles going around, gremlins had the hinkiest. "Lord High Decoratorius, Maker of Things and Breaker of Illusions. Says here, most people knew him as 'Ducktail.'"

Frank grunted. They got pretty lucky, all told, what with gremlins' habit of growing a little signature bit of hair. Kept folks from stumbling over those godawful names like something out of a Flash Gordon serial. Didn't take a detective with Frank's years to know exactly what had happened to Ducktail. Fact was, the east-facing window was wide open, and had it been morning, the sun would be making the rapidly drying remains glisten like fresh ambergris. A motion picture of the crime couldn't have told Frank more.

"Time of death was—"

"This morning," Frank said.

"Uh, yeah. That's right."

Frank nodded to himself and checked the curtains. The pull was a gold braided rope, making the window resemble a movie screen. He fished in his pocket for a pen, then lifted the cord with that, squinting at it. It glittered, like whoever made it had worked real gold dust into the thread.

"We'll dust it for prints," the rookie said.

Frank nearly laughed. Prints weren't something you found all the time anymore. Or even most of the time. Half the monsters out there didn't leave them, either for lack of fingers or some other cockamamie reason. Prints would still put away meatsticks, though—and if you looked hard enough, there was usually a meatstick involved somehow. If not a meatstick, then a zombie. That's who they were supposed to pop for these crimes, and the reason they all still packed lead in their heaters.

Still, something didn't ring quite right here. Frank stared at the cord. Specifically, at a silvery crust that ran up it in short streaks. Wasn't much of it, but enough that he couldn't stop staring. He gave it a sniff; smelled like a hard rain. He dropped the cord.

"Who else was here?" Frank growled at the kid.

"Huh? Oh, let's see. The housekeeper. She's a haunt-in. We have her over in the kitchen. We think there was one more, though."

"One more?"

"Follow me, Detective."

Frank followed the kid out into the front hall, then up the stairs. He wished that these rookies would just spit it out, but sometimes they ran into something they couldn't quite put into the neat and clean boxes of "upstanding citizen" and "punk killer." Or maybe they just loved a little bit of drama. They *were* in Hollywood, after all.

The place even *looked* like a gremlin's flop: a big old Victorian pressed flush up against Mount Lee. From the roof, Ducktail could have seen the *Hollywoodland* sign launch itself into the air every few hours, shooting off enough fireworks to make it seem like D-Day. It was quite a sight; Los Angeles was famous for it. Other than that, the house was as dark as a cave, with drapes that smothered every bit of light and warmth that got within spitting distance. Everything was low, too; furnished with a two-foot-tall inhabitant in mind. Meant Frank kept barking his shins on end tables at perfect shin-barking height, and he'd have to stoop uncomfortably to take a gander at all the pictures. The upper parts of the walls were decorated with expansive scenes of the desert at night. Pretty in the sort of way you didn't have to look at them all the time. Frank liked that.

The rookie led Frank through a half-open door. Heavy locks, all on the outside and bolted firmly to the wood, stood open. Frank didn't have to look to know what was in there, but he did anyway. The room was likely the smallest in the house; he hadn't done a comparison, but these usually were. The one window was barred with thick iron. Most of the room was taken up by a big, square cage, like something Barnum would have used to move a tiger. Inside was a fairly clean bedroll and a bucket that stank exactly like a bucket in that situation was supposed to.

"Guess it happened before he cleaned the bucket," Frank observed.

"What's this, sir?"

Frank looked at the kid for the first time. *Really* looked. He could have come directly from a cornfield. Blue eyes, blond hair, a body for the gridiron. His face was honest and guileless and in the next couple years he was going to burn every last bit of that out.

"Nursery," Frank said. Newfangled tradition with monsters. He'd never had one, but he was a rougher generation, already riding off into the sunset.

"Where's the crib?"

"Not that kinda nursery, kid. These days, you get monsters who want the whole experience. They got someone in mind, but they want to raise 'em first. They take 'em, put 'em on ice in one of these nurseries, then change 'em when they're good and ready."

"That's not illegal?"

Frank shrugged. "Search me. Alls I know is, good luck getting the DA to prosecute." He nudged the cage door. It creaked wide open.

"The cage was empty when we got here."

"I figured. We know who was in it?" He poked his head in, sniffing first the bars, then the bedroll. Sweat, mostly, and enough of it that if he smelled the same sweat again, he'd know it.

"Sure do. Neighbor called in a half-naked meatstick prowling around their property. We arrested him. He's waiting for you at the station."

Frank nodded. Easy enough to put together. The kind of case the LAPD ran on. Some monster was trying to give an ungrateful human the good life, and that human turned it around, melted him with the sun. Wouldn't be the first time, and Frank had solved cases like that. This time, though...this time something smelled off.

"Hey, Detective. You think we got him?"

"Got who?"

The kid looked around, like saying the words would summon the thing that went bump in the night. "The Monster Slayer."

Frank snorted. "Monster Slayer's a myth, kid. Press made him up to sell papers. Now where's this housekeeper?"

The kid's shoulders slumped. Everybody and his uncle wanted a piece of that case, but fairytales didn't get hauled before a judge. "She's down in the kitchen," he mumbled.

The kitchen was the one place that didn't have blackout curtains on the windows. Frank glanced outside and saw why: a canopy, formed from the branches of trees with multicolored sheets bridging the gaps. Blocking the sun in style. The backyard was an oasis, with multilevel pools, waterfalls over glistening rocks, and ferns that looked positively prehistoric. Lawn furniture, all done up in gold, shimmered by the pool.

A hiss that sounded like it was pulled from the neck of a cheesed-off dinosaur made Frank jump back like a startled cat. On the other side of the glass door leading out to the patio, a white bird beat its gigantic wings against the window, desperate to commit a second homicide in the place.

Its black-and-orange bill was open, hissing like a cobra Frank owed money to. Frank had been in the presence of things that wanted him dead more than a few times, but nothing had ever wanted it more than this bird. It pecked the glass with its massive bill and Frank had a vision of the whole thing shattering and that monster bird making good on its threat. He halfway reached for the gat under his arm—lead was good for birds too, if he remembered right.

"Don't be afraid." The voice was a sepulchral moan, and Frank turned to find a ghost floating in the kitchen. Her throat was cut, and she appeared to be bleeding spiders. Her eyes were haunted by the atrocities she'd seen in Hell. Frank sighed in relief. "She can't get in."

Frank jerked a thumb over his shoulder at the bird that was still entertaining fantasies of carnage. "What is that, a goose?"

"A swan," said the ghost. "My employer's pet. Meanest thing you will ever meet on either side of the veil."

"Why did he keep it?"

"He was a gremlin."

Frank shrugged. "Yeah, that adds up." The ghost smelled a lot like ghosts tend to: mist hovering over a graveyard. "Name?"

"Mourning Fogg," the ghost said, and spelled it.

"All right, Ms. Fogg. I need you to tell me everything that happened."

TWO

Frank let the ghost's statement rattle around in his attic like a phantom who just found where they kept the chandeliers. Fogg was a transplant from St. Louis, coming west with nothing but dreams and a small box filled with her mortal remains. Wanted to be a set decorator and wound up as a gremlin's maid. Just another Tinseltown dream turned sour in the harsh light of day.

He was still gathering cobwebs when he stepped out of the dead gremlin's house onto the sleepy Hollywood street. It was the middle of October in the City of Devils, meaning it was a little chillier and a little drier than the months around it but was otherwise unrecognizable as being distinct from the rest of the year.

"Detective?"

Frank looked around, momentarily unable to figure out where the voice was coming from. It was silky and rich, the kind of voice that should be on a radio. The crawling eye slithering up the sidewalk solved that mystery. They always had voices that should be introducing jazz standards or advising exhausted armies to surrender.

This one was dressed more than most, with a gray-checked collar and a small cape right under where her tentacles and eyeball met. The eye, though a couple feet across, was a fetching shade of green, complete with long, fake eyelashes. She was the closest thing to a cartoon Frank had ever seen.

"What?" he growled at her.

"Pearl Friday, *Los Angeles Minion*."

Frank's grunt of disgust could have curdled milk. "Yeah, I know who you are."

"I want to talk to you about the murder of Lord High Decoratorius."

"No comment."

"Detective Wolfman, isn't it?" she asked.

Frank stopped. "What do you want, Friday?"

"People deserve to know what's happening in their community."

"And you aim to tell 'em."

"That's why I'm here."

"Then what are you doing working for the *Minion*?"

"Is that your way of telling me *No comment*?" she asked.

"Chops like that, you could be a detective."

"I thought all it took to be a detective was pointing at the nearest human."

"A bleeding heart, is that it?"

The edge of a word tickled Frank's ear, but Friday swallowed it before she gave it voice. "We got off on the wrong foot. I just want to know if you have any suspects. A pillar of the community murdered, it helps to know the brave detectives of the LAPD are getting their man."

"Which makes me wonder how you got here so fast."

"Don't be naïve. It doesn't suit you."

Frank had to admit, she kind of had a point there. Any reporter on the crime beat worth the salt would be paying off somebody at the station. "Fair enough," he grunted. "What do you know about this..." he waved at the dead gremlin's house. Saying the name made him feel ridiculous.

"You'll talk to me?"

"Yeah, yeah. You know something?"

"Reputation, mostly. You read the gossip columns?"

"Do I look like I read the gossip columns?"

"No, but in a town like this one, petty gossip can be a motive as sharp as a blade, you know? Decoratorius doesn't have the best reputation, if you follow me."

"Find me a gremlin that does."

"More than most. He was a set decorator on a lot of big pictures. Good enough at the job that no one minded he was..." She paused as one crimson tentacle plucked a notebook from the pocket of her cape. She delicately turned the pages, and read, "...a scaly tyrant."

"Who called him that?"

"If you read the gossip pages, you'd know that. You got someone or not?"

"Not."

"So, what do you say, detective? Do I have a friend on the force?"

Frank fixed her with his full attention for the first time since the conversation began. "Way I look at it, you don't need a friend. You write whatever you're gonna write. I can't stop you. Only ones who can have mansions on Mulholland and offices with doors and such. Ask them who your friends are and let me do my job." He stalked for his car. Maybe a year or two ago, the wolf would be snarling under the surface, ready to be let off the leash. Not now. He was already too tired. Friday was a dime a dozen, and she had to know it.

Friday called after him: "We're all just trying to do our jobs, detective."

"If you figure out what that is, let me know," Frank muttered as he got into his car.

THREE

In the old days, the kid sitting on the other side of the table would have been in a zoot suit. Nowadays, meatsticks wore everything as tight as they could make it. Just a way to tease monsters, so the locker room said. Not that the kid was much to look at, but Frank didn't spend much of his time looking. A lot of monsters, all they wanted to do was make more of themselves. Frank figured he had enough trouble just living with himself, and didn't see the point in crowding the arena.

According to the file, the kid was Eduardo Carias of Watts. Eighteen years old, and looked either two years younger or ten years older depending on how the light hit him. He was still wearing what they found him in—namely a soiled undershirt and some jeans that smelled like they'd been run over six or seven times. No shoes. Carias was slumped in a chair, one hand cuffed to the table, and he just let it hang there like old laundry. He stared at Frank with eyes that the detective had seen on kids in France near the end of the war. They were hungry, hollowed out, holding pain they couldn't shake. Hell of a thing, those eyes.

"Tell me if this sounds right to you," Frank said. "Gremlin catches you out after dark. Maybe you lost track of time, maybe you were with a girl. Doesn't really matter. He catches you, zaps you with some cockamamie ray gun, and throws you in that cage. He keeps you a couple three days, teaching you what it means to be a green two-foot-tall menace to public safety, and somewhere along the road, he drops his guard. Just enough. You pick the lock with something he dropped or you smuggled in, then you show him the sunrise. That about the size of it?"

Eduardo Carias stared at Frank. Then, finally: "I don't know how to pick a lock."

"Sure, kid." Every meatstick knew how to pick a lock. If they didn't before the Night War, they sure as hell learned during. "I got the rest of it pat, though, didn't I?"

"The ghost let me out."

"The ghost?"

"Yeah, the glitch had a spook in the house." Frank let the racist terms slide. He'd used them from time to time himself, and he didn't feel right telling the meatstick to clean up his act. "She was a maid or something, I think."

Frank made a show of looking for the ghost's name. He didn't have to; it was already in his head. "Mourning Fogg, right. You're saying she let you out of the cell? Why would she do that?"

"Ask her," Carias sulked. Frank wasn't fond of the kid's attitude. Didn't change what had to be done, but he could have put a happier face on it.

"I'm asking *you*. Tell me exactly what happened."

"It was in the middle of the morning. I don't know, an hour after she brought me breakfast, maybe. It's hard to tell time in the cell. No clocks, just that one window. Then the door opens. I don't know what's going on, since it's daytime and the glitch never came in until nighttime. She's scared—and I mean *panicked*. Like you don't see a ghost. She opens up the cage and tells me to run. Don't need to tell me twice. I legged it out the back."

"The back. Bird didn't jump you?"

"Bird?"

"Yeah, he had a swan. Real mean bastard."

Carias frowned, then nodded slowly. "Yeah, saw it paddlin' around one of the pools. Didn't pay me no mind."

Frank wasn't sure what to make of that, so he just moved on. "On the way out of the house, you see anything else?"

"Why would I look?" the kid said with a huff. "Got out as fast as I could."

"Why didn't you go home?"

"All the way across town, from Hollywood to Watts, no money, no shoes?"

Frank had to admit, that wouldn't be easy. "Okay, so what then?"

"I was sitting in the bushes when the wolves rolled up."

Frank stood up. "So you didn't do anything to the gremlin?"

"Nope. Never touched him."

"You still haven't asked me to let you go. An innocent man does that."

The kid snorted. "You ain't gonna let me go. A monster's dead, you got a human. Just thought maybe you should hear my story before you feed me to the judge."

Carias kept staring at Frank with those hollowed-out eyes. It was the detective who looked away first. Wasn't like Eduardo Carias was wrong. This was exactly the kind of case that was supposed to be a gift. Easiest thing in the world for a wolf to close. It was like one of those Wally Wolfman cartoons, and Frank had his very own Marty Meatstick. He shook his head, leaving the room and shutting the door.

Frank walked back into the bullpen of Northeast Precinct. One of the busiest in town, it butted right up against the areas of Hollywood that belonged to the Sheriff's Department. The two packs had momentarily set aside jurisdictional disputes to mop up all the dead goblins and zombies in that gang war. The killing had slowed down—way down—since last Christmas, even if everyone in Hollywood was on Santa's naughty list.

Frank stopped by the kitchen on his way back to his desk. He needed coffee. Well, truth was, he needed something a hell of a lot stronger than coffee, but he had enough of a reputation without walking around a station filled with wolves reeking of hooch. The coffeemaker was one of the new ones designed by a mad scientist, so it had a radioactive sticker on the side.

Frank wasn't sure if he should be worried or not. Or more worried than he was, at least.

He poured himself a cup, then threw in some milk from the fridge. He took a sip and spat it out. Sour. Pulling the milk back out, he gave it a sniff and recoiled. Smelled like week-old yogurt that had been baking in the sun. *How the hell does a station of wolves not know when the milk's turned?* Frank scowled and shoved the milk back in the icebox. Someone else could deal with it. He dumped the paper cup into the trash.

Empty-handed, Frank returned to his desk. At least, there was allegedly a desk under all that paper. He thought that maybe he should excavate the area, but he'd have to work up to it. Only one section was clear, carved out around a picture of a beautiful woman, professionally shot and lit, looking winsomely over her shoulder. They called those head shots. Actresses had them, used them like resumes. His fingers ran over it one more time, and the name was picked out on a marquee, the way it never had been in her life. Sylvia Screen.

"Hey, Frank?"

He looked up. The speaker was Bud Hound, Frank's old partner. They'd been policing Sunset Boulevard together when the gang war was just beginning to heat up. Bud was young, athletic, and good with a heater, so he was destined for bigger and better things. Only right at that moment, he didn't look better. The bags under his eyes had bags.

"What can I do for you, Bud?"

Bud gave a look around, not quite at the people milling or the walls beyond them, but both at the same time and neither. "Hey, partner, whaddyasay we get a drink?"

Frank stared at his desk. The dead glitch would keep and the meatstick could cool his heels in lockup. "You're buying," he told Bud as he stood up.

"Least some things never change," Bud said, but the humor was washed out, like old paint.

FOUR

Bud drove and didn't speak a word on the way. Frank let him stew. Had to be something big; Bud was usually a talker. Back when they'd shared a car, his partner was always the one flapping his gums about something or other. Could be the way the Hollywood Stars blew another save in the ninth, or a tomato he'd spotted slinging hash at Musso and Frankenstein. He wasn't giving voice to whatever was on his mind; he was worrying it between his teeth until it or they would be ground down to nubs. Frank had a fair guess at what it was, considering what had been happening to wolves in Bud's line. Wouldn't see Friday's byline on a story about those, either.

There were at least half a dozen bars closer to the station than the one Bud picked, but those were wolf bars, the paint outside corroded away at piss-height. One whiff could tell you who drank there, from precinct to whether he walked a beat, worked narco, or whether breakfast was rare or well done. The piss might turn off other monsters, but it cut down on the roughhousing. That was good enough reason to piss on most anything. Maybe if someone had pissed on Hitler back in '39, they could have saved the world a ton of trouble.

The spot Bud picked was south of Sunset, right on the border of what was city and what was county. It looked like the kind of place where every down-on-its-luck monster drank away the last memories of being human.

It was the kind of place that wasn't dank on accident; it actively cultivated its dankness, nurtured it and allowed to grow into a miasma of dank, a place where dank ceased to be adjective and almost became a noun.

It was a joint filled with slumped tentacles and beaten-down scales. On one corner, a gremlin nursed a Rum and Bebop, muttering to himself in that queer way his kind did, lamenting a vehicle never wrecked or a candy never devoured. At the bar, a ghoul hammered some sludge in a milkshake glass that smelled like industrial runoff, probably ruminating on the corpse that got cremated before it could be dinner. Two stools down, a crawling eye blinked up into an eyedropper filled with amber fire; wouldn't be seeing a damn thing out of that peeper. None of the fellas there looked too happy with the road that brought them. When Frank glanced over at Bud, he saw the same look. Frank wasn't used to being the most chipper one in a room.

The other wolf picked a table in the corner that stank of booze and zombie rot. The waitress was a zombie, but if she was mobbed up, Frank was a Yorkie. Bud bought the drinks at least: rye, neat, two glasses of liquid gold. It would do. Frank lifted it to his lips and watched Bud gulp. His ex-partner could handle his booze, and with a wolfman's constitution he could do it like an Irish prizefighter, but he was slurping like it was a doggie dish.

"You copacetic, partner?" Frank asked, knowing the answer.

Bud smiled, but it looked more tired than amused. "Sorry. Had to get out of there. Walls have ears, you know."

"Work in a place with enough glass men, sure."

"You know what I mean," Bud said, fixing Frank with a gaze more haunted than a mummy's flop. Frank saw the steel that had been there before, rusting now, but still sharp enough to cut. Bud had always been more keen on kicking down doors and trading lead with the bad guys. It's what tapped him for the headlines, leaving Frank in the muck, where he belonged.

"Yeah, suppose I do," Frank allowed.

"You know Lou Garou?"

"Sure," Frank said. "One of your Wolf Packers, right?"

Bud chewed his lip. Technically speaking, membership in the Wolf Pack was a secret. Kept them from being bought by the same gangsters they were supposed to bring down, so the thinking went. Practically speaking, everybody knew who was on the team. Wasn't that they dressed that much differently than any other plainclothes dick. It was the way they stood: tall, proud. The way they looked at the world: through a gunfighter's squint. Hell, the way they wore their hats: slouched and cocked at an angle. They started to look like the same trouble boys they were busting, or at least the silver screen's idea of them. A Wolf Packer didn't have to piss on anything for another wolf to know whose it was; the swagger did the work.

"Wolf Pack don't exist anymore, partner. You know that."

"Suppose I do." Organized crime had been defeated in the City of Angels. The headlines had screamed "HERO COPS CAN REST!" Frank would have laughed or cried if he could still do either one. To an outsider's view, the Pack had been dissolved, the old timers put out to pasture and the rest of them put back onto the street as regular cops. Wasn't sure if Friday's byline had been on any of those. Probably, if she was covering the Hollywood crime beat.

"Yeah," Bud said, relenting and answering the earlier question. "Garou joined up after I did. Came over from 77th Street."

"Tough beat."

"You can say that again. Meatstick Mile is nobody's idea of a good time."

Frank could have disagreed with that. Plenty of wolves loved those beats. Whether it was Watts, Boyle Heights, Chavez Ravine, or anywhere else the meatsticks gathered, you could find wolves who wanted to wade in and crack some skulls. Wanted to make the peasants hide in their hovels like it was the Middle Ages or something. The wolves on Meatstick Mile could mostly do what they wanted, and sometimes maybe even solve a crime or two. Those weren't real cops—never were—but then, Frank reasoned, who was anymore? He didn't say this to Bud, instead going as diplomatic as he ever got. "Not that I don't mind having a drink on you, but what's this about? What's the story with Garou?"

"He's missing."

"Missing?" Frank stared at Bud, then motioned with his hand, a *Go on.*

"Exactly what it sounds like. Nobody's seen hide nor hair."

"How long?"

"Two days, maybe?"

Frank shook his head. "Wolves don't just go missing. Maybe on full moons, but that's in..."

"Four days," Bud said quickly. Frank nodded. Wolves could do that without thinking—the ones who didn't drink too much anyway. There was a certain pull a wolf could feel if he concentrated on it. Frank killed the last of his rye and held his fingers up to the zombie waitress. She dragged her rotting gams over and fetched him and Bud another round.

"Wolves don't go missing," Frank said, more forcefully.

"Wolf Pack ones do," Bud said.

There it was. Frank's face got hot, and he tried to put out that fire with another swallow of rye. "They don't, either," he said, but he said it softly. This was a raw place for Bud. It had to be. Sure, they were Frank's fellow officers, too, but to Bud, these were brothers. These were his *pack.* Frank cleared his throat. "When a Wolf Packer...it's public."

"A shootout," Bud said bitterly. "Looks all on the up and up, only a Wolf Packer catches a silver slug through the temple."

"Like that." Frank watched his partner, then lowered his voice. Sure, this place looked safe enough, but who could tell, really? "Partner, you need help getting out of town or something?"

Bud smiled, shook his head. "No thanks. I need you to find Garou. Can you do that?"

"Why me? You knew him better than I did."

"You're better at this than I am." Bud wasn't wrong. He was good at parts of policework, sure. The parts that came down to kicking in doors and shootouts with zombie gunsels. Wolf Pack kind of policework. He wasn't a detective. Not the way Frank was, at least.

Frank gave him a nod. He wasn't going to insult his partner, ex or not, with false modesty.

"And I know I can trust you," Bud said. This last was serious, and Frank knew what the other wolf meant. Anyone with a badge would have. It meant Bud knew Frank would never take a gangster's money, that he was a clean cop in a dirty town.

Frank could only nod mutely. "Garou have any enemies?" was all he could think to ask.

"Same as the rest of us, I expect."

A memory scratched at the inside of Frank's skull. "Didn't he lose a partner?"

Bud nodded. "Some of the Gobfather's hobs plugged him."

"You're thinking it's more of them?"

He shook his head. "The Gobfather's been pushing daisies going on nine months now. We've pretty much cleared out whatever was left of his mob."

"Yeah, I read the papers. You hero cops should be resting."

"Only we're not. We're..." he dropped his voice, "...catching silver left and right."

"I hear you, partner." He took another swallow, got to business. "I know I wasn't your first stop. What have you done already?"

Bud sighed, a tiny bit of relief showing through the clouds. "We checked the clubhouse first."

While Frank didn't know what the clubhouse was specifically, he could guess in generalities. The Wolf Pack had been a club before its dissolution, a secret society, like the Elks with machine guns. They had to have a hideout. The only cops in the city who couldn't be bought needed somewhere to go to unwind.

"We?" Frank asked.

"I," Bud said, with the tone of someone who wasn't looking for a follow-up.

"His house, too." It wasn't a question.

"You got it."

"He married?"

"Lou? Yeah."

"How married?"

Bud offered a ghost of a grin with that one. "Suppose we have a little bit of a reputation."

"Any outfit that'd have you."

"I wasn't that bad."

"I rode around in a car with you for over a year, partner. Sell it to someone else. Tell me about Garou's last girl. What's her name?"

Bud pulled the memory up through the fog. "Sea hag chorus girl." He pulled a little harder. "Bermuda Triangle. Hard to forget a handle like that."

"Where do they come up with them?" Frank wondered.

"Some people spend more than five minutes picking a rebirth name, Frank."

"Dumb custom," Frank said. "A name's a name."

"I'm just happy more monsters aren't like you. I don't know if I could live in a world with a bunch of Betty Vampires and Jim Crawling Eyes."

Frank scowled. "So this Triangle..."

"They broke it off," Bud said. "I think. We didn't always keep track. Just some nights we went out with wives and some nights with girlfriends."

"What'd you do on wife nights?"

"Went stag, or took somebody out for the first time. Couldn't have her spilling the beans to one of the fellas' ladies."

"Yeah, that'd be bad manners. Tell me more about this Triangle. You talked to her?"

Bud shook his head. "You think it was her?"

Frank shrugged. "If I'm starting somewhere, it's her and the wife."

"You're looking at this like a murder, Frank."

"That's what I do."

FIVE

rank stared through the windshield of his car. Night on Fountain Avenue was dark enough to forget that it was only two blocks from Sunset, the lambent carotid of Los Angeles. Traffic was sparse on the two-lane street. A lone phantom charger pounded down the road, its hooves striking sparks, the headless horseman on its back raising Cain. Frank sighed. In the old days, it was just hot rodders with zip guns. Now it was headless toughs with swords of hellfire.

He was parked under the boughs of a palm tree, in front of an apartment building. This late on a Monday, the lights were all off. The inhabitants were either asleep or hunting. Either one was legal, and neither was Frank's problem. He slouched low in the beat-up Plymouth. This was his own car; he was officially off the clock. The tree sagged, maybe sick. Maybe dying.

Frank watched the streetlamps glow through the dust on his windshield and he waited, turning the meeting with Bud over and over in his mind. This Garou thing didn't smell right. Wolf Packers didn't just go missing and they sure didn't die quiet. Bud knew that better than anyone, so if he said something was hinky, Frank was inclined to listen.

But Bud wasn't saying everything. That much was obvious. Something hung over him like a miasma, but Frank couldn't pick out the scent. At least his partner was smart enough to remember he was a piss-poor investigator.

Headlights haloed Frank's slumping figure. The lights in the rearview obliterated everything else, just two eyes like wounded suns. Frank heard an engine shut off, and the lights winked out. A human-shaped silhouette crossed behind the car, headed to his passenger side. A silhouette that was slender, or even emaciated, like a shadow caught between too many lights. Found the scent, too, a familiar one. Mostly rot, along with a generous spritz of *Catacombe*, still not enough to cover the baked-in cigarette smoke. Frank wished he didn't know it so well.

The door clunked, creaked open, and the figure sat. She was a zombie, and as lean as most of them were. With zombies, either they rotted the extra off, or they got a little bloated the way corpses did in water. Either way, it didn't do their odor much good. She was missing all the skin on the left side of her face, the side now facing Frank. The eye in that socket was disturbingly alive, a brilliant emerald green that might have been pretty if it had lids. White bone peeked from rotten bits of graying muscle along her cheek and jaw.

She was dressed sharply. It was a newer style, though, halfway between a suit and a dress. Some dames decided they were a bit closer to gents, Frank supposed, or wanted to be treated as such. The top of it was a pinstriped suit, tailored and tight over her skinny frame, complete with a cravat in a bold geometric pattern. Her skirt was loose enough to move in, and matched her jacket. Frank didn't see the fancy black oxfords on her feet, but he could smell the polished leather. He clocked the bulge of a roscoe under her arm, and he knew she'd be packing a pair of cold iron hatchets at the small of her back, too. She wore a collar around her neck, made of dented metal like the hull of a battleship, with a speaker at her throat. An unlit cigarette stuck from the end of a bone holder, and she clicked it against her teeth in measured patterns.

"Brains," whispered the zombie. Her name was Aida Parrish. Frank hated her like he hated no other creature on this planet. *Click-click* went the bone against her teeth.

"Detective Wolfman," crackled a voice from the speaker. It sounded like honey drizzled over barbed wire. The voice belonged to Sarah Bellum, the boss of every racket for a hundred miles from the comfort of her fortified home in Beverly Hills. It wasn't that she didn't like getting out, it was that she was a literal brain in a jar. She let her army of zombie trouble boys do the legwork for her. "You wanted to speak to me?"

"Ms. Bellum," Frank said. "Thanks for coming."

"It's always my pleasure to assist the Los Angeles Police Department in any way that I can."

Parrish pulled a lighter from her jacket pocket, flicked the top, and lit up. The car filled with stinking smog. Frank had the window down, but it wasn't enough. The zombie knew what she was doing to him. She liked it. She was showing the cop who was in charge, and Frank was too whipped to say much of anything. Frank's skin crawled. "You know the name Lou Garou?"

Parrish's head twitched, like she had to catch herself from doing a big take in Frank's direction. So that answered that. Bellum took her time: "A policeman."

"You know him."

"The sobriquet gives away the game. But now that I'm thinking of it, yes. I believe I've heard the name."

"He on your payroll?"

Bellum laughed. Eventually someone was going to have to tell her a real joke so she'd know what a laugh sounded like. Then again, maybe Frank was expecting too much out of a brain in a jar. "I resent your attempts to mischaracterize my extensive philanthropic work."

Frank snorted. "That's also a yes."

"It's a no. Detective Garou has never accepted my overtures of friendship."

"Is that why you killed him?" Frank didn't tense when he said this, and neither did Aida. Neither one displayed the slightest intent to go for their guns. Smoke from Parrish's coffin nail lazily spiraled up to the roof.

At least she'd knocked it off with the clicking.

"Killed him? You're jumping to conclusions, Detective. Why don't you start from the beginning and I'll see if I can help you. Unless you called me across town to insult me." Bellum's voice grew icicles on it at the end.

"Brains," murmured Parrish, backing up her boss's annoyance.

"You didn't cross a single thing," Frank snorted. "You're still sitting snug as a bug in your living room in Beverly Hills."

"True," agreed Bellum, the menace gone. "But poor Aida. She was planning to spend an evening at the Nocturnist. They have a coven of witches singing for them now that she adores."

Frank stared at the quiet street outside. "Garou's missing."

"And you're looking into it. He's Wolf Pack, isn't he?"

"So you *do* know him. Explains why he's never taken any money off you."

"Brains," said Parrish. A sharp burst of static came through the speaker, and the zombie started like she'd been shocked.

"Yes, well, we're lucky our fair city no longer needs police like the Wolf Pack."

"I heard. Organized crime has been eradicated from the city."

"As you say."

"Doesn't explain why all of those cops who were with the Wolf Pack have been catching silver. If they're not doing anything."

"A series of tragic accidents," Bellum said, and she didn't even attempt to feign concern. Frank could almost respect that. "But one of these didn't befall Garou, did it? If he'd experienced such an accident, would my associate be sitting in your car? I don't think so."

"No. He just up and vanished."

"I'm insulted that you would even dream I'd be involved with the disappearance of a policeman." Aida Parrish stuck the holder between her teeth, holding it there like Roosevelt.

"One you couldn't buy? Sounds like someone who might just disappear."

"No, were I truly interested in such a man, I would ensure that his death was quite public. Gunned down in the streets. A raid gone wrong, perhaps." Bellum paused. "Were I to even consider such a thing."

"You're saying you have nothing to do with it?"

"That is exactly what I'm saying, Detective. If you choose to contact me again over this matter, you won't find me nearly so pleasant."

Aida Parrish opened the Plymouth's door and put one foot on the street, then paused. "Oh, yes. Before I forget."

The zombie reached into her jacket and put an envelope on the dashboard. "Brains," she said around her smoke. Then she was out the door, slamming it behind her. As Frank stared at the envelope, filled with five twenty-dollar bills, the sound echoed like a coffin lid.

Six

Frank pulled his car to a stop on the dirt road in front of his house. He lived in Orange County, within sight of the county line if such things could be seen. The place he lived wasn't incorporated yet, just a rural road next to endless fields of orange trees. It was more space than he needed, than he really even wanted, but this far out, "big" was all they had. It was big enough for the wife and kids he'd never have. It was big enough to hold memories Frank would never make. Big enough to get lost in.

When it had been built forty or fifty years ago, the house had probably once been either for guests of whoever owned the land, or a nice place for a family of workers to keep an eye on the orange groves. It was quiet, it was lonely, and it was as remote as anything could be around Los Angeles. For that, Frank treasured it.

The house was an old Craftsman, and had seen better days. Frank knew he had half a dozen things he needed to do with it, but the truth was, he never let himself. There was always something more important to do at the station across town. Someone who needed to be taken off the streets. Someone who needed what little bit of justice Frank could give. So this house, what was supposed to be his piece of paradise, sagged beneath the weight of neglect.

Frank's house faced a dip in the land, the front porch looking out over descending rows of trees. Out back were even more rows, all the way out to the dirt roads where farmers' pickups threw tails of dust into the flat sky. It wasn't the Black Forest, but it was as close as this part of California got. Frank lumbered through the citrus haze and let himself in. He took off his trenchcoat and hung it on the rack by the door. His one concession to housekeeping.

His living room wasn't worth the name. A single chair faced the fireplace, with a table covered in old newspapers and some empty tumblers. Headlines blared story after story of the Monster Slayer, adding every corpse found in the city to his tally. To the right, a pair of built-in shelves divided the living room from a smaller room he never used and wouldn't know what to do with it if he did. It held some old boxes and a faint musty odor. A den, he guessed, and he was the only wolf with no use for one.

On the way through the dining room in the silent, dark house, he passed by the pictures on the wall without giving them a look. He knew the names of the smiling people there—*was* one of them in a few shots—but he didn't know them anymore. No one came to greet him.

It was just him. Probably always would be.

Frank went into his kitchen, opened up the icebox. The stink of ham turning made him recoil. He grabbed a beer and shut the door, then retrieved a TV dinner from the freezer.

The throaty *boom* of a shotgun echoed out over the groves. Frank sighed, then uttered a small curse. He left beer and meal on the counter and burst out of his house. The shotgun sounded again, followed by a stream of deranged cursing delivered in an Okie twang.

"Jack!" Frank called. The shotgun boomed again. Frank heard it chip some wood. "That better be a goddamn tree, Jack! You shoot my house, I'm gonna make a campfire outta you!"

Boom. Then the clatter of branches. Frank stomped through the trees. The light came from the moon overhead—nearly full—and a few distant twinkles from the closest neighbors. He caught Jack's scent through the trees first: like a hayride through a gunfight. He saw him next, moving in that jagged way his kind did, like their limbs weren't completely under control. He had a puffy silhouette, pinched off at the joints. His hobo clothes were ragged. Most important, though, was the double-barreled shotgun that he was presently stuffing another pair of shells into.

"Jack, what the hell are you doing? It's after dark!"

Jack Dawes turned his saggy face to Frank. He was a scarecrow, his face painted on a burlap sack with the kind of skill that suggested his creator shouldn't go for a career in art. "Goddamn crows, Frank! Goddamn *everywhere!* Goddamn *eatin' up my goddamn oranges!*"

"It's after dark, you daffy crop-jockey!" Frank barked.

"Crop-jockey? Goddamn doggie don't know respect!" Jack yelled back.

Frank didn't appreciate being called a doggie, but he didn't have much of a leg to stand on after the crop-jockey crack. "There ain't no crows," he pointed out. "It's after dark. You're shooting at owls. Or bats. Or, hell, vampires for all I know."

Jack's shoulders went slack. "What do vampires want with my oranges?"

"Nothing!" Frank told him. "The owls don't want anything with them either!"

"You okay, Frank?" Jack asked.

"No, I'm not. I wanted to come home, have a beer, maybe eat something with too much salt in it, and instead my neighbor is out here huntin' owl!"

"Like I said, my oranges—"

"Can't you scarecrows..." Frank gestured to his head and made a wooey motion with another hand in the direction of the trees. "...birds?"

"Takes practice," Jack said, crinkling self-consciously. "A lot of practice."

"So practice."

"A shotgun," Jack said philosophically, "don't require practice."

"I gotta differ with you on that one, Jack. And your monster powers ain't gonna end with me haulin' you into the station for disturbin' the peace or shooting me."

"Hell, Frank. I wouldn't shoot you."

"Somebody don't practice with a shotgun and starts firing it off willy-nilly don't have much of a say in what he shoots!"

Jack slung the shotgun over a shoulder. It was still broken in half, and that made Frank feel a little better. "I didn't know you had such strong feelings on the matter."

"No? Not after I read you the riot act every time?"

Jack sighed. It sounded like wind through corn. "You ain't a farmer. You don't understand."

"No, I suppose I don't. Just...it's nighttime. At least wait until you see the sun before you start shooting blackbirds, okay?"

"Sure, sure." Frank started walking back to his house. "Hey, Frank? You wanna talk or somethin', I'm just down the way."

"I know where you are, Jack."

"It's just that I found that if you don't talk about your feelings, sometimes you get to violence."

Frank stopped and turned. "Like shooting at owls with a .12-gauge?"

"That example feels needlessly pointed." Frank shook his head and stalked back to his house. "Okay, then! I'll talk to you later!" Jack called after him.

Back in the kitchen, he was grateful when the shotgun stayed silent. The TV dinner went into the nuclear oven—another one of those gizmos mad scientists made to make life easier, like the office coffeemaker—and was out inside a minute, piping hot and smelling as good as these things ever did. Frank took it and the beer into the living room. Right at the front of the house, where a wide picture window looked out onto the rows and rows of orange trees that were now just shadows in the dark. Jack was out there somewhere, stalking whichever imaginary threat to his crops. At least he wasn't shooting.

Frank ate his dinner while he stared at the shadows. Even inside, with most of his windows closed, he could smell the trees. That was nice. Sometimes, being a wolfman could be difficult. Always smelling more than you wanted to, but not quite as much as would be useful. A constant twitch at the edge of awareness. Out here, all he smelled was orange, and if you had to smell one thing, oranges weren't a bad choice. Though he knew the rows were perfectly straight, from his view on his chair they were canted, just a bit, and sometimes he could pretend they were an unruly forest rather than a crop in military formation. He felt small in his big house, smaller still by the endless fields outside.

Nothing added up with this Garou business. As much as he hated to admit it, Bellum had a point. If she wanted to press the button on a Wolf Packer, it would have been in public and her ganglia wouldn't be anywhere near it. Garou just up and vanishing made no sense.

Maybe he skipped town. That thought had some legs. Any Wolf Packer with a brain between his ears should have been thinking in that direction. When you build an elite squad to take out the mob, and then the mob wins, said squad should get out of Dodge.

Problem with that was the Wolf Packers were fighters to a man. They wouldn't put their tails between their legs, even if that was the smart play. And they sure as hell wouldn't take Bellum's money.

Frank tossed the aluminum TV dinner tray in the garbage along with the beer. The can was starting to smell a little ripe. He would think about trying to remember to take it out.

He lumbered into the bedroom at the back of the house. No pictures dotted the walls in here, and the bare patches in the dust where pictures had been were long since filled in. Only a few nails peeked from the wallpaper to show that anything had ever hung there at all.

Frank took off his jacket and threw it over a chair where several more were waiting for their comrade. He fished the envelope out of the pocket where it had already become rumpled. He dropped it in the corner of his closet on top of a pile of identical envelopes, all containing an identical sum. He'd forget about them until the next time Bellum paid him his rent.

SEVEN

L ou Garou lived in Burbank on a sunny suburban street that looked like the American Dream. The lawns on the avenue were as squared away as a Marine's haircut. Ceramic birds peeked from flowerbeds. A swan made Frank do a double take, and he was relieved when it turned out to be fake.

Frank pulled to a stop in front of Garou's address. Every one of the ranch-style houses was nearly identical save for what precise shade of yellow it was painted. On reflection, Frank determined Garou's to be a faded gold.

A concrete walkway formed a straight line from the street to Garou's front door. Frank knocked, and still didn't know what he was going to say. He wasn't even sure he was talking to a widow yet, though his gut insisted—over and over again—that he would be.

The door opened, and whatever words Frank had been prepared to say fluttered away like startled butterflies.

She was a looker, that was for sure. Sturdy, too. Frank liked that, though he had never seen a dame wear it as well as this one. She wore a halter dress, showing off shoulders with distinct muscles, and when she moved they rippled like a breeze over a pond. Her features were bold, with dark, arched eyebrows, chocolate-brown eyes, full lips, and a strong, dimpled chin. Her brown hair was in the short and curly Italian style. She put one hand on a shapely hip and regarded him with the faint curiosity of a sated predator.

She smelled clean. Not clean like a regular monster, where the smell was actually soap and shampoo and hairspray and perfume. Lulu Garou smelled like herself, a musky scent that called to mind the wild. The wolf inside Frank stirred from its month-long slumber. It was hard work, not leaning in and inhaling her neck. Frank had the self-control to manage.

"Can I help you?" she prompted in a voice like sweet butter.

"Uh, right." He cleared his throat. "Excuse me, ma'am. I'm Detective Frank Wolfman. I'd like to talk to you, please."

"Wolfman?" She raised an eyebrow.

"Yes, ma'am." Frank was used to it by now.

"About as creative as mine, I suppose," she said. "Lulu Garou."

"Yes, Mrs. Garou. I know. May I come in?"

"Of course." She stepped aside, gesturing into the home.

Frank came in, and only then remembered to step back out and wipe his feet. Not that they were especially dirty; he'd left the Orange County dirt on the pedals of the Plymouth. Frank's house was the lair of a bachelor who'd given up, and the only reason it wasn't in a worse state was because of how little time he spent there. Now, he felt a little grimy just being near the Garou place; it looked like a museum. As put-together as Lulu Garou was, he couldn't imagine her actually sitting anywhere. The furniture all matched, done up in a Chinese pattern, with plants embroidered into the cushions. The lamps were all Chinese style as well, with dragons holding up beige balls of paper and balsa wood. It was a classy joint, classier than Frank would have pegged Lou Garou for. It was a lead-pipe cinch which of the two of them had the taste.

"Can I get you something to drink?" she asked.

"No, I'm fine."

"I was having orange juice. It's freshly squeezed."

"Sure," he said.

Mrs. Garou disappeared into the kitchen and returned with two glasses. They smelled almost like home to Frank, but didn't look anything close to it. She set both on coasters on a coffee table. "Have a seat," she said, gesturing to a sofa that looked like it had never felt the imprint of a single rear end in its entire existence. Frank obeyed, though maybe that was because he didn't have it in him to disappoint a woman like Lulu Garou. He stared at the bubbles on top of the juice, but couldn't bring himself to taste it.

"Is this about Lou?" she asked, only she wasn't quite asking.

Frank nodded. "I'm afraid so."

Lulu set her glass down and folded her hands. Her knuckles turned white. "What happened?"

"We're not sure. When was the last time you saw your husband?"

She had to think about it. "Three days?

"You didn't report him missing."

"He wasn't, so far as I knew."

"He just went to work, never came home?"

She nodded, and a spark caught in her eyes as she made the realization. "You're wondering if his car would be here."

"I am," he said, surprised.

"It's not," she said.

"I'll need a description. License number. I can look for that. So, he's gone three days and you don't tell anybody?"

"My husband works...long hours." She paused, lowering her voice. "He was with the Wolf Pack, when they were still around."

Frank nodded. "I know."

"I was under the impression that was a secret."

"You knew."

She shrugged. "I'm his wife. He had to give me some reason he was gone for days at a time."

"So three days wasn't unusual."

"No, it was. It is. One day was normal. Two days was unusual. Three? Well, I was getting worried, and then a detective shows up on my doorstep asking me if I know anything."

Frank stared at her. Lulu Garou could have been sculpted by Michelangelo, down to those impressive shoulders of hers. "You don't seem that concerned."

Her lips formed a thin line. "I am. I'm also a policeman's wife. I spent over a year waiting for the call. All last year I thought it would come every night. Do you remember what it was like? Zombies and goblins shooting it out over Sunset?"

He cocked his head. He'd expected a derogatory term out of her. *Stiffs and hobs*, anybody else would have said. Especially a wolf's wife used to seeing them as the enemy and nothing more.

"What?" she asked him.

"Nothing," he said. "I just didn't expect... You're polite."

She offered a half-smile. "Lou uses the other words all the time."

"You don't."

"No," she said. "It's not right. Pretends they're less than you, and that's not true. Any one of us could have been one of them had something gone differently."

"I'm not much of a poet," Frank said, thinking about life as a goblin.

"That part would have been hard."

"Anyways, I *do* remember what it was like."

"Were you in the Wolf Pack?"

Frank shook his head. "Homicide. Been working Hollywood since before the treaty."

"How does that work?"

"We were half cops and half soldiers in those days. And half monsters, too, I guess."

"That's three halves."

"I'm not much of a mathematician either."

Lulu Garou chuckled. Her brown eyes sparkled, like dew on a moth's wings. "I can't imagine trying to solve a murder in a war zone."

Frank frowned, wondering why she would be thinking about solving murders in the first place. "It wasn't easy. But when the sti...the zombies and the goblins were rumbling, I see what you mean. But the Wolf Pack was disbanded back in June. He was still working late nights?"

Lulu shrugged, taking a sip of her juice. "He was still a homicide detective. He still had a caseload. And no matter what the papers say, there's still plenty of people dying around here."

"Tell me something I don't know."

"Is my husband officially missing?"

Frank cleared his throat. He wasn't sure he could lie to Lulu Garou if he tried. "Not exactly. I don't know if there's an open file or not. I was asked to find him by a friend."

"Yours or his?"

"Both."

"I don't know why, but that makes me feel a little better. Then this investigation is unofficial?"

"You could say that."

Lulu nodded, looking away for the first time. Frank thought he saw vulnerability there, but that could have been wishful thinking. He wouldn't know what vulnerability looked like on a woman like Lulu Garou.

"How did you meet?" he asked.

"You know those advertisements in the back of the *LA Minion*? *Monster seeking woman*? It was one of those."

"Those are usually for turning, aren't they? Mea...uh...humans looking to be turned by a specific kind of monster?"

Lulu nodded. "That's right."

"And you answered it. Meaning you wanted to be a wolf."

She met his eyes, and he saw the hardness in them. "I wanted to be a cop."

"What stopped you?"

"How many lady cops do you know?"

Frank frowned. "Lots."

"Meter maids?"

"Sure."

"I don't want to be a meter maid."

Frank wasn't sure what to say. He thought about picking up the glass of juice, but once again, he couldn't bring himself to. The glass was too nice for the likes of him. "You answered an ad, he turns you, and the two of you get married?"

"That's about right."

"Was it a happy marriage?" The laugh that jumped out of her surprised the both of them. "Wasn't supposed to be funny," Frank told her.

"It wasn't. It's just such a simple question with such a complicated answer. I don't think any marriage is completely happy or completely sad."

"Some of them are completely sad."

She chuckled, and this one stayed on her lips. "Well, we got married just after the treaty, in May of '53."

Frank raised his eyebrows at this. Humans who lasted through the Night War were tough customers. He guessed Lulu would be in her early thirties, but the War also had a habit of aging people.

"When were you turned?" she asked.

"'48."

"Early."

He nodded. "Right around the tipping point."

"You ever answer one of those ads?"

"Nah. No human girl would want to see this coming for her."

"You might be surprised."

"I don't like surprises."

The grin widened momentarily, accompanied by a happy crinkle in her eyes. "We had at least one good year. I went to the academy, even though Lou didn't want me to. Found out my career had a ceiling already figured."

"He didn't want you to? Didn't he know what you wanted?"

"Sure he did. He told me he thought I'd get it out of my system. He wanted..." she gestured to the immaculate house.

"This doesn't sound happy to me."

"I'm making it sound worse than it was. We got on fine."

"Did you notice a change in him?"

She nodded, her eyes looking far away. "Yeah. Starting when his partner died."

"That would be Phil Moon."

"Yes, Phil."

"You knew him?"

"I did. He was nice. Older. He and Lou worked together before they joined the Wolf Pack."

"Which was when?"

"A little over a year ago? Something like that. It was definitely after the trouble with the giant lizard."

Frank nodded. The end of August last year, three giant monsters—a lizard, an ape, and a dame—had slugged it out over the south side of town. Big sections were still mashed flat. A lot of folks had taken a powder and moved east for greener pastures. For any Angeleno, "the trouble with the giant lizard" was a reliable time marker.

"Phil died in January."

Lulu nodded. "I thought you would know the story."

"I do. I want to know what *you* know."

"Oh. Well, Lou and Phil were up around Chinatown, and they got in a shootout with some gangsters. Goblins, I think. Lou made it out. Phil didn't."

"And Lou changed?"

"He did."

"How so?"

"He felt...distant. That's the best way I can describe it. He was just always elsewhere. He could sit right where you are now and it would feel like he was a hundred miles away."

"That can happen to someone who's been shot at."

"Have you been shot at?"

"Sure. First by Germans, then by Americans. Humans, then monsters. The usual."

"You should think about answering one of those ads, Detective."

Frank found somewhere else to put his eyes. "Tell me about the distance."

"It wasn't all at once. It wasn't that the day after Phil was killed, Lou was a thousand miles away. For maybe a month after, he was here, or nearly all here. As time went on, he drifted farther and farther away."

"Are you certain it wasn't because of the Wolf Pack being disbanded? Or the...other?" Frank didn't know of a good way to point out that a lot of Lou's friends had been gunned down over the past couple months.

"There was some of that, sure. But I did see Phil's casefile on Lou's nightstand."

"The casefile?"

"Of that night."

"Why would he want a casefile for something that happened in front of his face?"

"You're the detective," Lulu Garou said. "I'm only fit to be a meter maid."

"Did you look at it?"

She shook her head. "He looked at it a lot. There was a picture in there. I saw it once when he put it down. A picture of a girl. Mexican, I think. Beautiful. She was on top of a hill somewhere, the wind in her hair."

"Not a goblin, I take it."

"Definitely not."

"Did Lou have any family? Friends?"

"Human family? No. Not that he talked about, anyway. If they were still around, he wanted to get away from them. All his friends were on the force. He was a cop, through and through."

"Right." Frank thought to himself. "You mind if I look around a little?"

"Be my guest," Lulu said. "I don't know what you hope to find."

"I don't either. Maybe just get to know him a little bit."

Her smile turned wan. "Good luck."

Frank rose, and pointed to the hallway. "What's back there?"

"Den, bedroom, bathroom. There's a sliding door out to the backyard."

Frank nodded and went off in that direction. The hallway was decorated with more vaguely Chinese-looking artwork. A few pictures, some from fifteen to twenty years ago, showed a washed-out family. Frank thought he might have recognized Lou Garou in those pictures, but he couldn't be sure. Those would be his; anyone turned as late as Lulu had been would have lost her keepsakes in the Night War. Other pictures were more recent. One showed the Garous on their wedding day. Lulu was radiant, but that was to be expected. Her smile was guileless and her eyes were wide. Lou Garou conformed to Frank's vague memory of him. He had that solid, mean look that a lot of cops had, and even when he was happy, the wolf wasn't too far underneath. He reminded Frank a bit of Bud, but Bud genuinely had good humor while Garou gave the impression of faking it.

Frank went down the hall into the bedroom. The bed was made, of course. He would have been shocked if anything was out of place in this home. Lulu Garou was a wolf, as much of one as he was, and here she was a living museum piece. That was certainly a motive for murder. Anything to get out and be the animal that kept the heart beating.

Even now, Frank wasn't certain he was looking at a murder. If Garou was smart, he blew town, and from the looks of things here, he wasn't leaving behind anything he cared about. As much as treating a woman like Lulu Garou like chopped liver might rankle Frank, he could see one of those strutting alpha wolves in the Wolf Pack doing it. Fit who they were.

Nightstands sat on either side of the bed. One was clean. On the other was a brochure for Little Monster House. Frank picked it up. The brochure promised, in bright colors and pretty pictures, to find the perfect person for any monster to turn. Whatever you were, from banshee to wendigo,

Little Monster House would match you with a human being to your specifications. Getting past that human's wards and spiriting them out to be changed was up to the monster in question. Frank put the brochure back down where he found it. He couldn't figure Lulu had much more use for it than he did, but she still wanted to look.

EIGHT

The Atlantis Club sat near the corner of Santa Monica and Fairfax, a squat three-story building painted an ocean blue, art deco lines making it at home in the neighborhood. Anchors, nets filled with starfish, and stuffed seagulls decorated the exterior. The whole thing was crowned with the name in an arc of lights, flanked by two neon seashells. Frank had never been inside. It was on the other side of the line, in the purview of the Hollywood Sheriffs, and he wasn't much of a swimmer. As he got out of the car, his hackles rose. No one watching him, but he felt like maybe they should be.

The conversation with Lulu Garou swirled in his head since he'd had it the day before. He didn't think he was ever going to shake her loose, but he'd have to try. If only to concentrate on the task at hand.

He walked up the concrete steps and through the big swinging double doors. The brass handles were done up like dolphins with seashells at the noses and tails. Inside, the decor was even more obviously nautical, like a boat turned inside out. The scents of salt and fish were strong, but not unpleasantly so. Managed to smell more like the open sea than the docks somehow. The wooden floors, swollen with years of moisture, creaked like the deck of an old ship as Frank made his way over to the front desk.

This place was built for gill-men and sirens, or fishies and sea hags if you weren't being as polite as Lulu Garou. Frank didn't have much of an opinion on the fish people; he never worked Harbor Division. Most of the sea hags he met were hangers-on in Hollywood, pretty girls with gills and pipes and dreams that never came true.

A pretty siren—she fit the type, good-looking but no knockout—on the other side of the desk smiled at him. For her, that meant baring a kisser full of teeth that looked like hell's own pincushion. Frank concentrated on her eyes, the water-filled goggles she wore magnifying them to the size of basketballs and making her confusion impossible to hide. Other than that, she was wearing a sailor suit that was either cute or sad, depending on one's proclivities. "Good morning, sir. Can I help you?" She had to be wondering what somebody without scales was doing there.

Frank sighed. He'd already been over the rigmarole trying to track Bermuda Triangle down. After calling all over town, another one of the chorus girls at Visionary Pictures had pointed him here. It was a place for those gill-men or sirens who didn't live on the coast to wet their whistles. And everything else.

He showed her his badge. "I'm looking for a customer of yours."

"Oh," she said. "Oh no. Has something happened?"

"It's nothing to be concerned about, miss." This siren looked about nineteen, and Frank was being generous. There was still enough of the old Frank in him that he didn't want to scare her over nothing. "I just need to ask her a few questions."

"Oh. All right. I don't suppose you need a membership for that."

Doors opened up on either side of the desk. The smell of the open sea billowed through, flexing some olfactory prowess. Lighter, drifting over the tops of the heavier aromas, he detected different plants, from seaweed to orchids and mangroves. He took half a step, hesitated. "Miss, you wouldn't happen to know where Bermuda Triangle is?"

Her face lit up. "Bermuda! Of course. She's probably in the lagoon. I'll show you." She slapped a sign on the desk that said, "GONE UNDER—BACK UP FOR AIR SOON." She smiled at Frank and led him through the door on the left.

His breath caught. He wasn't sure what he was expecting, but this wasn't it. A pool, sized for Olympians, dominated the room with only a narrow boardwalk framing it. The impressive thing was, in the center was an artificial island, an enormous rock poking from the center, ringed with smaller islands. Small trees grew in the crevices, and sea life clung to the rocks around water level. Gill-men and sirens basked on the rock or cavorted about in the swirling saltwater. In the waves and eddies, Frank thought he glimpsed swaying kelp and darting fish. Water periodically washed up over the wood he was standing on.

"Oh, Tethys Rock? Yeah, it's something," his guide said. "Before I saw it, I didn't think you could have something like that, you know, indoors."

"You said it."

She led him around the side. A few of the sea people stopped to watch the interloper, but most were content to ignore him. A shadow, bigger than a man, swam uncomfortably close to the boardwalk. Frank did his best not to flinch. "That a shark?"

"Probably," the girl said over her shoulder.

Frank hugged the wall and was grateful when she led him through another door. The boardwalks split into several pathways that wound through the room. This place was dark, contrasting to the summery lighting over Tethys Rock. Mangrove trees grew out of swampy waters and fireflies danced through the air. Gill-men swam through brackish water, surfacing only enough to expose their eyes.

His guide walked across the centermost boardwalk and found another door. This one opened up onto another bright room. Here, the boardwalk once again turned to skirt the room, but a white sand beach nearly swallowed it in places. A shallow lagoon took up most of the space, with the expected gill-men or sirens either in the water or lying out on the sand.

Frank's guide pointed to a siren lounging on the beach. Until he slapped eyes on her, Frank had nursed the faint hope that she wouldn't be there and he could put Bud's mind at ease. *Don't worry. Your pal's a louse. He left a hell of a woman to worry in Burbank and ran off with a fish.*

But Frank also knew he wasn't that lucky.

"Thanks," he said to the girl.

"Don't mention it." She gave him a little curtsy and left him there.

Frank approached Bermuda Triangle. She was slender and pretty—maybe even gorgeous— and delicate in a way that Lulu Garou never would be. Her skin was blue, lined with thick yellow stripes like a tropical fish. Her hair was long and black, and in the light, it shimmered green. She was dressed in a bathing suit in a bright Hawaiian pattern, all stretched out on a beach towel decorated with pastel carp. Her goggles sat by her hand in a small goggle-shaped container of water. Her eyes were shut, far too prettily for her to be dozing.

"'Scuse me, Bermuda Triangle?" Frank asked.

She opened one eye, squinting up at him. "Who's asking?"

"Police, ma'am."

She sat up, concerned, but not concerned enough. "Excuse me, I can't see you." She leaned over and plucked her goggles out of the water, keeping some in the lenses. Something about the way their peepers worked; they couldn't see through air very well. She donned the goggles carefully, then blinked fetchingly up at him. "What's this about?" she asked.

Frank glanced around. They were drawing looks, but none of the other fish people came over to investigate. "Somewhere we could have a little privacy?"

"Sure," she said. "Snack bar should be pretty deserted this time of day."

She got up, gathering her things in an oversized wicker bag and throwing it over her shoulder. She led Frank through another doorway, and here he found a small pool with tables and stools poking from the water. A snack bar, like one on any beach, stood against one side of the room. The menu was geared toward fish. A single gill-man worked behind the grill, but he wasn't doing much more than cleaning. As they walked in, he noted them and said, "We're not up for another hour."

"It's fine," Bermuda Triangle said. He shrugged and got back to work.

Bermuda hopped into the water, where it only came up to her waist. Then she climbed up a stool, putting her bag on the table. She sat demurely, legs crossed, looking expectantly at Frank.

He grunted in annoyance and reached out to the nearest stool. Through some judicious playing of "floor is lava" he was able to perch there without getting wet. He brought out his notepad, wobbling on the precarious seat. "You live around here?"

"Why, Detective, is that an appropriate question to ask a lady?"

"So I'm talking to a lady." Even without the goggles, he couldn't have missed the death glare.

"Wanna tell me what this about?" she asked again, already tired of him.

"Do you know Detective Lou Garou?"

She watched him, then: "You know I did. Otherwise you wouldn't be talking to me."

"Did?" He wasn't expecting a confession, but if one came, he'd take it.

"We aren't acquainted anymore."

"What does that mean?"

"It means I broke it off with him."

"Why?"

Bermuda gestured vaguely. "There isn't much of a future in dating married men."

"You broke it off when you found out he was married?"

"No. I knew he was married when I met him. Lou never took off his wedding band."

"You lost me. You knew he was married when you took up with him, but then you decide that it's a reason to break it off."

"Feelings change. You've been with a girl before. You have to know what that's like."

Frank grunted. He supposed he did know, but Susan had what looked like a good enough reason at the time. Something *had* changed. Once every full moon. "When was this? When you had your sudden change of heart?"

"Two months ago," she said promptly.

"August."

She nodded. "That's right."

"Got a new boyfriend?"

"It was two months. What kind of girl do you take me for?"

"The kind that takes up with married men."

Bermuda sat up straighter, and for the first time Frank saw real anger in her eyes. "Get something straight, Detective. Lou's married. I'm not. Any vows that got broke were on his end. I didn't do a damn thing wrong."

"Some people might call you a homewrecker."

"Wouldn't call Lou that."

"You sound like you disliked him at the end."

"No, it's not that. You're..." she shook her head. "Whatever reasons Lou had for cheating are his. I didn't ask. They never mattered to me. I liked him, and he liked me, so we were together."

"Until you weren't, when his being married suddenly mattered to you."

"Wasn't that," said Bermuda. "Not exactly. No matter what I thought about him, there's no future. What, is he going to leave her for me? What dame hasn't heard that story? So I left him."

"Looking for a single man this time?"

She shrugged. "Could be. Why do you want to know about an old boyfriend?"

"If you broke it off, what does it matter?"

"Humor me."

"Lou Garou is missing."

"What?" Her eyes went wide and her mouth went slack. Her demeanor, confident, even aggressive before, fell away in the face of pure surprise.

"Just what I said."

"What does that mean, 'He's missing'?"

Frank nodded. "We don't know exactly *what* it means, specifically. No one has seen him for a couple days, and folks are starting to get concerned."

"And you thought he might have run off with me."

"Crossed my mind."

"Well, as you can see, here I am." She gave a sweeping gesture that encompassed the Atlantis Club snack bar and immediate environs.

"I can see that." So far what she had told him agreed with what Bud had said. She, too, was holding something back, that much was clear, but yet again, Frank couldn't tell what. He sniffed the air experimentally, and caught mostly her scent. She smelled distinctly, but not unpleasantly, of the ocean. For the first time, Frank could not only understand but empathize with the attraction she might hold for a wolf. She wasn't his type, but he got it.

What he didn't smell was anyone on her, or the stench of a body. Couldn't take that to court, but it was something.

"I hope you have more leads than little old me," she said.

"You were the best one. Sorry I wasted your time. I'll show myself out." Frank got up and left the Atlantis Club on the same winding trail he took to come in. He sat in his car for a time, thinking about his next step. Something Lulu Garou had said kept worrying at his mind: He still had a caseload. Still had to officially solve Ducktail's murder. Frank sighed, and started the car.

NINE

Impulse took him to the county coroner's office. Frank was grateful for how mundane the place looked. It was in an industrial section of town, lightly scarred from the Night War because nobody wanted to live there even when absent other options. The thing was, when the war was won and the monsters were definitely in charge, probably around '50 or '51, things had started to change. Certain monsters thought they should be living up to the examples on the silver screen or some Transylvanian folk tale. They got creepy for the sake of being creepy. It was exhausting. So Frank was grateful that, at least for now, the place hadn't been turned into some goofy Egyptian pyramid.

Of course, with all the mummies downtown, that was only a matter of time.

Frank badged his way in and went down to the refrigerated basement. No matter what time of year, it was always winter at the coroner's office. The reason was sitting at his stainless steel desk with his feet up. Dr. Hannibal Winters was a wendigo, which meant he looked a little bit like a cross between a white ape and a body that had been left out in the snow too long. He smelled like frozen blood and he was crunching on something from a white paper bag.

"Afternoon, Detective," the wendigo said, not getting up. He had a trace of an accent that sounded almost Canadian. "What can I do for you?"

Frank walked over to the desk. The freezers were all shut tight, the dearly departed resting quietly—no longer a guarantee these days. He'd been around bodies long enough that he had no particular superstitious dread of them. Winters himself could be a little unnerving, though. Maybe it was the teeth, like a shark made dentures out of a sawblade.

"I had a couple questions about an old case."

"Sure," the coroner said, then held out the bag. "Ladyfinger?"

Frank didn't have to look to know Winters was being literal. "I'm fine."

The wendigo shrugged and leaned back in his chair. "Shoot."

"You do the autopsy on Phil Moon?"

Winters frowned, an impressive expression on a face that was little more than gray skin stretched thin over a malformed skull. "What is it with that one?"

"How do you mean?"

"I don't mean any offense, but being a cop isn't the safest of vocations these days, yet Moon's the only one you people want to talk about."

"Who else asked after him?"

"Detective by the name of Garou, and now you. Two's enough to make it something, especially because no other case gets more than a first glance, let alone a second or a third."

"I guess it is strange. Did you know him? Moon, I mean?"

"Sure. He worked homicide. I know all of you homicide fellas at least a little. I'll tell you this, I liked him better than I like Garou."

"What's wrong with Garou?"

"You don't know him?"

"Enough to say hi to."

Winters chuckled. "Can't imagine you being so chummy. Anyways, how do I put this? This isn't gonna get back to him?"

"When I'm not saying hi to him?"

"Point." Winters eyed Frank. Considering those eyes were yellow and glowing, it was quite a look, like being sized up by a pair of haunted lanterns. "Garou is...intense. One of those wolves that's never all the way a man, you know? I'm just glad he's out there, putting the fear into all the people that aren't me."

Frank nodded. "You liked Moon?"

"I didn't know him well, but I liked dealing with him more than Garou. I was sad to see him go, but you know, dangerous times and all that."

"You did Moon's autopsy."

"Sure did."

"Can you get the file?"

Winters sighed and regarded Frank, doing the calculus of energy expended finding the file versus arguing with Frank and maybe not getting out of it. "All right. Stay here."

He got up, unfolding his long and spindly body from the chair, and slunk off through the far door. He took his ladyfingers with him, and for that Frank was grateful. There was only so much a man could take. Winters took his time, leaving Frank in the arctic environs of the basement. He briefly considered letting the wolf out, if only for the fur.

When Winters came back, he handed a manila folder to Frank before plopping himself back down in the chair, crunching ostentatiously on his snack. Frank opened up the file.

"Well, Detective? You going to solve a case that was already solved back in January?"

Frank paged through the report. When they got Moon on the slab, they pulled a couple .38 caliber rounds out of his belly. Those were lead. Nothing unusual there; lots of gunsels packed lead. It would do the job if you used enough of it, and most wolves weren't going to get bent out of shape if they busted you with it. That wasn't what killed Moon, though. A single round, this one a silver 7.62mm, had perforated his heart. A perfect shot. Moon would have been stone dead before he hit the ground.

"Gut shot with a pistol, killed with a rifle?" Frank asked.

"Mmmhmm," Winters confirmed. "Caliber doesn't say much. Definitely a rifle, though."

"They don't usually carry rifles."

"How do you mean?"

"For their longarms, stiffs pack shotguns, tommies, that kind of thing. Hobs go even smaller. If it's a shotgun, it's sawed off. They like those grease guns, too. Not rifles."

Winters frowned. "Guess that *is* a little weird. Not unheard of, though."

"No, not unheard of," Frank said. Enough ordnance was still floating around from both Day and Night Wars that anyone could lay their hands on nearly anything if they wanted to bad enough. "You said this thing was solved. Who'd they arrest?"

"Nobody, so far as I know. Garou was there, and he fingered some of the Gobfather's thugs."

"Which ones?"

"Who knows? You see a three-foot poet with a gun, you figure he works for the Gobfather, not for the greengrocer, you know?"

"So Garou is there when Moon buys it, and he still wants to see the autopsy months later?"

"Yeah. I thought it was funny at the time. I told him so, but he just did that thing you wolfmen do where your eyes go a little red and you growl. That's when I thought that maybe I shouldn't find him funny."

"Smart decision."

"I *am* a doctor."

Frank paged through the report again, wondering what he was missing, what Garou had seen and he hadn't. "Did Garou say anything to you after looking at this thing?"

"Nope. He took it home—I wasn't supposed to let him, but you know, red eyes. Then he brought it back a couple days later in perfectly fine shape."

"Didn't change anything in it?"

"I don't think so," Winters said, mulling it over. "You think he's the type to do that?"

"I got no idea."

Winters stared at Frank, then asked, "What's all this about, Detective? Why are you digging up this case?"

"I'm just doing it because he did it," Frank said.

"And why'd he do it?"

"If I knew, I wouldn't have done it. Thanks for your time, Doc."

Wrong place, wrong time, wrong weapon. No wonder Garou was hung up on the case. But he'd been there. If he wanted to correct it, he could. The tension was stiff enough to snap, but Frank couldn't find where the damn thing would break.

TEN

In the summer, the cinderblock square of the Highland Park Station was an oven, but in October, it was damn near tolerable. Frank stared at the casefile in front of him. It was Phil Moon's. The case was still technically open. Nobody had gone down for it, but the impression was whichever hob had done it was rhyming in Hell. Frank read it over and over again. Garou's report was in his gruff voice. It was as everyone had said: Moon and Garou go up to the spot over Chinatown, get ambushed by hobs. Garou fights them off, but Moon takes one to the ticker. What wasn't in the file was the picture Lulu Garou had mentioned. Pictures of the site, pictures of some shell casings, all there. No girl. Frank was frowning at its absence when he felt a presence at his shoulder.

"Detective? Captain wants to see you." Frank didn't look up to see Officer Accalia, one of Captain Talbot's assistants.

He blinked and looked up after all. "Accalia?" She was small, with dark, Italian features. Nobody in their right mind would call her pretty and the uniform wasn't doing her any favors.

"Yes, Detective?" She stopped and stared at him expectantly, though without any particular interest.

He almost asked her to verify or contradict what Lulu Garou had told him. After all, Accalia was a cop, and she wasn't a meter maid. No, she was an officer. Who never left the station. Who served as an assistant mostly to

Talbot, and also to any other cop or detective who needed her.

"Never mind. Not important."

She gave him a curt nod and walked away. Frank shut the file and got up with a grunt. He touched the photo of Sylvia Screen once in a superstitious gesture he didn't care to break, then headed up the wooden stairs to the captain's office. The captain's secretary was an invisible woman—just a floating dress and glasses—who waved him in. Frank extrapolated the gesture from the motion of the watch on her transparent wrist.

Frank rapped on the frosted glass of the door's window, right over the gold lettering of the captain's name and title. "Come in," came Talbot's voice. Frank let himself in.

Captain Lon Talbot looked the part. He wasn't precisely heavy; he was just one of those people who would always have a couple inches and at least thirty pounds on anyone he spoke to. He wore a tailored three-piece suit that must have needed twice the fabric as a regular one. A chunky gold ring flashed on one finger—a Stanford class ring of which he was inordinately proud. Like a lot of wolfmen, he'd given up fighting the persistent five o'clock shadow and instead cultivated a neat beard that was a bit more salt than pepper. His hair was short, though not military.

Frank was unsurprised to see Talbot's right-hand man standing behind him. Lieutenant Temple Glass was the opposite of his boss, at least in terms of build. Lean and bordering on short, his suit was nearly as nice. He stood by an open window, a cigarette floating midair. The breeze carried the smoke mostly out the window, some of it washing around Glass's invisible head and hands, giving a ghostly impression of pinched features and slender fingers. Frank didn't know how Talbot tolerated the stink of the cigarette. With the change, most wolfmen quit and couldn't abide it after.

"Frank, sit down," Talbot said, gesturing to the chair opposite his desk.

Frank obeyed. "What can I do for you, Captain?"

"The Ducktail murder."

"Lord Decoratorius," Frank said, "yeah."

"You haven't charged anybody."

"I don't have the one who did it."

"There's a human in lockup," Glass pointed out. "Charge him."

"Eduardo Carias," Frank said. "I don't think he did it."

Talbot frowned. "Why not?"

"Kid said he didn't do it."

"Well then," Glass said. The lieutenant brought the cigarette to his transparent lips. For a moment, Frank could see the smoke as it washed into his mouth, and then it vanished, swallowed up by whatever made invisible men invisible.

"Glass has a point, Frank. One you should know as well as anybody. They all say they didn't do it."

"In this case I believe him," Frank said.

"If this were almost anybody else, I'd tell him to jump in a lake," Talbot said, "but you're not the sentimental type. Why do you believe the kid?"

"I can't see it. Gremlins are good about sunlight, but Decoratorius is standing in front of the window waiting around patiently while the kid he has locked up, who suddenly escapes somehow, pulls the curtains open? I don't know about you, but if somebody pulled the wall open in front of a silver bullet firing squad, I might move."

Talbot blinked like that revelation was news to him. Glass sucked in a lungful of smog. "So what do you want to do?" the captain asked.

"I want to take another run at the housekeeper. She was the only other person in that house, and either she makes me believe Carias did it, or I know for sure it was her."

Talbot chuckled. "Never knew a fella who loved humans like you do."

"Don't give a damn one way or the other about humans. Carias didn't do it, so he shouldn't take the fall."

"Nobody'd lose any sleep," Glass said.

Talbot waved it off. "Get it done. But if you can't get the ghost to cop to it, charge the meatstick, understand?"

Frank nodded, getting up. "Anything else, Captain?"

"That'll do. Thanks, Frank."

Frank left Talbot's office and made his way downstairs. The truth was, he wasn't thinking about the gremlin or the kid. He was stuck on Lou Garou, knowing there had to be a door he could knock on or a person to talk to. Someone saw Garou last, but Frank couldn't imagine who. He liked having a body to work with. Scents he could tease out, a scene he could reconstruct, eventually see it in living color in his mind's eye. He hated to admit it, but he needed help.

Like a ghost summoned from the self-doubt, Bud Hound stood at the bottom of the staircase. He didn't look great. He needed a shave, a haircut, and a shoeshine. And something that would stop his eyes from darting around. He looked like Jesse James about to get the business from Robert Ford.

"Frank, how you doing?"

"Good. You sleeping?"

"Standing up." Bud glanced around. "You got a minute?"

Frank nodded. "Let's take a walk." They emerged into the sunlight on York Boulevard.

"You got any news?" Bud spoke in a murmur, glancing back at the cement box that was the Highland Park Station.

"'Fraid not. Talked to the wife and the girlfriend and neither one knew where he was."

"Why would they know?"

"I figure a man don't leave town without settling the dame situation."

"Dame situation?" Bud asked, a grin creeping to his lips. "Been a while, partner?"

"Tell me I'm wrong."

Bud shrugged. "I don't know what was going on with Lou and the missus. The fellas all had different home lives, you know?"

"They were all stepping out."

"Sure."

"Makes me think that if he skipped town, he wasn't going to take his wife with him."

"Safer that way," muttered Bud.

"Why? You not telling me something? Did Garou know something that would mean he had to run?"

Bud shifted uncomfortably. "No." Frank didn't like that *No*. It didn't quite ring true. "No," Bud said more surely. "Nothing more than anyone else in the Pack knows. But those fellas getting the push ain't because they know something, it's because Bellum's settling debts."

"What about you, partner?" Frank asked. "If you ran, you taking somebody?"

Bud offered a wan smile, more pain behind it than Frank had ever seen. Just as quickly as it appeared, it was gone, and Frank had to wonder if he'd imagined it. "Nobody to take."

"Way I look at it, a man skips town, he's picking one of his girls, but it looks like Garou didn't pick either one. 'Less there's somebody I don't know about yet."

"Another one would be news to me, too."

Frank still burned with Garou making a fool out of that wife of his. Woman like that deserved more. "She didn't know anything. Triangle. The chorus girl, I mean."

"I told you, they broke it off."

"She told me the same."

"You tracked her down for that?"

"Is there something you're not telling me?"

"Like what?"

"Like why he would run. You're skipping around something. I can smell it."

Bud shook his head, and Frank nearly believed him. "I told you everything, partner. I swear. Just find him, all right? Soon."

"Working on it," Frank grumbled as he headed back into the station, leaving his old partner behind. He plopped himself back at his desk and started racking his brain. No other cops were clean enough to trust, and Frank didn't exactly have a deep pool of friends.

"Wolfman? You there?"

Frank blinked, looking up. What looked like a caterpillar hovered at head level by the side of his desk, wiggling with the words.

"Bosch," Frank sighed as his brain caught up to the incongruous image. Anonymous Bosch was an invisible man, but he liked to wear a false mustache so people knew vaguely where to look. Explaining the thought processes of glass men was above Frank's pay grade. Every last one of them was goofier than a gremlin on Halloween. "What can I do for you?"

"You know Tuesday Thorne?"

Frank blinked. "Sure, yeah. Ghoul, runs hexes for a couple covens on Hollywood. What about her?"

"She's dead. Struck by lightning."

"Has it rained? Never mind. She got hexed." Frank shook his head. "Almost had her on a murder. Bumped off a busboy over at the Gloom Room earlier this year, only I couldn't prove she swung the hammer."

"Yeah, I remembered. Thought you'd want to know some witch did the job for you."

Frank sighed. "Rather get her in bracelets."

The mustache was motionless. It was almost hypnotic the way it just hovered there. Finally: "What's eating you?"

Frank almost clammed up. But if there was anyone still clean in this town, it was Anonymous Bosch. The invisible man's reputation said he was a loner and a hardass, but he was as honest as they came. It was why nobody trusted him. "Looking for a witness," he said at last.

"Can't find him," Bosch said sympathetically. "Been there."

"*You* couldn't find somebody."

"It happens to the best of us."

"So you're not just hovering over my desk for your health. You got some advice."

"I have a fella I use sometimes. A private snoop. His office is over on

Flower."

"This private snoop got a name?"

"Nick Moss." A pencil levitated up over the desk and to a pad of paper where it scribbled down an address.

Frank squinted at it. "Funny name for a wolf."

"Not for a meatstick it's not."

"This fella's human?"

The mustache went up and down. Frank imagined that was a nod. "You bet, though you could be forgiven if you thought he was a wolf."

"What's that supposed to mean?"

"You'll see."

Frank pulled the paper from the pad and held it up, appraising the address, as though that could tell him anything. "How good is he?"

"Found *me* once," Bosch said.

ELEVEN

The snoop's office was south of downtown, perched on top of a laundry. A staircase led up the side of the building to a door with the words *Moss Investigations* painted on it in black letters that were almost even. Frank let himself in.

"Can I help you?" asked a siren from over the top of a copy of *Look*.

The room on the other side of the door was a little too big to be a broom closet, but not by much. An empty chair sat by the entrance on Frank's left, and to his right, a tiny table with an empty pastry box and a coffeemaker churning out a liquid that, from the smell of it, couldn't legally be called coffee. A frosted glass window hid whatever was in the room to the right, but if Frank had to guess by the smell, it was a jar of gasoline with a nervous condition. The secretary's desk took up most of the room, and behind her was a large aquarium with a few distinctly frightened-looking fish.

The secretary herself was pretty. Not quite pretty enough for the pictures, but that almost made her more attractive. She was real in a way that most women in this town weren't. Her fairly standard siren coloring wasn't too different from Bermuda's, though her stripes were in a different pattern. Less spirally, more bold. She kept her dark hair up under a scarf. Her goggles fit snugly over her magnified eyes. As Frank looked, he noticed a tiny shrimp flitting around inside one lens.

"I'm looking for Moss," Frank told her.

"Nick!" she sang out. "There's a policeman here to see you!" She smiled at Frank, showing off entirely too many razor-sharp teeth. As pretty as sirens could be, it took a special kind of fella not to blanch when they showed off their choppers.

The door to the office opened, and Frank had never been more unimpressed in his life. Moss was a short man, bearing a distracting resemblance to a weasel some joker decided to put into a suit. He looked like he was trying to cultivate a mustache, but his five o'clock shadow was thick enough that it was hard to tell. He didn't look great, either, with dark circles bruising the undersides of his brown eyes. When he took Frank in, he started, as though he was surprised to see him.

Moss was the source of that nervous gasoline scent, and close up it caught more like the wrong side of a bender. Whatever he'd tried to put on over the sweat was losing the fight. That nervousness poked the wolf. The little man smelled like *prey*.

"What's this about?" he asked.

"Let's talk in your office," Frank said.

"Yeah. Yeah, okay."

Frank squeezed into the office. It felt even smaller in here than in the front room. An overflowing file cabinet took one side of the room, and a desk even messier than Frank's dominated the center. Moss tiptoed around it and sat down in an office chair whose springs groaned like a tired old man. A filthy window peeked out over the traffic on Flower Street. Frank picked one of the chairs in front of the desk and parked himself.

He watched Moss closely, wondering what Bosch saw in the guy. The suit was actually fairly nice. It didn't fit him quite right, though. It was a bit too large, just enough to give the impression of discomfort. Something had happened to the snoop lately. Maybe he was sick.

Moss clinked when he moved, too. When the jacket flapped open, Frank realized why. Slender pockets, each one carrying a vial, were sewn into the inner lining. He also carried weapons under each arm, a pistol under one and a dagger under the other. Whether he could use them was another thing entirely.

"So what's this about?"

"Anonymous Bosch gave me your name."

"Oh." Moss relaxed a bit, but pretty soon he tensed right back up. Frank got the impression the guy was never truly unwound. "I, uh, I take it you want somebody found?"

"Say, you *are* a detective. Yeah, I'm looking for a wolf that went missing."

Moss frowned. "A wolf? As in a cop?"

"As in a cop."

"The LAPD isn't interested in finding him?"

"You want the job or not?"

"I want to know what you're throwing me into." For the first time, Moss looked almost keen.

"I'm not throwing you into anything, Moss. But if you take this, we didn't talk, and you're not looking for who you're looking for."

"You haven't even said your name."

"Wolfman. Frank Wolfman."

"What, really? Sorry, of course. Detective Wolfman. Right. Pleasure to meet you. This wolf I'm finding, what's his name?" Moss pulled out a pad and stubby pencil and was ready to write.

"Lou Garou." The pencil scratched to a stop. "You know him."

"Uh, is that by any chance a common name? Seems like it might be."

"Not especially. I'm talking about Detective Lou Garou. Works homicide."

"Used to have a partner named Phil Moon."

"You do know him."

Moss swallowed and set down pad and pencil. "I know him."

"How?"

"Uh...let's see...met him on one case. A councilman went missing... this was last year. A couple months after that, he hired me for a job."

"Friendly relationship?"

"Not exactly. I don't think he likes me much."

"Can't imagine why. When was the last time you saw him?"

Moss tapped the table. Frank couldn't figure out if the fella was stalling for a lie or just nervous. It was hard to read him past the jittery energy. "It was that case he hired me for. He wanted me to find Bosch. I found him."

"Yeah, Bosch mentioned that."

"What happened? To Garou, I mean."

"I got no idea. He hasn't been seen for a couple days. I talked to his wife, talked to his former girlfriend, nothing." Frank found Moss staring hard at him, and as soon as he noticed, the human looked back to the pad.

"Their names?" Frank rattled them off, along with addresses. "You got any idea on what might have happened?" Moss asked.

"If I knew that, I wouldn't be hiring some private snoop," he growled.

"Yeah, that makes sense." Moss thought it over. "You know where he was last seen?"

"He was at work last Saturday. Near as I can tell, he hasn't been seen since."

Moss looked up from the pad, met Frank's eyes for the barest moment before his gaze slid off and he was staring at his desk again. "Uh, so... Garou. Was he...how much do you know about his caseload?"

Frank couldn't believe it. "You knew Garou was in the Wolf Pack?"

"He never came right out and said it, but he didn't deny it either."

"Did anybody *not* know?"

"How secret is—doesn't matter. Point is, Wolf Pack means he's got enemies."

"Yeah. I shook that tree. Nothing fell out. Wouldn't be the worst if you did the same."

Moss sighed, staring at a framed picture that was face-down on the desk. Frank didn't ask; he didn't want to know what was going on in the weasel's head. "Yeah. Yeah, okay."

"You'll take the job?"

"I never told you my rates."

"You charge me what you charge Bosch. If it's different, I'll know."
Frank got up and went to the door. He put his hand on the knob and
paused. "How did you find him anyway? Bosch, I mean?"

"Long story," Moss said.

"What's the short version?"

"I finally checked the place he was hiding out in."

Frank shook his head. "Don't make me regret hiring you, Moss." He
went out the door, muttering under his breath, "Regret it *more*, I mean."

TWELVE

Frank sat on his front porch. The sun was low in the sky, just kissing the sloping fields of orange trees. He lifted the beer to his lips and took a swallow. Barely tasted it. His mind was far away, into the black distance beyond. Pawning off his work on a meatstick didn't feel right, but every which way he stretched, he found a brick wall. Garou had vanished into thin air. The Wolf Pack didn't know where he was, neither wife nor girlfriend knew, and it wasn't on Bellum. Bud's manner meant Garou had to be found *now*, and even if the whole thing stank, Frank wasn't about to leave his partner holding the bag. The thundering of Jack's shotgun echoed through the groves, but it was far enough away to be someone else's problem. Just like Garou.

A car crept up the road that split the groves into different properties. One benefit of living up on a hill in the middle of nowhere was that cars announced themselves in the day with trails of dust as they left paved roads for dirt ones. At dusk, as it was now, the glowing headlights gave them away. Frank watched it with a bit more interest when it took the turn that pretty much only led to his front door. The car was a '51 Starlight Coupe, and though the dusk light washed out the color, Frank knew it was seafoam green. A flashy ride, one for the pictures. Bud Hound's car.

The Studebaker pulled to a stop behind Frank's car and the heavy door thunked open. Bud got out, waving.

"I don't got anything new to tell you," Frank called out. "Made the drive for nothing."

Bud pulled a crate of Deerhead beer out of the front passenger side. "Oh, you want I should go home?"

"Might as well drink it," Frank grumbled.

Bud came up onto the porch and put the crate down between them. Twelve longnecks poked up. Bud grabbed one, bit the cap off, and spat it into the dust, sitting down on the empty chair next to Frank. They were quiet for a time, relaxing in the easy silence they'd built when they were sharing an unmarked car. The sun disappeared below the trees before Bud broke that silence.

"How've you been, Frank?"

Frank stared at Bud, then shook his head when the other wolf turned to look at him, grinning ear to ear. "Jesus, Bud. What's got into you?"

Bud shrugged. "Nothing," he lied.

"Yeah, okay," Frank said, putting aside his empty bottle and getting one of those Bud had brought. Like Bud, he bit the cap off and spat it into the dark. "It's just this morning, you were on pins and needles."

"You got something you want to tell me, then?"

"No, like I said."

"I figured. I ain't here to ride you for that. I wanted to come down here and have a beer with my old partner. That okay?"

"I won't stop you," Frank said.

"You're all heart, Frank. You ever hear that?" Bud said without malice.

They sat in silence some more. It felt right to Frank, being with Bud. Maybe that was part of whatever it was that made them wolves. Some piece that connected to nature in a way he couldn't consciously put words to. It had been so long since he'd had a partner, he didn't think he missed it, but sitting there with Bud put the lie to that. Only now, with Bellum's tendrils through everything, there were no real partners anymore. The scent of citrus hung heavy in the air, but a sharpness lurked in it, like a wasp in the fruit.

"This really is a nice place, Frank. Could use a woman's touch, but I can't think of anything that doesn't."

An image of Susan was bright in Frank's mind. "Nobody's volunteering."

"Frank, I've known you for, what, three years now? I haven't seen you with a girl that whole time."

"There's been women," Frank said, maybe a little too defensively.

"Sure, partner." He paused. "Heard from Susan at all?"

Frank shifted in his chair. Soon as it was out of his mouth, he'd regretted telling Bud about her. That was his own pain. Shouldn't have to burden anybody with it. Besides, he wasn't the first man to have lost somebody. That was what being a man was all about—taking the pain and bearing it. "Nah. She moved east. Kansas, I think."

"Has to be the first dame who started out in Hollywood and went to Kansas."

Frank shrugged. "I can't blame her."

"Can't blame her? Frank, she didn't have to leave. That was her choice. Did you want her to go?"

"'Course not," Frank replied. "Put yourself in her shoes. Her husband's police, so it's in her head somewheres that he might come home with some lead in him. Only he's on duty one full moon, and the crazy he's chasing turns out to be a wolfman. Next full moon, her husband turns into a monster."

"Frank, that happens every full moon."

Frank gave a violent shake of his head. Bud wasn't getting it, making like the world *hadn't* changed. Everything anyone thought they knew turned upside-down and a little over ten years later and the world wanted to pretend it was like it always had been. "Not back then it didn't. Most folks didn't know what was going on. They didn't have those home cages, nothing like that. All she knew was her husband turned into a monster. What do you expect her to do?"

Bud shook his head. "Dumbest move there is. Now she's not married to a cop. She's probably been turned already."

The wolf inside snarled at the thought. "Hope not. Hope she's still human."

"Ain't no future for them, partner. Best thing for her. Best thing for *you* is to stop thinking about her all the time."

"I don't think about her."

"That so? If I was to walk into that house, I'm not gonna find a single snap of her?"

"Nobody said you got to go inside."

Bud grinned. "Tells me everything I gotta know, partner."

"Should I go get myself a siren chorus girl?"

"Maybe someone a little more your speed, but sure. Don't think you could keep up with no chorus girl."

"Yeah, no argument there."

Bud's voice turned serious. "I'm not kidding, Frank. You should find somebody to look after you."

"I'm doing fine on my lonesome."

His partner sighed. "I'm not saying you ain't. But you could be doing better. A life's not really finished if you're only living for one."

"There a Mrs. Hound I don't know about?"

Bud coughed, staring into his beer. "Maybe I never met the right person. Besides, didn't seem fair, once I joined up with the Wolf Pack. Watching the way the married fellas...the wives were scared and they made the fellas more scared. We were walking into a silver rain damn near every night. Not right putting a person through that."

"What if she wanted to?"

Bud frowned. "Not a person alive is fine with their mister dodging bullets."

"No, no. I mean, you think a dame could be a cop? I'm not talkin' about a meter maid. I mean real police."

"There's a difference between loyalty and honor. I figure a woman knows the first one, maybe even better than we do. But the second one? That's what you need to be police, and I don't know a woman who knows honor like a man."

"Honor, huh?"

"Honor. Sticking with a gunfight you know you'll lose, or sticking with a case until it gets solved."

Frank grunted. He didn't have anything to add. "So you gonna find yourself a loyal woman, even if she doesn't have honor?"

"Maybe next week," Bud said with another grin that never made it past his mouth and faded as he turned his attention to his beer.

Frank felt like an idiot. The Wolf Pack didn't exist, but the wolves who had been a part of it were getting gunned down weekly. And there was still the missing one Frank couldn't find. "Yeah, I'll start then, too."

Bud reached his bottle over, and Frank gave it a clink. They watched the orange trees for a time, now mere shadows, and drank in the scents. Scents that could almost remind Frank of a time the world wasn't rotten to its core.

Finally Bud broke the silence. "You got family, Frank? Real family? Human?"

It was a hell of a question. One of the only taboos everybody could agree on. Even after the two of them had shared a car for over a year, put their lives in each other's hands, it wasn't a question Frank would have asked. In another situation, a different night, he might have told Bud to get lost. A lie would have dishonored them both.

"Uh...yeah. I got a nephew. Last I heard, he moved east."

"That's it?"

"So far as I know. Night War didn't really go well for everybody."

"No, it didn't," Bud agreed. He was quiet for a little while, before, "I got a sister. A crawling eye. Changed her name to Victoria Humor when she got changed." He shook his head.

"You went with Bud Hound," Frank pointed out.

"Yeah. Sounds like a cop name. I have a nose for crime."

Frank blinked. "Please tell me you never said that to anyone."

Bud blushed. "That's not important. Anyway, you named yourself Frank Wolfman. I bet you didn't even change your first name."

"It's a perfectly fine first name."

"Thought, partner. Some folks put *thought* into their names."

"For the sake of a joke."

"World's a joke," Bud said. "Anyway, my sister—"

"Why are you telling me about your sister? Oh, I see. Look, partner, I appreciate the thought, but crawling eyes aren't really my phase of the moon. Some gents can... What?"

"Frank, I ain't fixing you up with my sister. She's married."

"Oh. Good. Good for her. Congratulations."

"It's just...I bring her up because if something happens to me, I want someone around to kind of look in on her."

"Don't she got a husband for that?"

"You know what I mean."

"Why me?"

"I can trust you."

"When you left to join up with the Wolf Pack, I thought you was gonna get a better class of police in your life."

"I did. Then the Pack started getting gunned down. In the old days, it wasn't so bad. It was how we were supposed to go. A stand-up fight ain't nothing to be ashamed of. But now, it's all silver in the back. Anybody in the Pack is counting down, Frank. Every moon we howl at could be the last. It's why I need you, Frank. We're not in the same pack anymore, but we *were*. And that matters, right?"

"It matters, partner." Frank drank again. Back in the Day War, he'd understood what a pack was. Not really in those words, but he'd gotten it. It transferred over to the LAPD, and once they'd all been changed, it was assumed. Not something wolves had to talk about; it was something they knew in the parts of them that had to sing to the moon.

"Thanks, Frank. She'll be fine, but it's nice to know. You know."

"Sure thing, Bud. Sure thing."

They sat together and drank, with nothing else that needed to be said.

THIRTEEN

The ward box rattled and jumped in Frank's hands. It was made of holly, and he was pretty sure that wasn't for the sake of a pun. It was carved with runes, anointed with oil, and crisscrossed with cold iron chains. The city's shield, the lid inlaid with pewter, gleamed. Inside was the top half of a skull, most of an arm bone, and a little grave dust.

"Knock it off," Frank growled to the box, "or I'll tack on resisting arrest." It was a hollow threat. Any ghost that wasn't manifesting hordes of spiders or making the walls bleed wasn't going to get charged with anything. A little rattling was just because, near as Frank could figure, getting trapped in a ward box was about as comfortable for a ghost as a pair of silver bracelets would be for him.

He came in through the front door of the Highland Park Station, placing the box on the desk in front of the sergeant. "Mourning Fogg. Book her for the murder of Lord Decoratorius," Frank said.

The sergeant was clicking his typewriter when Frank heard a booming voice from across the lobby. "Frank, tell me you made an arrest."

Frank looked over to find Captain Talbot approaching him with a wide, glad-handing smile on his face. "Yes sir. The housekeeper. Ectoplasm on the curtain cords, and she as much admitted the whole thing when I pressed her."

"Well done, Detective. I trust the report will be on my desk in the morning."

"It will," Frank said.

"Don't sound so glum, Frank. You wrapped this thing up in time for the full moon. I always find I enjoy the time more when I don't have anything hanging over my head."

"I could catch a case tomorrow."

"Nonsense," Talbot said. "You closed this one, you're getting your day off. Then, after you blow off a little steam, you can come back a new wolf. The people of Los Angeles depend on you."

Frank made sure Fogg got into the ghost cell—just a wall of boxes like they had at the bank, carved with some runes—and got the officer on duty to open up Eduardo Carias's cell. The kid looked sullenly up from his bench. In the next cell over, a martian reached for him with flabby tentacles. Two cells over, a pair of zombies were staring and moaning "Brains" at each other. Either the kid didn't see or he had gotten used to it.

"Come on, kid. I'm springing you."

"Gee, thanks." Carias got up, bare feet slapping on the cement floor.

Frank walked the kid up out of the basement and to the front. "I'll give you a ride home."

"Stuff it, cop."

"Hey, I got you out of lockup," Frank griped.

"After how long? I told you I didn't do it."

"I got the one who did. Now come on. You're not gonna walk home on bare feet."

"Watch me."

Eduardo Carias walked away, drawing looks from a pair of ghouls on the street. "Keep walkin'," Frank growled at them, and they rapidly put together who he was and did just that. Frank watched Carias make his way up York Avenue. He shook his head. The kid was crazy, and he wasn't going to last. Made him like every other human in town.

Frank went back inside, plopped himself behind his desk, and started the hard work of filling out the report. He was an awful typist, and too often the report took more time to finish than the investigation. He had it done long after Talbot had gone home, and so just left it on the captain's desk.

Frank contemplated the long drive home in the front seat of his Plymouth. When he finally got moving and made the turn north rather than south, he refused to think about where he was really going. He knew that if he did, he would turn around and he didn't want that. He kept hearing Bud telling him to find a woman, and seeing Susan's face when she told him she was leaving. The citrus scent in the trees was bright that afternoon, or maybe it was his newly sharpened sense of smell. The crickets purred through the groves, and his wife was terrified. They didn't prepare you for living with a monster back then. *I'm going to live with my cousins,* she said, and he watched her pick up two bags, and march to the pickup waiting outside, shoulders squared but quivering. Her cousin was behind the wheel, ready to take her to Kansas or somewhere east. Everywhere was east. Frank didn't even protest. What was he going to say? He *was* a monster. Sometimes he wondered what would have happened if he had said something. Still couldn't think of what, though.

He went north, through the gap in the hills, into edges of the suburban sprawl north of the city proper. Somehow, he already knew the route by heart. He'd committed it to memory without consciously realizing he had, and it pulled him with all the mysterious insistence of the moon. Soon he was in front of Lulu Garou's home, staring at the gold paint, faded like her relationship to her husband. Only then did he start to wonder what the hell he was doing. He knew only that he had to be there. That his presence felt right in a way nothing else had.

He kept wondering as he went up her walk and knocked on the front door. The porch light came on, and then the door opened. Lulu Garou stood there, as dolled up as she'd been before, but her eyes were red and she dabbed at them with a handkerchief. Frank had to wonder, had she been crying the whole time? All for Garou? Her musky scent hit him like a heavyweight's right cross and he was having trouble putting one thought in front of another.

"Detective Wolfman. Did something happen with my husband?"

"No, ma'am. I'm sorry. I didn't mean to scare you." He paused, trying to think of what a sensitive man might say. "Are you all right?"

"Lulu."

"Ma'am."

"It's Lulu."

"Frank," he said.

"Well, come on in. I was just watching the news."

Frank followed her inside. The television was on, showing milling bandaged backs of mummies, and uniforms of police, some with the wolf fully out. Frank glimpsed some stone steps, and then thick ropes, maybe tentacles, draped down them. Frank didn't much watch the news; it mostly said what the folks in charge wanted you to know. This looked different. Like actual news.

"What's going on?" he asked, feeling like a sucker.

"Eden was assassinated," she said.

Frank frowned. It took him a second to place the name. "Gardenio Eden?"

Lulu nodded. "Yeah. He was killed after a speech."

Frank wasn't sure how one went about killing a gigantic carnivorous seed pod, but humans were pretty inventive. And they had a record of doing this kind of thing. "They catch who did it?"

"I think so. They arrested a human."

"Of course they did."

"You think it was a human?"

Frank nodded. "Stands to reason. It was a human last time." Everyone had a clear memory of that day. The news cameras had gotten the whole thing, and broadcast it over and over until the treaty had been signed. The indelible image was that of the human, later identified as Raymond James Fish, hurling the burning bottle at new President Rameses III and turning him into a pyre. Just before the Secret Service turned the wolves on him.

"That was right after the War. Feelings were a little more raw then."

'52 seemed like a lifetime ago. "The world has changed a lot since then," Frank allowed.

"Not enough."

"What did Eden do?" Now, the camera glimpsed the fallen plant between the rapidly shifting figures surrounding him.

"Nothing. He was sympathetic to the humans."

"Why would a human kill him, then?"

Lulu Garou shook her head, and said firmly, "They *wouldn't*."

"I'm sorry," Frank said. "I don't really follow politics."

"Then how do you know who to vote for?"

"I don't vote. One fella's the same as any other. Used to be Republicans and Democrats, now it's Americans and Liberties and...there's another one."

"Two more. Popular and Nocturnal."

"See? If I tried to vote, I'd just get it wrong."

"It's a vote. You can't get it wrong."

"I think you can. I think most people do. I take it you were going to vote for him," he said, gesturing to the TV.

"I was thinking about it. Him or Veritas." She sniffed. "I'm sorry. I just started and now I can't stop."

"Something like this can be a shock."

"It's not," she said. "I think that's the worst part."

"He's one monster. There will be others."

"Not like him. And this...I feel like we're back in the days of the Civil War."

"We're through it. Called it the Night War this time."

"Treaties don't end wars. Besides, Lincoln was killed *after* the end of the last one."

Frank shifted, uncomfortable. Lulu turned away, back to the television. Reluctantly, she shut it off, then turned back to Frank. "What can I do for you, Frank?"

"I'm sorry. I didn't know it was a bad time."

"Don't be silly," she said, drying her tears. "Do you want something to drink?"

"More orange juice?"

She smiled. "I could use something a little harder."

"That sounds good."

Frank felt wrong sitting down on Lulu's immaculate couch. He thought of it as hers rather than Garou's. He might have paid for it, but she was the one who lived with it. Frank was getting the impression that Garou had seen his home as a last resort. Hell of a way to think of a place like this and a dame like her.

The couch wasn't quite as immaculate as before. The cushion sported a dent Frank was certain would match the precise contours of Lulu's rear end and he forced himself to find someplace else to slap his eyes. Rings on the coffee table hadn't been cleaned up, nor had yesterday's newspaper, turned to the entertainment section. A photo of the touring Russian ballet, the graceful lines of the dancers turned abstract on account of the whole thing being upside-down.

Lulu returned from the kitchen with two glasses. Real ones, not the jelly jars Frank used. She handed one over, kissed it with hers, and said, "Mud in your eye."

Frank coughed. Having the undivided attention of a lady like Lulu Garou made it difficult to think straight. The liquor was sweeter than he was expecting. The orange peel and cherry floating among the ice should have tipped him off.

"Apologies, I should have asked if you were an old fashioned man," Lulu said.

"I wouldn't know how to answer anyway."

She chuckled. "I'm sorry you saw me that way. I feel silly." She nodded at the television, now off.

"Don't think anything of it." Broken up over some plant getting it, but at peace with her husband missing. Or so she projected at Frank.

Lulu sat down and Frank reluctantly did the same. "To what do I owe this visit?"

Frank's lie came so readily, he almost believed it. "I wanted to see if you remembered anything else. Anyone your husband mentioned. Anywhere…" He shrugged. She would have made an incredible cop. She was damn near impossible to lie to.

Lulu thought about it, or at least she pretended to. Frank wanted to believe she was innocent in all this. Just a neglected wife abandoned by a thoughtless brute of a husband. But the simple fact of police work was that before he could move on, he had to be sure Lulu hadn't done it. If there was even an "it" to be done.

"I can't think of anything, Det…Frank." She sighed. "Lou didn't really talk to me about those things. Didn't really talk to me about most things."

"I'm sorry to hear that."

"It's marriage."

"Tell me about it."

"Are you married?"

"Not anymore."

She nodded, sipping on her cocktail, eyes far away. "The full moon is tomorrow. If he's going to turn up, it's then."

"You seem awful calm about this, Lulu."

"I don't know how I'm supposed to feel," she said with a resigned shrug. "Lou already had a foot out the door. Had for a long time. Now that he's gone, I'm worried for him, but I'm also relieved. I don't have to wonder anymore."

"Wonder about what?"

"About him. About where he'll land on everything I want."

"Little Monster House?"

She chuckled, her cheeks reddening just a bit as she stared into the murky depths of her cocktail. "That was silly. I knew it was silly when I took the brochure."

"But you still took it."

"I still took it." Another shrug. "Part of me thought that if we found someone to turn, I could have a little company. Somebody to talk to."

"It's a crime he didn't jump at the chance to talk to you." Frank realized what he'd said a second after it passed his lips; it was his turn to look away and hope she didn't see it burning on his face.

"You could always arrest him for it. If you find him."

"Charges would never stick."

Frank felt her staring at him, and he fought not to wither. Lulu Garou was a beautiful woman, but it was the contours of that beauty, her strong frame and heavy features, that spoke right to Frank's soul. She was the kind of woman who should be leading a tribe of barbarians through a fallen Rome. And here she'd been cooped up in this museum.

"Got plans?" she asked him.

"Plans? Track your hus...track Garou down. Find out where he's been."

"No," she said. "For the full moon."

"Hard to plan those kinds of things."

"You aren't one of those wolves who locks himself in a cage on those nights."

"No, no, no," Frank said quickly. "Usually I just let myself change out in the orange groves around my place. I hunt, like you're supposed to. Wake up in the dirt, smelling like blood and oranges."

"That doesn't sound so bad."

"What do you do?"

"I've been staying inside. Lock all the doors."

"That's a good way to wake up with a broken-down door."

"I had a witch put some wards on it. Keeps me inside."

Frank watched her. "You're a wolf."

"A wolfman."

"Six of one," he said.

"No, it's not the same. I'm a wolf*man*. We're not like gill-men and sirens, or witches and mad scientists, where we're separate. We're the same monster, you and I. But it's different for you. You're a cop. You keep the city safe for twenty-eight days. On *one* night you go out and get some blood under your claws. I'm a housewife. I was turned because my husband was a wolfman. On paper, I'm the same. In real life, I'm not."

Frank absorbed it all. "If it was up to me, Lulu, you'd be out there under the moon like the rest of us, howling to beat the band."

She looked away, and Frank imagined she was picturing herself doing all the things they were supposed to as wolves. As wolfmen. She could be the barbarian woman he saw under the pretty dress and coiffed hair. The woman Lou Garou never wanted her to be while he was out making time with a siren. Frank had to concentrate on his drink again, because he was staring. Lulu Garou was easy to stare at.

"Frank?"

He looked up, found her dark eyes on him. He saw the edges of pain, of real humiliation there, but also determination. "Yeah?"

"Have you talked to my husband's mistress?"

Frank swallowed. "You know about her?"

She smiled sadly, the edges of those other feelings crashing down over her features. "I do now."

Frank coughed out some good whiskey. "Can't believe I fell for that one," he managed to mutter.

"It's all right, Frank. I suspected. I'd have to be the dumbest woman alive if I didn't."

That's motive, Frank's cop brain pointed out. He didn't want to believe it. "It ain't all right."

"I made peace with it. The other Wolf Pack wives...we all knew, but we talked around it. It was just something we all accepted—as long as our husbands didn't flaunt it."

"Hell of a way to live," Frank said.

"I don't need your judgment."

"I ain't judging *you*." He swallowed the last of his drink and put it down on the table. "Thank you for the drink. I should be getting home."

She nodded. "It was nice to see you, Frank."

He spent some time on the way thinking about what she might have meant.

FOURTEEN

Lulu had moved into Frank's mind, and she'd brought all her stuff. He knew he was mooning over her like a lovestruck kid, but he couldn't stop himself. Even catching up on paperwork, his thoughts slipped to the feel of her gaze on him, the smell of her body, her posture when she was making a point. He leaned back, rubbing his eyes. Blinded already. If he was really lucky, Garou *had* left her. Skipped town ahead of Bellum's hitters, and ready to start a new life in a new town with a new girl. And Frank could...even with all of that falling into place, he couldn't picture it.

Didn't help that it was the day of the full moon. He and every other wolf in the station could feel it pulling, already bringing with it the red dreams of the big night. Tempers were frayed to breaking. Everyone was a step away from going for the throat. *Any* throat. Frank wanted to eat something raw and glistening, but he was stuck with paperwork and schoolkid daydreams of an impossible woman.

"Detective?" The speaker was the desk sergeant, scratching at the thick growth of beard that often came with the moon. "You got a visitor at the front."

"Visitor?"

"Yeah, short guy, kinda nervous. Smells like bad coffee and gasoline."

"Moss," Frank growled. "Yeah, send him over."

The sergeant nodded, and a moment later, Nick Moss wandered into the bullpen, craning his head around. He looked like a rabbit caught in a wolf den—which is exactly what he was. The wolf in Frank wanted to chase the little man, and on a day like today, he was even more inclined to listen. Maybe over a moor, if there were such a thing nearby. Instead he stood up, grunted "Moss!" and beckoned the meatstick over.

Moss put on the jets, his steps staccato. "Detective Wolfman, hi."

"You could use a damn phone if you don't like police stations."

"Thought I could bring you the news personally."

"Not here," Frank said, glancing around.

"Yeah, yeah, okay."

Frank had the impression that he could have convinced Moss to have the meeting inside one of the sea monster tanks at Neptune's Kingdom, just as long as it meant they left the station. He led Moss out the door, hoping not too many of the wolves present saw him meeting with a private snoop, let alone a meatstick. Wouldn't do for his reputation.

Frank walked down York. The station gave way to a line of houses, and from there, a market at the corner. They were both silent as they turned and headed into the hilly suburban streets behind the station. Plenty of people would see them talking, but very few would be cops. They wouldn't catch the significance. From a distance, Moss could pass for a wolfman.

"Uh, Detective?" Moss ventured.

"You wanted to talk to me, so talk."

"Oh. I...uh, I didn't realize we were...okay. Garou is missing."

"I know that, Moss. Why did you think I hired you?"

"No, no," Moss shook his head. "That's not my point. My point is that he's *missing*. I shook every tree. Talked to everyone I could who didn't have a badge. No one knows where he is."

Frank stopped, turned to Moss and fixed him with a glare. The wolf was snarling right underneath his skin. "Are you telling me that you can't find him?"

Moss quailed, but nodded. "That's exactly what I'm saying."

"Bosch said you were a bloodhound. Said you found *him*—an invisible man."

"That was, um, well, every case has its challenges, and in that one...
see, there was this phantom—"

"I ain't asking for the story."

"Sorry, I didn't know what you're asking for."

"I'm asking you to do your goddamn job, you twitchy meatstick. I told
you to find Garou."

Moss stank of fear, but it was hard to tell if it was because of what he
was saying, or general nervousness. Moss smelled like prey every day of
his life; Frank had noticed it back at the meatstick's office. But on the day
before the full moon, the wolf demanded Frank do something about that
smell. "You've only been looking for two days."

"I know. I also know when it's a lost cause. Look, I'm sorry, but Garou
is missing and he's going to stay that way."

"You don't have to sound so happy about that."

"I'm not! I'm not. I'm sorry, actually. I wish I had better news for
you."

Frank shook his head in disgust. "Don't know how you have Bosch
snowed, meatstick."

"I'm sorry?"

"He thinks you're a real detective. Should have known you were just
some flimflam man. My own fault for hiring one of you." Frank started to
walk away, leaving Moss on the street.

"About that?" the weasel ventured.

"About what?" growled Frank. He thought if he stayed on that street
with Moss, he was going to do something that wouldn't be strictly legal for
another six hours or so.

"You hired me; I did work the case."

"File a claim," Frank told him. "See where that gets you."

He was seething as he stalked back into the station. The world felt a
tiny bit smaller and a little bit hotter. The moon, the anger, had given him
a couple more pounds of muscle, a thin coating of fur, and the beginnings
of fangs. Not a full change, but close to it. Ready to let the wolf out all the

way and really put the hurt on someone. The night couldn't come quick enough.

"Was that Nick the Stick?"

Frank's eyes took a second to focus. He hadn't been looking at the reports in front of him, but he imagined it might have looked that way. Bud Hound stood by his desk, concerned, maybe, and just as furry as the desk sergeant was. Bud tended to grow a seven o'clock shadow if the wolf got anywhere even close to the surface, and today, it was going to hover right under the skin until it burst out.

"Nick the what?"

"The Stick."

"I s'pose." Frank knew right then he wasn't going to get anything done. "C'mon, partner. Let's get a drink. We need to have ourselves a conversation."

"You said it."

FIFTEEN

Bud tapped the Formica table, and the sound was too hard and crisp to be made by a fingernail. Thick hair, nearly fur, poked from his cuffs. His jaw worked on an underbite. It was easy to spot the wolves on the day before the full moon, and one of the reasons Frank chose this diner to talk was that there weren't any there beyond him and Bud.

The waitress, a gray-skinned ghoul, took their orders timidly. It was the timidity that almost made Frank lash out. When she left, he concentrated on what he had to say. Words stuck in a throat that only wanted to howl at the coming moon.

"So what's this Nick the Stick malarkey?" he growled at Bud.

Bud's finger stopped tapping. The fingernail was definitely a bit longer, yellower, and sharper. He'd be carving a divot into the table, but the owner of the diner wasn't going to say boo. "Nick the Stick. The little weasel you were talking to in there. That was him, right?"

"That's what they call him?"

"That's what I always heard. They call him that on account of he's a meatstick. And his name's Nick."

"Thanks partner, I put that together."

"Right." Bud colored a bit. "Where the hell are our drinks?"

Either the ghoul heard or luck was on her side. She put a mug of coffee in front of Frank and a bubbly glass of red soda pop in front of Bud.

Bud grunted a thank you and even flashed what might have been a smile if he hadn't had his fangs. He took a swig of his drink.

"Don't know how you stand that poison," Frank said.

"*When only one thing hits the spot, when the victims don't taste so hot, have an ice-cold Plaaaaasma,*" Bud sang, just like in the commercial, if the dame who sang the jingle had a rabid badger stuck in her throat. He lifted the cup up and gave Frank a wink, sipping the blood-flavored soft drink. The wolf in his face receded a little bit.

"They make that stuff for leeches," Frank pointed out.

"Doesn't mean it's not tasty."

Frank shook his head. "If any of the fellas saw you—"

"They'd make me disappear?" Bud said.

Frank felt like he'd been shot in the gut. "Yeah. Guess you're right." He shifted in his chair, desperate to change the subject to something that didn't hurt. "Who is this Stick fella, anyway?"

"You're meeting with him, don't know who he is?"

Frank shrugged. "This is your chance to be the better detective."

Bud gave him the finger. "Stick's some kind of gangster."

"Him?"

"I know. Wouldn't know it to look at him, but he's one of the brassiest meatsticks you'll ever see."

"Him."

"Him. Used to hang around the Nocturnist."

"Him."

Bud nodded. "He was even seeing one of the skin-dollies who worked there."

"*Him?*"

Bud laughed. "What can I tell you? Weasel-y waters run deep, I guess."

Frank shook his head, trying to square this with what little he knew of Moss. The truth was, the little meatstick looked too scared to be in the same county as a monster, let alone walk into a roomful of them at night. Especially the crowd the Nocturnist drew.

"So this Stick is a gangster? Doesn't look like he works for the Gray Matter, and she's the only game in town."

"Nah. I think he was with Mickey Cohen's outfit before he got sent upstate."

Frank fixed Bud with a stare. "He wasn't seeing one of your girls, was he?"

Bud choked on the soda. "Nothin' like that. The one he was with was a real ice queen type, you know? Didn't much like the fellas."

"Didn't much like *you*, you mean."

"A lady doesn't like me, she doesn't like fellas."

"Okay, so this meatstick is a gangster, and you knew it, and you never brought him in."

"I thought it was funny, myself. One night I was at the Nocturnist, and the Stick comes in like he owns the place. You know how meatsticks are. He takes a table, and he has that skin-dolly—real willow tree, her—bringing him drinks all night. Writin' notes to each other like schoolkids. I ask around a little bit, and I get the story. I bring it to the Wolf Pack and you know what I hear? He's okay. This fella, this gangster, he's *okay*. We don't worry about him."

Frank frowned. "That *is* funny."

"You said it."

"Who said no? Moore?" Detective Lieutenant Hunter Moore was the one publicly known member of the Wolf Pack: its leader.

"No, it was Lou Garou," Bud said, and then his eyes widened as he put two and two together and, yep, it made four. "Wait, is that why he came in? You think he has something to do with it?"

Well, now I do, Frank thought, but he shook his head. "No, no. Nothin' like that. Unrelated matter."

"Unrelated. How'd you find him?"

"Bosch turned me onto him. Uses him to bird-dog witnesses from time to time. Get this, your gangster is a private snoop."

"Makes sense," Bud said. "Lot of these trouble boys get a dick's license so they can carry silver and whatnot."

"Bosch swears by him."

"Could be. Any meatstick who can score a skin-dolly and shows his face at the Nocturnist has something—" He gestured, indicating that whatever something that was, it was likely located in the neighborhood of his lap. "Dunno what, but it's definitely something."

The food arrived, two steaks, damn near raw. The ghoul stuck around only long enough to make sure they didn't need ketchup. It took a little bit of energy for Frank to use his utensils. Bud didn't bother; he just picked up the slab of meat and tore chunks off it with his teeth.

"What's your interest in the Stick, anyways?" Bud asked.

"It ain't important."

"New CI," his partner said knowingly. "Smart. That's why you were always the brains of the operation."

Frank let Bud go right on thinking what he was thinking. Hiring a possible gangster to find Garou wouldn't go over well. "Caseload never stops."

"You'd think people'd be better behaved in the City of Angels."

"Anybody still call it that?"

Bud chuckled, slurping down a chunk of meat. "Ones who see it on TV maybe?" The other wolf dropped his voice and glanced around. "Any headway on Lou?"

"Sorry partner. You ask me, he left town."

"He didn't leave town," Bud insisted.

"I'm telling you, partner. I looked. Garou's a fart in the wind."

"If you was him, you'd take the wife or the ladyfriend, right?"

If I was him, I wouldn't leave the wife. "Not everybody shares your priorities, partner."

"I'm telling you!" Bud slammed his fists on the table. It was so sudden, it pulled a dangerous growl from Frank's throat. The diner went silent, everyone in it watching the two wolfmen but doing their best not to look. Frank swallowed the snarl and held out a hand to placate Bud.

"I'm okay," Bud said. Then, more to himself: "I'm okay."

Conversations started up around them, but they were soft, tentative. Everyone had an eye on the door just in case the full moon came early.

"Help me here," Frank said. "How can you be so goddamn sure he didn't skip town?"

Bud shook his head. "Trust me, partner. You gotta trust me. Lou wouldn't just leave without telling me."

"Telling *you?*"

Bud flinched. "Telling *somebody.*"

"One of the Wolf Packers, you mean."

Bud nodded. "He didn't skip, and he didn't catch some silver during a raid. Only one thing left."

"I could sit on Triangle," Frank sighed.

"They broke up."

"He broke up with his wife. He just forgot to tell her. If he was going anywhere, it's with Triangle."

"Did you check the motels?"

"What, every roadside Hausferatu?" Frank couldn't picture a well-heeled Wolf Packer like Lou Garou staying in one of those roadside shacks, but stranger things and all that.

"No, no," Bud said, waving the silly idea away. "The *motels.*"

"You know I don't use those, Bud. Someone didn't do it, making 'em sweat in a box while I work 'em over is gonna make 'em say they did. Then I got an innocent mug on the hook and a guilty man free. It's for the birds."

Bud smiled. "If you was wondering, that's one reason I came to you."

"You're breaking my heart."

"Look, the Wolf Pack used motels. I ain't proud of it, but we were fighting a different kind of war. One of those hobs ain't gonna turn over a new leaf because you put him in a cage. No, he'd have six different leeches showing up cryin' about his rights."

"How many hobs are buried outside of those?"

Bud looked at the thin red juice on his plate. "More than a couple. Wasn't just hobs."

"I figured."

"Point is, we got some motels that nobody but the Wolf Pack knows about. If Lou was gonna hide out, he'd pick one of those."

"Why's this the first I'm hearing of these things?"

"They were the first place we looked when we figured Lou was missing. Wasn't at any of them." Bud saw the question before Frank could ask it. "Doesn't mean he ain't there *now*."

"You're thinking he's moving around."

"Could be. Maybe he ducked us when we came looking. Or maybe he got held up somewheres else and went there. I don't know."

He fixed Bud with a penetrating stare. "What ain't you tellin' me, partner?"

Bud stared right back. Frank saw his old partner there. "Nothing you need to know, Frank. Trust me on that one."

Frank sighed. "I wish I knew how you could be so damn sure he's around."

"Maybe it's hope."

"Didn't think there was any of that left in this town."

SIXTEEN

Frank took the list of locations from Bud, scratched onto a napkin. They felt like the handle of a coffin. These places offended the very heart of him, but every single cop knew they were out there. Hell, he knew where the ones for the Highland Park Station's homicide bureau were—an abandoned house up on the end of Washburn. The yard behind a garage on Figueroa. A shack on Elephant Hill. No matter what his other sins were, he'd never use one of those places.

And his other sins were going to drag him under anyway. He'd made that deal. It was foolish to think he could do any kind of good after what he'd let happen. Still, he held onto this one part of himself. He'd never use a motel.

When he started his car, he didn't head to the first address on the list. No, a lead had been scratching at the back of his mind. Wolves like Bud couldn't walk away from a fight, but Frank couldn't walk away from a clue. Not until he had it between his teeth, until he'd cracked it and tasted the marrow. That was the impulse that led him to following the crazy who turned out to be a wolfman, and it was the same impulse that made Bud think he was a good cop.

He hadn't told Bud. Bud was keeping his own secrets. So was Moss. Everyone in this town had something eating away at their souls from the inside. Garou had it too, and once Frank figured out what that was, he'd know where Garou had gone.

Moss was the lead. His connection with Lou couldn't be a coincidence. Moss copped to knowing Garou, to a single job. One job didn't buy him the goodwill that keeping the Wolf Pack off him would cost. In any case, *something* was definitely off.

The October night would soon swallow up the city, and with it would come the bedlam of the full moon. Frank was going to grab what little time he had, try to catch the clue that hovered maddeningly just out of reach. He drove to Flower and parked down the street from Moss Investigations. Frank didn't have to wait too long before Moss came out and got behind the wheel of a beat-up old Ford Coupe. Frank watched the meatstick carefully, trying to chase out speculation, and only see what was in front of his eyes. The initial read he'd had of the little fella had to be off somehow. If he was a gangster romancing a meat golem, he couldn't be as squirrelly as he appeared. Those stitched-up dollies could take a man's head off with an errant backhand. No telling what one could do in the boudoir.

Some meatsticks—called Daaés after some dame who made time with a phantom in a movie—got off on the danger. Liked sharing a bed with a monster, even. Moss didn't smell like that kind. He smelled like one of those who would piss himself at the first sign of trouble. It didn't square. Nothing did.

Moss knew something, but it could be anything.

The snoop pulled into traffic, and Frank let a few more cars and a spectral charger ahead of him before following. Moss headed downtown. Before long, it was obvious that he wasn't heading into Boyle Heights, one of the few human neighborhoods this far north. He was running parallel to the western edge, heading for Chinatown. Moss took a few more turns, passing the arched rooftops, taking a side road into the hills overlooking the neighborhood. Frank cursed. On the drive here, there had been enough traffic to mask him, but this road was deserted. He'd be made in a second.

Frank pulled over and slumped low in his seat, watching the road Moss had disappeared down. He was playing a hunch, but he'd done that more than once. Some of the other wolves said it was letting the moon drive, but that wasn't right. Only place the moon drove to was blood.

Moss might be a shady character—maybe a gangster, maybe not—but that didn't mean he'd bumped Garou off. For all Frank knew, the meatstick was the one hiding him. He reminded himself not to *want* any outcome. Just pursue it all until he found one.

Frank's hunch paid off. In the dying light of the day, a car crested the hill in front of him. He slouched lower than the wheel and watched as Nick Moss drove by, a bit too fast, heading south. Frank waited until the car's taillights were pinpricks, then started his own car, going to the top of the hill before pulling over and getting out.

He stood on one of a series of hills overlooking the shantytown that clung to the bottom of Chavez Ravine like fungus. The street said the Ravine was no place for a monster, that the meatsticks there were feral, that they never came all the way back from the war. Up here, the only inhabitants were ghosts, and for once Frank wasn't being literal. The place had once been a neighborhood straddling the dirt roads, but the Night War had utterly destroyed it. Humans had taken this high ground and dug in with their machine gun nests and ward dumps and had laid out the red carpet for the monsters' heavy artillery. Some of the houses had been smashed into ruins. Others had been flash-melted. Martian death rays could turn wood into liquid in a single pass, and they had gone to work here, transforming homes into abstract art. The place was eerie, an outdoor memorial to a war that was trying frantically to be forgotten, but stung like a bit of glass caught under a fingernail.

A realization hit Frank with the force of a physical blow.

This was right about where Moon had his ticket punched by hob gunsels. Coincidences happened every day, but not this coincidence and not today. Moss had a reason for coming up here.

Frank sniffed the air. He didn't get much more than exhaust from the roads below, a whiff of smoke from a chimney, the distant spice of Chinese food. He started walking, stopping every twenty feet or so to test the air again. It was slow going, and he hardly noticed the sun inexorably sinking into the horizon.

The moon stalked him as sure as he might stalk a rabbit. Its shadow crept over him like an oil slick, its blood-scented breath was hot on his neck. Frank didn't feel it, didn't clock it consciously because the hooks in his mind that would catch it were being sanded away by the moonrise. As night gathered, he wasn't hunting a witness. He was hunting prey.

Frank's steps, growing ragged and uneven, took him deeper into the hills. He wondered if the battle here had ever had a name. Probably not. The Night War wasn't something anyone liked getting too specific about. It was a rejiggering of priorities. Put monsters on top, where they belonged, and that was the end of it. If they named this place, they'd have to start thinking about all the people who didn't make it through. No telling where that kind of thing would end up. In a hundred years maybe, the Night War wouldn't even be called that. It'd have some soft euphemism that'd melt in a vampire's mouth.

Frank's body reacted before his mind consciously registered what he was perceiving, stilling him in preparation for pursuit. He sniffed, the wolf telling him that *prey* had been there in the recent past. Frank didn't notice the subtle red cast in his vision either, or the way everything was already a little smaller, a bit warmer. The important thing was what filled his sharpening sense of smell.

That godawful cologne. Moss stank like he'd been swimming in La Brea. Like his new ladyfriend was an oil well. Like his hair tonic was forty weight. Frank caught that now, lingering in the air, as reliable as an arrow.

Frank sucked it in. It was only a touch, carried on the breeze coming down from the hill. He loped up the slope, no longer pausing, ready for the final chase where he would bring his rabbit to heel and exult in the hot blood in his mouth and the weakening struggles in his mitts. The scent was a trail leading him to a specific point, exactly where Moss had stood. If the full moon hadn't been so near, he might have missed it. The wolf wouldn't let him.

He stopped at the top of the hill, and he knew he was close. The cologne beckoned to him, sure as the steam from a fresh-baked pie in one of those Marty Meatstick cartoons. A road ran over the top here, half-covered by blown dirt and the odd tumbleweed. Frank knelt. Footprints, bare impressions in the dust but pregnant with the stench of that cologne led from the side of the road in the direction of a fallen house.

Frank inhaled, then sneezed as Moss's noxious scent filled his nose. He crouched, hunched over, his fingers curled like claws. *This* had been Moss's destination. After telling Frank that Lou Garou was lost, he had waited until the end of the day and driven to the top of this nameless hill in Chinatown and...

...another scent wrapped tendrils around the first. A small, confused growl popped out of Frank. The scent was earthy, with a touch of spice. Not floral at all. No, this person smelled like an herb garden at the bottom of a witch's den. And it was a woman. The underlying musk, calling to Frank's wolf, told that story clearly enough. It was a gorgeous scent, and *alive*, so very alive. As natural and musical as Moss's was obnoxious.

Movement grabbed his attention. A shape freed herself from one of the houses. She paused, like a mouse that's heard the screech of an owl. The human part of Frank's mind, growing weaker, quieter by the second, registered that she was beautiful. A Mexican girl, maybe nineteen or twenty, with hair like a crow's wing. She stared at him in terror, ready to bolt. She was a rabbit. And Frank was now a wolf.

He took off after her as the curtain of the moon pulled over his mind. Then she was gone. Vanished into nothing. The animal in Frank turned to another pursuit; hers wasn't the scent he wanted to bathe in. Wasn't the one howling in the dying light of day.

The sun winked and vanished below the horizon. The choir of the wolves serenaded the ascendant moon.

SEVENTEEN

Colors faded. Frank didn't notice. He didn't think of colors much once the moon rose. He forgot the words for them, and he wouldn't have seen much point in them anyway. The only color that mattered was red, and he got that in the ripe coppery scent of blood, in the twitch of prey right before it ran, in the feel of rending flesh under his teeth and claws. *Red* had left the realm of the abstract and become immediate.

Frank was more than he was. By the light of day, he might have said less. The moon had a way of shifting priorities. All that mattered now was the undeniable power in his limbs, the razor-keenness of his senses. He was powerful in a way he wasn't when the sun was in the sky. More than that, he was *free.*

Frank loped through the city. The houses were shut up tight, all of them. Though many were packed with prey who would have been helpless against him, they weren't what the moon called. He sensed the two-legs, those like him, and the four-legs who *weren't.* They prowled, and fought, and hunted on the same night streets as he did.

He caught their scents on the wind first, often the ghosts of their former presence. He hunted for the one scent he wanted, but he couldn't find it. Memory, hazy beneath the pulsing of the moon, drove him north. The scent was there, beckoning just out of reach.

The howls in the air helped guide him as well. There were those like him, the ones that still had a bit of human in them. Caught somewhere between a howl and a scream. He threw his head back and unleashed one of these into the sky, to let all the others know that he was there, and he was not one to be trifled with. Others were indistinguishable from the howls of wolves, and those brought Frank's blood to a hotter simmer. Those wolves shouldn't be anywhere near the territory of his kind. It was like they'd pissed on all those corners for nothing.

Frank had never been overly concerned with territories beyond his own. The orange grove surrounding his home was clearly marked out, not that there were any wolves who made a habit of invading. Now, a part of him, spurred by that *red*, wanted him to stick around in this place, far away from his home, to show the four-legs what he thought of them. On another moon, he might have, but this one compelled a different journey.

The wolf's lair had tickled his animal mind as sure as the clues had tickled the mind of the man. Now, there was no part of the man to keep him from heeding the call, from asking the questions that would keep him in his gray existence. He had been caught outside, and far too close.

Frank didn't feel the distance, but he ran for miles, far enough to exhaust any human being, or him on any other night. As the mountains on the southern edge of the Valley opened up before him, he passed a melee. A huge group, half of his kind and half four-legs, tore into each other. It had to be a slight of territory, these things always were. The howls of his kind tugged at him, demanding he stay here and find the *red*. Only one urge was stronger, pulling him past with the dulcet tones of a siren.

Leaving the streets behind, he climbed into the hills. The constructs of humanity weren't for him, not tonight. He howled again, his own half-scream. This time, he was answered.

He smelled what he had been hunting from the beginning, what had pulled him on this long trek through the city when his mind and his human heart were buried under fur and bone. The scent was strong, alluring in its musk. It wasn't so much inviting as dragging him bodily through the hills. He couldn't have resisted the call if he tried, and he never even considered trying.

He howled again, and this time *she* answered.

Not all red was violent.

This red called to him as surely as the others. Her scent was even stronger, and he caught images of her leaving it along this path. Summoning him. Bringing him to her den. The howl carried with it the same invitation, the violent demand that pulled him bodily to his eventual destination. This wasn't a howl of triumph. She was summoning.

Finally he saw her. She stood at the top of a rise, a black shape against the luminous moon. Fitting, since the moon had driven them both to this place. Frank howled again. He watched her throw her head back and answer him. Though she was close now, his steps slowed. He growled deep in his throat, and she heard him.

She was crouched, like him. The change had made her bigger, stronger. She was covered in a thick pelt of black hair. Fangs jutted from her jaw. Her eyes blazed. Frank no longer thought of beauty. It was her scent that held him now, the glorious musk that needed him.

He paused at the top of the rise. Her hands twisted into claws. Like him, she wore the remnants of clothing, shredded first by the transformation and then by her activities of the evening. She snarled at him. He snarled back. He belonged here. She agreed, but she still might fight him anyway. That was how they did things.

He lunged at her, and she at him. They fell to the earth, scratching, biting, tearing until the two of them found the red the moon demanded from them, and they kept finding it until their bodies gave out utterly.

EIGHTEEN

Frank awoke in the chill of the morning. He lay flat on the dirty ground, dew clinging to the yellow grass on the hill. The air was still blue. The sun had yet to completely rise, and all that was left of the night before was a dim memory. As usual after a full moon, he could only recall base impressions. He tasted blood on his lips, but not as much as usual.

He'd only slept long enough for the moon to lose its grip on him and for the man to take back his form. Might as well have been a week for the time it took his body to regain some pliability. Blinking the sleep from his eyes and sitting up gingerly, he saw that only a few rags somehow had clung to him through his rampage. The only thing intact was his shoulder holster. Those things were designed to hold up to nights like this. He felt a little ridiculous, an armed naked man sitting on a hillside.

A shape stirred next to him, and Frank whipped his head around before he even considered what might be there.

What turned out to be *who*, and the impressions of the previous night started to return. He had made his way halfway across town. He'd been called, and he found her.

It was Lulu Garou in the altogether. She was stirring as well. Not a single scrap of clothing clung to her strong limbs. Rapidly fading scratches and bites crossed her neck and back. Frank knew he shouldn't stare. No matter what had happened during the full moon, it didn't really count, socially speaking. Those of them with the wolf in their veins needed a night without a memory. Not staring at a nude Lulu Garou was perhaps the most difficult thing Frank had ever done, and he had lived through the Day War in an American tank.

"Sorry," he muttered, turning away, and hunting around for a bit of cloth to cover himself. He found a scrap of pants that could kind of serve as long as no one looked too close. Like every other wolfman, he wore suits made out of elastic materials, but those only covered your day-to-day transformations. A full moon transition and a night running through town could chew any outfit apart.

"For what?" Lulu asked. She sat up, not making a move to cover herself. Her muscles rippled like sunlight on a pond.

"I didn't mean to...uh, you know, stare."

"Frank, you did more than stare."

Abruptly, the rag he had over his crotch was too small to completely hide him. "Yeah, I know. That was then."

"Do you regret it?" He felt her gaze boring into the side of his neck. It had been a long time since any woman had seen him like this. Years.

"Hard to regret anything you do on the full moon," he said.

"That's a yes." Lulu stood up, and in the blooming light of the morning, she was magnificent. Frank wasn't prone to poetry, but for the first time he wished he was. A woman like Lulu deserved poetry. Here, he couldn't even tell what rhymed with Lulu. All he could do was stare at the tiny shadows pooled in the dimples in the small of her back.

"Lulu," he said, and had no idea what to say next. Sure, the monsters had taken over, but there still hadn't been a collective agreement on how to treat everything. Besides, "having sex with someone while the both of you were half-beast and in the back of your mind you still think she might have killed her husband and also if she didn't, she might be married" wasn't a scenario one ran into on the regular.

"See you around, Frank," she said, making her way downhill. Maybe she didn't care if anyone saw her, or maybe she was doing it to show Frank what he was missing. As Frank watched her go down the hill toward civilization, he thought of a third possibility. She'd been married to a louse who cheated on her, and now she was free. She'd gotten a chance to do something for herself, and Frank had fouled it up.

Was married. Frank had started to assume Garou was dead, and couldn't make himself hurt for it. Not as he watched Lulu getting smaller and smaller.

He realized pretty quickly that he was on the hill overlooking Lulu Garou's neighborhood, not too far from a road. He scrounged around the hill and found what had been his pants. Now they were a pair of ragged britches, and when he put them on, he had to hold them up with one hand. He hadn't been too careful when it came to taking them off the previous night. Or there was the chance that he hadn't been the one to remove them at all. He unzipped the safety pocket hidden inside the hip pocket and pulled out his spare callbox key. He had that, at least.

He got to his feet, feeling ridiculous. Here he was, like some kid freshly turned, rutting like an animal. *And*, he reminded himself, *couldn't even keep from screwing that up*. Not that he had any idea what he wanted with Lulu Garou. This wasn't the kind of thing that ended with happily ever after. He couldn't see any ending happier than the one that just occurred.

The shreds of the rest of Frank's clothes were scattered over the area. He didn't see a single piece that could have belonged to her. She had prepared for this, been ready to unleash the wolf on the hills of the city. He wished she had worn something, if only that he could have held onto her scent. Something to remember her by. A woman like that *deserved* to be remembered, even if he was as much of a louse as her husband.

NINETEEN

The callbox held Frank upright, carrying the weight of his long night that had lasted years. He muttered into the receiver, giving the dispatcher his location, and angrily nixing an offer of pants. On the streets around him, werewolves and wolfmen sheepishly made their way home after a night of pack hunting under the full moon, now solo. He didn't make eye contact. Same etiquette as a locker room. They all knew what they were about, and Frank was no exception.

In fifteen minutes, a black-and-white pulled up, and Frank poured himself into the backseat with a pained grunt. The driver was in uniform, cap resting on an invisible head. On the night of the full moon, the station was turned over to the few non-wolfmen on the force, mostly invisible men and doppelgangers. Not that they did any crimefighting, mind. They locked the place down, waited out the night, then fielded calls like the one Frank just placed.

"Good night, Detective?" the glass man asked.

"Mind your damn business," Frank suggested.

The uniform took the hint. Frank was one of the first in the station. The fellas who'd been at it all night were moving through molasses, and most of the wolves weren't ready to say goodbye to the moon. Down in the locker room, the hiss of the showers signaled the red scents of a full moon being unceremoniously smothered under soap. Couldn't drown a night like that one all at once. The telltale smells were still under there if a wolf had a mind to sniff at it. Frank knew he should shower, if only for Lulu's reputation. That was part of being a wolf—the next morning washing away the red nights, but knowing it had happened. He wanted to hang onto the scraps of Lulu's scent that clung to him more than he had wanted anything in a long time. He'd never have her, not really, but he could pretend for a few more hours.

He opened his locker and found two suits waiting for him. He shucked off the rags that had managed to cling to him like the last survivors of a shipwreck, extracting only his callbox key, and tossed them in the garbage. He hung his shoulder holster on the locker's hook. Yeah, they were designed to last after nights like that, but the straps now sported scars that Frank was pretty sure he could measure precisely against Lulu's claws. The holster might look like leather, but it was actually some miracle material designed by a brainiac. It was incredible stuff, but even that couldn't stand up to a wolfman deep in his moon. Or her moon, for that matter.

Frank picked one of the clean suits from its hook, pulling it on over his pleasantly aching muscles. Its scent, fresh laundry with just a little bit of a locker room's mildew and bleach aroma over the top, chased off the worst of the pungent slurry he wore from last night. A few splashes of cologne on his wrists completed the change. Any other wolf would smell that long before they sniffed out Lulu. Only Frank would know she was there and he could keep her on his skin for a little bit longer.

Turned out he was a sentimental old cuss. Surprised even him.

He jogged up the stairs, shocked to find more energy in his legs in than he'd had in a long while. He pointed at a uniform loitering at the top of the wooden staircase. The kid in it had that slight waxy scent all doppelgangers carried, like a new candle. "You."

"Yes, Detective?"

Frank tossed the kid his keys. "You and your partner, go get my car. Left it on the hills over Chinatown." He gave the kid as close to an address as he could.

The doppelganger stared at the keys, eyes baggy after a long night. He nodded. "Yes, Detective."

"Leave the keys on my desk, will you?" Frank didn't wait for confirmation. He walked into the bullpen as the radio squawked on the wall, calling wolves that hadn't yet come in from the moon. "Highland Park Station? Come in, Highland Park Station?"

Frank grabbed the speaker from the wall. "Detective Wolfman, go ahead."

"We've got a call. Fountain and Vine. Brains."

"On my way."

A murder wasn't exactly good news, but Frank would take it. A murder would get his mind off the scraps of scent resting on his chest like the exhausted hand of a lover. He grabbed a car from the motor pool and gunned the engine over into Hollywood.

The place in question was a cinch to find. The sign was neon, dead in the cool light of morning. It said *Brains*, but truth be told, a good number of joints in the city bore that handle, or else the same word in some other language. Frank learned the word *Cerebros* when he tried to order a beer in a Mexican joint, and hadn't that been an unpleasant surprise. Restaurants, bars, drugstores, boutiques—well, as close to a boutique as a stiff could get—had signs with that word. Point was, a lot of places were called that because it was the only word the vast majority of its clientele could say.

Hell of a world the monsters had made.

A pair of uniforms stood sentry on the sidewalk near the first responding black-and-white. Normally, they would be shooing away rubberneckers, only the full moon had seen to that for them. The street was still a ghost town, even now.

Fountain and Vine was smack dab in the middle of Hollywood. With Sunset a couple blocks up and Santa Monica a couple down, this corner was where nightlife, showbiz, and the underworld all got stitched together into the golem that was Los Angeles. Prime real estate for a zombie place.

"Detective?" ventured one of the uniforms. He was an invisible man, so the worry was in his voice and on his scent rather than on his face.

"Yeah, I'm here. Whadda we got?"

"A bloodbath," said the other one. He had the same waxy scent as the fella back at the station, but another part of the smell made Frank do a double-take. This doppelganger was a Germanic mountain of a woman, at least at the moment. Frank almost dismissed her to talk to the glass man. Lulu's sadness appeared in his mind, a snapshot of disappointment.

"First one?" he said to her.

She snorted. "Been working this beat a year and a half, sir."

"Right. Who called this in?"

The doppelganger pointed across the street. "Gremlin over there runs a TV repair shop."

"He got a name?"

"It's about sixteen words long and sounds like he should be running some tiny country in Europe. He goes by Spex."

"Spex. Right." Frank looked over at the cramped shop where the call came from. A security gate was still down, the window blacked out against the sun. Gremlins were night owls. When the sun turned you into goo, night owl was the only reasonable thing to be. Frank pictured the little monster peering out that window as the howls reverberated around the city, the one time a month a gremlin prayed for dawn, and getting more of a show than he bargained for.

This particular Brains was an automat. The front door was glass, now in tiny crystalline fragments all over the filthy sidewalk and a few feet of linoleum floor inside. A cashier's till sat right by the door, but no cashier manned it now—just a mottled stain on the wall behind where a head should be. Wasn't red, exactly, more reddish, with plenty of green and brown thrown in. Looked like someone had taken a month-old slop bucket and tossed the contents against the mint-green wall. Frank had seen enough zombies get their tickets punched to know what he was looking at.

He ducked under the door handle and into the dining room, his shoes chewing glass. As always, the scent told the story. The strongest smell was dead zombie. Well, dead*er* zombie. One of the fun parts of having a wolf's senses was being able to distinguish between the mundane stink of a walking corpse and the deeper stinging stench of a corpse who'd moaned his last "Braaaains."

Frank rounded the corner of the counter and found the source of the smell, slumped up against the wall and staring at his lap. The twice-deceased zombie wore shirtsleeves, suspenders, slacks, some nice loafers, and was missing half his melon. Gunk from his shattered head spilled down his collar, over his narrow shoulders, pooling underneath him in a sticky morass. One look at the dead fella told the story, up in black and white on the screen in Frank's mind. The killer had blitzed the front door, grabbed the cashier, and slammed his head against the wall. Plaster and skull cracked. He'd been dead before he hit the floor.

A .45 automatic, same kind he'd had in the service, waited snug in a holster just beneath the countertop. The cashier never had a chance to grab it. Frank slipped it from the leather for a closer peep.

"What are you thinking, Detective?" the uniform asked.

"That I might like a little quiet." Frank slid the clip from the weapon and touched the bullet. It didn't burn. The doppelganger gasped like she'd touched a hot stove. "What?" Frank demanded.

"*Now* you want to know?"

"Out with it, flatfoot."

"That's a cold iron load," she said, nodding to the bullets.

"Figures," Frank said. Cold iron worked on doppelgangers the same way it worked on hobs, and the same way silver worked on him. The Gobfather had been pushing up daisies for the better part of a year, but the city still had its share of trouble boys with a penchant for rhyming and magic tricks. If this place was what Frank thought it was, having security with goblins in mind was to be expected. He returned the gun to its place and stood up, his knees popping like champagne corks.

The movie he was building in his mind spooled out the first reel. The first monster came through the door and punched the cashier's ticket. No other corpses lay in the front of the automat, meaning it was as empty as it ever got—just like it should be on a full moon. The cashier never pulled his heater, so the red carpet was out for the killer.

Frank inhaled, then sneezed violently three times.

"You okay, Detective?" the doppelganger asked.

"Dog pepper," Frank growled. Once cops could ID crooks on their scent, the crooks started carrying stuff to hide their smell. Same way masks had been a part of stick-ups since the first highwayman requested a stand and deliver. Frank plugged one nostril and blew it out, then the other. Wouldn't get rid of the pepper that was already up there and making his eyes water, but it made him feel better anyway.

The back wall of Brains was the usual semicircular automat dispensary. Frank peered through a few of the windows and saw that the place wasn't lightly named. Helpfully, the options were labeled, letting a customer know the source of the brains and if any special sauces or seasonings had been used. None of the labels said "human." This place wasn't rich and fancy enough to pay for legal human brains, and if it was what Frank was thinking it was, they wouldn't have courted trouble by offering those anyway.

Through the little windows in the front, past the pies on display, and through the back windows of each individual compartment, Frank could see a little bit of what he assumed was the kitchen. A few dark shapes loomed back there, but nothing moved, and he couldn't catch a solid scent over the pepper and cooked brains. So he followed the line of the windows to the swinging door and nudged it.

The scent hit him harder this time. A dead zombie's final breath hung in the air like a week-old steak in a graveyard, dog pepper buzzing beneath that like a swarm of angry bees. Blood was next, fresh. What Frank thought of as "real" blood, not whatever sludge came out of zombies like yogurt whenever they sprung a leak. The door swung open and he saw why: the inside was painted with blood. It dripped and pooled on the walls and floors like a slaughterhouse. The scent reached into Frank's nostrils and shook the wolf that had been sleeping since the moon set.

Frank stepped inside, catching a whiff of wolf. Not a werewolf. Wolf*man*. *Not* himself, and it sure wasn't the glass man or the waxwork. A wolfman had been in this room. Frank wished he was shocked, but the revelation was waiting patiently in the corner as the evidence mounted. In the blood splattering the doorway was the confirmation, lurking in a scent not even the dog pepper could kill. A wolfman had bled.

At the other end of the room, most of a zombie clutched a sawed-off shotgun. He looked like a piñata that had been stuffed with roadkill and then spun around by an over-enthusiastic child. His clothes, his appearance—Frank couldn't do more than guess.

The second reel of the movie clacked along in his mind. A wolfman, probably the same one who had punched the cashier's ticket, had gotten the bad end of a hogleg. Then that wolfman's friends, his pack, showed the zombie why that was a bad idea. Shadowy shapes on the flickering screen as Frank put one, maybe two more wolfmen at the scene.

Frank crossed the room, but proximity didn't do much to reassemble the jigsaw puzzle that the zombie had been torn into. He knelt by the shotgun and leaned in for a good sniff. The scent bit back, knocking him on his heels. "Silver," he grunted.

"Who's packing silver rounds?" the waxwork asked.

Technically speaking, silver was just as legal or illegal as anything else that could kill. A silver license was easy to come by—too easy for many wolves' liking. Maybe the one thing werewolves and wolfmen could see eye-to-eye on. So as legal as silver was, the reality was a bit different. If a wolf caught you with it, every *i* better be dotted and every *t* crossed. Cops were always looking for an excuse. A zombie with a record, and Frank would be damned if the dismembered fella didn't have one of those, was liable to get half a dozen extra charges tacked on to the legit ones. A zombie packing silver meant business.

And he'd suffered for it.

The armed zombie wasn't the only one who'd bought it. Another one, a portly cook who looked like he'd been fished out of the bay after a week of floating, got an easier death. One of the killers cracked his head on the counter like an egg. Frank squatted down and stared at the man. He took in the surprise on his bloated face, the hands nowhere near a weapon that could do a damn thing to a wolf on his moon. The greenish-black stain on both counter and floor, like an oil slick made of fish guts. Frank's searching gaze snagged on the zombie's gold wedding band. For the first time, anger lit a spark in his chest.

The doppelganger took a step back.

Frank blinked. "What?"

"You growled."

"Wasn't at you. Officer..."

"Facie. Prima Facie."

"You ain't gettin' the wolf."

Facie nodded, and Frank could tell she didn't quite believe him. He straightened up, stepping respectfully past the cook to the other door set onto the left side of the back wall. The movie ticked out a few more frames. The zombie with the shotgun had come from there, ready for trouble. He'd given one barrel to the first wolf through the door. The second and third were on him before he could pull the trigger again. Then one of them, maybe a fourth, offed the cook, just because.

"We know who the stiffs are?" Frank asked.

"One by the door was a Rictus Grinn. Fella here was Baron Saturday." She gestured to the dead man who'd formerly carried the hogleg. "He," here she pointed at the cook, "went by Diaz de los Muertos."

"Lemme guess. Muertos is clean. Grinn and Saturday have records."

"We haven't checked more than their wallets, but my partner and me know them two. I dunno about records." Facie shifted uncomfortably. Frank wasn't going to make her say it.

"They might have some connections in that regard," he said.

She nodded, relieved. "Something like that."

"Got it." He went to the back door and nudged it open. What should have been a pantry, or maybe a walk-in freezer, was a bare, white-walled room. A shiny metal table, the kind butchers used to ply their trade stood in the center, entirely naked. Frank didn't have to sniff it to know brains had never touched its steel surface. A heavy safe squatted in one corner, its door open, empty. This was a counting room; Frank had seen them more than once, back when the mob war had been raging. One of Bellum's stash houses; there was no telling how much cash had been in here before the thieves cleared it out. It was a hell of a score, no doubt about that, and the Gray Matter would be ready to tear the city apart looking for the wolves behind it. The thieves had picked one of the most complicated and painful ways to commit suicide.

"What the hell happened here?" Facie asked.

"Moonlight special," Frank told her.

"What's that?"

"On full moons, wolves lose control. We get stronger, faster, tougher."

"I stay in the station on full moons."

"Smart. Anyways, some wolves go find themselves a witch who ain't too particular about the kind of hexes she sells. They get hexed just enough so's they keep some control, and then they pull a job on the full moon."

"When there are no cops."

"Got it in one."

"A moonlight special," Facie said, trying out the term.

"Don't throw that around," Frank warned. "It ain't popular to know about. Wolves are supposed to *be* the law, not break it."

Facie snorted and caught herself, a momentary flash of fear over her broad features. Frank let it go. She was right to laugh at that, and it was right that he should take it.

"You don't think these were cops?"

"There's no cop in the city dumb enough to hit this place," Frank said.

She nodded. Frank knew they were both thinking the same thing: *What cop would rip off his own boss?*

He didn't envy the wolves who'd pulled this. He'd caught the case— and he'd be getting it from both sides to bring these fellas in. Frank wasn't going to cover for them, wolves or no. Self-preservation, sure, but the cook had clinched the judgment. He didn't deserve that.

Frank dropped to a crouch and inhaled. A mildewy scent that lined up with what he'd gotten from Saturday lingered in this place. Tough to reconstruct it completely; a zombie smelled a little different on the inside than the outside.

Another scent tugged at Frank's attention, beckoning him along insistently. He frowned, inhaling more deeply, trying to catch it. He walked to the safe and took another breath.

His blood turned to silver as he recognized the scent of one of the wolves who had been in this room.

It was Bud Hound.

TWENTY

Frank emerged out on the sidewalk, trying not to show the near-panic coursing through his veins like a wildfire made of mercury. He wanted to get into his car and floor it to Bud's, demand to know what the idiot was thinking. Make sure he got the hell out of town before he ended up with silver poisoning. It wasn't likely that anyone would recognize Bud's scent over the dog pepper, so at least they had some time. It was only spending more than a year in a car with the fella that gave Frank the chance to manage it. Still, Bud couldn't hide from this forever. Either the money would burn a hole in his pocket, or some other cop would catch his scent, or somebody would blab, and the whole city would know he pulled the moonlight special. Unless Bud left town *yesterday*, there was no way out for him.

He felt like someone had dumped a bucket of melted snow over his head, the icy water chilling every godforsaken nook and cranny. He'd had those moments of raw terror before. Lived them while he was driving a tank up the Italian boot. There was usually the quick flash of panic and then the reflexes would take hold and he could get to work surviving. This, though...this was sustained, and the closest Frank could come to it was dancing with a kraut Tiger, knowing their shells would tear right through a Sherman's armor while the Sherman needed to catch the Tiger on the ass. It was so close, right down to the out-of-body feeling of being more worried for his buddy in the next tank over than himself. There was no way to get behind the panzer and open her up with his cannon. No, Frank could only sit there, trying to stop his mind from spinning up every awful thing that could happen to Bud.

When you ripped off Sarah Bellum, that was a mighty long list.

Frank's belief in any higher power would be considered mildly blasphemous. The crux of it was simple: if a situation could be made worse, it inevitably would be. So when the cherry red Packard rolled up and disgorged Pearl Friday, ace crime reporter for the *LA Minion*, Frank was less surprised and more suicidally resigned. She wore her lacy cape at the base of her eyeball, clutching a notebook and a pen, her other tentacles propelling her with disturbing speed over the sidewalk.

"Detective Wolfman," she said with a smile in her voice, "fancy meeting you here."

Frank tamped down on the stark panic that threatened to flood his lungs. "I got no comment."

"I don't know why you insist on seeing our relationship as adversarial."

Frank looked her up and down. Maybe she had a point. He didn't know how Bellum's tentacles reached into the papers, or if the bigwig who owned them had a beef with her. The *Minion* had spat out the Gray Matter's line that organized crime was kaput in the City of Angels, but that line served a lot of masters.

"What do you want to know exactly?" he asked.

"How many victims?"

"Three," Frank said. He ran through the scenarios in his mind, didn't see how any of the three connected to Bud outside of their untimely deaths, so he listed them off.

"Zombies?" she asked.

Frank gestured at the sign. "Zombie joint, zombie victims."

Friday looked up at the sign, then at the shattered door. Her scent, mostly a floral bouquet, gained a chemical spike. Fear. She'd put two and two together. "Got any suspects?" she asked.

"Not a one."

"Has to be wolves, right?"

A Studebaker screeched to a stop and Captain Talbot stepped out of the passenger side, straightening a disheveled suit. Glass emerged from the driver's side, a cigarette floating by the end of one cuff. His features were a ghostly silhouette as he stepped through the swirling cancer smoke. No Talbot without Glass.

"No comment," Frank growled. "We're done here." He lumbered over to his boss.

"Frank, you talking to the press?" Talbot asked, dabbing at the sweat on his forehead.

"She showed up. I was just giving her the brush-off, but she's got a right to be here."

"Letting dames write for the papers," Glass said, pausing as the cherry on the end of his coffin nail went bright, "what'll they think of next?"

"What are we looking at here, Frank?" Talbot asked, his eyes following Friday as she peered into Brains. Facie's invisible partner kept her on the street with the rest of the gathering rubberneckers, but a crawling eye could see a lot with that giant peeper.

Frank kept the story short and his voice low. The panic was a lot like the wolf; Frank kept it on a tight leash and maybe no one would notice it seething. He felt Glass's transparent attention on him, looking right through the lie. He straightened up and scolded himself inwardly. He couldn't give away the game. Keep the press and the brass off of Bud's back.

"Glad you drew this one," Talbot said, lowering his voice and leading Frank off to the side. He leaned in conspiratorially. "Someone trustworthy, I mean."

Glass stood a pace away. Frank's nose itched from the billowing cigarette smoke. He nearly barked at the lieutenant to take his cancer stick somewhere else. *That's a good way to avoid suspicion, yelling at a superior officer.* So instead, Frank took it, his eyes watering and nose twitching, a cough stuck in the back of his throat.

"Yes, sir."

"What do you see?"

"It's a moonlight special."

"Christ," Talbot swore, eyes flicking to Friday. The night was far enough away that they'd had time to gather. "Anybody else know?"

"Nope. Gave the victims to the eyeball, but they don't lead anywheres I can see. Just a couple jobbers at an automat."

"Good. Good man." The captain patted him on the shoulder. The other wolf was gigantic. He couldn't tell if Talbot was meaning to loom or if he just did it naturally. The frigid panic told Frank to *do* something about it, either open the captain up or bolt. Took a lot to keep himself in place. "Get a scent?"

Frank shook his head. "Enough to know we're looking for wolves, but they used dog pepper."

"Thank God for that," Talbot said. "Well, we have some time."

On the sidewalk by them, the cigarette fell from an invisible hand, and the shoe ground it out. Almost immediately, the pack came out of Glass's jacket and he was fishing another out. *Those things are gonna kill him,* Frank thought.

"Time, sir?" Frank asked, mostly to keep the captain talking and off noticing that he was more squirrelly than a balam in church.

Talbot cleared his throat. "I don't suppose I need to tell you what this place was."

"Not my first day out of the nunnery, sir."

"Of course. Well, you can imagine that the owner is quite upset. There's a rather substantial cash reward for the culprits."

"We're doing that?" Frank blurted before he could stop himself.

Talbot's eyes narrowed. "There a problem?"

"No, no. Just caught me off guard is all."

"Mmm," Talbot hummed, not buying it. "Well, maybe if you knew how substantial this cash reward was, you wouldn't be so off guard. Let me put it this way, Detective. We could split it and still have more money than we'd know what to do with. This is the kind of money you leave to another generation. Get me?"

"For this? Bel...*she* must have twenty, thirty places like this all over the city. This is just one."

Talbot glanced around, eyes snagging on Friday, who was trying to coax a statement out of Facie's partner. Glass took the hint and wandered away, trailing smoke like a locomotive, and intercepting the reporter. "It ain't the money, son. It's the message. Says she doesn't own this town like she wants to. Says she can be taken for a ride. One wolf does it, and soon it's another. And another. And then you got yourself the Gobfather all over again."

Frank nodded. "I get it."

Talbot wasn't done. Frank got the impression the captain had started the ball rolling on some thoughts that had been rattling around in his head, getting in the way between him and sleep. Words he wanted someone else to believe because he couldn't. "The city's at peace, Frank. We finally caught a break. More money in our wallets and fewer bodies on the street. We're winning here. Someone cracks this lid, though, and we're right back in it. Don't look at it like we're doing this for a reward. Look at it like we're keeping the peace and we're getting paid back for it the way we should."

The thing was, Frank had said those same words to himself. Right when he made the call and took the Gray Matter's cash. Only Frank knew for damn sure it was a lie. Because one of the bodies that dropped smiled at him from a picture on his desk every day.

He didn't put a voice to any of that. "What if the wolves we're looking for have badges?" he murmured.

Talbot blanched. "A criminal's a criminal, right? Let's say a brother wolf puts his wife in the hospital. You looking the other way?"

"We all look the other way on that one, Cap. And you know it." On the movie screen in Frank's mind, he caught Lou Garou giving Lulu a taste of the chin music, and he felt taller, bigger, ready to show Talbot what it really cost.

Talbot took a step back. "Bad example, Frank. You know what I mean. And of all my men, you're not the one I thought I would have to make this case to." The captain sighed. "Frank, there's a reason I'm glad it's you here and not one of my other detectives. You're ten times smarter than anybody else in that station. You know what we're buying here. You see the big picture. The hurts we can stop and the hurts we *can't*. And that look on your face says you know it's one of the second ones."

"Makes me about as popular as an ogre at the opera."

Talbot cracked a grin. "I knew you'd see it the right way. When we rolled up, I told Glass, 'Thank God, there's Frank. This thing gets done the right way.'"

"That reward, did it specify dead or alive?"

"Alive is more money. A lot more."

"Got it." Frank's stomach turned. Didn't take a brainiac to know what would happen to someone brought in alive.

"Good, good. Glad we understand each other, Frank. Now, you got any leads?"

He shook his head. "I know it's wolves. That's about it so far. I got one of the uniforms canvassing."

Talbot loomed in close, eclipsing the street with his bulk. "You didn't catch a scent, did you, Frank? Somebody familiar maybe?"

Frank held onto the wolf's leash with the strength of a dead man. He kept his face perfectly blank, desperate not to betray the one friend he had. "No sir. Like I said, dog pepper everywhere. Sneezed out half my brains in there."

Talbot leaned back, nodding, but Frank couldn't read the old man. Couldn't see if he bought what Frank was trying so goddamn hard to sell. "Who did you say's canvassing?"

"Facie. She was working last night."

"You want a wolf?"

"Nah, she got the call, and she don't know enough about wolf business to ask the questions we don't want answered."

"Good thinking, Frank." Talbot patted him on the shoulder again. The moon was on the wane, but enough of the red washed over Frank and for a split second, he wanted to snap.

"Okay, Captain. I'm gonna get to work."

"You find something, you call me first, all right? Any time. We circle the wagons, turn them over together."

Frank nodded, not saying anything because he was too busy swallowing a growl.

"One last thing," Talbot said. He dropped his voice. "You think it was cops?"

"Too early to tell," Frank replied. "Sometimes it's tough to see the difference, you know?"

Talbot chuckled. "It'll be a lot easy when your wallet's a good ten pounds heavier."

"That's what I'm gonna tell myself. Talk to you soon."

TWENTY-ONE

Frank stopped at the scene long enough to tell Facie to report to him when she was done with the canvassing. She nodded and gave him a "You got it." Frank didn't much care about what she'd find; he suspected it would be nice and vague. Nothing to conclusively tie Bud to the scene.

Because there was no way in hell Frank was giving Bud to the Brain. Wasn't a lot of justice to be had, but Frank knew that no one deserved the kind of pain Bellum's stiffs could dish out. Bud was a friend. A packmate even. Frank might take a piece of Bud for the dead cook, but in the meantime, he needed to find his old partner.

Frank radioed into the station and asked for Bud. No surprise to find he hadn't reported in. Not exactly a sick call. Plenty of wolves had themselves a hangover after the full moon. They all got joshed for it by the glass men and the waxworks, once the moon was far enough in the rearview that things wouldn't turn red. Bud's absence wouldn't be noted until afternoon at the earliest, once all the wolves who were going to trickle in already had. Frank had a tiny bit of wiggle room, but Bud's scent lingered at the scene. The amount of money Bellum was dangling meant that whoever else recognized *eau de Bud Hound* would switch his conscience off and sell him to the Gray Matter.

Bud's flop was in Hollywood, a little Spanish-style bungalow not far from Sunset. Frank had to fight a lead foot all the way there. No reason to tip his hand just in case the tickle on the back of his neck wasn't his imagination. No one other than him could have sniffed Bud out this quickly. As long as his old partner hadn't been wearing a nametag or pissing on anything, he was safe for a couple hours. *Maybe if I keep telling myself this stuff, I'll get to believe it,* Frank thought.

He knocked on the front door. "Bud, it's Frank," he said as loud as he dared. "I'm alone."

The house was silent. Frank knocked again and listened for his partner rustling around. He sucked in some of the neighborhood smells. Nothing said brainiacs or zombies, or Bud standing on the other side of the door, for that matter. Just flowers, a freshly-mown lawn, the ghost of some piss from the Hollywood Sheriff's Department, and bacon burning in a frying pan a few doors down.

Frank tried the knob. The door opened. He stood at the threshold, sniffing the air. He sifted through the smells of the house—Bud, some old takeout, air fresheners instead of actual cleaning products—mingling with the smells from outside. His mind supplied the mildew-stink of zombies, a picture of one of Bellum's corpses crouched in waiting behind the door with a silver-packed heater. He forced himself through the panic, smelled what was actually *there,* beyond the air fresheners and the food spoiling in the wastebasket. The overwhelming scent was Bud's, baked into the house, the combination of wolf, beer, and that dumb cologne they made for wolves that was supposed to be barely detectable but Frank swore smelled like flowers dipped in ammonia. He caught the edges of other scents—a slight fishiness, something herbal—but nothing overwhelming. Nothing that screamed a presence in the house.

"Bud?" he called. No answer, but Frank hadn't really been expecting one.

He stepped inside. He couldn't shake the foreboding. The house felt full, no matter what his nose was telling him. His partner—or the one sent to kill him. Shutting the door behind him, he let the wolf off the leash, just a bit. The monster inside him growled in relief as the world grew a bit smaller. The scents bloomed in his mind. Still no corpse with a .45 clutched in his rotting hand that Frank could tell.

Bud's house was small, and Frank knew that it really only existed as a place for his partner to take women to. It wasn't big, because Bud never had the slightest desire to start a family. In the old days, Frank had razzed him for that from time to time, but the truth was Bud knew what he wanted. He wasn't like Frank, living alone in a family's house in the sticks, dreaming of the one who'd left.

The small foyer had a coat rack that held Bud's coat and slicker. Those would be staying put until the rains started in November or December, then back up on the rack for another year. To the left was a nook with a circular table and two chairs. The scents here were stronger, one chair for Bud and one for his ladyfriend-for-the-day. The side that smelled more strongly of Bud had a mug half-filled with cold coffee and a copy of the paper, opened to sports. He either left suddenly, or was that much of a slob. Frank would buy either.

Beyond that was a narrow kitchen that didn't smell too strongly of the man of the house. A door at the end opened out into a small yard with a single orange tree growing in the far corner. On impulse, he went out, plucking an orange from the tree. With fingernails that were almost claws, he stripped away the peel, then dropped the whole fruit when a wasp struggled free of the rotten innards. Frank's foot came down on the whole mess. He went back inside, then to the living room. What he saw stopped him cold.

The fireplace, set in the far wall, had been decorated. No, not decorated—turned into a message that couldn't have been more obvious with a stamp and an address to Bellum's Beverly Hills estate. Whoever came through the doors, wolf or corpse, would be Bellum's creature, and hell, that included Frank in his own way. The wolf slinked back into its den inside, putting the leash back around its own neck. Frank scarcely noticed as he took hesitant steps toward the altar Bud had left behind.

Right in the center was a big picture of a bunch of wolfmen all wearing their human skins, dressed in nice suits with fedoras slouching on their heads, arrayed in front of a pair of Packards parked kisser to kisser. Some carried longarms, others pistols. A few smiled, but most were striking a pose for the camera, looking as close as they could to the Old West gunfighters that they all grew up idolizing back when you could still worship a meatstick. Frank leaned close to the picture and matched a few mugs to handles. Bud knelt in the foreground, a cocky grin on his puss, a .45 in one hand just like one of Bellum's trouble boys.

Hunter Moore, the lean and grim public face of the Wolf Pack, stood in the center, about half a head taller than everyone else. Lou Garou and Phil Moon leaned against a Packard, shoulder-to-shoulder on the right-hand side, both toting shotguns.

This was a portrait of the Wolf Pack. Such a thing didn't officially exist, what with the idea that Bellum or someone else—back when there was a someone else—would use it as a hit list. Once the Wolf Pack was dissolved, a few surfaced. After all, why worry about organized crime when the papers all said it was gone?

Frank stepped back and took in the other pictures surrounding the central group shot in a mosaic. Some were framed newspaper headlines, proclaiming a Wolf Pack bust or a shootout with Bellum's, or Mab's, or Cohen's gang. These never featured any of the wolves other than Moore, and instead concentrated on the lurid images: a bullet-riddled car with two dead zombies slumped over the seats, sheet-covered goblins in a theater lobby.

The other wolves who had knocked over the stash house would be in the central picture. He went from face to face, wondering which of them had been there. Which of them had killed Bellum's people. Which one had killed the cook. Whoever came through the door was supposed to make the connection. It was a taunt. *You can't get all of us*, the picture said, *but we sure as hell got you this one time.*

Something pulled Frank's attention to the right-hand side of the display. Bud's badge glittered on a shelf, just in front of an article about a bust that left four zombies dead. Wherever Bud had gone, he would no longer need it. He wasn't a cop anymore and never would be again. Frank's hand went to the badge of its own accord, his fingers fluttering like moths. He couldn't pick it up. It was Bud's, the same as his name, and Frank had no right to move it.

He moved off to the rest of the house, leaving the message for Bellum. Bud wasn't there, and no stiffs were waiting. Zombies would have tossed the place, and his partner would have come out of hiding by now. No, if Bud had a brain in his head, he'd already skipped town with the rest of his crew and would be spending Bellum's cash on a beach someplace. Or maybe a moor. Wolfmen had a thing for moors. It was the dank.

Bud's bedroom was clean, the bed made. Frank snorted. Trying to put on a good face. He knew he was going to have company. Squares, a bit darker than the surroundings, suggested that pictures had been taken from the walls. That was a relief; meant Bud was planning to be alive, somewhere he would want to keep a memory or two. When Frank opened the closet, he found the frames, stacked neatly against one side. In terms of clothes, the pickings were sparse enough that he guessed there was a suitcase packed with the balance.

One picture sat on Bud's bedside table. Frank picked it up. It was a glamour shot of Beth Keene, a banshee Bud had dated back when he and Frank had been partners. They were long since broken up, and Bud had never carried any sort of torch for her that Frank was aware of. She was a looker, but they all were. No reason to have her mug on his bedside table.

Frank picked up the frame, turned it over, and opened it. Along with the picture and a slab of cardboard keeping the shot straight, a folded piece of paper tumbled into his hand. He put everything else down and opened it. A note. And it was addressed to him.

Frank—Figured you could sniff this one out when no one else could. If you found this, you know what I did. Hope the job went as clean as when we drew it up. Hope you're not too cheesed I did it. I hope you can understand why. I want you to get it. There's no place in this city for good cops. The city belongs to the Gray Matter now. Best you can do is get out, so that's what I'm doing. Got myself enough money to start over where nobody knows me. Maybe a place where the cops are cops and the gangsters are gangsters. You should do it too. Get out while you can, because they'll kill you. They kill all good cops.

Frank dropped the note into his lap, loathing writhing in his stomach like a serpent. What would Bud do if he knew?

If he knew Frank was as rotten as the rest of them?

Bellum would never kill one of the police she bought and paid for, especially not one who'd already proven his worth. Frank was completely safe, and he had never hated that fact more.

Frank reassembled the picture frame and put it back where he found it. He folded the note up and stuck it in his jacket pocket where it weighed him down like a lead slug.

TWENTY-TWO

Back when Bud was seeing Beth Keene, she'd been a chorus girl at Visionary Pictures. In the meantime, she'd gone and got herself a record deal under the handle "Beth Keene and her Sunset Scene." She was no Perry Como, in Frank's estimation, but she wasn't bad. Her repertoire was mostly love ballads, pop ditties, and haunting dirges describing a dire fate. The normal stuff.

She wasn't in her old flop, a bungalow just off Melrose she shared with a pair of ghosts. She'd moved into the Chateau Marmont, a sure sign she was on her way somewhere, whether up or down. The ghoul at the front desk was a funereal brunette whose old-world elegance gave the "Chateau" part of the name a touch of authenticity.

He showed her the shield. "Ma'am." She smiled thinly and set aside the coffin catalogue she'd been perusing. He nodded at it. "Ordering up lunch?"

"Broke up with a boyfriend," she said in monotone. "Need somewhere to keep him."

He frowned at his badge. "You can see this, right? You know I'm police."

"Oh, I know. What you need to ask yourself is, 'Did this ghoul confess to murder or is she merely a delightfully deadpan darling?' How about it, *dick*? Which one am I?"

Frank grunted in annoyance. "Just fill the damn thing with lye or you'll have to dig him up in a week."

Her eye sparkled like a knife in the moonlight. "Good to know. What can I do for you?"

"I'm looking for Beth Keene."

"She in some kind of trouble?"

"Could be she offed her boyfriend."

The ghoul's mirthless grin quirked. "I'd say that's unlikely." She gave him Beth Keene's suite, directed him to the elevator, and went back to her reading. Frank had to hope he hadn't just abetted a murder.

Beth's suite was on the top floor. Frank stepped out of the elevator onto the burgundy carpets and hunted around for the right numbers. His keen ears picked up a melody and he followed that, and sure enough, there was Keene's door. He rapped at it, with full knowledge that this was a shot in the dark. Keene's picture hadn't meant Bud was hiding out here. It was pup bait.

The melody, having been tickled out on a piano, stopped, and Frank caught a whiff of cigarette smoke. He sneezed once and cursed whoever thought lighting plants on fire and sucking on them had been a good idea. The door opened into the goggle-eyed face of a phantom. She was short and stout, and though it was tough to tell with their weird sunken faces, Frank had the impression she was relatively young. She was dressed in a black gown that fit like a sack, and her dark hair was piled up in a complicated artichoke. A cigarette dangled from her gray lip.

"Yes?" she asked. Her voice was high and clear, and didn't look like it could come out of her.

"Beth Keene in?"

"Who's asking?"

Frank showed her. "LAPD."

The phantom's eyes bugged out even more. They had to be holding on for dear life. "Is she in some kind of trouble?"

"Nothing like that, ma'am. I just need a few minutes of her time."

"Come in, have a seat."

The central room of the suite was cluttered, making it appear more like an apartment than a suite in a hotel. Of course, that was the whole point with a flop like this. Damn thing was an artist's colony in the middle of Hollywood, because the folks who came out west liked to pretend art still happened around here. The phantom directed Frank to a chair, though she had to move a stack of sheet music about as tall as a gremlin. The music was deposited across the room on the piano, which sat next to the exit out onto the balcony. Cigarette smoke ambled its way to the curtains, but not quick enough for Frank's liking.

The phantom bustled off and returned a moment later with Beth Keene. She looked just the same as Frank remembered her, except that her death shroud was a little nicer and her hair had been done. Like all the women Bud dated, Beth was a looker, assuming you could get past the way that her jaw would sometimes unhinge and she'd howl a portent of doom. She had blonde hair in a stylish bob, and eyes that sparkled like ghost lights over a swamp. Her stems stopped about halfway down her calves; so Frank supposed she was one of the few women Bud ever dated whose legs didn't go all the way up.

"Yes, Detect...do I know you?"

"You do. Any chance we can talk in private?"

She beckoned him out onto the balcony. Frank was grateful, as the smoggy air cleared up. The room faced the rising hills of Hollywood, and Frank could look out west to where the studios had carved their fiefs from the city.

"I've forgotten your name, I'm sorry," she said.

"Frank Wolfman."

"Bud's partner."

"The same."

"What's this about?"

"It's about Bud." Frank shifted. He turned away from the city to measure what he was going to say on Beth Keene's mug. "You haven't seen him lately, have you?"

"Bud and I broke it off..." She had to think about it. That wasn't information at her fingertips. "Around two years ago, I think? We haven't had occasion to speak since."

"Bud had a picture of you by his bedside."

Beth laughed, a sound at once musical and chilling, like a violin's funeral. "He what?"

"Picture of you. It was your old head shot, one you used when you were still hustling for gigs at the clubs."

"I remember it. It's a nice photo. Why would Bud have it?"

"I asked myself the same question. You're a looker, but..."

She laughed again, and caught herself. "I'm sorry. Bud was never much interested in how I looked, good or not."

"How do you mean?

Beth's eyes flicked to the suite, and Frank's nose easily plucked out the poison threads of the coffin nail. The phantom was in another room, not listening in. "Bud doesn't care what a lady looks like."

"Sure he does. Bud only ever dates tomat...uh...lookers like yourself."

Beth sighed. "You don't know."

Frank swallowed a growl of annoyance. "You're talkin' in circles about something. Spit it out."

Beth glanced at the billowing curtains, but really, she was looking through them, at something Frank couldn't see. "Bud and I were never really together the way you're thinking of it. The truth is, I'm not interested in the fellas that way."

"Oh," Frank said. He was old-fashioned enough to be shocked by the admission. "That don't seem to matter too much in the modern world," he said diplomatically. "I seen men and women, all different kinds, who... uh...stick to their own kind."

"It matters," she said, and with another glance far away, launched into a story. "You ever hear the way a man's heart is through his stomach? That's not entirely true. Men like watching a pretty woman sing a song, and when they do, they daydream. They think that the woman, though she's singing to an entire room, is actually singing to them personally. So when you're a singer, if you want your career to go past crooning for souses in local watering holes, you have to let the saps pretend they got a chance with you."

"You're saying Bud pretended to date you so that your fans would think they had a chance."

"Something like that."

Frank's frown deepened. "I don't get it. What was in it for him?"

"You're telling me you don't know?"

"Out with it, lady. I'm just about losing my patience here."

Beth looked at him with such amused pity that Frank felt like the wolf should maybe take the lead in the conversation. He had to remind himself that he was scratching an itch he knew wouldn't go much of anywhere.

"Bud wasn't interested in the ladies."

"Sure he was. Got himself in trouble over a dish more than once."

"A sham. A put-on. Bud was pretending. He and I, we had ourselves an arrangement, and it lasted until...Bud had a hard time accepting who he was, and he could be a bit abrasive at times. Besides, stick around long enough and folks start asking about wedding bells."

"No, see, Bud was—"

"Not exactly who you think he was."

Frank shook his head. It didn't square. Bud was a hound, just like his name implied. He was *always* talking about ladies. Kind of cheesed Frank at times, even. "Okay, okay. Let's say I think you're being square. Why's he trying to hide this? Not like he has fans who think they got a shot with him."

Beth caught a surprised laugh, and had the decency to look contrite. "You got a lot of queer wolves at the station?"

"Course not."

"Why not?"

"I don't think the fellas would be too keen on the showers if they turned into..." Frank trailed off, not particularly wanting to follow that line of thought.

"There's your answer. That ladies' man reputation you keep going on about, Bud wore it like armor. I helped him wear it for a period too, and then we broke it off. You came here asking why he had a picture of me, and I don't have the foggiest. I never expected to see him again in my life."

TWENTY-THREE

It squared. That was the problem. As much as Frank wanted to say Beth Keene was jilted, angry, or just plain dizzy, it squared. He wanted to feel the resistance of "Oh no, not Bud. Bud's not that way," but her words had a click to them, the feel of a missing piece of a puzzle Frank had never known he was working.

Didn't lead to Bud, though. Whatever was going on in Bud's personal life, Frank had to make sure he got out of town. The grimy feeling that clung to Frank, transferred on those monthly envelopes from Bellum and Parrish, would never fully go away. He had to do one good thing. One thing he wouldn't regret. One thing that proved the Gray Matter didn't own his soul.

He found Officer Prima Facie in the motor pool at Highland Street Station, waving her over as he got out of his car.

"Detective," she said. "I was looking for you."

"Found me," Frank replied. "What came from the canvass?"

"Whole lotta nothing," she told him. "One eyeball witness was the one who called it in, the gremlin who owns the repair shop."

"Right, Sex."

"Spex."

"That makes more sense. Slightly. He didn't see nothing?"

"Nothing we can use. He saw wolfmen, but beyond that? Not much."

Facie pulled a notebook from her breast pocket and flipped over several crinkling sheets before getting to the one she wanted. "According to Spex, he was awake and working on a television. Tried to tell me what was wrong with it, but I think you'd want me to skip that. Anyway, just after midnight, he hears a crash, then a bang."

"Crash and a bang? What is this, Morse code?"

"Glass breaking from the door, bang from the zombie getting his head caved in on the wall. That's what I figure."

"Okay," Frank said, gesturing to her to get on with it.

"Right. So Spex goes to the window, and it takes him a bit to open it. He has metal shutters down."

"At night?"

"Better safe than sorry, I guess."

Frank thought about the puddle of gremlin on the Persian rug and nodded. "He might have a point there."

"He gets there in time to see a commotion inside the automat. Doesn't get a clean look at exactly what's going on. More shapes than anything, but he does hear what he said was like a car backfiring. Well, he said 'car cough' and I had to work it out. Gremlins, you know."

Frank nodded. He did know. "That'd be the shotgun."

"Yeah. Not too long after, he sees four shapes coming out the front. He gets a better look at them this time thanks to the streetlights. It's wolfmen, of course, but more than that, not much."

Frank held up a hand and asked a question that wouldn't have occurred to him a week ago. "Wolf*men*?"

"That's what he said. You think it was ladies?"

"Don't hurt to ask."

"He said wolfmen. I can double-check, but he didn't get the best look. He can't even get fur color because it's too dark to tell. Said they were dark, wouldn't commit to brown or black. They're wearing pants and that's it. One of them is half-carrying one of the others."

"Half-carrying."

"You know," Facie said, miming putting an arm over her shoulder and bearing the weight.

"The fella was hit by the shotgun."

She nodded. "They pile into a Bel Air that's out front—probably gray, could be black—and speed off east."

"One of the wolfmen was driving."

"Thought that sounded funny, too, so I double-checked. Yeah, and he was...you know." Her features took on the look of melted wax, reshaping themselves into a reasonable facsimile of a wolfman on the full moon.

"Yeah, that's the hexes they were under that let them do that."

Her broad, clean face returned. She whistled. "Hell of a hex. Can't imagine just any witch could set it up."

"Need a good witch."

"Sounds more like a wicked witch, you ask me."

"Hard to tell the difference sometimes. What have you spread around?"

"Nothing yet," she said. "Report's yours."

"Keep it that way. What about your partner?"

"He wasn't with me when I talked to Spex. Had him checking with other shopkeepers along that stretch."

Frank nodded. She had good instincts. "Hey, you seen Bosch?"

"Has anybody?"

"I was just starting to like you."

"I think he's inside," Facie said. Frank turned to go. "Wait, there's one more thing."

He paused. "What?"

"A minute or two after the Bel Air with the wolves gets away, two cars pull up in front of the automat. Black Packard 400s, zombies behind the wheel and in the back. A zombie comes out from the automat, gets in one, and they all go after the other car."

Frank swore.

"Detective. What's going on here?"

"I don't know yet," he lied. He was a louse for lying to Facie, but if anything, Bud's note proved he was that and worse. "I know I don't like it. You let me worry about the paperwork, all right?"

"You got it."

Frank left Facie outside. He found his keys next to the picture of Sylvia Screen, pocketing them before heading over to Bosch's desk. The invisible man had his nose in some paperwork, or, at least, the mustache floating in front of the desk implied the location of Bosch's nose.

"What can I do for you?" the invisible man asked.

"Can I have a word?"

"Sure," Bosch said. The chair scooted out, apparently of its own accord, and the mustache floated up to something approaching head height. Bosch wasn't a tall fella all told, but an invisible man didn't have to be tall. Amazing the kind of violence a glass man could do if he had a mind to it, and a lot of them ended up that way. Something about not being seen. Bosch, though, was as level-headed as they came so far as Frank knew.

Frank led him back outside to the motor pool, found his car and got behind the wheel. The passenger door opened and the mustache floated its way in. Frank sighed. Even a glass man of Bosch's otherwise spotless character could be hard to take.

"Ain't you cold?" Frank asked.

"Sure, a bit. Ask me again at Christmas."

"You could put on a coat."

"And you could not howl at the moon so much."

"Yeah, okay."

"Did you call me over here to give me crap, or was there a deeper purpose?"

Frank looked around the parking lot. No one was lingering, no one was staring. Didn't help. Frank still felt his hackles raised. They would know. Somehow, they would know. Those walls had eyes, ears, and a phone line to the Gray Matter.

"I was gonna buy you lunch."

"Shoulda led with that. You can make fun of my mustache all you want."

"Didn't think a hamburger would get me that much," Frank said, turning the car over and merging onto York Boulevard.

"Hamburger? Thought you were springing for Musso and Frankenstein."

"On my salary?"

"Didn't think money was a worry for you," Bosch said.

And then Frank was back on the knife's edge. Wasn't that Bosch was with Talbot and the others—it was that he *wasn't*. Of *course* Bosch would be the last honest detective in the LAPD. Just Frank's luck. "Yeah, well, you learn something new every day," Frank grumbled.

He felt Bosch's attention on him like a life jacket stuffed with lead. Bosch knew Frank was bent. Even if he didn't know, he could see it on Frank's mug. Bosch had to know everybody was bent unless they proved otherwise. And Frank, working homicide for the Northeast, wouldn't go long without being bought. He'd have tripped and fallen on a silver bullet just like all the Wolf Packers.

He drove Bosch over to On the Hoof, a hamburger stand a couple miles distant from the station. It was an enclosed kitchen with a counter and stools around the front end, set in the corner of a parking lot, with a few outdoor tables and plastic umbrellas to complete the setup. A couple cars were parked around, mostly packed with ghouls, eating greasy food out of white cardboard boxes. The menu was posted right above the window, and there were only five things on it: hamburgers, cheeseburgers, French fries, Plasma Cola, and strawberry shakes.

Frank waited for the wendigo ahead of him to rattle off his order—six hamburgers, no buns—before stepping up to the window and ordering from the cook, a crooked-toothed ghoul in a stained apron. A few minutes later, he was carrying a couple boxes of burgers and fries to the car. Frank liked this place. Most of the wolves did, and they tended to like it more closer to the full moon. The meat had a gaminess to it and the cook barely waved it at the grill. Kind of made Frank wonder what sort of hooves the meat used to have, but even "hooves" might have been a little too optimistic.

"Didn't know you meant this place," Bosch said.

"What's wrong with this place?"

One of the burgers levitated out of the box. "If you don't know, I ain't gonna convince you." A bite vanished from it, momentarily visible, then mercifully vanishing before it got too masticated. "So, what did you want to talk about?"

"Nick Moss," Frank said, picking up his own burger.

"What about him?"

"Of all the private dicks in town, you send me to a gangster?"

"Moss isn't a gangster."

"Sure he is. Goes by the handle Nick the Stick. Hangs around the Nocturnist, and there's only one kind of meatstick does that."

"He was seeing one of those waitresses there," Bosch said. A brace of fries floated from the bag, scooped some ketchup, and vanished in two stages.

"What kind of meatstick is a girl like that seeing?"

"Look, Frank. I'm telling you, Moss is on the level. Well, as on the level as anybody else in this town."

"What's that supposed to mean?"

"Either you already know that, or you should get fitted for a Girl Scout uniform."

"Yeah, okay." Frank looked down at the burger. He still hadn't taken a bite. His appetite had abruptly fled as soon as he started talking to the other detective.

"I know the street says Moss is a gangster," Bosch said, his voice softer. "I looked into him. Believe me, I had reasons. He makes his living mostly finding missing people, sometimes serving process for leeches, other stuff. Private eye stuff. He's not making book, there aren't any rackets. He hangs onto the reputation because it keeps him safe after dark. Monsters aren't going to hassle a meatstick they think will fill 'em full of daylight."

"You sent me to him..."

"Just like I said. I went undercover last year trying to bring down the

Gobfather, and I went deep. Nobody could find me. Well, somehow Moss did. I never really figured out how he did it, either. I know he isn't much to look at, but he's got it where it counts. Anyways, after that, when I need to find somebody, I'll throw him some work. He's like a bloodhound. Never let me down once."

Frank stared at the congealing meat in his hand. "What did you mean that you had reason to check up on him?"

Bosch's mustache turned. Frank realized the invisible man was looking out the window. "You don't want to hear this."

"Maybe I do."

"I tell you this, it doesn't leave this car. You understand me?"

"I get you. Spill."

Frank felt Bosch staring. "All right. The reason I was under, the reason I went missing, was that the Gobfather had some detectives on his payroll." Bosch fell silent but the stare remained, heavy as a hand on Frank's neck.

"Go on," Frank said, his voice dry.

"I had to figure out who it was before I came up for air or I was a dead man. Well, Moss figured it out, too. I had it narrowed down to two fellas and Moss cut that in half." Bosch trailed off, the floating mustache going still. He took a deep breath, something Frank registered as the gust of greasy breath.

"Who?"

"Moss cut me out of it. Said it was because the rat knew my scent. Left me behind. Went up for a meeting with him, and when he came back, he didn't say much. Were you in the war, Frank?"

"Which one?"

"Yeah, okay. Day War, I served in the Pacific. And you know, morning after a battle, nobody would say nothing, but you could see in their eyes something happened. They were hashing it out in their heads, the things they had to do, the moments that death almost caught them. Well, the next morning, Moss had that look in his eyes."

"I've seen it," Frank said.

"Yeah, figured you had. So you know enough not to ask any questions. I put it together once I saw the news."

"The news?"

Bosch took another breath. "What I'm going to tell you doesn't leave this car, okay?" he repeated. "You don't tell the captain, you don't tell your priest, you don't tell anybody who...you don't tell *anybody*."

"Yeah, I got it. Mum's the word. Who was the rat?"

"Phil Moon."

"Moon? He was Wolf Pack."

Bosch snorted. "You think the Wolf Pack don't have rats?"

"Well...yeah."

"It was Moon. Moss got Moon and his partner up over those hills in Chinatown and the two of them rubbed him out, then cooked up some cockamamie story about hobs."

Frank imagined an M1 in Moss's hands. He'd know how to use that weapon. Anyone in the service did, and Moss didn't look like he could have dodged it and didn't sound like the type to.

"You're sure it wasn't hobs?"

"Positive. Moon was in the Gobfather's pocket. Why are they picking off their pet cop? Especially right after Mab gets the push? They have bigger fish to fry."

"That's how Moss knows Garou," Frank chewed on the words. They tasted right. Only now it didn't make sense that Moss would turn out the lights on his pal. He wouldn't keep it quiet for nine months and then decide to turn to blackmail. Moss or Garou.

"So like I said," Bosch told him. "Moss ain't a gangster and he knows how to keep his mouth shut."

"Enough to rub out a cop."

"A dirty cop," Bosch said.

Frank nodded. *As if there was any other kind.*

TWENTY-FOUR

rank dropped Bosch off at the station, the whole time haunted by the image of Garou staring at his partner's autopsy report. Even if Moon was dirty, they were still partners, they were still pack. It was a place the man and the wolf intersected, a concept both understood. Pack was pack, no matter what. Garou had to live with what they did. Or maybe he didn't. That would certainly square with everything Frank knew. Garou wasn't going anywhere, and if he was, Frank barely cared. He had his own pack to worry about. When Bud was bound for someplace far away, Frank could solve the mystery of Lou Garou's whereabouts. He had his teeth into it, and couldn't let it go if he'd wanted to. He'd become a detective because he had to *know*, and the wolf only strengthened that need. An ungnawed bone had the sweetest marrow.

He drove into the suburban neighborhood of Silver Lake, a collection of Spanish bungalows clinging to a series of hills on the edge of a crystal blue reservoir. His destination didn't stand out particularly from any of the others. It had the same postage-stamp lawn, the grass as tight as a Marine's haircut. A bird of paradise plant grew next to a picture window. The window itself showed nothing, just a line of black between the drapes. Frank parked on the street and knocked on the front door.

He had knocked a third time when the door opened.

Hunter Moore was an impressive man. He had a gunfighter's lean silhouette and the squint to match. He'd always worn his suits with style, but not so much that he looked bought. He'd always been the kind of fella you'd want on your side in a scrap. Old, sure, but aged into whipcrack leather and battered gunmetal. He wasn't so much past his prime as he threw into doubt that primes mattered at all.

But the man who opened the door was Hunter Moore's ghost. He'd always been lean, but now he was downright skeletal. His skin was usually darkened into the same Los Angeles tan every cop sported after a year or so on the job. Now he looked like the belly of a fish who got out less than most fish. He was dressed in an undershirt and old pants, a bathrobe thrown over that, and none of it laundered. His stubble was white and patchy. His hair was thinner than Frank remembered, just some downy white clinging to his skull, waiting for an excuse to give up.

"Whaddya want?" Moore demanded. It was a far cry from his clenched-teeth press conferences where he looked like he was challenging the city to meet him at high noon. His breath stank like the underside of a distillery.

"Lieutenant Moore?" Frank asked. Even he couldn't believe this was the same wolf, even if it looked a little like him and lived at his address.

Moore snorted. "Ain't a lieutenant anymore."

"My name's Wolfman, I was—"

"Wolfman? Should have spent more than five minutes on the name."

"I get that a lot."

"Why are you darkening my door, Wolfman? I remember every man who ever worked under me, and you ain't them."

"I wanted to talk to you about some of them."

Moore sighed. He squinted out at the bright street, as though resenting that it was there at all. "Yeah, all right. Come in." The old wolf turned around and returned to the dark, like a spirit tired of manifesting.

Frank stepped past the threshold and the scent of the place hit him all at once. Mostly booze, but with some unwashed man, mold, and the clean, nutty scent of roaches. It was a minor miracle the outside looked as good as it did. The lights were off, with only dusty threads of sun peeking in.

"You wanna snort, Wolfman?" Moore asked, already in the kitchen.

Frank was about to demur that he was on duty, but he didn't think he should start this conversation with a lie. "Sure."

Moore's living room wasn't unfurnished—he had a coffee table and a sofa and a recliner and they were all in good shape. He even had a television, though it was an older model. It wasn't that there was no evidence of someone living there, either. The table had rings from carelessly placed drinks and the paper, opened to the crossword. It was that no one *lived* there. The pictures on the wall were generic hotel-room art. The crossword didn't have a single mark. The house felt empty in no way Frank could really put a finger on. In some ways, it reminded him of home.

Moore came back from the kitchen holding a pair of coffee mugs. The scent was overpowering, bad coffee strangled with rye. "Mud in your eye," the old wolf said.

Frank tipped the mug back, but only sipped. Moore barely noticed, returning to his place on the recliner. Frank sat down on the sofa. It wasn't as clean or as unused as the one in Garou's house, but they were of a kind. That was for sure.

"So who are you?" Moore asked.

"I work homicide out of Northeast."

Moore nodded. "Yeah, name rang a bell. Couldn't tell if I'd heard it, or it was just because it's Wolfman."

Frank nodded. So Moore had been looking at him for the Wolf Pack. Looking at him and passing over. Hard to know if he should be offended or not—or if that decision had saved his life. "I used to be partners with Bud Hound."

Moore's expression darkened. He sipped his coffee. "How's Bud doing? Haven't talked to him in a dog's age. No offense."

Frank didn't need his fifteen years on the job to know the old man was lying. "Bud was with the Wolf Pack."

"Can't say one way or t'other," Moore said, "but the Pack don't exist, so maybe it don't matter."

"Why did you pick Bud?"

Moore turned, and for a second, Frank saw the old gunfighter behind his eyes. Not so much looking *at* Frank as looking *into* him. "When I was recruiting, I was looking for a good mix. I wanted some real detectives, the ones who could put puzzles together for everybody else. I wanted drivers. I wanted loyal men. Most of all, I wanted fighters, all of them. Not just the ones who'd seen action in the Day War. I took fellas who were changed late in the Night. The ones who knew how to fight monsters. That's what we were after."

"Bud's a fighter," Frank said.

"That he is. Give you a lot of trouble as a partner?"

"Some," Frank allowed. "He was never in it for the police work."

"No, he wasn't. Bud was one of my cowboys. In the good old days, he would've worn a star when something needed to be done, but other than that, he'd be in the saloon, drinking and carrying on with the dancing girls. We need more wolves like Bud." Moore fell silent.

Frank let the comment about the dancing girls pass without comment. Bud had been wearing a mask good enough to fool him, small wonder it had Moore snowed too. "I can understand that."

"Only not anymore. No mob in the City of Angels." Moore shook his head. "Can you believe that? Damn near went full moon when I saw that headline. One outfit wiped out the others, now they own everything and everybody. And they bury everybody who don't show 'em throat."

"Dangerous to talk like that."

Moore fixed Frank with the stare, a bruised challenge. "Oh? You here for that? I been shut up plenty, but if you think you need to do it with silver, go ahead."

"No. I'm not...I don't do that. I'm here because of Bud."

"What about him?"

"I think you know."

Moore's eyes narrowed. "Tell me right now, Wolfman. Tell me what you plan to do with Hound if you find him."

Frank stared right back. "I'm going to help him get the hell out of town and never look back."

Moore stared for a few moments longer, and then the old gunfighter fell away, revealing the broken-down man underneath. He dropped his gaze and went back to drinking, turning away. "Ask your questions."

"Did Bud have friends in the Wolf Pack?"

"We were closer than friends in the Pack. All of us."

"You know what I mean."

"I suppose I do." Moore thought about it. "I remember him hanging around Wolfgang Howell and Lou Garou. Thick as thieves, those three."

"Garou's missing."

"What do you mean, 'missing'?"

"That's how this whole thing started. About a week ago, Bud comes to me asking me to find Garou. He just up and disappeared."

Moore shook his head. "A week? No, no way Garou... Have you found him?"

"Nope. He vanished into thin air. Then last night a group of wolfmen pull a moonlight special on a Bellum stash house in Hollywood. I figure Garou was supposed to be with that group. So it seems like a funny time to disappear."

Moore took a deep breath. "If they're hiding, they might go to the clubhouse."

"Clubhouse?" Second time he'd heard that word. Bud said they'd checked it for Garou and Frank had let it drop from there.

"Take Vermont into Griffith Park. Drive until you can't. Then go northeast. Ignore the trails, and before long you're gonna find the scent markers. Go long enough, you'll find a little shack out there. It was the Pack's place to unwind. If there's one spot in the entire city someone in the Pack could go and never be found, it's there."

"Got it. Thanks." Frank got up, setting the coffee-flavored booze on the table. He had the suspicion that Moore would drink it. Frank needed to get out of this house. It was beginning to strangle him. He got to the door when Moore spoke.

"I shouldn't have told them about her."

"About who?" Frank didn't turn. He wasn't sure he could look at Moore again.

"Wyeth Wyrd. The cook at the Nocturnist. You need hexes to pull a moonlight special."

"How'd you know she could do it?"

Moore swallowed, and nearly whispered, "Because she gave me mine."

Frank left Moore to his empty house.

TWENTY-FIVE

It was October, so at least the sun wasn't trying to beat the life out of him. Instead, the air was dry enough to strike a match off of, and the grass had all shriveled into kindling. The earth beneath was cracked after a long summer. So even if it was cool enough that Frank left his jacket on, he needed a drink within ten minutes of leaving his car. Whiskey or water, didn't much matter which.

He had parked where the road ended, just like Moore told him. The dirt here was rutted with old tire tracks, nearly obliterated by repeated use. Frank straightened his hat and headed off what he figured might very well be northeast. The terrain of Griffith Park was rough. Damn near wild, really. During the Night War, humans were always hiding in the hills and gullies of the park. Monsters, mostly the wolves, had taken it upon themselves to ferret the meatsticks out. Frank had never been a part of all that. He had things to do in the city. Just because the humans had gone crazy didn't mean crime stopped. There were still a bunch of law-abiding monsters who needed the police. There were times he even believed his reasoning.

The park itself didn't belong to the werewolves or the wolfmen. They fought over it in the best of times and it always got bloody on the full moon. It'd never be settled. Could be they liked the fighting more than the having. Wolf meant cop, sure, but the werewolves were a different kind. In the old days, Frank thought of them as the ones who let the rules slip, who did what they liked and called it law later. But that was him now. That was all of them.

Frank stayed the hell away from the park as a rule. From most of the wild places. Back when he was a meatstick, he'd never been one for the outdoors, but then he was changed, and the wolf was in his veins. Wolves liked nature, at least for something to piss on. He felt the pull, but dug in his heels. He'd live on his own terms at least in this, to hell with what the moon wanted.

It figured that the Wolf Pack would have made their hideout here. They were the kinds of wolves who liked a scrap, and they could always find one in Griffith Park. On a rise, Frank caught his breath. He'd been heading steadily up, climbing where the slopes were at their most gentle. Game trails crisscrossed the ground, between the larger collections of leaves and thorns. The soft rosemary scent of the hills washed over him, beneath it the smells of animals, their spoor, their decay, their musk. Coyote was the most persistent stink, a rotten milk odor that clung to the hill. They were smart enough to give wolves a wide berth, but they weren't going anywhere just because a bunch of half-wolves raised Cain every month or so.

Frank found himself pausing frequently on his hike. His shoes weren't built for this. Dust clung to his pantlegs and coated his lungs. He wondered if another wolf might have found some appreciation in the terrain, or in the view of the city. It had changed. Not just the devastation of the war, but what had been rebuilt. The oil derricks of the old days had been largely replaced by spheres of crackling lightning. The gothic movie palaces all along Hollywood Boulevard were also new, as the monsters started building what everyone kind of expected them to. The skyline included traffic, too, from homemade gremlin flivvers to the stately flying pyramids of the cats and the massive tripods of the martians. Go down to the coast, he might catch sight of a fifty-foot bathing beauty, or an ape the same size. Maybe it was beautiful.

He thought of coming up here with Lulu. Human, probably—though on the full moon, he thought of her barbarian physique doing battle with the werewolves, and he found his own wolf liking the idea. Frank might not be able to see the city's beauty, but he sure as hell could see hers, enough to awaken the poet in Frank's bruised soul. Well, awaken the closest thing he had to a poet there. A drunk Frenchman who could appreciate a decent limerick, maybe. Yeah, Lulu made Frank wish he could think of a single thing that rhymed with orange.

But he couldn't. All he could see was the Brain's ganglia wringing the life from this place.

He was one of those ganglia. Bought and paid for by the Brain herself. He wasn't dancing to her tune right at the moment, but why? *Am I trying to balance some kind of ledger?* he was wondering. It was almost funny, Frank even entertaining for a moment that he had any nobility left, or that it could be balanced. Save one wolf, did that mean Sylvia Screen could draw another breath? Could star in the pictures she thought she would when she stepped off the bus?

"Partner, if you're not in this goddamn shack, we're gonna have words," Frank muttered. He kept walking. Piss smells crept into the tapestry of the hills, pulling him along. His nose twitched, and he felt faintly *wrong*. He shouldn't be doing this, because someone else had staked out this territory—and unless he wanted a fight for it, he should find another way to get where he was going. That was the wolf, growling its two cents from its place deep inside him. He advised it to shut its trap.

This was the right track. It was hard to explain, but wolfman piss smelled different than werewolf. The latter was a bit muskier, the former a little more astringent. He caught the edges of beer that had been passed through a system, accounting for the origins of the urine. Werewolves usually smelled more like the remnants of blood than of Coors. In any case, that wasn't the kind of conversation Frank would have had with a ladyfriend, even if he had one.

He wasn't sure how long he'd been following the marking scents when he spotted it: a wooden shack, set into a flat area against a hill, easy to miss, hiding in the expansive shade of a California oak. The shack appeared pretty well constructed, and that impression didn't change as Frank approached it. It was unpainted, made of simple wooden beams with no insulation, but it didn't look like it would fall over without a lot of work. The kind of thing that would have housed pioneers in another era. It was almost a cabin, really. From the outside, he couldn't imagine it was more than one or two rooms. An outdoor oven of sorts had been built next to it, just cinderblocks stacked up around a firepit with a metal grill over the top. It would have charred meat, which was all a wolfman needed an oven to do. Vegetables were really more of a garnish. A sack of garbage slumped up against the side of the shack, food turned to maggots and rotting in the sun.

The scents nearly knocked Frank on his ass, drowning out anything creeping in from the hills. The wolves who spent their time here had liberally marked it. No wolf, or coyote for that matter, could come anywhere near this place and not know who called it theirs. Frank could dimly pick out Bud's scent—got to know that after his old partner's habit of pissing in any convenient alleyway while they were on the job—as well as a host of others. Like any wolves who'd formed themselves into a pack, their scents began to smell like each other. Or maybe it was because they all drank the same brand of cheap beer. Crushed empties were scattered in the dust.

The plain wooden door was shut, a faded gold-colored welcome mat out front nearly shredded into strips. As Frank approached it, the wind shifted, and he stopped dead in his tracks. The scent slithered through the narrow gaps in the walls, from under the doors, and through one of the barely open windows.

Death.

It wasn't simply the stink of a dead man. That smell didn't do much more to Frank these days than let him know he had some work to do. But there were degrees of dead man. Say, a phantom got plugged full of enough holes that he finally died and spent some time outdoors cooking up a funk—wasn't all that bad. Here, now, Frank smelled more than simple blood and decay. He smelled spilled marrow. He smelled bowels turned inside out. He smelled wounds cooked in silver. Death was close, and not a pretty one.

Frank paused to steel himself before opening the door. It didn't help. When he turned the knob with his forefinger and thumb—avoiding smudging what prints could be there—and saw the ruin they'd made of the wolfman inside, no amount of preparation would be enough to armor him. He turned away, swallowing the burning gorge that tried to force his way out of him. Not looking didn't even do much; inside, the scent was so strong that his mind supplied the image of the hapless cop twisting in unspeakable agony.

Frank breathed slowly, acclimatizing himself to the sight, an inch at a time. The Frank who went into the shack and the one who left it would be slightly different. The kill inside was the kind of thing that cauterized a bit of you. Burned it away like a silver knife.

He took in the rest of the shack first; everything except the carnage. There were, in fact, two rooms. The main room was where the atrocity had taken place, judging by caked splatter baked crusty and maroon in the heat. Most of the wolfman—now a man, only barely recognizable—lay on an old sofa nearly soaked through with everything that could come out of a body. Two other chairs, arrayed opposite and around a dusty old rug, as well as an overturned table, were the only furniture in the place. A door in the back opened into a bedroom with two cots. The scent was far dimmer in here and Frank took a moment, breathing in the mustiness like pure mountain air.

Then he turned back to the body. The initial horror had faded into a dull ache. This kind of thing was never exactly common, but from time to time they found a zombie or a goblin who'd met his end in unimaginable pain. After the Gobfather died and the last remnants of his gang had dried up, there hadn't been much of a call for this kind of outrage. Bellum and her corpses didn't have anybody left to torture.

Now Frank stared at the face, or what was left of it. He let himself ask the question he'd been frantically hiding from since the instant he knew there was a dead wolf in this place: Was this Bud?

It didn't smell like him, but he was smelling more of the inside of this fella than the out. The wolfman's face was only recognizable if you happened to be Picasso. He didn't look to have a stitch of clothing on, but Frank couldn't imagine that anything would have stood up to what happened to the rest of him.

Frank's stomach lurched as he realized what he would have to do. He approached the ruin on the couch, trying to tell himself that it wasn't a person anymore, that the wolf was past pain. It was all over and done with. If justice was coming, Frank would be the one carrying it out. He swore at himself. *Just like a man hit with artillery*, he thought.

Yeah, countered the voice, *but that happens all at once.*

He leaned close. The body eclipsed the world. It wasn't just the nauseating sight of it, but the way the terror permeated his senses. Frank felt himself growing, the room becoming hotter, and he let out a hushed snarl. The wolf wanted to run; even it wasn't so dumb that it would stay and fight against an enemy capable of this.

The new explosion of scent proved Frank something he also knew: it had been zombies who worked the wolf over. A particular scent caught his attention, almost lost in everything: cigarette smoke, decay, and *Catacombe* perfume. Aida Parrish had been here. He didn't think she was the one who did the knifework, but she had been in that room when it was being done.

Rage sank its claws into Frank, and the wolf burst from his flesh before he could stop it. He threw a leash around it, wrestling it down. *Don't destroy the damn scene!* he snarled at the creature inside him. *We need to know everything!* The wolf whined, its lips rippling over its teeth, but it slunk back into its den inside his mind. Frank stayed where he was, breathing slowly until the man was all that was visible on the outside.

Aida Parrish. This was on him, too. He hadn't used the blade, but he had let it happen. This time the wolf burst free with an agonized howl, and

Frank used every ounce of control to fling himself from the building and out into the dry hills.

He wasn't sure how long it took him to come back to himself, but when he did, he was halfway to his car.

TWENTY-SIX

The sun sank into the sea and red seeped throughout the sky. *Why should it be any different?*

Frank stood outside the shack, trying to ignore the stench of the body and the pop of flashbulbs behind him. A few uniforms had spread out over the hills, listlessly searching for something, anything, to tell the brass what they already knew. The whole thing was a sham. Frank only wondered how many of the wolves on the hill knew it. How many pocketed cash, and how many were too scared of the ones who did.

He needed a drink. He probably needed to eat, too, but his stomach had turned into a rock the second he'd found the dead man. The only thing that would stay in his gullet would need to be strong enough to burn out an infection. Rye, maybe. He was a jagged mass of nerves, needing to run or fight, and being unable to do either. If that wasn't Bud, it could be unless he was found. And if it was...he couldn't think about that. Bellum would put the same pain on all the Wolf Packers who'd done the moonlight special. It was only a matter of time.

Aida Parrish. The wolf inside him didn't think with words. It thought with impressions, colors, tastes, and textures. It came close to adding its voice to the name, though it spoke more in the sensation of teeth tearing through neck muscles. As much as Frank wanted to make her pay, as much as he needed it, she was untouchable. She sat at Bellum's right ganglion.

"Frank?" The voice was Talbot's. Frank turned, seeing his captain approaching somewhat cautiously. The smoke from Temple Glass's cigarette swirled around the entryway, forming an ethereal gate between the sunset outdoors and the carnage within. The invisible man's thoughts were, as always, his own. Frank couldn't imagine he felt the slightest guilt over a brother officer's gruesome murder.

"Yeah, Captain?"

Talbot came up alongside Frank, his fingers hooked through his belt. "Kind of beautiful, isn't it?"

Frank frowned before realizing the boss was talking about the skyline. "I don't see it so much anymore."

"You could use a vacation." Talbot chuckled. "Can't exactly picture you enjoying a beach in Aruba."

"I can't either," Frank agreed. He tried to imagine a vacation that wasn't him drinking on his porch and throwing empties into the orange grove, but his dreams weren't up to it. He knew other fellas would go places, but they usually had people to go with. Wives, girlfriends, some human they were changing. Frank flashed on an image of Lulu Garou in a bathing suit stepping out of a pool. A cough forced its way from his throat as he tried to keep his mind on the here and now rather than the never-would-be.

"Well, maybe you should start. Think about using that reward money. Get away for a bit, you know?"

"That what you're going to do?"

"Maybe. Might be nice to get out of the city."

"Way I hear it, most folks go to places where the sun shines. Don't know what you do when you're *from* a place like that."

"You have a really dim outlook on the world, Frank."

Frank stared at the reddening haze on the horizon. "You saw the wolf in there. What they did to him."

"I did."

"We know who it was?" Frank blurted the question so he wouldn't hesitate.

"Wolfgang Howell," Talbot said.

"You're sure?"

Talbot nodded. "I identified him myself and one of the patrolmen confirmed. You might have seen him puking his guts out in the ditch over there." The smell of that lingered too—French dip sandwich and potato salad, unless Frank missed his guess.

"Who was he? Howell, I mean."

Talbot looked around. No one was near. He dropped his voice anyway. "Former Wolf Pack."

Frank didn't have the energy to feign surprise. "Oh."

"Now, you can stop me here if you've heard this one," Talbot said. "But you knew about this place, and knew enough to check here. That tells me you've figured out the moonlight special was former Wolf Packers."

"I suspected."

"Mind my asking why?"

"M.O.," Frank lied. "Looked like the kind of efficiency cops would go for, and if wolves hit Bellum...had to be the Pack."

Talbot nodded. "Bit easier for me. I just looked around for the men who didn't show up to work, who didn't call out, and weren't home when I sent someone to check."

"Yeah, that would have been easier. Wolf Pack? All of them?"

"Yep." Talbot paused, fixing Frank with a stern look. "Now, Frank. We're on the same page here, right?"

"What were the names?" Frank knew one for certain, but he hoped and would have prayed if he thought anybody were listening, that somehow Bud had been missed.

"Hold on. We need to be clear first."

"Captain, is this my case?"

"For now," Talbot said. "If I think you're not going to handle it the way it needs to be handled, I'll do it myself. We both know how this ends, Frank. The only question you and I need to answer is how much we benefit from that."

"It's still *we?*"

"It can be, Frank. I just need you to tell me exactly what you plan to do."

"I know what we talked about before. But you saw Howell, right? You saw what they did to him? How much money is worth that?"

Talbot sighed, and for a moment, the pain in his eyes flared like a match. A match that quickly went out. "Don't look at it like that. The ones who did this aren't going away. If we raise a stink about one dead cop, what do you think will happen to us? I have a wife. We're looking at Little Monster House, gonna start a family for real. I got more than just me to think of, see. So the way I see it, we got two options. Either we join Howell in that shack, or we get a lot richer. And a little safer."

Frank wished the captain didn't make so much damn sense. "I hear you."

"Good. So what are you going to do with the information?"

"My job. Find the wolves who did it and tell you."

Talbot watched him, then nodded. "Good. Good, that's good." He took a deep breath. "The men that are missing are Sylvester Bullet, Mark O'Beast, and..." he paused again. "Bud Hound."

Frank let himself flinch when he heard the final name. He didn't know Bullet or O'Beast beyond a hazy recollection of faces that might belong to them, but no reaction to Bud would tip Talbot off. "Got it."

"I know you and Hound were partners. You can't let that muddy things."

Frank looked into Talbot's eyes and lied. "It doesn't. I'll find them." He started walking.

"Where are you going?" Talbot called after him.

"Getting started, sir. Still a little daylight left."

"Thanks, Frank! I knew I could count on you!" The worst words the captain could have chosen, echoing out over Griffith Park.

TWENTY-SEVEN

The Nocturnist's art deco sign was bright in the velvet evening. Frank only ever came to this place on work, so once a week tops. An exaggeration, sure, but cram in that many of the city's troublemakers and get them hopped up on prime hooch and somebody was going to bleed.

Moore had mentioned Wyeth Wyrd, and Frank knew her as the Nocturnist's cook. Finding out she hawked hexes on the side was about as shocking as finding out that gremlins didn't like the beach. A witch with Wyrd's gig could sell in Hollywood's best real estate to the movers, shakers, and earthquakers on all three sides of the law. There was the open question if Nyx Nocturne, the owner of the club, knew what Wyeth was up to. But Frank didn't have any illusions; Nocturne would have her lawyer cover for anything. She kept her nose just clean enough to stay out of a cell, and dirty enough that everybody trusted her. Maybe she was the only person in the city Bellum couldn't touch.

If Frank was going to lean on anybody for information, it would be Wyrd herself.

He parked a few blocks away and walked to the front of the club, passing the alley that ran by the side entrance. He and Bud caught a murder there a couple years back, one of Bellum's zombies bumped off by his girlfriend. She thought she was gonna make some kind of life with Bud, of all people. It was funny at the time, and if what Beth Keene had said was true, tragic. That night had been a wake-up call for Bud. He really cleaned up his act, or else he exercised better judgment when it came to which dames gave him cover. Moore brought him on to the Pack only a few months later. For Frank, it had been just another case. For Bud, it had changed everything. Funny how the world was like that.

Frank walked through the big double doors into an interior chamber where the ogre bouncer waited, farming his drool. Frank badged him. The palooka opened the inner door and waved him inside. Frank was ten feet in before he reflected on how weird the ogre's passivity had been. As if the bouncer was expecting him.

The far wall was the stage, done up to resemble the front of one of those medieval castles everyone thought vampires lived in until they found out that the leeches liked Beverly Hills same as anyone with money. The band—mostly phantoms because this club could afford it—performed on a stage designed like a drawbridge. Murals of the night sky with a full moon lording over everything covered the walls. Silhouettes of trees gave the room more depth than it needed.

As Frank entered, he passed cages on either side, where wolves—real ones—paced back and forth and bats hung from the ceilings. He turned to the right, and on his left was the stage and a series of tables for the high rollers. Tiers of tables rose on his right-hand side, for the less well-heeled. Balconies jutted out from the walls. There were private rooms upstairs, though giving a damn about privacy in the Nocturnist was almost quaint. Everyone was welcome there, which meant evenings could get a little strange.

One of the meat golem waitresses the place was famous for burst through the swinging doors from the kitchen. She was a looker—they all were if they wanted to work here. Sometimes Frank wondered why the meat golem ladies tended to be pretty while the men mostly looked like they'd lost a fight with a pickup truck and a sewing machine, in that order. He didn't wonder about it long; some of the fellas liked skin-dollies, but Frank would rather play with fire. No pun intended.

This one was fairly tall, sporting the curves of half a dozen dames. Her face didn't quite line up, but it gave her a little character. She was dressed in the uniform of the place, a halter and some shorts barely worth the name, along with fishnet stockings and a pair of heels that could bludgeon the ogre outside. Her long black hair was done up in victory rolls, the silvery streaks from her temples looking like swirls of ice.

Frank waved her over. She pointed at some stitches on her chest. "Yeah, you," Frank told her.

She clomped over. Didn't matter how graceful one of these dames could look, she always had shades of an elephant just learning to walk. She put a hand on her hip and cocked an eyebrow at him, an eyebrow set a bit higher than the other, giving her a perpetually ironic look.

A memory flitted through Frank's head—Moss made time with a dolly. Might be this was her. He couldn't imagine how that might matter. "Looking for Wyeth Wyrd. She in yet?"

The skin-dolly's face went slack, something between surprise and horror.

"What?" Frank asked.

She looked around and let loose with a hiss, the one sound the ladies could make. That was another thing. The men could talk, sort of, but the women could only hiss. Mystery of life, Frank supposed. Or else they wanted it that way. She beckoned back through the swinging doors she had only recently popped out of.

The kitchen was spacious, with high ceilings. Zombies bustled busily around the long metal counter, grabbing tureens and chopping vegetables, and generally being a clattering nightmare. Zombies in a kitchen was generally a bad idea, but if Nyx Nocturne could keep Bellum off her back, she could do the same to the health inspector. The scents, though, those were lovely. The spicy cinnamon of fourmi—giant ant meat to the hoi polloi—along with the dense meaty scents of sauces filled the air. He didn't see Wyeth around anywhere, and he couldn't help wonder why the waitress had brought him in here. Wasn't like he could talk to the zombies—they were just moaning "Brains" at each other. One of them, in chef's whites, looked to be in charge, but his vocabulary would be nearly as limited as the skin-dolly's.

The waitress pulled an order pad from the wall and pushed back into the main room. Frank gratefully followed her, the sounds and smells already beginning to make him feel small and penned in. With the sudden cessation of the heaviest of it, old cigarette smoke joined the bouquet as though asking to be recognized. Figured. Anybody was welcome here, and that meant smokers too, enough that it had bled into some of the fixtures. Frank could swallow his irritation.

The skin-dolly was writing, and when she finished she held up the pad. Her penmanship was lovely, damn near calligraphy. *Wyeth was murdered.*

"What? How?"

She turned back to the pad. *I don't know. She was at home w/ coven. Got news when I came in.*

Frank shook his head. He might believe in coincidences, but he didn't like them and sure as hell didn't trust them. The meat golem gave him Wyeth's address. He thanked her, and she got back to work. He could see it in her now—the annoyance with her workload was going to hold her through the day and whatever sadness and fear would be held for later.

He knew exactly how she felt.

TWENTY-EIGHT

Wyeth Wyrd had lived in a cozy bungalow court at the foot of Mount Lee, a mile or so from Ducktail's flop. As Frank pulled up, the Hollywoodland sign was flashing its multiple colors and getting ready to spray its ordnance at the moon. The monsters who lived around it had either never heard kraut artillery or else they were fit to cut out paper dolls.

The bungalow court might've been charming enough if not for the thunder of the sign rattling its gremlin-designed mayhem into the sky. Four bungalows were situated around a central courtyard planted with the local flora and crisscrossed with a walkway made from irregular stones. A bubbling fountain stood in the center of it. Frank guessed it probably wasn't water in there, both because of what water did to witches and because it was oozing a thick smoke over the ground. Something moved around just under the surface, much too big to fit into such a small space.

The door of one of the units closest to the street opened and a Venusian mantrap slithered out. All told, the plants were fairly rare sights. They got around with a combination of pulling themselves with thick green vines they used like martian tentacles, and their twitching mass of pale roots. A collection of leaves and flowers bloomed along the central stalk, and at the top sat a massive seed pod lined with thornlike teeth. They talked with a big leaf where their tongue should be. Frank obstructed the guy, even if the writing mass of greenery made him more nervous than a witch in a rainstorm.

"Excuse me," Frank said.

The mantrap's seed pod reared up like a cobra. "What do you want?"

Frank showed him the shield. "I'm looking for Wyeth Wyrd's residence."

"Oh, of course. I'm sorry about that. It's just...what happened to Eden..."

"Don't worry about it. Wyeth Wyrd?"

"That one." A tentacle pointed to one of the bungalows in the back, and the rest of the plant made a move to go around Frank.

"A moment," Frank said. "What's your name, sir? Or possibly ma'am."

"Lavender Flowers."

"Were you here when it happened?"

"No, I was at work."

"I thought she was killed at night."

The mantrap winced, the mouth that Frank could have easily fit inside twisting unpleasantly. "She was. I work at night."

"Where?"

"Visionary Pictures. I'm a set dresser."

"Set dresser?"

The mantrap's tone dropped a couple degrees. "Films need plants."

"Who do I call to check on that?"

"You can talk to Orbus, the director, half a dozen grips, a few electricians..."

"Okay, okay. I get it. Did you know the victim?"

"Wyeth? Not well, but I knew her. I rent the place from the coven. I usually pay Winnifred. She's the crone."

"Where's she?"

Flowers indicated one of the back bungalows. This one was partly grown into the root system of a live oak.

"So what happened?"

"I got home this morning. We were shooting up at the studio, but the whole place was locked down. You know, for the..." The mantrap nodded to where the full moon might have been. "They let us out in the morning, by the time I got home, the police had already arrested Willow Wyrd."

"That the maiden?"

Flowers nodded. "Yeah. I don't really know anything else. I went out back and got to sleep."

Frank followed the mantrap's gesture and saw a postage stamp of a jungle behind the bungalow, complete with a now-empty hole. "And now it's back out to work."

"About the size of it," Flowers said. "Is this going to take long? I don't want to be late."

Frank stepped aside. "Get to your job. I'll be checking the alibi."

"I think the other detective already did, but be my guest." The mantrap wiggled down the street, heading for Franklin Avenue where the red car stops would be located.

As Frank walked through the gateway into the courtyard, that same eerie sensation that had grabbed him at Moore's sank its claws into him again. Death had left a hole in each place, physical and spiritual. More places had those holes than folks wanted to admit. Better dance between them, ignore them, and hope you don't fall in.

Frank gave the fountain in the center a wide berth and knocked on the door inside the tree. It looked like the house had been built first and the tree grown around it, but the bungalow wasn't old enough for a tree that big. A little witchcraft went a long way.

The door opened to reveal a hunched-over woman who must have spent her spare time cultivating warts. She was piled high with layers of shawls and leaning hard on a gnarled staff. Witches radiated feelings the way a lightbulb gave off light, and with crones it was always fear. Now, Frank wasn't scared, but Winnifred Wyrd made him more nervous than he liked to admit. He felt like a dog snarling at a new person, no one quite knowing what was provoking the animal. The crone looked up at Frank with rheumy eyes, and he held up the badge to forestall whatever spicy greeting she had planned.

"Wolfman, LAP—Jesus!" Frank's greeting was cut short as a fat bird pushed past the crone, wings spread and a homicidal hiss snaking from its beak.

Winnifred Wyrd laughed. "One bird, and all that steel's gone in a second!"

"Ma'am, I'm going to have to ask you control your fowl."

She set her staff, a gnarled length of wood that could only come from an enchanted grove, in front of the beast. The swan pressed its breast against it, looking for an opening to bite Frank. "When I incarnated Cygne here, I was a maiden. Quite the looker, then. Everybody thought, *Oh, she's pretty, got a pretty familiar.* They didn't know."

"That swans are mean bastards who hate the world."

"Exactly," she broke into a graveyard grin. "Now, whaddya want, young fellow?"

"Like I said, I'm LAPD. Name's Wolfman. I'm—"

"Spend a lot of time on that name, did you?"

"A long weekend. Talked to a priest, even."

Winnifred Wyrd snorted. "I'm bereaved. Besides, ain't nothing to tell you I ain't told the other wolf."

"Who was that, ma'am?" Fear stuck that *ma'am* in his mouth.

She plucked a card off a big wooden toadstool by the door and handed it over. The swan continued to batter at the staff barrier, but couldn't move it. Frank kept one eye on the bird and used the other to take a gander at the card. The name said "Lobo Solitario" on it. Frank knew the gent; he was a good detective. As good as anyone could be these days, at any rate. He handed the card back. "I understand, Ms. Wyrd. Just had a few questions of my own."

Her eyes might be watery, but a keenness glinted in them like a blade at the bottom of a river. "We can start with how they fingered one who didn't do it?"

"We can start wherever you like. Can I come inside?"

"No. You can follow me. Got a feeling you're gonna want to sniff around where it was done." She paused. The air around her drew close. Like one of those summer days when the sky is about ten feet off the ground and it felt like being cooked from the inside. Frank focused on the crone's eyes and pretty soon that was all he could see. They were the color of the dry leaves on the underside of her live oak. They seemed so big, and when she spoke again, her voice was all around him, the consonants scraping at his insides. The swan's hiss joined her words, and now it was more than hate, it was a command. "You're gonna get the ones who done this."

"They made the arrest," he told her. "I can't do anything about it." Though he wanted to, deep inside, where the words scored his soul.

"You let me worry about Willow," she said. Now her voice sounded like the scratching of branches on a window. "The ones who done this, the killers. You see they get what's coming. I ain't got Kali here, but you'll do. You'll do."

"I will." Frank wasn't sure if the crone made him say the words, but he didn't think so. When they were out of him, he felt the breath surround him and slam shut like a cell door. And then Winnifred Wyrd was in front of him, small and gnarled as before, and the sky was back up where it was supposed to be. The swan sat primly next to her, shaking its tail feathers and folding its wings close to its body.

"It's done," she said.

Frank coughed, looking around in embarrassment. The street was quiet, a dry breeze riffling through the leaves. "Can you tell me what happened?"

Winnifred Wyrd nodded to the gate. "I don't sleep much anymore. Sign I should start thinking about maybe moving beyond." She snorted. "That ain't happenin' now. Tell you that. Willow ain't ready for motherhood, and she damn sure ain't no crone." She hawked and spat into the foliage.

"This was last night?" Frank prompted.

"Mmm. After midnight, I should think. I heard the car on the street, and then steps coming up here. Car left, going fast. I didn't think much of it."

"No?"

"Wyeth gets visitors late at night. Happens when you're a witch doctor. Figured it was that and went back to what I was doing."

"Which was?"

"Cooking." She left it at that, her tone implying that was probably for the best.

Frank pointed at the other house in the back. "This is...was...Wyeth's?"

"Mmmhmm. I let the noise go. Left that business to her. But then I hear another car pull up. Now, *that* was unusual. That time I went to the window." She gestured to one facing the courtyard. Frank stood by it. The view wasn't ideal, being partially blocked by the branches of the tree her house seemed to be growing inside, but he could see large sections of the walkway and Wyeth's front door.

"What did you see?"

"Zombies. Five of 'em."

Frank fished a notepad and stubby pencil from his pocket. "Describe them?"

"They were...a type. You know the ones. Fancy suits, nice hats. The women were in skirts, but it's the same kind of suit."

"Guns?"

"I didn't see any, but it was dark and my eyes don't work so well. Heard 'em later, though. Besides, you ever see a zombie like that didn't have a gun?"

He thought of Diaz de Muertos, but wasn't going to correct her. "How many men? How many women?"

"Three men, two women. A woman was in the lead, so that was nice. She had half the skin of her face gone. Saw the light from the street on her bone." Frank didn't need that bit of clarification. He figured who would be in the lead there: Aida Parrish. He hadn't caught her scent, but sniffing anything specific in a witch's garden other than herbs was next to impossible anyway.

"Any distinguishing features on the others?"

"I think one of the men was missing his eyes. Another one looked chewed on. More than most of them, anyway. It was dark. Anyway, they kicked in the front door and that's when I heard those gunshots." The crone shuddered with the memory. It was the first time Frank saw the mask drop. He understood why she was keeping it up. Let it fall and she'd crumble when she needed her wits most.

"Heard some shouting. 'Brains' and the like, so guess who that was. Some commotion around the back. Then next thing I know they're dragging somebody out the front gate. Willow's door opens then, and I think she's ready to fight. Don't have to tell you how dumb I thought she was being. They put a couple slugs into her house and she went inside. Then the five zombies and the one man they were dragging get into the car and they're gone."

"Then?"

"I checked on Wyeth." She swallowed, her eyes going distant.

"What happened?"

"They shot her. Takes more than one bullet to down a witch, but not a lot more. We ain't meat golems. Anyway, those stiffs did the job and then some. Willow came up and joined me, a sobbing wreck, the poor thing. Held her until the wolves got here. And you know what they did?"

"They arrested Willow," Frank said. "Ms. Flowers told me."

"Arrested *Willow*," Winnifred said. "What witch do you know uses a gun?"

"Let alone bumps off a member of her own coven."

Winnifred gave him a *There you go* gesture. "Bunch of zombies come in here, kill my mother, and the wolves decide my maiden is going away for it."

"I'm sorry."

"When I told you about the woman in the lead, I saw your face. You know her."

Frank didn't see the point of lying and didn't want to test a crone. "I know her."

"Then she's the one you need to get."

Frank nodded, his mind going through what Winnifred had told him. "The ones who got here before the zombies, did you see them? Hear them at all?"

"Kept hearing one man's voice talking low, and the other one kind of moaning. Sounded like two men, but I can't be sure. Kind of a growl to both voices, but it being a full moon, I guess that's not strange."

"What happened to that second man? The one that wasn't in the car?"

Winnifred gestured to the house. "You're welcome to look for him."

Frank paced around the side of the house. The boundary of the bungalow court was a wooden fence. Trees growing by it would have made it an easy climb. He went to the edge and sniffed. He sneezed a few times as the aromatics from the garden hit him, but he smelled what he was hunting for. Bud had gone this way.

He relaxed, finally becoming aware he had been clenched like a prizefighter's fist. Bud had gone over the fence. He might have kept going. He might have got away.

"Thanks for your time," he said to Winnifred Wyrd as he left the court.

"You do what you're bound to," she called after him, "or evil will come visit."

"Evil damn near moved in," Frank muttered.

TWENTY-NINE

Frank left the witches' bungalow court with the hex coiling around his soul. Getting Solitario to walk away from a bust, especially when the one who did it held his leash, well, that was about as hard as everything else Frank had to do.

"Fancy meeting you here, detective." Pearl Friday slithered out in front of him, her presence hidden by the greenery at the border of the witches' domain.

"What do you want?" Frank growled.

"Same thing you do."

"I doubt that."

"Detective...you have to know running into me isn't a coincidence. We're working the same case."

"I'm trying to solve it."

"Oh? I heard this was Solitario's collar."

"Now how in the hell could you know that?"

He heard the smile in the crawling eye's voice. "Come on, Frank. Let me buy you a drink. Get off on the right foot for a change."

"Fine," Frank said. "But I ain't talkin' to you here."

"I know just the spot."

"Fine, I'll follow you."

He didn't know what to expect, where a reporter might want to spend her time, but this was never on the table. Maybe he didn't know as much as he thought.

If not for a certain giantess, the ogre would have been the biggest dame Frank had ever seen with his own two eyes. She was on rollerskates, and legally should have been classified as a train. When she bodychecked a siren into the railing, it had roughly the same effect as a locomotive shrugging off a carelessly parked car. Frank stared at the swirling spiral of dames on skates all hammering into each other at dizzying speeds and completely forgot that he was with Pearl Friday until she spoke.

"You wanted someplace private to talk," she said.

She wasn't hard to hear, even over the roar of the crowd. This gym wasn't huge, and most of the space was taken up with the wooden roller-rink and the bleachers. The air could have been wrung out like an old washcloth. The scents were of the bodies on the track, the breath of the crowd, and the fresh buttery bouquet of popcorn, being sold a nickel a bag by a grinning ghoul.

"So talk," Frank growled. He allowed he didn't see many zombies in the joint, and those he did were focused on the action in the center.

Not that he blamed them. More than one of the skating ladies was Frank's type. Lulu Garou would have liked this place, he thought, though he wasn't sure if he should tell her. Felt vaguely embarrassed over the whole thing.

"Okay, okay. You're looking into the Wyeth Wyrd case, despite it not being yours and an arrest already having been made."

"What's your point?"

"That you know as well as I do that the maiden didn't do it."

"She's gonna go down for it."

"Then what are you doing there? What brought you to that door?"

Frank watched the swirling mass of femininity bump and shove on the rink. "What are you looking for here? The Gray Matter owns the *Minion*, doesn't she?"

"Not to my knowledge."

"Then why the headlines? The ones about organized crime being a thing of the past?"

A choked off syllable sounded in the air. A lie, she'd thought of a lie, and started to speak it, but checked herself. "Money. The one you're talking about...she doesn't own *everything*. She owns an awful lot, sure. But not everything. There's too much. Sure, eventually they'll get it down to where one can own a city like this one, but we're not there yet. No mobs means more money. And let's be fair, once the Gobfather turned up dead, they were only off by one."

A siren that looked more kraken than fish absolutely leveled a petite vampire. "Okay. So maybe you're onto something there."

"In the Decoratorius murder, they brought in a human. But word is you let him walk and arrested a ghost instead. Why?"

"Kid didn't do it."

"Never bothered the LAPD before."

"Bothered me."

"Maybe that's why I'm here," she said, the huge globe of her eye turning to the action on the rink.

"I ain't a crusader, if that's what you're thinking. Wasn't like some bigwig offed the gremlin. It was his own maid. That money you're talkin' about? It's not moving anywhere for some haunt-in. Far as they're concerned, a ghost ain't that much different than a meatstick."

"If it didn't matter, why'd you do it?"

"Didn't say it didn't matter. Just said it doesn't make me somebody lookin' to spit in the Gray Matter's eye, if she even had one of those."

On the rink, a gremlin slipped though the blockers and raised her arms over her head in triumph. Her team hoisted her up on their brawny shoulders for a victory lap. Frank found himself clapping, though he couldn't imagine why.

"Cops knocked over a stash house," Friday said. "One of 'em got hit with silver, so they went to the nearest witch doctor, which was where the button men caught up with them. That witch doctor got caught in the crossfire. Bellum doesn't want her zombies going down for that, so the LAPD pins it on a maiden who doesn't look like she could pick up a gun, let alone use it."

Frank clamped down on a big reaction. Friday would have made a hell of a detective. "Put all that together, did you?"

"Gotta admit, it fits pretty well."

"You planning on writing this, then? Last time I checked, the *Minion* wasn't exactly keen on the idea of crime in our fair city."

"I don't know if it'd get past the editorial desk if I did. It's like you said, this is one witch either way. One of them mixed up with exactly the kinds of crooked cops the city doesn't want."

The wolf was halfway out before Frank could leash it. "They ain't crooked."

Friday quailed in the face of his sudden anger. "Right. I didn't mean crooked in that way."

"Maybe the only cops in this town who ain't," Frank muttered, turning away. Shame threw the wolf back in its den. Getting mean with an eyeball was low; one sharp object and they were screaming for the hills. Frank carried ten of them on the ends of his hands.

"A year ago, when the goblins and zombies were dropping each other every week, I used to wish one of them would win. It's like I wished on a monkey's paw."

"Get the damn thing back."

"When the Gobfather was bumped off, they made an arrest. You know that?"

"I didn't," Frank said.

Friday chuckled without an ounce of humor. "Zombie. He was out the next night and the whole thing was scrubbed. It's like it never happened."

"You ever try to write about it?"

"Sure did. Editor killed the story. Then you know what happened? The Gobfather had these...I don't know what to call them. They called themselves the Goblins Three. Ran a hat shop in Hollywood called

Redcaps. Anyway, they were the Gobfather's right hand men. Months after the Gobfather was rubbed out, someone offs them, one after another."

"You think it was the zombie who got pinched?"

"Or the Monster Slayer."

"Thought you'd know better than that. Monster Slayer's a fairy tale."

Friday shrugged, and on a crawling eye, that gesture was impressive. "Okay, fine. Had to be someone in *that* organization, but does it really matter which one gave the push?"

"And nobody cared because the ones who bought it were trouble boys."

"I keep thinking that eventually I'll find a story, a big enough one, that the editors can't kill. That wasn't it. This one? Feels different to me."

"And then what? Free of those who run things?"

"Maybe."

"Pipe dream, Friday. You have to know that." Frank got up.

"But what if it's not? If you find something, give me a call." An eye that big, it was impossible to miss the pleading in it.

"Maybe I will," Frank said.

"I almost think you mean it."

"I almost trust you." Frank gestured at the rollerskating dames. "Hell of a thing that is. How'd you find it?"

"By paying attention to the stuff no one else does."

THIRTY

As Frank stalked through Highland Park Station, images of Howell, of what they'd turned him into, kept intruding. Details he wished he could forget but knew he never would. Whenever he passed a wolf in blue, another flash on Howell's ruined body went up on the silver screen in his mind. They were all guilty of it. Either they took the Gray Matter's money or they let someone else do it and still looked the other way.

Bellum and her corpses had escalated things. They were seeing what they could get away with, and once they knew what was in play, they'd look for the next line and cross it too. The Night War changed all the rules, but the world had thought the changes wrought after it would stop there and things would proceed as normal—albeit with a few more tentacles.

An easy lie they all told themselves.

Frank started off downstairs. Most of the cells were occupied, but it didn't take him long to find who he figured had to be Willow Wyrd. She barely looked fifteen. Her auburn hair was long and straight, still a bit tangled from sleep. Her face was round and freckled, and he imagined she looked nice when she smiled. Now, with her eyes red and watery, and dried snot under her nose, she looked impossibly young.

"Willow Wyrd?" Frank asked, though he didn't have to.

"Yeah?" Her eyes widened. "Giskie! Where's Giskie?!"

"*What's* Giskie?" Frank asked.

"My familiar. He's a fox. So big," she held her arms out to approximately fox size, "red, and very cute. They took him away! I can feel him, but he's cold, and scared, and—"

Frank held up a hand. "Don't worry, Miss Wyrd. The familiar's fine. We got a little kennel, keep magic from...he's fine."

"Please. You don't understand. I didn't *do* anything. Just put Giskie in here with me, I promise I won't cast any spells. I don't have anything to use with them anyway."

"Sorry. Policy. Look, I talked to Winnifred Wyrd."

"Then you know what happened!" The girl shot up from the bench, grabbing the bars, her tiny knuckles turning white. "You know I didn't do it."

Frank glanced at the sergeant on duty. The lazy lech was thumbing through a copy of *Twilight Visitor*, and just barely holding in the wolf whistling. He wasn't about to look up for anything, up to and including a martian death ray. "Yeah, I know. I'm gonna see if I can get things straightened out. Get your familiar back to you."

"Thank you, Mr.—"

"Detective. Detective Wolfman. And don't thank me yet, kid. I said I'll do what I can, not that I was a genie."

She sniffled and nodded, returning to her seat. Frank tapped the bars in farewell. He couldn't imagine someone taking a look at Willow Wyrd and thinking she could jaywalk, let alone plug a member of her own coven. It took all kinds, sure, but there were limits.

Frank marched into the bullpen with a fight in his steps. Lobo Solitario was at his desk, putting some paperwork away. He had a look like a relieved groan from sitting down on a sofa, but in human form.

"Solitario?"

The other detective looked up. He was a little soft around the edges, but there was steel in his brown eyes. His skin was dark, and there had been a time when that mattered. Or mattered *more*, anyway—it was getting harder to ignore that those old barriers were still there, just not brought up in polite society. Frank had used his nightstick on fellas that looked like

Solitario back in the riots of '42. Hell, that had been half the reason he enlisted. Had to be better skulls to crack overseas.

"Wolfman—what do you want?"

"Heard you caught the Wyrd case."

"Caught and closed, old man."

"Yeah. You fingered the maiden for it."

"You got it." Solitario said it a little too loud, and the way his eyes darted around was like he was hunting for an audience he wasn't sure he had. The bullpen was pretty empty. The shift would change over, with only a few of the night owls hiding from home in their cases.

"Come on. A maiden pushes the button on her mother? A witch don't bump off her own coven."

"This one did," Solitario said, and locked eyes with Frank with an unspoken *Go with me on this one.*

Frank hunkered down, speaking quietly. "I just talked to the crone. She has five armed zombies barging into the house and then some gunshots. It don't take Sam Spade to know what happened."

Solitario dropped his voice too. "First off, what are you doing talking to my witnesses?"

"You closed it, remember? Thought somebody should work it."

"You sweet on that maiden or something?"

"I don't know her from Glinda. Alls I know is the crone saw something and I caught a scent backs her up."

"Fine. What do you want me to do? Walk right into the Nocturnist and slap cuffs on the first stiff I see?"

"It's your job."

"Oh, really? That how you would do your job? Because I seem to remember a case involving the same Miss Parrish where the evidence went—"

That was all Solitario got out. The wolf burst out of Frank, and he was yanking the other detective out of his seat by his collar. Solitario's wolf wasn't far behind. Black hair exploded from his face. His jaw stuck out, lower canines extending and sharpening. His brow thickened, ears suddenly pointed. He grabbed Frank with hands now twisted into claws. The two of them careened around the room, snarling and crashing into desks and filing cabinets. Two wolfmen throwing down almost fought like men—albeit men with anger throttling their higher functions and a handful of razor blades. Frank didn't have a clear memory of anything other than the red, the desire to tear this other wolf limb from limb. Hands closed over his shoulders and around his sides, and then there was daylight between him and Solitario. Cops held him and Solitario apart while they snarled and snapped like angry dogs.

"Break it up, you two!" Captain Talbot shouted. "Acting like a bunch of damn Sheriff's wolves!" He held onto a struggling Frank from behind, a uniform in front with his hands on Frank's chest, while a detective and a uniform held onto Solitario. The other wolfman let go of the wolf first, shrinking, the fur vanishing back beneath skin. Frank found he was having trouble, the red sticking its claws too deep. Howell wanted a pound of flesh and Frank was the only one out to collect. Talbot took his voice down a level. "I know it's been a long day. I know it's been rough. But I can't have two of my detectives fighting like junkyard dogs in the bullpen."

"I'm fine, Cap," Solitario said. The wolves holding him loosened their grips and he nodded to them, straightening his clothes.

"Good man," Talbot said, and Frank could swear he heard surprise in the voice. "What about you, Frank?"

"I'm..." It came out as a growl. Frank focused on the wolf, throwing a leash around its neck and dragging it down inside. "I'm jake, Captain."

"Now I don't give a good goddamn what this beef was over, but it's buried now, got it?"

"Got it," Solitario said.

Frank nodded.

"Shake," the captain commanded.

Solitario stuck out his hand. "I think we understand each other, right, Frank?"

Frank nearly took his throat for that. He kept the wolf down by grinding his own teeth down to nubs. "Yeah." He took the other wolf's hand and didn't squeeze that hard. They understood each other. Too damn well.

THIRTY-ONE

Frank knew what he was doing as soon as he got into his car. Later, he would do his best to pretend it was an impulsive decision, that he had chosen without choosing. But he knew. As someone once said, the wolf wants what it wants.

He headed north and leaned hard on the gas. The night had barely started, so it wasn't deep enough to blame the moon or the wolf or the... anything. No, this was Frank. What he wanted. Needed, really.

Lulu Garou opened her door at the first knock. She stared at him, her face unreadable. "Didn't think I'd see you again, after you got what I wanted."

"Didn't get what *I* wanted," Frank told her, staring back.

She considered, and he could see her weighing the next twenty seconds in the way she appraised him. Finally, she stepped aside. "Well, come in. Can't have the neighbors talking."

Frank walked into the living room. *The Pilar O'Heaven Show* played on the TV. Pilar, the bathing beauty of the southland, shimmering in a figure-hugging gown, was in the middle of a sober interview with a young-looking vampire, tiny next to the giantess's famous fifty foot frame. They were jawing about Gardenio Eden; Frank figured the leech had worked for the plant. Lulu turned off the TV.

Frank could smell her. He tried not to, but there was no turning off the scent. Her body, the heavy earthy scents that came with being a wolfman. Hell of a thing to call her; she was all woman. Beneath it, he fancied he could smell himself, still clinging to her from the night before.

"Can I get you something to drink?"

"You have rye?"

"Vodka."

"Have to do."

She returned with two glasses of orange juice, the stinging scent of vodka lurking inside. Frank swirled it around, took a taste. Not what he was used to, but he didn't mind it. No, he didn't mind it one bit. Would have been the easiest thing in the world to drink that forever. Out of the corner of his eye, he saw Lulu open her mouth to speak. He cut her off, terrified that she might throw him out.

"Nick Moss," he said.

She frowned. "That name supposed to mean something?"

"He was an associate of..." Frank faltered, pushed on, "...of your husband's."

"Who is he?"

"A private snoop. Works out of a closet on Flower Street. Little fella, kind of looks like a weasel who got into the coffee."

"Not ringing any bells."

"He's human."

"Now I *know* I've never heard of him. Didn't know there were human snoops."

"Just the one."

"Why would Lou be working with a snoop?"

Frank shrugged it off. That truth was a little too complicated to just go blurting out. He wanted to tell her. A woman like Lulu Garou deserved all the secrets, and it was a crime she'd spent most of her life knowing none of them. "He might have been an informant. Word on the street was that he was connected with organized crime."

"Funny, I heard that organized crime was a thing of the past."

"Yeah, I heard the same thing."

"So why are you asking me about this gent? He have something to do with Lou's disappearance?"

"I don't know," Frank said truthfully. "Could be. I know he and your husband were pals, or something like that."

"You think this Moss is hiding Lou?"

Frank shook his head. "No. I don't." He took a deep breath. "Last night, a group of four wolfmen pulled a moonlight special."

"I don't..."

"It's when wolves hex themselves before a full moon. They can stay in control, kind of. These wolves did that, and hit a Bellum stash house."

"Last night? You said Lou's been missing since—" she supplied the date with a shrug. She was right. Grief, stress, and all of those big emotions they didn't have names for, they made time pass in a fog. Frank imagined that there were times Lulu felt like she had been alone for years, and other times she felt like her husband was right outside.

"Yeah. I think it was originally a five-man job."

"And Lou was the fifth man."

Frank nodded. "Only he goes missing, and his pals panic. One of his pals was my old partner. They want me to find him."

"They?"

"The cops. The mob. Everybody."

Lulu shook her head. "So Lou went missing *before* the job? And the other four went through with it?"

"That they did. Probably too tempting a prize. Can't say as I blame them." Frank shook his head. "That kind of money could make a robot take up swimming. These fellas? They were honest cops. I can't say for sure, but I don't think they took a dime of money from the Gray Matter before last night. And they were so goddamn honest that they stole from *her*—not anybody else, anybody safer—so they could skip town with their souls intact. I think their honesty made them bent."

He wasn't aware he was shaking until Lulu put a hand on his shoulder. "Are you all right, Frank?"

"I don't even know what that means." He stared into the depths of the cocktail and wished it were pure vodka. Then, at least, it would have been transparent.

"Do you take money from..." she trailed off.

Frank thought about lying, but he couldn't. Not to her. He nodded. "If they come to you, give you the chance, you have to take it. The ones who don't get silver poisoning pretty quick. So they came to me, and I took it like I was supposed to. Thought it wouldn't mean much. I wasn't on organized crime detail. They weren't even killing each other much anymore, not since the Gobfather got his Christmas present. Figured it was just the cost of doing business. I keep my head down and I keep doing what I was doing."

Lulu's attention was a lead weight on him. "It didn't stay that way."

"Nope," he nearly whispered. He had gone this far; might as well give her the whole thing. "One of the underbosses, a zombie dame by the name of Parrish, she bumped off a hob. A remnant from the Gobfather's days who didn't get the message that it was time for poetry enthusiasts to leave town. I get a visitor not too much later, the kind of visitor who's missing some skin and don't smell too good."

"A zombie."

"Yeah," Frank said. "This zombie's got Sarah Bellum on a radio. Tells me that the evidence against Parrish needs to be lost. And I figure, what's one hob more or less? Wasn't like we were talking a citizen here. So I do it. Without the evidence, Parrish is on the streets. Only that wasn't the end, because it's never the end."

Frank cleared his throat. He couldn't look at Lulu for the judgment he'd see in her face. The judgment he deserved. "So maybe a week later, Parrish decides she's going to finish what she started, or maybe the goblin spots her when they're out. I never got the whole story. I don't think it matters. Anyways, Parrish carries a pair of tomahawks. They're made outta cold iron, perfect for hob killing. She's known for them in the wrong circles. So she comes across a hob at the Nocturnist—friend of the last one—

and goes to work. He doesn't go down without a fight, and in the middle of everything, one of those tomahawks ends up in the chest of Sylvia Screen."

"Who?" A reasonable thing to ask. Nobody had heard of Sylvia. Nobody kept her name like Frank did.

"She was a doppelganger. Fresh off the bus from Bisbee, Arizona. Handle like that, she thought she was going to be a star. Just had some snaps done for the studios. I bet her prospects were sky high. Her first week in LA, she went to the Nocturnist and never came out again."

Lulu swallowed. "What happened to Parrish?"

"Not a thing. Her lawyer argued manslaughter in the act of self-defense. Wrong place, wrong time. It was the hob's fault for starting things."

"He didn't—"

"He wasn't around to rhyme different. Only story they got belonged to the zombie and a couple other witnesses who backed up her statement. Can't prove it, but each one of those witnesses is at least a thousand dollars richer. Sylvia's dying goes straight from the night I decided to take that money right up to where this silly kid with stars in her eyes gets caught between two gangsters with a beef."

"You couldn't have known that."

"Specifics? No. But when I took the money, I decided that *my* life was worth more than anybody else's that might cross Bellum and her thugs. Turned out that person was Sylvia."

"Why did you become a cop in the first place?"

"Didn't think I would have to answer that for you."

"I know why *I* want to be one. I don't know about you."

"Sounds stupid, but...I wanted to be the one who was there for the dead. They can't do it anymore, so it's on me to find out what happened and make sure whoever did it gets their just reward, whatever that is. With Sylvia—"

"It's on Parrish. You know who did it."

"Yeah," Frank said. "And can't do a thing about it. I put a slug in Aida Parrish, I'm dead. Bellum would probably come for everybody I loved, too, if there was anybody still on that list."

"I don't know if I should feel insulted or not."

Frank blinked, looking up at Lulu for the first time in what felt like years. Her expression was serious, but she was looking at him. *At* him, in a way he seldom felt anyone ever did. She was seeing the man he was, and she was still looking. "I'm sorry?"

"You came here tonight, after last night. Seems you had something to tell me."

"I don't think your husband is alive."

She nodded, thinking it over. "I think I think that too."

"This is a chance, Lulu. You should pull up stakes. Go back east. There's a lot of 'back east' to choose from."

"Want me out of your town that much?"

Frank shook his head. "I think there's a place out there somewhere where you can be a cop. And there, wherever it is, you won't be owned by anybody else the way I am. You can do the job the right way. The way it's supposed to be done. The way you've been wanting to, and the way I know you can. You just gotta take this chance for what it is."

Her eyes glittered in the dim light of the living room. When she spoke again, her voice had rust on it. "I'm not going to leave tonight," she told him.

Then she turned and walked down the hall to her bedroom. Frank followed her.

THIRTY-TWO

Frank didn't want to look at the clock. It was a couple hours later at least. He knew if he pinned it down, it would mean it was time to end, and he didn't want that to happen. He wanted to lay there, in the rumpled bed, holding Lulu Garou. Her head was pillowed on his shoulder, one hand on his chest, her body fitting into the contours of his.

"Well, we can't blame that on the full moon, now can we?" Lulu said.

And for the first time in a long time, Frank chuckled. "No, you can blame me for being a cad."

"You were a perfect gentleman."

"I don't think perfect gentlemen make time with married ladies."

"You mean widows," she said, and they were quiet for a time. Frank couldn't figure out if that made it better or worse. In a way, she was only evening the scales, even if Lou Garou was alive. "I knew about Lou," she said finally.

He didn't have to ask. Their minds were running along the same tracks. The only ones open on this side of midnight. "How?"

"I didn't know for certain, but I *knew*. He was careful, but you can only have so many late nights before they begin to add up. Only so many scents that linger."

"Why didn't you leave him?"

She rolled onto her back and Frank immediately missed the warmth against him. "I don't know. I should have, maybe. I kept wondering what my life would be if I did. I wasn't anything. Just some housewife. If I wasn't that anymore..." she finished.

"You shouldn't feel that way," Frank said. He hated Garou for doing that to her. Nobody had that right.

"Maybe I should do what you said." She looked at him, and he turned to face her. In the dark, her eyes glittered like gemstones. "Go east. Colorado, maybe. I always liked the sound of Colorado."

"Yeah."

"What about you?" she asked him. He wanted to hear an invitation in her voice, but it wasn't like that. They'd shared something, sure, maybe even something special. But he couldn't imagine her wanting anything beyond it.

"I need to find Bud, my partner. He was on that moonlight special, and if Bellum finds him..." He shook his head.

"Maybe he skipped town already."

"Maybe," Frank said. "Feels kind of silly to hope."

"It's what you're telling me to do."

"You're right." Frank sat up, turning away from her. This was Lou Garou's side of the bed he was on. He stared at Lou's nightstand, where Moon's autopsy report had sat, then out the sliding glass door to the dark lawn outside.

"Where are you going?"

"Home," Frank said, standing. He hunted around on the floor for his pants. He and Lulu hadn't paid much attention to where the clothes had gone, so long as they were off.

"You don't have to," she said, and winced. He heard the twinge of desperation in her voice. The worst part was, he shared it. But he just couldn't stay and had no way to explain why.

Instead, he made a joke and regretted it instantly. "What would the neighbors say?"

"You're right," she said, and they both knew he wasn't. "I hope you find your partner."

"And your husband?" Frank pulled on his clothes.

"If there's anything to find. I suppose it would be nice to tell him why I was walking out."

Frank paused in the doorway. The bed was warm. Lulu Garou was warmer. He wanted nothing more than to go right back where he was and wake up with her next to him.

This wasn't his life. He had no right to it. "I'll do what I can," he said to her.

He left Lulu in her bed and just like that she was a thousand miles away. The street was quiet. All the monsters were either asleep in their beds or out finding a human to turn. He drove south.

A martian tripod strolled through the city, its cabin light glowing a bright blue. He passed two floating step pyramids, each one making its stately way in one direction or another. A few gremlin flivvers rocketed through the skies, each on the precipice of crashing in an entirely different way. Frank found himself missing the old days, when the only thing up there would have been a plane, or maybe some owls.

Not that it took his mind off Lulu. He could still smell her on his skin. Could barely smell anything else. He rolled the window down, and it helped, just a bit. She was still with him, swirling around him in a delicious aura that drowned out all other smells. He knew at any point, he could simply turn the car around and go back to her. He also knew that he couldn't.

The city gave way into the orange groves of home, but the citrus smell didn't do much to banish Lulu; now it reminded him of the cocktail she'd mixed. By the time he pulled his car to a stop in front of his house, the lure to return was almost too much to fight. Almost.

His house was dark in front of him. Empty, and remained so even once Frank was inside. He had nothing at all, just another man's wife. And he'd told her to leave. Frank couldn't. He still had more to do. What was done to Howell required an answer. He heard the voice of Winnifred Wyrd in his mind, commanding him to do what he wanted to do anyway.

Somehow, Aida Parrish was going to whisper her last "Brains."

Frank let himself in the front door. Later, he would blame the woolgathering for why he was completely flatfooted. He was exhausted anyway. Long day, and there'd only be another long one ahead of him, then another. Frank went down his empty hall. That was when a shadow in the dining room shifted and a familiar odor finally battered through the cloud of Lulu Garou enfolding him in its soft embrace.

"Hey there, partner," Bud Hound said.

THIRTY-THREE

Bud sat at the dining room table like he was invited over for a proper dinner party. Like Frank hadn't been all over town trying to find him since getting the call early that morning for the stash house the idiot had knocked over. He was dressed in nothing more than a pair of ragged britches, hanging on by a literal thread. An open can with a spoon sticking out sat on the table in front of him.

"Damn near gave me a heart attack," Frank griped. Despite the dark, his keen eyes got most of Bud's face. He definitely got the smell—his partner reeked of a long day, beans, and what beans tended to do to a body, Lulu's heavenly scent finally at bay. "Now you're stinking up my house."

"Sorry about that. I was hungry enough to eat the tires off a tractor, and I get to your place and find nothing to eat but a can of beans from before the war." Bud nodded at it, the lid bent back, wafting the only thing even close to a pleasant scent into the room.

"Didn't know I was having company," Frank growled.

"Almost didn't. No, don't get the light."

Frank stopped at the switch. "Were you followed?"

"No. Don't think so, anyway. Been here for a couple hours, and they'd have come in by now. But...uh...feeling a little squirrelly."

"Suit yourself." Frank moved away from the wall. His eyes went to the pair of windows looking out over the shadowy orange groves. Nothing moved out there, and he looked away before his imagination came up with something.

"Where were you, partner?" Bud asked.

"Looking for you."

"That's not what you smell like," Bud said with a grin. "She got a name?"

"You keep your mouth off that," Frank snarled.

Bud put his hands up. "Hey, I'm just happy you got a name on your dance card."

"Where were *you*?"

Bud had the grace to look a little guilty. "Wasn't sure anybody knew I was missing yet. Thought we'd have at least a day."

"I got the call for your moonlight special. Smelled you in that place."

"We used pepper!" Bud protested.

"When somebody stinks up your car for the better part of a year, pepper don't cut it."

"You didn't tell, did you?"

"No. But Talbot worked it out. I don't know if you thought this job was a good idea or not, but it didn't exactly go like clockwork."

"We were a man short."

"Garou. Yeah, I figured that out."

Bud looked at Frank with real admiration. "Always were a hell of a detective, partner."

"Let's see how well I did. You, Garou, Sylvester Bullet, Mark O'Beast, and Wolfgang Howell plan to knock over a Bellum stash house. Then about a week before the job, Garou disappears. Maybe he skipped town, maybe he turned rat."

"Lou ain't a rat!" Bud protested. "Sly and Mark thought he might be, but those fellas didn't know him like I did. He ain't a rat."

"Fair enough. But you need me to find out what happened so's they can know it too. I can't find him by the deadline, and the four of you decide to pull the job anyway. You got the hexes from Wyeth Wyrd, the cook over at the Nocturnist, after Moore gave you her name. Then the four of you go in. At first, it's just like you drew up, but when you get into the back, one of the zombies had a shotgun. Howell took the hit."

Bud shook his head admiringly. "Yeah, that's what happened. Wolfgang got hit in the shoulder. Spun him around, and the way he started howling we knew it was silver. Mark and Sly lost it. Tore the gunsel up.

"And Diaz de Muertos too."

"Who?"

"The cook."

"Wrong place, wrong time. Cook for a Bellum stash house ain't where you go if your nose is clean."

Frank growled low in his throat. "He didn't have a gun, partner."

"How were we supposed to know that? We see Wolfgang catch silver and we just went to it. That's how the Pack always was. We couldn't wait around to get shot. We had to attack *first*."

"Goddamn it, he was just a cook!"

Bud stared at him, eyes going glassy. His tone was a fragile challenge. "You check into that? You know that for sure?"

"No," Frank admitted. He didn't know for sure. He'd never checked. And he wasn't changing a damn thing now. Not Bud's mind, not Muertos's fate.

"All right then." Bud looked away, swallowing hard.

"So after that, you get the cash and you get out, to your car," Frank said, getting rolling again. "Only you were followed. Wolfgang was hurt, you had to get him to a witch doctor."

"Sly and Mark were going to let Wolfgang die," Bud said. "Bastards. They didn't put it like that, though. They just said the silver wasn't gonna do more than it already did. He could be fixed later, after they got out."

"Threw your lot in with some real winners."

"They got wives," Bud said, shaking his head. "Mark's got a wife, I mean. Sly's got a lady. Those two were waiting for 'em. It was Wolfgang's bad luck he got shot."

"Not with you in the car."

"No, I made 'em take us to Wyrd. Couldn't think of anyone else...the hexes, they keep you in control, but it's still not all the way. Her hexes meant I had her scent, maybe? They dropped us off there, told us they'd leave our shares at a spot we all knew. Same place we planned the gig. Then they left."

"And while you were waiting on Wolfgang, the zombies came."

"Yeah. Packing silver. They started shooting, and I just ran. Left Wolfgang behind, jumped over a fence, and spent the rest of the night and all day getting out here. Sometimes I wish you lived closer to the city, but right now, I don't think there's a place I'd feel any safer."

Frank knew he must have made a face, because Bud was staring at him. "What?" Bud asked.

"They got Howell," Frank said. He didn't elaborate. "Found him at your clubhouse in Griffith Park."

"What'd they do to him?"

Frank shook his head. "Don't ask me that." The horror washed over Bud's expression. He swore softly. "You'd have stayed, I would have found the pair of you," Frank said.

"Yeah. Maybe."

"This ain't gonna be news, but Bellum knows who it was, and there's a reward out for each of you."

"Figured as much."

"Noticed you ain't asked who we can trust."

"I'm looking at him," Bud said with a wan smile.

"Great," Frank muttered.

Bud traced circles on the table. "You really couldn't find Lou, huh?"

Frank shook his head. "Thin air, partner."

"Maybe the Monster Slayer got him," Bud said.

"C'mon. The Monster Slayer is a spook story."

"They got a task force for a spook story?"

Frank almost stopped himself, but he couldn't. "Don't get bent out of shape, but I gotta ask. How do you know Garou ain't a rat?"

"I just know." Bud's voice broke. He didn't know, but he needed it to be true. He was trying to put words on the way the world should be.

"I went and saw Beth Keene."

"Why'd you do that?"

"You left the note with her picture. Thought maybe there was more to it than that."

"Nah. I figured you'd know we broke up so it would catch your eye as wrong. I was right."

"Thing is, I talked to Beth Keene."

It hung in the air, solid as one of them. "And?"

"She told me...about you. About what you were to each other."

"And?" Frank smelled fear. Over everything else, it was clear and sharp and coming off of Bud. The man was terrified of what would come from Frank next. Not the zombies coming to fill him full of silver.

"I don't give a leech's eye tooth about it, partner. Alls I want to know is if I was lookin' in the wrong place for Garou this whole time. Do you know he wasn't a rat because you two were...?"

"No," Bud said, swallowing. "Lou wasn't...look, some of the guys were...some were like me...some were like me some of the time. Lou was... like me one time. Maybe he was drunk enough that night, I don't know. But that was it. I kept thinkin' maybe he could figure it out on a permanent basis if we went some other place. I don't know. Maybe I'm a fool. Could be he really liked dames. Not just pretending, the way I...thing was, he didn't ever give me up to the other fellas."

"If they was all..."

Bud snorted. "The ones who were like that some of the time? They were the worst ones. Gotta be the wolfman of the papers, you know? Gotta be the tough guy. Tough guys don't...you know...with each other. So you keep it secret, and sometimes they get drunk enough. And hell, there were the ones who never knew."

"They knew. You smelled my ladyfriend on me."

Bud grinned. "So she's a ladyfriend now."

"You're killin' me here, partner."

"Frank, I'm serious. You were always a friend to me. Hell, right now you're the best friend I ever had. If some dame's makin' you happy, I'm happy."

"You're makin' me misty."

"That's how I know Lou ain't a rat. He wouldn't give up another wolf no matter what."

"Where did they park the cash?" Frank asked, changing the subject.

"You ever watch that show *Silver Sixgun*? The set's still up. This whole town out in the Valley."

"I'll take your word for it. Money's there?"

"Hidden," Bud said. "I know where, and no offense, I'm not *saying* where until my mitts are on it."

"Should I take that personal?"

"Everybody knows the whole department's on the take."

Frank stared at Bud. "You trying to ask me something, partner?" After what Bud shared with him, had he asked, Frank would have come clean. But something else had grabbed him.

"It's got me...what?" Bud frowned at him, the thought derailed.

Frank was holding his finger up, barely paying attention to Bud anymore. He caught a scent, a scent that had no earthly business being within acres of his flop. It oozed through the citrus haze and scratched at the back of his throat. Cigarettes. "You smell that?"

Bud shifted uncomfortably. "Sorry about that. It's these beans...I think they went bad."

"Not that, you nitwit." Frank gestured, as though that would help.

Bud sniffed the air. "You got a neighbor who smokes?"

"Just birds," Frank muttered.

"Huh?"

Frank didn't elaborate, instead going to the windows. He peered out into the darkness, through the lines of trees. Flitting shadow, nothing more. He let the wolf off its leash now, and the stink of cigarette smoke yanked a cough out of his throat. His eyes, though, they sliced right through the murky black outside. Lean shapes stalked through the orange grove. Moonlight slid over the barrels of long guns clutched in their hands. This ambush might have worked, but Aida Parrish wasn't ever leaving her smokes behind.

"We gotta get the hell out of here," he growled.

Bud rose from the chair, changing, enlarging, hair bristling from his face and hands. Only changed did he catch the scent of the shapes. He muttered a spicy curse, and then, "They're gonna be packing silver."

"No kidding." Frank moved to the front door, back hunched and knees bent. They had to get to the car; only way they were going to slip the noose. As soon as he got his hand on the doorknob, a shape flitted past the window set in the door, others slinking through the darkness beyond. Frank backed through the archway into the dining room, a subvocal snarl rippling his lips, nearly running into Bud.

"Guess we fight our way out," Bud said, and it was impossible to tell if he was smiling or baring his teeth in preparation of sinking them into a hitman. *Probably both*, Frank figured.

"Sucker play," Frank said. He threw a leash over the wolf's neck, and it retreated to its den reluctantly. It felt the danger, calling to the savage urges inside him. Frank needed his faculties, needed to make rational decisions of when to run and when to fight, not surrender to an animal. The sharp senses, the strength, the reflexes, those would have been great if he had one of Wyeth Wyrd's hexes, but she was dead and her killers had arrived to clean up after themselves.

He pulled Bud into a room that would have been a guest room if he'd ever had a guest. Or a bed in there. As it was, it was a repository for old boxes. Some of them were Susan's things. Some of them were filled with what they'd bought together, stuff that was supposed to be out in the house. The kinds of things that turn a house into a home. Frank lost the use for those the second Susan stepped into her cousin's pickup and struck out for parts east.

He moved up to the bay windows and put his back to the wall, peeking out over the groves. The orange trees were arrayed like soldiers on a parade ground outside. Nothing moved. He nodded to Bud, then to the window. Bud was still changed, and his eyes shone silver in the moonlight as he leaned close to the window, sniffing. "Clear," he said. He grabbed the sill, ready to throw the window open.

"Not yet," Frank whispered, putting a hand on Bud's arm.

His partner frowned, but didn't protest. The wolf receded from him, but as always, it left a beard behind. Frank's heart thundered in his chest. It was like being in the black of the war again, krauts moving out beyond the lamplight, getting closer, murder in their hands. Bellum's corpses closed in, and Frank had to let them. Move now, and it was all over.

A bang, followed closely by the splintering of wood, reverberated from the front of the house. A moment later, the same sound came from the kitchen, where the back door was. Frank nodded to Bud, and his old partner yanked upward on the window. It groaned, but not louder than the groans of "Brains" coming from living room and kitchen. They were in his house, the damned gunsels were *in his house*.

Bud hopped out of the window first, and Frank followed. The grove was clear. Bud pointed to the front of the house. Frank nodded, and once again called to the wolf. He hadn't put the thing away very well, or for very long. It came snarling back, and Frank found himself loping through the citrus-scented dark momentarily unsure if he was predator or prey. Bud was right next to him, also wearing the beast on the outside.

Frank's car waited out front and a single zombie stood by the driver's side door, cradling a shotgun in his skinny arms. Frank was momentarily disappointed to note that it wasn't Aida Parrish. She'd be inside with a bunch of stiffs between her and him. Their rendezvous was going to have to wait.

The zombie saw them too late. He shouted the one word he knew and brought the gun up, but Bud was already on him. The shotgun boomed, taking off a bough of a nearby tree. Oranges, whole and in shredded pieces, rained onto the dirt. The corpse's hat fell to the ground with a heavy thump—Bellum's zombies wore steel-reinforced fedoras to protect their noggins. Bud grabbed the side of the zombie's head and slammed it into the car's front fender. He dented the car, sure, but he dented the zombie much worse. One would still run. The other never would.

Frank tore open the driver's side door and nearly hurled Bud through it, diving through after. Zombies called out from the porch as Frank slammed the car into gear and dropped his entire weight on the gas. The tires threw up a rooster tail of dirt as the guns at the door started popping. Bullets hammered into the steel fenders. The back passenger window exploded, showering Frank and Bud with glass. No silver touched them. Then Frank's car was slithering all over the road, barely under control as he burned for the main road.

Bud let out a howl of glee. The wolf followed the howl, and Bud was fully human on the seat. Frank wasn't sure when he changed, but only then noticed skin rather than wiry hair on the backs of his hands.

"Just like old times!" Bud whooped.

"The hell are you talking about?"

"The Pack, Frank! You woulda fit right in, let me tell you."

"Glad I never did."

"Sour grapes, partner," he said as Frank hit the main road and turned. In the distance, the rainbow lights of Los Angeles at night twinkled. "Where are we going? Pick up the money?"

"Got a stop first. There's one fella who might know where Lou Garou is. High time the two of you met."

THIRTY-FOUR

As the Plymouth roared along the dirt tracks through rows of orange trees, the buzz of combat receded from Frank's blood. Bud stared out the window, drumming out some rhythm on the door. The confession wasn't forgotten, but as for Frank, he didn't know how to take it. Bud didn't like ladies, but that didn't really matter in the scheme of things. *So why does it make me feel like I'm sitting on a bed of nightcrawlers?* Frank wondered.

"So who is this fella? The one you're taking me to?"

"Moss."

"The gangster?"

"He ain't...okay, I'll catch you up." Frank spilled what Bosch told him. Most importantly, that Moss and Garou were pals—though Frank held back what he suspected about the murder. No telling how Bud would take that. The headline was that the little meatstick was hiding something. Might be hiding Garou.

"Lou wouldn'ta left us in the lurch like that."

"Could be he got cold feet."

"The Wolf Pack don't get cold feet."

"Garou was smart, right?" Bud had to nod. "Okay, so maybe he figured the one thing I've been thinkin' since I caught your moonlight special. That *robbing Sarah Bellum is about the dumbest damn thing you can do in this city.*"

Bud shrugged. "Moss hides Lou because they're pals, then he helps him out of the city?"

"Meatsticks got ways. They're always sneakin' people around borders, and if anybody's got those connections, the first place I'd look is a gangster."

"You're all wet," Bud said, but there wasn't a lot of conviction behind it.

The orange groves fell away to the low buildings of south LA. They passed through miles half-cleared of debris, streets cracked and disused, the whole place overgrown with dandelions and cattails. A scar of sorts, a place the city had been hammered flat and the junk hauled away. It was a remnant of the time the three giant monsters had slugged it out, and the city had just kind of left it, a barren laceration reaching in from the coast.

"You know, they're making a movie about that," Bud said. It was like he could read Frank's mind, but then, there wasn't much else to look at around here. Just the wasteland that comes with a trio of giants settling things the old-fashioned way.

"Gonna hire Imogen Verity or something? Put her on miniature sets? Have her fistfight an iguana?"

Bud laughed. "They were talking to the dame herself. She's got a show now and everything."

"Yeah," Frank said, thinking of the little he caught at Lulu's house. "Could you play yourself?"

"I wasn't there for this."

"If they made a picture about the Pack."

"Sure, why not? I know all the lines."

"The hell you do. You still get a script."

Bud waved that off. "Besides, it don't matter what you say, so long as you have the mug for pictures. I tell ya, Frank, this was wasted in the department."

Frank snorted. "Yeah, you missed your calling."

"How about you? Could you play you?"

"Nah, nobody wants to see this."

"No argument there."

Frank pulled over at the edge of where the devastation gave way to a relatively intact cityscape. A single phone booth stood alone in front of a boarded-up old watering hole. Drinking down here would be sad enough without looking at miles of broken masonry and crumbling streets, where the only real feature was three different kinds of footprint. "Sit tight," he said, getting out. Bud slumped low in the seat, but nothing was on the streets this close to morning, not down here. Nothing here to hunt, nothing here to stalk. It reminded Frank of stretches of Italy in the Day War. They worked hard to repair things, but there was so much that it would never be fully fixed. The scars would always be around if you knew where to look. Frank paged through the tattered yellow pages, hunting for a name. There it was, just like he knew it would be. Humans had to be listed in the book; it was a law. Moss lived on Juniper Street in Watts.

Frank got back in the car and leaned on the gas. Watts wasn't too far from the wasteland. Activity picked up a little, but dawn was so close that a lot of the monsters had gone home. He found Moss's house on what might have been a sleepy street in any other time. Now, the few monsters who hadn't given up by now prowled over rooftops and through alleys, hunting for a broken ward in their house of choice. Moss's place was in significantly worse shape than most of them, crudely vandalized with the word DAAÉ inscribed in jagged, angry letters next to a broken window repaired with wood and tape.

A lovely young woman lounged on the dead lawn, watching the door with a longing expression. Though it was chilly, on the edge of cold, she was dressed in a summer halter dress, a picnic basket open beside her. She turned as Frank pulled up in front of the house.

"Can I help you?" she asked as the two wolfmen got out of the car, with the implication that the only help she'd like to offer was a different address.

"Not here for you," Frank said, brushing past her to the short cement staircase up to the tiny porch. She smelled a bit like a candle doused in Chanel. Then the stink of wolfsbane hit him. He nearly turned tail and ran, but it was old. He could stand it, just barely.

"What gives?" she demanded.

"What's a girl like you doing in a place like this?" Bud asked.

Frank didn't have to look to know she was smiling up at Bud. He could hear it in his voice, and there was the fact that Bud looked like the grown-up version of every girl's high school quarterback boyfriend. Bud was barely dressed, too, showing off his chest like some weightlifter. Why he insisted on wearing the mask even here was beyond Frank. Could be Bud had been wearing it for so long, it was a reflex.

"What kind of girl do you...oh my god!"

Frank turned, and saw that the doppelganger on the lawn had turned green, the back of her hand to her nose.

"Sorry about that," Bud said. "The beans were—"

"You finished?" Frank hammered on the door.

The doppelganger retreated upwind of Bud. "What do you want with Nick? He's not in any trouble, is he?"

"He your boyfriend?" Frank asked, gesturing at the DAAÉ.

"I wish," she said, deflating. "He's such a dreamboat."

Frank jerked a thumb at the house. "Nick Moss lives here, right?"

She sighed. "Uh huh."

"Short fella? Kind of weasel-y?"

"To the untrained eye," she said archly. "The word, that's from the neighbors. Didn't like him making time with a skin-dolly, you know. Between the two of us, Nicky could've done a lot better than her."

"I can see that," Bud said, checking the doppelganger out some more.

"Could you stand over there, please?" she said.

"Knock it off, partner, she ain't buyin', and neither am I," Frank snapped.

Bud threw his hands up and stalked away. "I'll just wait in the car."

"Crack a damn window!" Frank called after him. Bud answered him with a single finger.

"Seriously, is Nicky in trouble? I can vouch. He's been here all night."

"Nothing like that. I just need—"

The inner door opened, leaving a screen between Frank and the house. Old or not, the wolfsbane kept Frank from opening the screen and hauling Moss to the other side.

That's who darkened the doorway, of course. Moss, eyes filmy with sleep, cheeks covered in beard, dressed in an old pair of pajama pants, a stained undershirt, slippers, and a bathrobe that looked like he'd gone a few too many rounds against a giant moth.

"What's going—" Moss's eyes went wide when he recognized Frank. "What do you want? I thought we were done."

"We gotta talk," Frank told him.

"Hey, Nicky! Sam already left, and I don't think I can bounce this palooka for you."

"It's fine, Mira," Moss said in a voice that weighed a thousand pounds. He turned his attention to Frank. "You didn't pay me for the last job."

"Yeah, I got money now," Frank lied.

Moss sized up Frank, and there was something in the way he stood that raised the detective's hackles. "I need a shower."

"No kidding, but we ain't got time. Need you now, Moss."

"And you're gonna pay me this time?"

"Yeah. Triple your rate."

Moss nodded, trading the bathrobe for a jacket, hat, and a leather holster from the coatrack next to the door. He pulled on the holster first; a cross-shaped dagger under his right arm, and an honest-to-god Luger under the left. Then the jacket went over that, making soft clinking sounds. Then finally the hat.

"All right," Moss said, stepping out the door. "Let's talk." Frank took an involuntary step back. A meatstick leaving the safety of his wards in the middle of the night wasn't what anybody would call common.

"Nick! Are you gonna be okay?" Mira called. The histrionics were a bit much; Frank figured that's why she was spending her nights on a lawn in Watts rather than at some party in the hills.

"Yeah, I'm fine."

"I'll wait for you!"

"I don't even know what you mean by that."

"Oh, like...I'll wait for you." She said it quieter, and looking up, waving, like he was on a ship.

"Okay?"

"Well, I mean. I have work." She checked a watch on her slender wrist. "Oh, poop. I have to be on set in an hour. I really thought you were going to let me in tonight."

"Why would you think that? You've been camping there for a year."

"Your mirrors have been in better shape." She pointed without looking, shuddering the whole time.

Frank followed the gesture. She wasn't kidding. The mirror by the window was only a few stubborn shards clinging to the frame.

Moss sighed. "I just bought that one."

Mira sighed back. "Getting a girl's hopes up. I know you like monsters."

Moss's shoulders slumped. "Come on, Wolfman. Take me for that ride you want to take me on." He trudged to the car, then paused. "Mira, you going home before work?"

"I suppose."

"Tell Ser about this, would you?"

She nodded. "The mirror? Of course."

"Not the mirror." He gestured to Frank and the car. "This."

"Oh! Oh, I can tell her about both." She waved. "Have fun!"

Moss climbed into the backseat of the car. "I don't think she really understands the gravity of this situation."

"Do you?" Frank asked, sliding behind the wheel. Bud turned around to regard Moss.

"Not sure how much I care."

"I'd say that's the booze talking," Bud said, sniffing the air.

Frank sniffed too. "Oh, Jesus, Bud."

"Sorry. I'm telling you, partner, you need to check your cupboards once in a while. You could kill somebody with those things."

"I think they're killing *me.*"

Frank stepped on it out of Watts, going north, toward Chinatown. With the windows down, he couldn't smell much other than the city. That was a blessing. He kept an eye on Moss in the rearview. The little weasel was quiet, but tension rode in every muscle and tendon.

"I never could figure it," Bud said. He was still turned around in his seat, so he could look Moss in the eye. "Two-bit meatstick gangster like you and a hero, a real one like Lou Garou says hands off."

"Garou hired me once."

"To find Bosch," Frank supplied.

"Right. Which I did."

Bud scoffed. "What I'm trying to say is, you and Lou was friends."

Frank watched Moss's eyebrows reach for the sky. "What?"

"You and Lou Garou lured Phil Moon up to that spot over Chinatown and the two of you plugged him," Frank said. Time to let Bud in on it. The reaction, and the fear from it, could prove useful. Bud's head snapped around. He felt his partner's incredulous gaze on him, but Frank couldn't look now. Couldn't break momentum. "Cooked up that story that the hobs did it. What I can't figure is why you kill Garou nine months later. You got away with it. Clean. Both of you."

"I don't kill cops," Moss said. His voice was hard, but jagged. Trying to keep it together.

"You do, this is a shorter trip than I thought," Bud growled.

"You killed Moon," Frank said.

"I didn't kill Moon," Moss said. And Frank believed him. He couldn't see a lie in Moss's eyes, hear it in his voice, or smell it on him. They were the only car tooling along these empty streets. Garou killed Moon. A shudder worked its way through him as he pictured a wolfman putting silver through a brother in the blue pack.

"Hey, Frank. Why don't you pull this car over? I'll get the truth out of this meatstick." Frank saw Moss move, just a twitch in his hand. He nearly went for something, and only barely stopped himself. Bud caught it a second later and a growl rumbled through the car. Had Moss gone for his heater, he could have already painted the windshield with Bud. The little fella was fast.

"That is the truth, partner," Frank said.

"I can see what the truth is and what it ain't."

"Cool your jets." Frank said this to Moss as much as he did to Bud; he wasn't sure Bud's ego was going to let him see that the meatstick had him dead to rights if he wanted it. Hell, he had them both. Frank had a spooked rattlesnake in the backseat and if he didn't start acting like it, he was going to get bit. "All right, Moss. Then what gives? I know you're holding out on me. What was it?"

Moss's eyes flicked between Bud and the back of Frank's neck. "Look, you hire me to find Lou Garou, all right? First rock I turn over, and it's nothing but cops and gangsters. You aren't paying me enough for that kind of trouble. In fact, you didn't pay me at all. You want to know what happened to him? I think you've known from the start and were trying to find someone who would tell you different."

Bud's shoulders sagged. Moss wasn't wrong. Didn't smell quite right, but the broad strokes were there. "Okay, Moss. Okay."

Moss looked from Frank to Bud and back again. "So what gives?"

"What do you mean?" Frank asked.

"Well, uh, neither one of you looks like you're ready for duty. Him, he looks like he just crawled through half the backyard gardens in the city during a full moon. There are bullet holes in the side of your car, and I'm pretty sure I'm sitting on the back window here."

"You did say he was a detective," Bud grumbled.

"I feel like I sat down in the second reel of a picture that's only halfway in English."

"You don't get to know—" Bud started.

"We have to get Bud out of town," Frank cut him off.

"Partner! What are you doing?"

"You think anybody listens to him? You think anybody believes him?"

Bud stared at Moss. "I guess not."

"Sorry," Frank said into the rearview.

"What for? Nicest thing a wolf's ever said to me."

"Bud's on the wrong side of the Gray Matter."

"And you drag me into it. Wonderful. Well, skipping town is the smart move," Moss said. "But she's got eyes everywhere."

"Yeah, every stiff in the city," Bud growled.

"Not them. She's got *some*, sure, but she likes you to think she's got more than she does. Keeps you on your toes even when she's not around. And it makes you beat on zombies, turning them against you and toward her."

Frank stared at Moss in the mirror so long he nearly crashed the car. That was the smartest thing he'd ever heard out of a meatstick's mouth. He tried to reconcile that with what he'd seen thus far.

"Right," Bud sneered. "Corpse don't break the law, they got nothin' to fear."

Moss snorted. "Heard that one before. You want to get your partner out of town without a bullet in him, he's gonna need some help."

"What kind of help?" Frank asked.

"I have friends who might do it. It'll cost you."

"That's fine," Bud said. "We're just about to pick up my money."

THIRTY-FIVE

As dawn broke, the car wound its way through a break in the hills at the western edge of the Valley. An Old West-style town slouched in the distinctly California environs. The buildings were steadily falling apart, but with the weather in the southland and *Silver Sixgun* only being off the air for a little over a year, it was still in reasonably good shape. Everything was blanketed in a thick layer of dust and crinkling leaves from the live oaks.

The road came in between two buildings, neither of which would have passed as authentic from this angle. There did look to be enough room for interiors, but Frank also saw bits of tape sticking to plain boards, and more damningly, more than a few stenciled-on factory markings on the wooden planks. The other side of the street, where the classic saloon stood, was a lot more convincing. Frank stopped the car.

They opened the doors and stepped out. Bud passed gas loudly. Sounded a little like a train, the way it got steadily louder before trailing off. "I was holding onto that one," he said.

Frank caught the edge of it and took a step back. "Good thing too. Woulda killed us."

Moss, his jacket lightly clinking in the early morning breeze, had moved to the corner, peering at the nearest building's façade.

Bud gestured at him with amusement. "Look at the meatstick. Like he's never seen a set before."

Moss frowned at the wall, turning to look across the street. Then he jogged over. If he heard Bud, he gave no sign.

"Hey Moss, what did you sniff out?" Frank called, trudging into the dusty thoroughfare.

"Bullet holes," the little man said, indicating the wall, then pointing across the street.

Frank sniffed the air. Smelled like the hills; he caught a whiff of corpse-stink, but it wasn't fresh. "You smell that?" he said to Bud.

"I told you already, it's the beans."

"Goddamn it. I'm going to talk to the meatstick."

Frank stalked out into the middle of the street. A tumbleweed somersaulted over the dust right in front of him.

"That's not a great sign," Moss said.

Frank wasn't going to get into it. He climbed up onto the wooden sidewalk in front of the saloon. Moss was right; a few bullet holes pockmarked the wood here. He couldn't exactly eyeball a caliber, but he was willing to guess they had come from the barrels of the .45s Bellum's corpses seemed to like so much.

He looked at the sidewalk: glass from the windows covered it in a thin layer. He looked up and caught Moss's gaze. The meatstick was thinking the same thing he was.

Bud joined them, sniffing the air. "I don't smell Mark or Sly," he said.

"I do, but not like they're here."

"You use this saloon here?"

"Sure," Bud said. "It's the biggest building around, other than the hotel. They built up the inside more for shooting, too. Only the bank and the sheriff's office have complete, y'know, interiors. Hotel's got a few rooms, but most of the buildings are just fronts."

Frank nudged open the saloon's double doors. The room was thick with dust. But just as strong a smell as the dust was the stink of animals who had made this place their home. Then, fresher but fainter, he smelled wolf. And blood.

Pathways had been carved in the dust, enabling Frank to follow in the footsteps of the Wolf Packers who had used this place first to plan a caper, then as a place to hide. They went to one table, littered with several empty cans of Plasma and a few Deerhead bottles. The silver screen in Frank's mind brightened with the image of the five wolves planning the moonlight special around that table, conversation going late into the night as they threw back their drinks. Any wolf worth his moon could solve this thing with one visit to this hideout. The Wolf Packers wanted them to, just like the altar Bud had left for the investigators. It fit.

Frank followed his nose. Farther from the table, the dust was less disturbed, and he could almost see individual footprints in it like one of those instructional manuals on how to waltz. It was the blood-stink that drew him. Bud followed behind, his breathing shallow. Moss was by the wall, his weasel eyes hunting out more bullets embedded into the wood.

Bud got there first. Halfway into the room, he caught a scent and took quick strides to the far wall. He was staring down at the floor when Frank came up alongside him. Blood caked the floorboards here, thick enough that whoever had done the bleeding hadn't had much left over. Sprays touched the walls as well. The last reel of the movie in Frank's mind clicked as he saw the wolf here, standing at first, catching slug after slug before collapsing, his own heater falling from a nerveless hand. The stiffs had shuffled in not long after, huddling up around the dying wolf.

"Mark," Bud said, his voice catching.

Mark O'Beast, one of the missing wolves. "You're sure?"

"Yeah."

"That leaves Sylvester Bullet still in the wind. You want to see if you can catch his scent?"

Bud nodded and shuffled off, brushing through the swinging door of the saloon. He was damn near catatonic, and Frank was praying he didn't come to the conclusion that Frank had.

Moss came up next to Frank, looking at the pool. "They just stood here, watching him die?" he asked.

"If he was lucky. They could have started cutting."

Moss shuddered. "Your friend shouldn't be sticking around."

"No kidding. Don't say nothing about what we saw in this blood, got it?"

The human nodded. Frank found Bud out back, staring into the dappled shade of the hill. "Sly went this way, I think. I lost his scent. Can't get it back, but I think he made it out. I think."

"Let's get your money, partner."

Bud nodded. "It's this way." They walked around the saloon, through a little alleyway half-blocked with prop barrels. Moss came out of the saloon's double doors, looking ridiculous in his jacket, pajama pants and old slippers. Bud walked across the street to the building marked *Bank*.

"Wait, the money stash was in the bank?" Frank asked.

"Yeah."

"That didn't seem, I don't know, obvious to you?"

"Or so obvious that they'd never guess it."

"You're either the smartest dumb guy or the dumbest smart guy I've ever met."

"It's a living."

The door of the "bank" didn't latch anymore, and rattled whenever the breeze touched it. Bud went in first, revealing a finished interior set for whenever the denizens of this particular town needed to put up with a bank robbery. Based on the westerns he'd seen over his lifetime, Frank figured that was at least a weekly occurrence. The central room was bare, with dusty floorboards and old tape-marked spots for actors to stand. The bank featured only a single window. Bud easily vaulted the desk and landed on the other side. It took Frank a bit more doing; he had never been the kind of athlete Bud was. Moss leaned in, peering at the alcove where the fake teller would have conducted his fake business. A few phony gold bars were scattered, forgotten on the floor, along with some old leaves blown in from outside.

Bud went to the back of the room and knelt, sweeping aside the detritus on the floor and pulling up a loose floorboard.

"Thought it was going to be back in the safe for a second," Frank said.

"Nah, we had a cot back there."

"You're kidding."

"We figured if we needed to lie low, it should be in a *safe* place." Moss snorted.

"I should shoot you for that," Frank growled at Bud.

"At least *he's* got a sense of humor," Bud said, gesturing at Moss. He turned back to the exposed place and set about removing more floorboards. It looked to Frank like the first one had to come out before the others could budge. It was reasonably ingenious, and Frank was confident that Bud had had nothing to do with its design. When he had a pile of floorboards, Bud leaned in close, his arm disappearing to the shoulder. He hunted around for a few seconds, then pulled up first one, then two, then three identical khaki canvas bags. A fourth bag was a completely different shape.

Bud opened one up, revealing stacks of cash. A low whistle escaped Moss. Frank had never seen that much money. Explained why Bellum was so steamed. In a way, it made him feel a little better; he didn't like the idea that the Gray Matter was operating on anything like principle. Nobody could afford to lose this much—and if they could, they wouldn't have noticed its absence.

"Yeah," Bud said, in response to Moss's whistle. "We waited until right before the weekly pickup before hittin' 'em. Lou and Sly had worked out when there would be the most money in there. We needed enough to set up five fellas for life."

"You crazy son of a bitch."

Bud frowned, ignoring Frank's comment. He opened the other two khaki bags and sifted around in them, then sat back on his haunches.

"What's eating you?" Frank wanted to know.

"This is all of it."

"You sure?"

"Well, no. But it *looks* like all of it. Means Lou and Sly didn't take their share." Bud put one of the bags back and had picked up another before

Frank stopped him.

"What the hell are you doing?"

"They might come back," Bud said, his voice tense.

"I don't think they will."

"They *might*." This time his voice nearly snapped, and Frank let it lie.

Bud tucked the other bag back in the hiding place. He opened up the final bag, extracting a suit and a pair of shoes and socks from a similar collection. "Getaway clothes are all here too," he said, putting them on over his tattered shorts. When he was finished, he replaced the clothes bag and all the boards, then swept the bars and leaves back over the loose boards. It was like the three of them had never been there. He picked up the bag of cash, cinching up the top. "Moss. You say you know how to get me out of town?"

"Like I said, I have some friends who'll probably help you, yeah. You can afford them now."

"And they won't talk?"

"I trust them a hell of a lot more than I trust you."

Bud grinned. "I dunno, Frank. He's starting to grow on me."

"Yeah, like a fungus."

"I was thinking like moss."

"Jesus, Bud. Your gas stank less than this."

THIRTY-SIX

Moss directed them into the winding hills of Hollywood, along narrow avenues where showbiz types had settled. The Hollywoodland sign flew into the air with a lot of pops and fizzles, the light show lost in the dim fingers of dawn. The car slithered around on sinuous roads, past houses built for the rolling hills. Either they were nearly invisible from the street and extended down the slopes, or they rose up like towers on the elevation. Some of the houses up here had been built before the Night War, but a lot had been built—or rebuilt—afterwards, so you got the kinds of architecture that really spoke to the fangs and tentacles set. That meant Gothic castles, Egyptian pyramids, and gleaming high-tech fortresses.

Moss pointed out a house on the downward slope that looked a bit like a flying saucer had crashed into the hill in the middle of an oasis. Palm trees framed the central disk of the structure while the morning light reflected off the numerous windows like a cut jewel.

"You taking us to see a martian?" Bud wanted to know.

"They bought it from a martian, I think," Moss said. "Everybody mind your Ps and Qs, okay?"

Bud passed gas loudly. He still hadn't let up. There couldn't be any air left in him. "Excuse me," he said.

"Maybe he could wait out here?"

"Get moving, Moss. I'm sure whatever gunsel you know stinking up the hills has smelled a lot worse than Bud."

"Sure," Moss said, getting out of the car.

Frank followed, not sure he should be so confident going in someplace he couldn't roll down a window. Bud joined him, holding the bag of money by his side. "Hey, partner," Frank said. "Take out a bundle, leave the rest in the car. Safer in there than with whoever this lowlife hangs around with."

"Yeah, good idea." Bud fished out a single stack, then threw his jacket over the bag, joining Frank just in time for the front door to open in response to Moss's rapping.

The woman who opened the door was a knockout. Even in her dressing gown, her hair in curlers and under a scarf, not a smudge of makeup on her face, she could have stopped traffic. Her hair was glossy and black and her eyes were a clear gray that showed the kind of faint disapproval that made Frank want to do better. She smelled like flowers in a windowbox. Her lip curled when she saw Moss. "It's you," she said, with the tone of someone noticing what they'd stepped in. A bluejay fluttered from inside, alighted on her shoulder, and cocked its head. Somehow, it too looked less than thrilled by what it saw.

"Hi, Verb," Moss said. Her expression hardened. "*Verbena*, sorry. Lil home?"

"Just what do you think you're implying?"

"Implying?"

"That our maiden might be *out*. With a *gentleman*."

"That's never been any of my business."

"At least we agree on something."

"So, she *is* home?"

"Why are you dressed like that?" she asked.

"It's a long story."

"It always is with you."

"Can I come in or not?"

The witch—Frank knew a witch when he saw one—sighed and rolled her eyes theatrically. Only then did she appear to notice Frank and Bud. "What's that?"

"They're why we're here. Listen, Verb...ena. We need to come in."

"We're here to pay you," Frank grunted.

"Does it look like we're hurting for money at the moment?" Verbena inquired archly.

"Well, no..."

"We just need a few minutes of your time," Bud said with a grin. "Then we'll be out of your hair."

Verbena stared at Bud. Frank had never been jealous of the attention Bud got from women until this moment. A looker like this Verbena could turn a man to jelly. She wasn't even specifically Frank's type, but he had the hunch she was everybody's type. "You should let *him* talk," she said finally. "Come in."

She stepped aside and waved them in. Frank, Bud, and Moss all took off their hats as they filed inside, hanging them on a rack by the door. The foyer was set in marble, opening out beyond to a large, semicircular room that took up the bulk of the back part of the house. The wall was entirely windows, looking out onto the Hollywood Hills, framing the eclectic architecture of the rich and famous like an exhibition. Curtains, like those in a movie theater, bordered the windows. The walls were decorated with framed posters like you'd see outside nightclubs. A large, semicircular sofa was set in a depression facing the windows, and behind that was a long table inlaid with arcane runes and set with candelabras.

Verbena nodded to the bluejay and it leapt off her shoulder, wheeling deeper into the house.

Bud was by the wall, peeping at a picture of a close harmony group of absolute lookers crowded around a microphone like they planned to whisper something scandalous into it. He snapped his fingers and turned from it to Verbena, his face lighting up. "I *knew* I recognized you! You play at the Nocturnist!"

"Played there last night," she said, shooting Moss a withering glare. "I *was* getting my beauty rest."

"Looks like you got more than enough to me."

Verbena was about to respond when the bluejay fluttered in and landed on her shoulder. It whistled a short tune and she nodded. "Lily and Hy will be here in a second." Then she sighed. "Don't suppose anyone here is hungry."

Frank's stomach gurgled. "Don't want to put you out, ma'am." Something in her presence made him add the *ma'am*.

"It's Verbena," she said. "And it's no trouble, I *am* supposed to be a mother after all."

"Started young," Bud said. "I'm starving. Eggs, toast, any part of a pig that you can put some char on, whatever you got."

She stared at him. "Is that it?"

"Oh yeah. Coffee, too." Verbena scowled and left the room, presumably for the kitchen.

"You better hope she doesn't poison it," Frank muttered.

"I'm hungry and she asked." Bud's rear end expelled a thunderous rattle. "And maybe with some real food, I can stop doing that."

Moss retreated from Bud like a meat golem at a house fire.

A moment later two more witches came in. One was a redhead with sparkling green eyes. The other had platinum blonde hair and eyes like an angry glacier. A robin perched on the shoulder of the redhead and a white sparrow did the same for the blonde. Both dames had a bright, floral scent, undercut just a bit with the scuzz of a nightclub and both were the kinds of dames that made a fella want to sack Troy.

"Nick!" exclaimed the redhead with a happy smile. "What brings you all the way out here?"

"At this hour," said the blonde pointedly.

"I'm sorry about that," Moss said to her. "These two woke me up before dawn. That one needs help, and it seemed like the kind of help you could...

uh...help with, I guess."

The blonde regarded them imperiously. Frank felt a flutter of fear, but nothing like Winnifred Wyrd could muster. This crone—if she even qualified—wasn't interested in cultivating that mystique. "I suppose you should introduce us."

Verbena came into the room, holding a tray of a few steaming bowls and mugs. "You're getting stew," she announced, putting the whole shebang on the table.

"Thanks," Frank said.

"Okay," Moss said, gesturing to the three beauties in dressing gowns. "These are the Salem Sisters. You've got Hyacinth, Verbena, and Lily. This is Frank Wolfman and Bud...something. Never got his name."

"Hound," Bud said, grinning at Hyacinth. "You know, I love blondes."

"So do I," she said without missing a beat. She stared hard at Bud, a slight frown creasing her brow. Bud quailed, and if he had a tail, it would have been between his legs. Hyacinth turned to Moss: "Those are wolf names."

"They're cops," Nick said. "Or they were. I'm unclear on the specifics."

Hyacinth looked Bud and Frank over. "Either one of you responsible for what happened to Willow Wyrd?"

Frank shook his head. "No. Different flatfoot."

"You know she didn't kill Wyeth."

"You're damn right I do. Unfortunately, the detective whose case it actually is don't believe it, and I don't think tryin' to punch it into his head did much good."

Hyacinth's eyebrows went up and she uncoiled, just a bit.

"Oh gosh," Lily said, holding her nose and retreating from Bud.

"Sorry about that," he said without much shame, sitting down at the table, grabbing a bowl and spoon, and going to work on the food. Around a full mouth, he croaked, "This ain't bad!"

"High praise," Verbena said. She turned to Frank. "Come on now. Eat before it gets cold."

Bud finished off one bowl and pulled another one to him. "Moss, you're not eating this, huh?" He swallowed the rest of the words along with about half the stew.

Frank sat down at the table, nodding a thank you to Verbena, and he started to eat. It was good, though lacking a little in the finesse department. Still, it had been a long time since a woman had cooked for him.

Hyacinth turned to Moss. "Is there a reason you brought two cops to our house at the crack of dawn?"

"We need to smuggle Bud out of town."

"What are you mixed up in, Nick?" Lily asked. There was real concern there. Once again, Frank had to take another look at the little man. He caught glimpses of what Bosch and this dame seemed to see in the little weasel, but they were gone quick, under the generalized tides of nervousness.

"Blame him," Moss said, gesturing at Frank.

Hyacinth stared first at Frank, then at Bud. "There is something around the two of you. Some bad mojo, like a miasma."

"It's the beans," Bud said, his voice wadded with stew.

"You said it, sister," Frank said. He could feel it, the same as her. His hackles had been up since the zombies had come to his house. This caper was shadowing them, and it would until they got Bud on a train out of town.

"I was thinking of some way you could hide them," Moss said. "Like the hex on that mummy."

"That hex is above our paygrade," Hy said, then sighed. "But I think we could whip something up. I'll gather some things together." The crone— and Frank felt guilty even trying to apply that word to her—swept out of the room with her sparrow.

"It's not free," Verbena said to Frank.

Bud slapped the stack of cash on the table. "That enough?"

"I'll say," Lily blurted.

Verbena glared at her and took the money off the table, flipping through the bills. Her eyes widened momentarily, and she locked eyes with the redhead and gave a silent whistle.

"Let me know if there's any extra," Bud said.

"There won't be," Verbena said, slipping it into the pocket of her housecoat.

"Nick, are you okay? Really?" Lily asked, her voice low.

"I'm fine, Lil. I'll be happier when he's out of town."

"I meant about Jane."

"Oh."

"Have you called her yet?"

"I don't even know where she is."

She put her hands on her hips. "If only you knew somebody who finds people for a living."

"I don't even know what I'd say to her."

"Something's always better than nothing," she soothed, but whatever this was, it stopped when Hyacinth came back into the room holding an elaborately carved wooden box. It reminded Frank a bit of the ward boxes they used to arrest ghosts. All this hoodoo looked alike to him.

"All right, Lily, Verb, you two sit down. Nick, you and your friend stand over there, please. We don't want you in the way while we're hexing."

Frank got up, holding the bowl. "Can I put this in the sink?"

"You're sweet," Verbena said. "I'll get it later."

Hyacinth sat down at the head of the table with Verbena on her right and Lily on her left while Frank and Moss stood by. The crone opened up the box and a powerful aroma of half a dozen strong herbs billowed into the room. Frank's eyes watered, but he was grateful it drowned out the stink of Bud's ass.

"How does this work?" Bud asked, putting the empty bowl aside next to the other one. "Gonna make me invisible?"

"Nothing so gauche," Hyacinth said primly. "It makes you harder to notice. If someone is hunting for you, they will still find you."

"There *are* people hunting me. That's why we're doin' this," Bud said.

"It will buy you some time," Lily said with a placating smile.

"These fellas are pretty persistent."

"Then move around," Verbena snapped.

"Verbena is right," Hyacinth said. "You should spot anyone looking for you first and be able to react accordingly. Get out of the immediate area."

"They aren't going to lose track of me, are they?" Bud asked, gesturing to Frank and Moss.

"They're here now," Lily said. "It's kind of like seeing a magic trick. If you know how it's done, it doesn't fool you."

"Witchcraft is a magic trick," Bud mused. "I always knew it."

"We'll be happy to show you how much of a trick," Verbena said with a smile that would have been at home on a shark.

Hyacinth removed a dagger, a pestle and mortar, and a few dried bits of plant. "Grind these up," she said to Lily, who quickly obeyed. "Verb, imagine you'd like to do the honors." She passed the mother the dagger.

Verbena turned to Bud. "Hold out your hand."

"Aw, nuts."

"It won't hurt much," she said, and nobody believed her.

Bud held out his hand, and Verbena passed the blade over his palm. He grimaced as the skin parted like butter. Lily handed over the mortar of ground-up herbs, and Verbena put Bud's bleeding mitt over it until he dropped some red in. Verbena took the mortar back and set it between the three witches. Bud picked up a napkin and held it to his bleeding hand, maintaining a poker face. Frank knew Bud wasn't going to show much pain in front of dames, especially not a trio of tomatoes like the Salem Sisters. The old pride was strong, and maybe stronger for it being part of the mask.

The three witches began to speak in a language Frank didn't know. The few times he'd watched a witch build a hex, they'd talked like this. It sounded Egyptian, or more to the point, what the pictures told Frank Egyptian sounded like. Every now and then, Frank heard Bud's name in there, but said with an accent that almost made him sound exotic.

Hyacinth, Verbena, and Lily held hands, the mortar of herbs and blood between them.

A spark lit the stuff inside the mortar with a spark, and the air exploded with the scent of charred and highly seasoned gamey meat. The aroma went through a transformation, burning away even the smell itself. For a moment, the char was the center of it, but then, through it, like a window, everything else vanished. It was the closest thing to "clear" that a smell could be. It made Frank think of the way a clean, though not freshly cleaned, window should smell. Present, but not distinctive in any way.

"It's done," Hyacinth said.

"I don't feel no different," Bud said.

"Do you normally have trouble finding yourself?" Verbena asked.

Frank stared at his partner. There was something ever so slightly *off* about him. Tough to put his finger on, but Bud didn't look like himself. The nose was a little different, or the eyebrows were thicker, or his jaw wasn't as square. Only when Frank really thought about it, comparing memories of Bud to the Bud sitting in front of him, they were identical. "It's working," he said.

"Of course it's working," Hyacinth huffed.

"I never doubted you," Bud said with a grin, and Frank watched all three witches soften, just a bit. That grin had loosened more than its share of legs. He turned to Frank. "Let's get to Union Station. Got a bag waiting."

Frank, Bud, and Moss turned to go. The maiden stopped Moss with a hand on his elbow. "Take care of yourself, Nick."

"Sure, Lil," he said, and Frank could tell he didn't mean it.

"Thanks, ladies," Bud said. "When next you see me...well, there won't be a next time."

"Don't think I'm forgetting this," Verbena said to Moss as he walked out the door.

"I never bet on anybody forgetting anything," he said with a weariness Frank felt.

THIRTY-SEVEN

Union Station was an art deco edifice not far from downtown, and on the short list of most attractive buildings in the city. It had been built in the '30s, and though it had sustained some damage in the Night War, it was quickly repaired, then refurbished. Union Station was a Los Angeles landmark, oftentimes the first glimpse a new arrival had of the city. Civic pride and all that; who cares if there was a meatstick shantytown only a few miles away in Chavez Ravine? Couldn't see it from the train platform, so it didn't matter. Out of sight, out of mind, as the saying went.

Moss got out of the car, his head popping this way and that like a prairie dog who knew there was a hawk around here somewhere.

"Didn't think it would end this way," Bud said.

"It ain't over yet, partner," Frank said.

"Happy face, Frank. I'm a train ride away from being away from all this. You should think about getting a ticket for yourself."

Frank hesitated. "Got some work here."

"Bring that dame. The one you won't tell me about."

Frank couldn't hold back the image of him and Lulu Garou boarding a train and going east. Maybe north. Anywhere but here. He realized that Bud hadn't spoken, and he turned to find his old partner looking at him with soft eyes. He put a hand on Frank's shoulder. "Think about it. This place is too rotten, and if you stick around, you'll be as rotten as everything else."

Frank smiled thinly. "Bit late too worry about that."

"If it was too late, you'd already have turned me in."

If Frank could have left in that moment, returned to Lulu right then, he might have gone. But he couldn't, and he knew because of that, he wouldn't. The Wyrd curse still wrapped around his soul, prodding him to do something he wanted to do anyway. "Come on, partner. Let's get you out of town."

"Yeah," said Bud, and Frank saw in his eyes that the other wolf knew it too. Only then did Frank remember Moss and found the meatstick standing a few feet away, pointedly not looking at them. A feeble attempt at privacy, but there. He abruptly hated Moss more than he had ever hated a meatstick. The two wolfmen got out of the car.

Frank started for the station's front doors, Bud falling into step next to him with Moss behind. Since it was still relatively early on a Sunday morning, the crowd was light. Monsters came in and out of the building, hailing cabs or making their way to the red car station across the street. A pair of vampires stepped outside, opening their parasols against the sun. A crawling eye held the door with one tentacle and placed a shaded monocle over its massive pupil. A trio of fur-clad ogres sat on the curb, watching the pedestrians with faint interest. Frank tracked faces. Was anyone paying undue attention to the three of them? What was undue attention when Moss was wandering around in ratty plaid pajama pants and slippers? He paid especially close attention to the zombies—and they were everywhere, some in suits and dresses, others in custodial jumpsuits. A brainiac rattled by in one of their little carts. The hackles on Frank's neck hadn't gone down since the previous night at least, but they were at full attention now. He kept waiting for a finger to be leveled and a sepulchral "Braaaains!" to tell him the jig was up.

Union Station opened up into a vaulted room with square wooden chairs set into the floor. Monsters waited for their trains here, reading newspapers or magazines. The ticket kiosks were in the back, lit up like the betting windows at Santa Anita. Bud started to head over baggage check when Frank spotted trouble.

They were witches. That much was obvious, mostly due to the black gowns and tall, pointy hats. All three were young, barely out of their teens. Two were fair skinned, one of them with black hair, the other with a fall of red curls. The last had light brown skin with a dusting of freckles over her nose and hair that went to auburn. An owl perched on her shoulder. The other redhead cradled an inquisitive rat, while the brunette wore a snake around her neck like a scarf made of muscle.

And they were staring at the three of them, pointing without looking like they were pointing, and giggling to one another. "Hey, partner," Frank muttered out of the corner of his mouth, "the Gray Matter got witches on the payroll?"

"She's got everything on the payroll. Pretty sure she's got her tentacles into this martian. Why?"

"Nine o'clock."

"Oh, shit."

Because the three girls were heading their way. They kept up their nudging and giggling, two of them prodding the brunette forward. Bud squared himself and Frank joined him, ready to let the wolf out. He was still old-fashioned enough to not like the idea of painting the walls with three girls, but he reminded himself, they weren't *girls*. They were *witches*. And a witch was never something to take lightly.

The three witches brushed right past Frank and Bud, intercepting Moss like he was the sick old sheep at the back of the herd. Then the brunette started jabbering.

"Excusez-nous, monsieur. Vous êtes bien Nick Moss, n'est-ce pas?" It was French. Frank spoke only enough French to get some grub in his belly, and this wasn't that. He could swear he heard Moss's name in there.

Frank gaped at them, then at Moss. The meatstick looked just as baffled. "Uh, quoi?" Moss's French was as poorly accented as his wardrobe.

"Vous êtes bien Nick Moss! Oh, je le savais! Tu vois, Cherie! Je te l'ai dit, c'était lui!" the brunette said to the others.

The redhead with the owl said, "Je ne peux pas croire que nous rencontrons le Nick Moss!"

"Moss?" Frank said, "What gives?"

"Search me," Moss said. Then he switched to his terrible French. "Salut les filles. Je suis détective licensié."

All three of them burst into musical laughter. "Je ne peux pas y croire," said the brunette. She fished in her gown and removed a small leatherbound book, opening it to a blank page. "Monsieur Moss, puis-je avoir votre autrographe s'il vous plaît?" She handed him a pen.

"My...uh...sure." Moss took the pen and signed his name in the book, along with what looked like a "Best Wishes."

The brunette looked at it and clasped it to her heart. "Vous ne saviez pas ce que cela signifie pour elle," confided the witch with the owl.

"Elle a vu toutes vos scries," said the witch with the rat.

"Uh, okay. Enjoy," Moss said, favoring them with an unsure smile as he disentangled and walked around them.

"What was that?" Bud asked.

"I'm telling you, I got no idea," Moss said as the three of them began to move.

Bud shook his head. "You live a strange life, you know that?"

"I might have figured that from time to time, yeah."

At baggage check, a ghoul who must have been seven feet high took Bud's claim ticket and returned with a bag. Bud took it, tipped the fella a few bucks.

"Here it is," he said. "My whole life in a bag."

"Other than all those pictures you left behind."

Bud grinned. "Knew you'd catch that. What I wouldn't give to have seen Talbot's face when he saw it. Or any of the others, really."

"I'm sure it got their goat."

"It was all I could do. Just nice to let them know that they don't own everyone and everything."

"So where are you going?"

"From here, Utah maybe? From there, who knows? Gonna move around until even I forget where I am."

At the ticket kiosk, the robot behind the desk beeped at them and handed over Bud's ticket to Salt Lake City. Bud turned to Frank and gestured to the kiosk. "Last chance. We're already here."

Frank shook his head. "Let's get you on that train, partner."

Bud nodded. They headed for the main tunnel leading to the tracks. "You're gonna finish this, then?"

"Get the ones that did in Howell?" Winnifred Wyrd appeared in Frank's mind's eye, and the invisible chains heavy on his soul. "Yeah. I'll do that. I don't know how, but I will. As for the rest of it...I don't think there's any way to burn the rot out of the department."

"You said it. Remember the old days? We thought we had it bad when Bellum and Mab were beefing in the streets."

"Wasn't too hard to close those cases," Frank mused.

"Yeah, you had it real easy back then. In the Pack, sure, we were catching more than our share of bullets, but it was *fun*. Like it was supposed to be, good guys on one side, bad guys on the other, a hail of lead in between. We were all doing right. Who'd a'thought that Mab getting bumped off would be the beginning of the end?"

"We thought it was Christmas," Frank said.

"It *was* Christmas," Moss said.

Frank turned around with a scowl. He'd forgotten Moss was even there. "Why don't you give us some space?"

Moss held up his hands and backed off, but the moment was gone. Frank was done talking.

The tunnel was long. At regular intervals, other tunnels let up and out into the sunlight, to the platforms and the tracks. They found the one whose placard matched Bud's ticket and went up to the surface. The first steps out of the underworld and to a new life—only Frank would be going back under soon enough. At least Bud would be free.

Bud shook his head. "Didn't think we'd be carting that meatstick around so long."

"Thought he had something. Won't make that mistake again."

"Least he got me that hex," Bud mused. "Still can't square him being pals with the Salem Sisters."

They emerged into the light. Tracks, like the angry stitches on a meat golem's kisser, sliced the platforms into smaller pieces. Passengers, monsters of every stripe and even a few humans, waited for a train that would take them away from this place. "Almost there, partner," Frank murmured.

If he were the superstitious sort, he might have thought that saying those words was what did it. No. It was just bad luck, the same bad luck they'd had all night. Lean shapes emerged from the tunnel behind just as the words died on Frank's lips. They moved with an unmistakable shamble, their hats set on their heads at a rakish angle. Three zombies, all wearing pinstripes. Frank didn't have to get close to know what they were whispering at each other.

"Hey partner," Frank murmured.

Bud swore. "They got us made?"

The zombies stepped onto the platform, their buggy eyes sweeping the waiting passengers. One of them snagged on Frank, but moved on almost as quick. "I don't think so, but you remember what the witches said. We stick around and they'll get us eventually."

"Hey, fellas?" Moss said.

"We see 'em," Frank growled.

"You see *them* too?"

Frank followed Moss's nod—he was grateful the meatstick had enough sense in his weasel head not to point—and saw pairs and trios of more pinstriped corpses coming out of the tunnels on the other platforms.

"Train's coming," Bud said. "Thank God for small favors, right?"

The train was one of those new mad scientist jobs that crackled with the lightning clawing all over its surface. It flashed in the distance, features just becoming recognizable. "Let's move," Frank said. "Nice and easy."

Bud nodded, gripping his luggage in one hand and slinging the bag of cash over his shoulder like a knapsack. Moss fell in behind them.

"Stay put," Frank said to the meatstick. "Way you're dressed, you'll draw them over here like a gill-man to a debutante ball."

Moss backed off, and Frank watched as the zombies eyed him hungrily. Frank and Bud started to make their way down the platform. The tracks disappeared into the horizon, running through one of LA's more industrial areas. In the later days of the Night War, a decent-sized human encampment had formed there, big enough that the monster government was unsure of what to do with it. Eventually, they sent the wolves in, but by that time the humans had cleared out. Same story all over back then. Frank sometimes wondered if Susan had found her way to one of those camps. She had to be. In Kansas, or wherever she'd ended up. That's all there was for humans, and she had picked that life. Dumbest choice a human could make.

Frank glanced behind him. The zombies stalked their way down the platform. They had already overtaken Moss. The little meatstick was shadowing them.

Cold breath chilled Frank's neck. It was the wolf, telling the man in the driver's seat that death was coming. The wolf pulled his attention pulled to the right, across several platforms. His eyes met another pair, one wide and staring, the other milky and dead.

Aida Parrish stood on the other platform, staring right at Frank. He couldn't tell if he saw betrayal or amusement on her half-face.

Frank swore. "I should have left you alone, partner."

"Brains!" Parrish called from the other platform.

The other zombies looked to her, then followed her rotten finger. The ones on their platform filled their hands.

"Come on!" Frank called.

He didn't have to. Bud had reflexes honed by a year in the Wolf Pack. He was already moving, his body thickening with each step, fur bursting from every slice of exposed skin. Frank figured he should follow his former partner's lead; he could use the extra oomph. And wouldn't mind being more willing to rip one of these corpses apart.

The train drew closer. Blue bolts writhed over its chrome art deco surface. It might as well have been a million miles away, and it sure as hell wasn't going faster than a silver bullet.

"Brains!" shouted one of the zombies on their platform.

The zombies on the next platform over hopped down into the gravel by the tracks, making their way across.

Frank pulled his pistol. A crack sounded behind him. He instinctively flinched, the high-pitched whine of the round zipping past needling his wolf-sharpened ears. The monsters on the platform screamed. Some hit the deck, others got up and ran. He chanced a look over his shoulder and saw the three zombies in pursuit doing their best to wrestle past a panicked martian.

Another gun boomed, the round pinging off metal close by. Frank whirled. Two zombies were clambering onto his platform from the next one over.

He fired. The first bullet whined off the zombie's fedora, taking gray felt with it and revealing dull steel underneath. The second bullet caught the zombie in the shoulder, knocking her off the platform and into the dirt.

The second zombie nearly got to his feet, but a brown blur leapt past Frank. It was Bud, pouncing, knocking the zombie flat on his back. "Brai—" the zombie started. He never got the rest of his thought out because Bud tore the steel-belted hat off his head and crushed his skull with it.

The train was almost there, brakes squealing as they strained to bring it to a halt. The lightning arced off it, scorching the dirt as it passed.

On the other platform, Aida and her two men fired their pistols. The bullets kicked up around Frank, and he hunkered down. "Bud!" he growled.

Bud yanked the heater out of the fallen zombie's hand, put a bullet over the side of the platform—Frank assumed at the zombie he'd wounded—

then came up squirting lead at Aida and her men. Didn't do much more than make the zombies scatter, but at least it silenced their guns for a second.

A cascade of partly muffled shots came from behind and Frank turned in time to see the blubbery mass of a martian fall to the platform, filled with enough bullet holes to give him a good cross breeze. A martian could survive that; the real danger to him would be infection. The zombies stepped over the twitching gray heap with death in their eyes and brains on their lips.

The martian out of the way, Frank gave them something to think about. When his roscoe clicked dry, one of the zombies was on the deck, struggling to get up, and the others a bit heavier for the lead in them. Wasn't enough. The two on their feet brought up their guns, but they didn't count on Bud.

Frank's partner was in his element. That much was obvious from the way he exulted in the carnage. Frank had never thought it before, but he wondered now if Bud had been born in the wrong time. Had he lived in an era where he could have made a real living at dying, a medieval knight taking back the Holy Land, say, or a Viking plundering the English coastline, maybe he'd have had a better time of it. *No*, Frank figured, *he'd just find a different way to die.* Really, that's all anyone ever did across the span of history.

Bud tore into both zombies, and it wasn't just to stop them. He lingered, pieces of them flying to splatter against the concrete. The other zombie protested with a "Brains" and pulled himself away, but he wasn't going anywhere. Bud's happy savagery was the worst of what the other monsters thought wolfmen were capable.

Bullets whined around Frank and Bud. Zombies flooded across the track, trying to beat the oncoming train. Charred ozone filled Frank's senses.

Aida Parrish wasn't among the advancing corpses. Frank found her on the same platform standing still with the arrogance of a warlord. Her skirt blew around her legs, but other than that, she was a statue. Her heater was leveled, her head cocked so that her good eye stared down the barrel. That side of her face was a grinning skull.

Frank called out to Bud, but it was too late. His partner was in the midst of tearing hapless zombies apart.

If he had run. If only he had run.

Parrish's pistol snapped and Bud spun around like a top. Frank caught an image of his face, still changed, the shock sitting strangely on the brutish features. The agony hadn't hit him.

It would. It was a silver round; lead didn't cause a bleed like that. What Frank would always remember was Bud's expression. He couldn't believe what had happened. This wasn't how it was supposed to end, wasn't what happened to the hero at the shootout. Bud had lived a charmed life. Hadn't heard "no" very much, and this was the hardest "no" a man ever could get.

Parrish's gun barked again and Bud's head jerked as though on a spring. Then he collapsed onto the deck and was still.

Frank ran for his old partner, even though it was pointless, but Bud had been in Frank's pack and that would always carry meaning in the wolf's soul. He had to be with Bud, there for him at the moment of dying, so his friend would know he wasn't alone.

But something heavy slammed onto the back of Frank's neck and he ate pavement. The world went cacophonously silent. He knew that if he hadn't been changed, he'd be counting sheep, and the last one would be made of silver. The wolf was gone now, knocked silly. His hands were entirely human; he wouldn't have any help for what came next.

He rolled painfully on his side. Two zombies clambered up the side of the platform. The legs of another, who'd been behind him, loomed over his prostrate form as across the platform, he barely glimpsed Aida Parrish, watching him with faint pity.

Then she was eclipsed. The train, crackling and popping, pulled into the station. The two zombies who'd been climbing vanished, save for a greenish streak that ran the length of the platform.

Frank pulled himself onto his back like a doomed turtle. His killer was merely a silhouette, tall and lean, topped with the brim of a fedora. A gold watch glittered on his skeletal wrist. The gun, smooth and black, faded into view, the barrel bigger than his whole world.

THIRTY-EIGHT

The whisper-moaned "Brains" would be the last thing Frank ever heard.

Not much of an epitaph, but the most common one cops got these days. At least it would be a clean shot, a silver bullet through the noodle and then nothing. Only one thing still burned: Winnifred Wyrd's hex crackled over his soul. Aida Parrish would get away with it. Again. Forever.

"Get on with it," Frank snarled. "I don't got all day."

The zombie wasn't much more than a shadow. The gun came up a fraction of an inch, a minute adjustment of aim, and the decision made. The murder would be done in plain sight on a train platform, an execution in front of a city. Frank had no illusions. He wouldn't be mourned, just his own stupidity at getting on the wrong side of the Gray Matter.

He didn't close his eyes. He wanted the zombie to see the contempt in them, ruminate on it during the late nights when a body was alone with his demons.

A second silhouette closed from behind, a soft clinking following it, leveling a pistol with a needle-like barrel point blank under the brim of the zombie's hat. Frank's brows knit. *This ain't how it goes.*

A snap echoed over the platform. The zombie's head jerked, and his body collapsed like a house of cards. The shape leaned down to Frank, holding out an empty hand, and the figure behind it swam into focus.

"Moss?" Frank said. Santa Claus would have been a less surprising savior.

"C'mon, get up," the meatstick said, hauling Frank to his feet. Frank's head throbbed from where the zombie had sapped him, his senses wobbling back on their own time. Whatever had hit him—he assumed the butt of a heater—it hadn't been silver. It'd heal, assuming he didn't catch even more punishment.

"Bud," Frank said.

"He's gone. We're gonna be joining him if we don't get out of here."

Frank leaned on Moss as they ran down the platform, paralleling the train. He didn't hear any more gunfire, but screams and moans of "Brains" rang out all around. The tunnel yawned open in front of them. They slipped past the glabrous mass of martian, listlessly crawling in a direction that didn't much matter. Then came what remained of the zombies Bud got his claws on, scattered in chunks all over the platform. Bud himself lay not too far away. Human now, his eyes wide with surprise. Frank wanted to stop, do something. Close the man's eyes, maybe. Say a prayer. Even just touch his hand. He couldn't just leave his partner like that.

Then they were past, down into the darkness of the tunnel, turning into the central passage, where panicked monsters ran everywhere like chickens who'd just met their first grenade.

"Get offa me," Frank growled at Moss.

"Suit yourself." Moss let him go.

Frank staggered, suddenly entirely responsible for his own balance. He was already healing, but his brain was still sloshing around like a drunken sailor, and likely would for a little while yet. That zombie had really rung his bell.

"Move faster," Moss said.

Frank chanced a look behind. Zombies in pinstripes were just making their way down the ramps. Aida Parrish stood two tunnels away, and between the other monsters running to and fro, she didn't have a shot.

"Not a bad idea," he said, but the ground was heaving under his feet.

He followed in Moss's path as well as he could, bashing into the white tiled wall to his left and panicked pedestrians on his right. Frank looked back again, nearly falling. The zombies advanced through the crowd like sharks, dead eyes fixed on him. Pretty soon, they'd be close enough that there wouldn't be room for another monster between their silver and their quarry.

"Moss? It's about time to fight. Moss!" This last was a hiss as the little weasel turned on the jets and darted through the crowd. Frank cursed the cowardly meatstick and increased his own pace, as though that would do any good. He felt like a poorly maintained bumper car on the highway with the number of monsters he was caroming off.

Then he saw what Moss was up to. The three French witches stood in a semicircle, listening to Moss yammering on, all three with stars in their eyes. Frank still couldn't figure out what the hell was going on there—Moss wasn't much to look at and a witch wouldn't turn him anyway—but he wasn't going to look this gift weasel in the mouth.

"Des zombis?" asked the redhead with the rat. "Oh, je les vois!"

"Thanks, girls," Moss said. "Uh...enjoy LA."

They giggled, even as they were fishing in their purses for something or other and beginning to mutter in that weird language witches used for hexes.

"Come on," Moss said.

Frank stepped a little straighter as he passed the three witches, and he chanced a look back; he *had* to know what they were cooking up. The witches waited until the zombies were right on top of them, then all three blew handfuls of shimmering dust in the gangsters' faces. The moans of "Brains" came close behind, but the zombies were unable to do anything but meander in confused circles. Frank damn near smiled at the sight. The witches, giggling madly, scampered away through the crowd.

"Gonna have to thank your friends for me," he said, coming up next to Moss.

"I'm telling you, I've never seen them before in my life."

Frank shook his head. "That was weird, even for this city."

"You're telling me," Moss said. They made it out into the main hall. Frank scanned the crowd, but when he moved his head too fast, his gorge rose in the back of his throat.

"You see any more pinstripes?"

"Nope," Moss said. "Doesn't mean we should start loafing."

"Don't have to tell me twice."

Moss looked over at Frank. "Doesn't look like you took a bullet."

"If I did, we wouldn't be havin' this conversation."

"Yeah, good point."

"Say, what the hell took you so long?" he demanded. "They were shooting forever before you showed up."

"Had to switch out my ammo to lead," Moss said. "Silver's hard to come by."

Frank stood up straight—or as straight as he could muster—and fixed Moss with an appraising look. "You pack silver too?"

The gun was away now, waiting in its holster under Moss's left arm. The fingers of Moss's right hand twitched. Looked like a gunfighter's move. His sweat was ripe in the air between them. "Yeah," he said.

"Probably smart," Frank sighed, and watched the tension evaporate from the man.

They emerged into the sunlight. No zombies came through the parking lot at them. Frank broke into a jog, Moss at his side. They got into Frank's car, and he had to stop as police cars, sirens on, barreled into the parking lot. He drove away without slouching too much. When the train station was a block away in the rearview, both he and Moss let out a long breath.

"That a Luger?" Frank asked, partly to think about anything other than what had happened on that platform.

"Huh? Oh, yeah it is. Why?"

Frank shook his head. "Haven't seen one of those in eleven years."

"You'll never guess where I got it."

Frank snorted. It was nearly a laugh. "I bet."

Moss shifted in his seat. "I'm sorry about Bud."

"Bud made his own bed," Frank growled. The sadness was there, reaching out with its inky tendrils. He would beat it back with anger. "Don't have to lose any sleep."

Moss nodded. After a second, a soft but exasperated sigh escaped him. It was so quiet Frank had the idea that he was trying to suppress it. "What?" Frank demanded.

"The cash. It's still up on the platform."

"Hell of a gift for the first person who finds it."

"Better not be Aida Parrish. Hopefully that hex the witches dropped on her keeps her tied up in knots for a while."

"How do you know Parrish?"

"Hard to be in my line and not know her."

Frank nodded, watching the road and wishing he could watch Moss's face. There was a story there. There always was. Instead, he said, "When were you over there?"

Moss understood the shorthand. "I dropped in the night before D-Day."

"Dropped in?"

"I was Airborne."

"You were one of those who jumped out of planes?"

"Yeah. I more fell out of the plane, but they trained me to jump."

Frank shook his head. "We all thought you were fit to cut out paper dolls."

"Probably was. The pay was pretty good."

"You were happy to jump out of a plane for some extra lettuce?"

Moss shrugged. "Hitler wasn't gonna kill himself." He paused. "Well, that's what we thought at the time anyway."

Frank laughed then, a loud bark, a sound made by a man unused to it. Moss jumped in his seat, calming down when he realized what happened. "I drove a Sherman," Frank said.

"Frank's tank?" Moss said.

The memory wasn't soft exactly, but it was warm. It made Frank think of a worse time, back when he still had it in him to wish things could be better. "What do you think they called me?"

"No kidding. Your human name was Frank?" Moss winced. "Sorry about that, I know it can be a sensi—"

"Yeah, I was Frank back then, too. When I got turned, I didn't want to have to get used to a whole other name."

"Makes sense."

"Only now I got to soak up grief from every mug thinks I didn't do enough work on it."

"They can jump in a lake," Moss said. "World's tough enough without worrying what other folks are thinking the rest of the time." He stared out the window. "You drove a tank, huh? France?"

"Italy, then Germany," Frank said.

"You thought we were nuts for jumping out of a plane. We thought you had a screw loose, going up against those goddamn panzers in a Sherman."

"You're telling me, but I made it through the whole thing in the same one."

"Got a friend upstairs, I guess."

"Used up three lifetimes of luck is more like it," Frank said.

Moss fell silent. Frank guessed he'd made the same connection Frank did the moment the words left his mouth. There wasn't any luck left, and every breath Frank had been drawing was borrowed.

He drove back into Watts, pulling up in front of Moss's vandalized flop. Moss got out of the car. A few people out on their lawns on this Sunday morning looked over at the two of them. It was hard to miss the sullen hostility in their gaze. Moss's shoulders were hunched against it, like he was standing in a storm. He took a few steps toward his ramshackle house and turned.

"Your partner was right."

"About?" Frank growled.

"Get out of town."

Frank nodded at the scrawled DAAÉ over the house's surface. "Maybe you should take his advice."

"Nowhere to go," Moss told him. "Good luck."

"Hey. I owe you some money."

Moss considered. "No you don't."

Frank grunted. He nearly said something else, not to thank the meatstick, but something around that. Moss was already walking away, and Frank would be damned if he called after him. Instead, he drove home. He thought a hundred times that returning to his house was a dumb move. If they wanted to bump him off, they could be waiting. Frank figured they were welcome to it. He and Aida Parrish had a score to settle, and if she showed at his place, well, that was a touch more convenient.

Frank drove through the city until the citrus-heavy air enfolded him. He was almost at peace, but a few questions remained, irritating him like silver dust in his clothes.

He pulled up in front of his place. From here, the only sign that Bellum's corpses had been by was the door hanging open, the lock broken. Frank got out, sniffing the air. Zombies had definitely been about, but if he wanted more than that, he'd need to let the wolf off its leash. After the night and morning he'd had, the thought made him want to collapse. He was so exhausted his blood was yawning.

Jack Dawes stepped out from the trees, shotgun cradled under one arm. "Frank? You okay?"

Frank waved him away; at least he wasn't shooting. The scarecrow stood at the edge of the grove, not coming any closer. He swayed only a little, the straw of his body crinkling beneath his burlap clothes.

Frank stomped up his porch, then paused in the doorway. He didn't hear anything, and only smelled faint traces of decay. Most places in the city had that stench at the edge of their profile. Zombies were everywhere, and they all stank.

He found bits of evidence that the zombies had been there: a few pictures knocked off the wall, an overturned end table, his bedroom door lightly dented from a foot. Mostly, he already lived in enough squalor that it barely registered.

He went into his bedroom, and was asleep before he hit the mattress.

THIRTY-NINE

When Frank opened his eyes, the room was dark. He sat up, sleep partly gumming his lids shut. His mouth felt like he had been licking a fire hydrant. He looked over at the clock and found that it was four in the morning. A glance out the window at the orange grove told the same story; the deep blue air might have looked enchanted if Frank still had any poetry in his soul.

He stripped out of his clothes, showered, and dressed in something marginally cleaner. He gave his place a once-over, even poking his head into the attic, half expecting a cadre of zombies or wolfmen waiting to give him the bump, only they wanted him to have a decent night's sleep first. Everything was quiet, and the house was as empty as it would be. In a way he couldn't have explained if there was anyone to ask him. It didn't even feel like he was all the way there.

Bud had been right. Frank should leave town. Parrish could finger him from the train station. But he knew he couldn't, not with the hex wrapping tendrils of need around his insides.

That was an excuse; he'd stay anyway. It's what made him who he was, and if he gave that up, might as well do the work for Parrish and Bellum himself. He had to balance the books somehow. *How?* That was the question that tormented Frank. He was a wizard at unraveling someone else's schemes, but didn't have the spark of creativity for his own.

And he was out of people who he could trust to help him.

Going home had been dumb; going to work was dumber. Frank drove into the station anyway. He had nowhere to go, nowhere to hide. The only thing he could do was play it as dumb as he could, and hope Talbot wasn't so deep he fed Frank to the Gray Matter. It was all a bunch of tragic mistakes, and the blood was on the hands of those too far out of reach to hold accountable.

Frank's hackles rose as he walked into Highland Park. Hard to tell if it was legitimate danger, or if his body was merely reminding him that leaving the safety of his orange groves was a bad idea. Frank found himself asking *What would Bud do?* and then chuckling to himself. Bud only ever thought one thing through in his life, and it had been the thing that got him killed. Frank just had to hope the call hadn't gotten to Talbot, or that there was enough of him left. Just until Parrish's long goodbye was arranged.

Frank sat down at his desk. Sylvia Screen smiled at the camera, her dreams dancing behind her eyes through all the parts she would never play. It wasn't just Bud and his pals who needed payback, or Wyeth Wyrd even. It was this innocent girl, resting uneasy for justice that had taken too damn long already.

"Detective Wolfman?" It was Accalia, the captain's assistant. "Captain wants to see you in his office."

Frank did his best to ignore the ice radiating out from his heart. He gave Accalia a gruff nod. Time to see what Talbot knew. He took a last look at Sylvia before lumbering from the bullpen and up the wooden stairs and knocked on the door to Talbot's office. A shape missing some parts opened the door. Glass, wearing one of his fancy suits, a cigarette dangling from his invisible mouth.

"Lieutenant," Frank said.

"Go on in," Glass said, exiting with a cloud of cancer like exhaust from a train's smokestack, hauling a cough out of Frank's throat. That smoke would cling to his suit for the rest of the day. He shut the door behind him.

Talbot, sitting behind his desk, nodded sympathetically. "I know. It's a filthy habit. I've tried to get him to quit, but..." He spread his hands, showing how helpless he was in this situation.

Frank nodded back. "No trouble, Captain. Just not used to getting it in the face like that."

"Ain't that the truth." Talbot motioned the chairs on the other side of his desk. "Why don't you have a seat?"

Frank obeyed, doing his best to feign nonchalance. Then he started to wonder if he shouldn't try to fake some concern instead, or allow the real nervousness through. *What's more believable?* his overheated mind demanded. "Probably want an update," Frank decided. Sounded pretty neutral.

Talbot cleared his throat, looking down at his desk. It was clean, with a neat blotter under his hands and some gold pens glittering in a cup by his right hand. Wasn't an ounce of policework on that desk. "I take it you haven't heard, then."

"Heard what, sir?"

"Bud Hound was killed yesterday."

Frank swallowed, putting in the pause he knew Talbot was looking for, and keeping a white-knuckled grip on his emotions. That place where he'd kept Bud was still raw, and the only way he kept it from burning too bad was by not looking at it. Blubbering in front of his captain wasn't going to solve a damn thing, either. "What happened?"

Talbot scowled in obvious distaste. "A shootout at Union Station. Hound was with someone at the time. Hound didn't make it out, but his friend did."

Frank tried to keep his eyes on Talbot's steady gaze. It was like trying to press the wrong sides of two magnets together. "They know who he was with?" he asked, and he knew he missed whatever blend of concern and curiosity would have sold it.

"We're assuming Sylvester Bullet," Talbot said, looking back at his desk with concern.

"Bullet? They catch him?"

Talbot shook his head. "Disappeared after the shootout. I'm sorry about your old partner."

Frank nodded, his hands balling into fists. "Thanks. Don't know what to think here. Seems like he did a very dumb thing and got his ticket punched."

"That's it," Talbot said, too quickly. "That's exactly it. You're not responsible for Hound. He did what he did. Tragic, but nothing anybody could have done."

"Wait, sir. Why Bullet? Last I heard, both he and O'Beast were in the wind."

Talbot shifted. "We found O'Beast."

"Where?"

"Which part?"

"Oh."

Talbot coughed. "We would tell his wife, but she's vanished as well."

The wolf woke up, lips pulling back over its teeth. "They're not... they're not looking for her, too, are they?"

"No, no. Nothing like that," Talbot said, but Frank knew that assurance was empty. While it was unlikely Bellum would go after family, it wasn't out of the realm of possibility. It wasn't that Bellum was cold-blooded; she just didn't bother having blood at all.

"So it's just Bullet."

"Smart money says Bullet got away. Crazy son of a bitch." Talbot shook his head, chuckling ruefully.

"Almost sounds like you admire him."

"I don't admire his brains, but his wolf? Sure, I can gaze in awe at that."

Frank settled back in his chair. For the first time in the conversation, he felt a semblance of calm. "Is that all you wanted to tell me? Our little search is over?"

"Yes. It's far from a perfect ending, but we don't get to pick those. It's really a shame."

"They were good men once, sir," Frank said, nodding.

Talbot blanched, then recovered, but not quick enough that Frank didn't notice. "They were. It's too bad they chose this way to flout the rules. It's done now, at least." Talbot's thick fingers found one of the pens, drawing it from the cup, and tapping it against the blotter. "Frank, I know you gave this one your utmost and it was hard for you. I want you to know I saw that when the time came, you were a soldier. I don't forget that kind of thing."

If Frank's veins could freeze solid, they just had. "I'm police first and last."

"First and last. I like that. I don't think the others—Bullet, Hound, O'Beast, and Howell—would have agreed with you. When it came time to choose, they picked another option."

The money was the same. Came from the Brain, went to the cops. The difference was, they took it and gave nothing in return. We give her our souls. Frank nodded in agreement, even as those words ran through his mind.

"When one of us—a wolf—does that, there's nothing else we can do. Leave the pack, face the consequences of that decision. Don't you agree?"

"Completely, sir," Frank said.

"I'm glad to hear it. You can get back to work."

Frank got up and made his way to the door.

"Frank?" Talbot said. "Keep closing your murders. That's what matters."

"Yes, sir," Frank said, and he left. A half hour later, he was in the hills, walking the scene of a dead ogre.

FORTY

Frank stared at the house in front of him. A modest bungalow in Hollywood, it could have been the home of any number of middle class actors and crew. He wasn't certain what compelled him to seek it out, let alone drive over, or knock on the door. It was after dinner, and Frank had spent the day on his ogre case, but his real case was never far from his mind.

The door opened, and Pearl Friday stood on the other side. She was naked, though Frank had no idea if that was inappropriate or not. Ironically, there wasn't much on a crawling eye to ogle.

"Detective Wolfman?"

"Can I come in?"

"Sure," she said, slithering aside.

Frank lumbered into her house. It had a comforting, den-like feel, with every square inch of wall that he could see covered with either art or an overflowing bookcase. The scent in here was of old papers and the words covering them. Friday gestured through an archway into a cozy living room, and Frank sat down on a chair that was barely more than some cushions with a wooden frame. The curtains were drawn, but Frank wasn't going to put his back to anything that wasn't a wall. The walls were decorated with framed newspapers, most of the headlines bugling some development in the Bellum/Mab dust-up. Happier times, as funny as that was.

"To what do I owe this visit?" Her tone was guarded, a shard of curiosity lurking beneath.

"Suppose you've heard about what happened at Union Station."

"The shootout, you mean?"

Frank nodded with a little grunt of confirmation. "You write the story?"

"No. A colleague covered it."

"What's the official line?"

"Disgraced former cop tries to rob the train station."

Frank snorted. "And people buy that?"

"It's in all the papers," Friday said. "You want a drink? I could use one."

"Why not?"

Friday left the room, her tentacles making wet sounds as she squirmed over her hardwood floors. Frank got up, peering at the papers. Many of the pictures were of the hits, a perforated zombie or a goblin laying in the street. Sometimes a sheet covered a piece of them, but it was never enough.

Not a single picture of Sarah Bellum of course; she hadn't been seen in public for years. Irony there, she ruled the city but never ventured out of her compound. Her gunsels, sure. Aida Parrish glared from a crowd shot over an article about the crimewave in Hollywood.

A headline blared *GOBFATHER SLAIN. A Dark Christmas Present for the Fairy King of Crime.* Two pictures ran below it. The first was of the Gobfather himself, bleeding under a sheet. The second was a picture of him in presumably happier times, at the Nocturnist, pretending he was something other than a vicious killer. His date was an elegant Chinese woman with the graceful lines of a swan, so beautiful that Frank had to remind himself to breathe.

"She's a looker," Friday said. She stood in the archway at the entrance to the room, holding a tumbler in one tentacle and an eyedropper in another, both filled with a liquid the color of gasoline. From the smell, it packed the same kick.

"Who is she?"

"The Gobfather always had a woman like that. The kind that they had to invent poetry to describe. They stuck around for a few months and then they vanished, never to be seen again."

"Turned? Murdered?" Frank asked.

"Most of them, I don't know. A couple—the last two—were murdered. One of them caught a bullet up in the hills. Another one got caught in the middle of a hit. This was right around the end of last year." Friday moved closer, handing him the tumbler. He accepted it gratefully.

"Sorry to hear it."

"So was everybody. Wasn't a single monster who wouldn't give their best tentacle to turn one of them. That one, he called her the Golden Swan. She was a dancer. Performed at the Nocturnist from time to time."

"She one of the murdered ones?"

"Vanished. Went where all the others ended up, I expect."

Frank grunted. "Damn shame."

"I'm sure you didn't come here to talk about the Gobfather or his women."

"I came to tell you a story."

She climbed onto her couch and squeezed a single drop into her eye. "I happen to like stories."

Frank sat down in the chair, and he laid out the story of the moonlight special from beginning to end. He left Moss out but told the rest as faithfully as he could, every sordid detail held up for inspection. When he was finished, both of their drinks were empty. He toyed with the glass in the silence.

"What am I supposed to do with that?" Friday asked finally.

"I don't know. There's no evidence of any of it. Quote me and they'll kill me and then smear what's left. Nobody else will talk. Guess I just needed somebody to know about it." Frank looked at the eyeball on the other side of the room. "If you could, *would* you write about it?"

"I don't know."

"Can't blame you for that." Frank got up with a sigh. "Take care of yourself, Friday."

"You too, Frank."

"Bit late for that, but what the hell."

FORTY-ONE

By Thursday, Frank had the case solved and Fenestru the Furious in cuffs. The bust had gone well, all things considered. Frank had been cautious, taking a handful of uniforms, making sure Prima Facie was among them. She deserved to get some experience under her belt, and Frank hadn't been disappointed in her performance. He wanted to call Lulu and tell her that Facie was proof she didn't have to worry about those old standards, but then he saw the other unis joshing about her while Facie was busy frogmarching the ogre to the back of the armored paddywagon. They tolerated her to a point, but it didn't mean anything like the way Frank wanted it to.

"Can it, you mugs," Frank growled as he walked past.

Only that didn't work, either. He saw it in the way they were looking at him as they whispered like schoolboys. They all thought he was making time with her, and nothing he could say would make them unthink it.

Frank slouched in the front seat as Facie drove the paddywagon back to the station. He turned the handling of the ogre over to the uniforms—let them figure out how to get Fenestru into the reinforced monkey cage they kept for ogres and the like. At least the ogre wasn't putting up a fight. Only swung her club around a little and barely clipped one officer. For an ogre, that was coming quietly.

"Facie, get her booked," Frank said.

"You got it, Detective."

He went back to his desk, ready to write up the report. It was the simplest of cases. Fenestru had been married to Khugbolf the Beast of the Hills Whose Number is GRanite-2237. Khugbolf had been stepping out on her, raiding the ogre tribe on the other side of Mount Lee. She got fed up, caved in his skull, and left him for the coyotes and other things that lived up in the hills. Her alibi had been broken with a little work, and Frank knew what he had. And now another murderer was where she belonged. Not the murderer he wanted, but at least it was something.

Frank's phone rang. "Wolfman," he grunted.

"Detective?" The voice was unsure, and to Frank, it sounded like that was not a usual state of things.

"Yeah, Detective Frank Wolfman."

"This is Bermuda Triangle."

It took Frank more than a second to place the name. "Miss Triangle. What can I do for you?"

"Is there any way you can see me?"

"Come into the station any time you like."

"In private. I live in Hollywood."

Frank leaned back. It was Thursday, and he'd just wrapped a case. He could write the report up tomorrow. "Yeah, I could do that," he said. "Be there as soon as I can."

He grabbed his jacket and left the office. His car was still at the body shop, getting the bullet holes fixed, so he was driving one from the motor pool. He wondered what the hell Bermuda Triangle was going to tell him. Nothing made sense about Garou's disappearance. He didn't turn up dead, and Bud swore he hadn't gone rat. Maybe he sniffed something wrong on the job and left it, and his girl, behind. Never told the others out of shame.

Frank kept himself from spooling out a movie. Queer it with speculation, and he'd have nothing. Hear Triangle out, and add her story to what he knew. Wouldn't be perfect, but it would be close enough for a matinee.

He knocked on her door, and it opened on a different girl than the one he met at the Atlantis Club. Not literally different, but whatever had happened in the last week or so had aged her. The confident creature practically daring Frank to make a move was gone. She'd dwindled down to a nub like an overworked candle. The bags under her eyes could have used some porters to carry them. She wore a dressing gown decorated with darting fish and a scarf over her hair with all the style and elegance of a woman who never expected to see sunlight again. She was holding a mug, but from the smell, the coffee was only there for color.

"Detective, come in."

She turned around and swished inside. Even her grief couldn't entirely rob her of her pelagic grace. Frank followed her in. The living room, decorated in a beach style, was disheveled, like a drunk's haircut after a long night. What caught Frank's eye, though, was a suitcase sitting in the middle of the floor, like Bermuda was isolating it from everything else. It didn't belong, and if it got too close might infect the rest. Triangle sat down and crossed her legs. She revealed a lot of skin, but there was no allure there. The gesture was too filled with careless regret.

"Take it you want to amend your statement," Frank said.

"Was that what I gave before? A statement?"

Frank shrugged. "Next best thing, I guess."

"You never found Lou, did you?"

"No, I didn't. Near as I can tell, he turned to mist like a vampire."

A single flutter of rueful laughter shook her. "I should have known he was a louse. Should have known."

"I ain't gonna argue with that one."

"How many times has a woman in my situation told you, 'He said he was going to leave his wife'?"

"I may have heard it from time to time," Frank allowed.

"He did tell me that."

"Oh, I have no doubt about that at all."

"You met her."

Frank coughed. "Yeah, I met her."

Bermuda nodded, appraising him. "And?"

"And what?"

"Is she pretty? Smart? Is she anything that would make you wonder why he was cheating on her with me?"

Frank shifted; as far he was concerned, cheating on Lulu Garou should be the textbook definition of insanity. But his opinion of Lulu's charms weren't helpful here. Instead: "In my line, I seen a lot of cheating. In both directions. I learned pretty quick that it's not about the one he's cheating with, or the one he's cheating on. It's about him. He wants something he ain't gettin' and doesn't have the guts to let the wife go do the same."

"That's really it, isn't it?"

"I'm not gonna tell you he didn't love you. Maybe he did. Probably he did. And I'm not gonna tell you he didn't love her. All I can say is you shouldn't give yourself a black eye over it. Everybody makes their choices, but it's up to the ones left behind to live with 'em."

She sat with this for a little while. "You were married." It wasn't a question.

"Didn't work out."

"Does anything?"

"I'll let you know if I see something."

She nodded, chewing on what he said. "I was lying to you the other day."

"I know."

"Why didn't you haul me in? Make some threats?"

"I was looking for Lou Garou. The department wasn't. Still isn't, really."

"That doesn't strike you as strange?"

"Wish it did. For all Garou was..." Frank gestured around the apartment, "he was an honest cop. These days the department isn't losing any sleep when one of those goes missing."

"Oh," she said.

Frank laid out the first reel of the movie. "Way I figured it, you and Garou broke ties maybe a month or two ago. Wasn't safe to be seen together. He would have said something like that. But the plan was a week ago you would get on a plane, or a train, or a boat, or something, and you would go meet him somewhere you two had picked out. You make up new names, easy enough now that folks are supposed to change 'em, and you live off some score he was promising. That about right?"

"That's the size of it," she sighed. "It was a train. I took it down to San Diego, like I was supposed to. Waited for him at the motel he told me to. From there, we were going to go south of the border. He said the money we would have would stretch down there. Only he never showed. I waited three days." A pause. "Where is he?" The last was choked, a sob she was going to keep lodged in her throat.

"I wish I knew," Frank told her. The one bit of this caper that didn't fit. Bud swore up and down Garou didn't sell them out, and the man had no reason to. He was going to leave town with his girlfriend. He had a life ahead of him. The question would gnaw at Frank, the way those kinds of questions always did to a detective. They always had to *know*. It was in the damn job description, and the ones that didn't feel that way washed out.

"Well," she said, nodding at the suitcase, "that's his luggage. It's all yours."

"You don't want to hang onto it?" Frank asked. "Something to remember him by?"

Bermuda Triangle shook her head. "I'll remember what I need to, and maybe I can forget the same way."

Frank picked up the suitcase, carrying it to the door. He stopped, because he had to tell her. He was down a little farther on the path than she was. "You're not gonna forget," he told her.

"I know," she said. "Sometimes a girl has to lie to herself."

"Sometimes a fella has to do the same."

FORTY-TWO

Frank hadn't touched the suitcase since putting it in the closet next to the stack of envelopes from Bellum. He wasn't sure why, but he couldn't open it. It was the last connection to the five Wolf Packers who'd gotten themselves underwater, and never came up for air. Opening the case would be admitting that it was over, the mystery would never be solved, that Garou was well and truly gone. And when this thing was truly done, Frank would have a decision to make. What to tell Lulu. What to do with her.

He was putting the finishing touches on the arrest report for Fenestru the Furious when Accalia appeared at his shoulder. "Detective? Captain's got a case he wants you to handle." She handed over a slip of paper with an address written in Talbot's neat hand.

"I should be off rotation," Frank growled.

Accalia put her hands up. "Captain wants you on it. You want to duck some work, maybe close fewer cases."

"Yeah, that'd make me a lot more popular." He looked at the report. "Facie around?"

Accalia didn't entirely hide her smirk. "Think I saw her in the motor pool."

Frank nodded, picking up the report. He found the doppelganger right where Accalia said she'd be. "Facie," he said by way of greeting, putting the file in her hand. "Just caught another case. Finish writing this up for me, will you?"

"Not a problem, Detective."

Frank paused. "Can I ask you something?"

Facie shifted uncomfortably. "I don't date...cops," she said.

"No, not that," he said in annoyance. "You thought...?"

"Lot of talk in the locker room...I didn't...I'm sorry."

"Don't give it a thought. It's about...you're a lady."

"Well, that explains my underwear."

"You don't make this easy."

"Ain't my job."

"No, it ain't," he agreed. "You're a lady cop. You gotta know they're never gonna let you do anything real. So why are you here?"

"I don't follow."

"Doppelganger like you could put on whatever face she wants. Go be a big movie star."

"This is the face I want," she said, gesturing to her square-jawed mug.

"Not quite what I meant."

"I do get to do some things. I got to arrest an ogre yesterday. I get to finish a report today. Later, maybe I get to help a citizen on their worst day. I get to *do* things."

"Not as much as you should."

She shrugged. "If I stop doing them, then whoever comes next starts from square one. Besides, every now and again, one of you wolves gives me a shot."

Frank nodded, wondering if any of that would make a dent with Lulu. If any of it really mattered. "Thanks, Facie."

"No problem, Detective. You get what you wanted?"

"Never can tell," he told her, climbing into a car. "Keep your powder dry."

She threw him a salute that never would have passed in the service, and Frank drove for the crime scene. The last week was a weight on him that he didn't think he'd ever get out from under. He felt the cracks running through him, multiplying, joining each other in a spiderweb that would soon cover every bit of him. He could only hope a single bit of himself would be intact. But for what? That was a question he never had the answer to, and it seemed pointless to answer it now. No one stabbed Bellum in the occipital and lived to retirement age.

No memorial for Bud, not with the papers tarring him as dirty and deranged. He'd said his goodbyes already, and it wasn't like his old partner would know who put roses on a stone. When it all quieted down, if it ever did, maybe Frank would find out which unmarked plot of land they'd planted him in. Then he'd say the things he had to in order to stop thinking about it, or maybe screw up the guts to do what Bud did and get the hell out with some of Sarah Bellum's cash. It was still waiting in that fake bank deep in the Valley.

The car went into the hills. Frank noted absently that he wasn't all that far from the Salem Sisters' flop. Those three seemed to have it all figured out. He envied that. Maybe it was easier for witches than for the rest of them, especially when you looked like they did. Frank had to shake his head. They were something, those three. Their hex hadn't been worth a damn, but beggars and choosers and all that.

The house was at the end of a winding street; the only sign of any structure was the top of a wooden staircase. A black and white loitered at the end, two unis leaning up against the side. Frank pulled to a stop and got out. It was early enough that white haze still clung to the sides of the shallow canyon. The calls of birds trilled through the scrub and trees. The other houses on the street were silent. Might as well have been empty.

Frank nodded to the unis as he headed for the stairs. They barely looked at him. Already on their lunch break. The short flight of stairs led to an outdoor deck. The house was a bit like the Salem Sisters' place, but anyplace in the hills was going to dedicate as much wall space to windows as they could. Only reason to live up here, he supposed. This spot lacked the style of the other, and was mostly a glass box secured to the canyon walls with steel beams. Gold fixtures gleamed on the walls, saying wealth but not necessarily taste. A bistro table and chairs sat on the deck, along with some potted ferns. Frank opened the front door.

The perfume hit him in like a right cross. Frank had to steady himself against the doorjamb. Whoever had lived here hadn't been a wolf, that much was clear, not if they bathed every surface in pure, chemical flowers. Probably smelled nice to other monsters. It shoved a spike up Frank's sinuses, right into his brain, and explained what those two wolves were doing waiting by their car. He silently swore at them. They could have said something. Weren't ever going to stop being patrolmen with that attitude.

He opened the door wide, vainly hoping that some of the thunderous stench would make its way outside. It mostly just made the doorway stink. Frank pulled a hanky from his pocket and stuffed it up against his nose. It was barely a shield.

He walked in, finding a dining room next to a kitchen. Everything was perfectly clean and squared away. Didn't look like a struggle had happened in here—ever. In fact, he had trouble imagining anyone using this kitchen for anything other than an image of what a kitchen might be like. Some monsters were like that; martians especially tended to be compulsive about their cleanliness. Frank supposed that if a single cold could kill him, he might take cleaning more seriously, too.

He paused at the picture on the wall, of two white birds taking flight over a lake. Hotel art, reminding him of something that would be hanging in Moore's place, or hell, his own. He couldn't ruminate, not with the perfume shoving nails into his sinuses. Getting out of this damnable scent was the priority, and sorry to the poor monster who had died in it. Later, once he got officers to air the place out a little, he could take a proper look and start piecing together the film of the crime in his mind. He could call Facie. This wouldn't bother her. Or he could make the two jokers at the top of the hill earn their pay. In the meantime, he needed a preliminary look at the body. Something to get him started.

He walked through the door and into the living room. It was bright from the floor-to-ceiling windows along one wall, but the light was flat and cold. The carpet was thicker than the coat of a Scottish sheep, almost the same color as the haze outside. The couch looked like it never knew the touch of a single living rear end. Frank didn't see a body. Must be in one of the bedrooms. Normally, he could have sniffed a dead monster out without much trouble, but this damned perfume was clogging his senses.

Frank paused, looking at the picture hanging over the couch. It was a landscape; rows and rows of orange trees on rolling hills stretched out into the distance. The sky was a flat shade of blue, the sun was a yellow disk. Frank didn't know art, but this looked like something that should be hanging in a hotel, not in a ritzy flop like this.

Maybe a room away, a door opened. Frank tensed, but it was already too late. Zombies in pinstripes and fedoras shambled into the room, letting him know which part of his anatomy they intended to air out. There were six of them, carrying pistols all lazily leveled at Frank, as though they would shoot him but didn't care too much about it either way. At the back was Aida Parrish, an unlit cigarette clamped between her yellowing teeth. She pulled it out by the holder and whispered, "Brains," to him.

He couldn't think of a single way to respond.

The collar at her neck spoke instead. "Good morning, Detective," came the whiskey-deep voice of Sarah Bellum.

Frank felt like he'd just swallowed a lump of lead. Knowing he was going to die was one thing. He knew that feeling well, but it had been some time since it settled into his belly. It wasn't a feeling he relished, but there was a certain nostalgia to it, a feeling he'd nurtured in the simpler times when he'd been surrounded by friends, back in the Day War, before the monsters.

No, what bothered him was the sense that he had *lost*. That in this struggle, this game, this battle, Bellum had well and truly won. She'd gotten away with all of it. Murdered three cops and bought all the rest. She was always out of reach, but Aida Parrish hadn't been. *She* could be dealt with, and the hex still gnawing on Frank's soul needed her to be.

Not anymore. Sylvia Screen would be unavenged. So would Bud. Howell and O'Beast too. So would Frank, but he never deserved avenging.

"Brains," Parrish whispered. She sounded almost betrayed.

"I thought you were smarter than this, Frank," Bellum said. "You had a good thing going. Money in your pocket. Keeping things or—"

Frank pulled his gun. He wasn't especially fast, but then, no zombie was ever going to outdraw Doc Holliday. Surprise alone—no one moved while Bellum was pontificating—got the heater half-clear of the holster. Then the zombies' instincts kicked in. The gunshots hammered Frank's ears. Gunpowder erased the stench of perfume, and he had just enough presence of mind to be absurdly grateful for that simple fact. A crash rang out behind him, then white-hot pain exploded in front of his eyes, and when something approaching wobbling vision appeared in them, he'd been turned around, spun by the impact of a bullet. In front of him, the sky yawned wide. A breeze kissed his face.

Another spear ran through him, and he lurched forward. One step, then two, crunching over broken glass. The world tilted crazily, and the next thing Frank knew, he hit the ground below with a wet thud. Above him, the cantilevered house loomed, gunsmoke wafting from the broken window. A moment later, dead faces appeared, peering down. Frank barely glimpsed them as he rolled down the steep hill.

Every revolution of his body brought another explosion of agony. Frank couldn't control himself. He tumbled over dirt, over rocks and brambles, only coming to a stop when he slammed into a tree with a bone-jarring smack. That yanked another cry of pain out of his lungs. It didn't abate, either. Two blades of fire, one in his left shoulder, the other in his right side, steadily twisting their way into his brutalized body.

This wasn't the first time Frank had caught a bullet. He'd taken a rifle shot to the leg outside of Rome; his own fault, he figured, since he was sitting on his tank at the time. The bullet had torn up the meat of his calf. Strange part was he didn't really feel it. At first it was like being punched by Joe Louis, and then, nothing. His leg was numb even as it leaked his life out all over the tank's armored hide. Medic said that was normal when they patched him up. Fellas could walk around missing half a face and not feel a thing until they dropped dead. Frank had walked with a limp until he'd been turned.

This didn't feel like that. He experienced the fire of these bullets burrowing into him. This was *silver*. The metal hated him. It wanted him to suffer and so he did. He lay there, unable to do anything other than breathe. He'd be a dead man without some help. Fast.

Come on, Frank. The words were in his mind, but they were in Bud's voice.

Oh good, he thought in his own, *I'm cracking up. That's just what I need.*

They'll be coming to finish the job, Bud's voice said.

Frank lay on his right side, wrapped around the tree where it had caught him right in the chest. He imagined his ribs must ache, but he couldn't feel anything over the screaming agony in his shoulder and flank. The hill reached up and behind him. He craned his neck, and in the distance, he could barely glimpse the house. His vision went wobbly, stuttering like a film strip that had jumped the track.

The corpses would be on their way.

He might have chuckled at the thought of zombies trying to handle the slope that had just rolled him like a bowling ball, but making any sound other than an anguished moaning was going to require more willpower than he had left.

Move, Bud's voice told him.

Frank listened. He raised his right leg up and nearly blacked out when the silver dug its claws into him. He felt like he was being operated on while playing football. He tried again with the left leg, getting purchase on the trunk. A narrow pine tree. He watched a line of ants he'd disrupted, frantically looking for their new scent trail. *Sorry, fellas*, he thought at them. *I'll be out of your hair in two shakes.* He put his right arm on the trunk, and clear as day, he saw Lulu Garou. For her, he would get up.

On the hill, up and behind, he heard calls of "Brains!"

Frank let out a choked cry as he got to his feet. He held onto the tree, bark rough beneath his grip. The hill was wild, damn near a forest. He couldn't see the corpses, but he knew they'd be taking their sweet time. A tumble like the one Frank took could easily be fatal to them, assuming they lost their steel lids.

The tree Frank had hit was nearly at the bottom. A break in the foliage revealed the sidewalk below. Only a few steps. He inched forward. His legs didn't give out, but the steps shook the wound in his side. Not much to be done for that. If he stuck around, they'd have put enough silver in him that he'd qualify as flatware.

He took a bad step at the end, or else his body gave out, and collapsed in a heap. Planting a leg under him, he pushed himself up. The calls of "Brains" grew louder on the hill. Zombies were slow, but Frank couldn't outrun them in this condition. He staggered like an old wino down the street. He didn't know where he was going. Just away from those sounds. Away from the knowledge that he really had lost, now and forever. Bud's voice barked commands in his head, but they were distant. He could only make out individual words. Words like *Run*. There were other voices, too, whispering just out of reach.

Then, coming out of the haze of agony, Frank saw salvation.

The callbox was on the side of a telephone pole. Frank reached into his pocket. It was wet in there, squelching against his fingers. When he brought out his key, it shone bright like rubies. He fitted it into the lock, tore it open, and called the one person he could think of who might save him.

"Moss Investigations," said the chirpy voice on the other end of the line.

FORTY-THREE

The silver had taken root, the pinpoints turned to thorns of fire radiating from the places the slugs rested inside him. He managed to loosen his shoulder holster enough to get a bit of the leather in his mouth, and biting down on that was the only way he wasn't screaming. His gun was long gone, dropped either in the house or on the hill. A heater was worthless to him in his present state, and the wolf was cowering and whimpering inside as the silver bored inexorably closer to his heart and lungs. If Bellum's corpses found him, there wasn't a single thing Frank could do about it. Couldn't even give them a final, defiant line to exit on.

He'd stuffed himself in some kind of laurel bush and couldn't do much more than lie there. Lie there and try not to scream. The sidewalk was within reach, and just beyond was the street. Keeping his eyes fixed on the concrete, he waited for the worst cavalry in the history of the term. He'd close his eyes for a second, the pulsing white of his agony eating him, then open them immediately only to find a bird or ladybug suddenly there. Blink again, and they were gone like they'd never been.

He couldn't be sure if he actually heard the moans of "Brains" or if it was his imagination. From time to time, he did see feet or tentacles passing on the asphalt not three feet from where he lay, but none stopped. He thought he was hidden well, but he couldn't tell. Then a tire screeched to a stop in front of Frank's bleary eyes. The wheel well was dented, rust showing through the paint. Paint that somehow managed to not really be a color at all, despite having all the properties of one.

The door slammed, and legs ran around the side of the car. "Frank! Frank, where the hell are you? Frank!"

Frank could almost have laughed. The goddamn meatstick showed. He actually showed. He spat out the strip of leather, permanently dented from his teeth. He wanted to yell, "Here!" But all that came out was a groan.

That didn't matter. A moment later, Nick's weasel face hovered above his. "Holy..." The gumshoe shook it off, horror giving way to resolve. "Okay. I gotcha." Frank felt Nick's hands go under his armpits, and he let out a hideous moan as the wound in his shoulder jostled. "I'm sorry, Frank. No other way to get you in the car."

Frank thought he nodded, but he wasn't sure. He didn't have much control of himself. As Nick dragged him over the sidewalk, he groggily turned his head and saw a phantom staring, her mouth in a horrified O. He didn't even have the strength to wave to her.

Nick managed to open the back door and wrestle Frank into the car. He lay there, on the dirty backseat, and he was almost comforted. Help was close.

The detective jumped in the front seat and started the car. "Hang on, Frank. Gonna get you to someone who can patch you up."

"Salem," Frank murmured.

"Sorry, big fella," Nick said. Frank felt the car lurch forward. The engine sounded like an old man with a two-pack-a-day habit, but the car was moving. "I might take you to them if you needed a salve for hemorrhoids, but pulling silver out of a wolf is a bit above their paygrade. Don't worry. I know somebody. She's not far."

Frank managed to feel a little disappointment at not seeing the Salem Sisters again. They would be a hell of a final sight for this world. Closest things to angels Frank would ever slap eyes on, anyway.

He blinked a few more times, shadows playing off the fraying roof liner of Nick's car. Then they were stopped, and a breeze brushed by his face, and a dog was barking thunderously somewhere close. Nick was talking, but he couldn't quite hear it. Then the back door opened by his head, and Frank looked up to see a meat golem.

From his vantage, she was huge. A lot of them were, even the dames. There was a lot of this one, bursting out of the silk dressing gown wrapped around her curves. She had a pretty face, even if it didn't quite line up, and she looked at Frank like he was last week's ham. She turned to look down at Nick, an eyebrow cocked.

"Silver," he said. "You don't pull it out of him, he's dead." Her gaze went from Nick to Frank, and Frank watched the wheels clicking in her head. "C'mon, Betty. He'll pay you double," Nick said.

Betty gave a silent sigh, lifted Frank out of the car, and put him over her shoulder like a sack of flour. Frank might as well have been a foul-tempered teddy bear for all the effort it took her. He groaned as his wounds bit back, but all told, it was better than being dragged. Watching the ground go by from his position, he saw what had been barking: a stitched-together wolfhound that was now following them, sniffing the air. Frank didn't need to be reminded that wolfhounds were called that because they had been bred to hunt wolves.

Nick's car was parked in a driveway next to a small house. He'd pinned in another car, one a little bit nicer and sporting a candy apple paintjob. Frank didn't get much else, because his vision went smeary. Then he was inside. Thumps, maybe a door, nails clicking on hardwood floors. The scent of blood strangled his senses. the world was tumbling over and over, and he was on a table.

The meat golem—Betty—stood over him, her dressing gown streaked with blood. She clicked on a powerful light, and he heard a clatter. The scent of disinfectant and old blood filled his senses. He blinked, long and slow, and she was holding a laminated card in front of him, decorated with serifs like the dialogue cards from an old silent film. *This is going to hurt*, it said. Something made of wood got jammed between his teeth. He bit down eagerly.

The burning turned to screaming, swallowing up his entire world. He was never more grateful when oblivion ate him up.

FORTY-FOUR

Frank wasn't sure if it was the voices or the ache throbbing in time with his heartbeat that actually woke him. He had vague memories of the blinding light, of cool steel probing in his shoulder and side, a relief after the scorching shriek of silver. He felt like he had surfaced after an extended time underwater.

He was shirtless, wide bandages wrapped around his two major wounds. The others—the scratches and bumps from his trip down the hill—throbbed and ached. They should already be knitting, but they were fresh. The silver had robbed him of the wolf-borne recuperative powers. He healed like a man now, maybe forever.

The table he lay on wasn't what you'd call comfortable. A bit of investigation revealed that it was stainless steel, a morgue table. Frank was stiff as a corpse, but whether it was from the table or the fact that he'd been trying to shake the reaper's hand, he didn't know. All he *did* know was that he felt like he'd been run over by his own tank.

The light was off, but Frank could see the room a bit. It was a laundry room, complete with a washer and dryer. It had also been partly converted into a makeshift surgery. He wasn't too surprised that Nick knew a back-alley doctor. Frank was a little surprised that he himself didn't.

The voice was a room away, and it belonged to Nick. "I'm sorry, Betty. If there was anywhere else to take him, I would have."

Frank couldn't hear the response—probably because Betty couldn't speak—but when Nick talked again, he knew the meat golem must have written something down and showed it to him. That's how a lot of them communicated with the outside world.

"I don't know. She left town." A pause, probably more writing. "I haven't looked. I thought...I don't know what I thought. She needed some time, maybe." Another pause, and now Frank could make out the faint scratching of a pen. "She's the one who left, Betty." A brief pause. "Maybe we are, but I don't see a lot of other options right now."

The door opened, and Frank fought to sit up. The two points where the silver had gone in blazed for a moment, but swiftly settled into the same pulsing ache that kept time with his ticker. Betty stood in the doorway, still in her bloodstained dressing gown. Now that Frank was no longer leaning on Death's doorbell, he was able to take her in. She was something else, like a Halloween pinup girl. He couldn't tell if the look in her eyes was concern or annoyance.

"I'm good for the money," Frank grunted. He didn't tell her he had a year of dirty cash from Bellum he was dying to unload. She nodded, then held out the neckline of the dressing gown and cocked an eyebrow. "Yeah, I'll pay for that, too."

She nodded, then came to his side, touching the bandages, holding up a finger, then pointing at a calendar on the wall. The picture was of an Alaskan Malamute, panting happily. "Change the bandage once a day?" Frank ventured.

She touched the end of her nose, then picked up a notebook, scrawling something on it. She held it up for Frank. *You can stay here until dark. Then I want you out.*

"You'll never see me again," he promised her.

She nodded, rubbing her fingers together. Nick produced some cash and handed it over. She made a *Come on* motion and he peeled off a few more bills.

"Don't worry," Frank said. "I'll pay you back."

Betty counted it, folded it, nodded, and gave them a smile before swishing her way out. Frank had to admit, it was nice watching her go. As she closed the door, just beyond the threshold Frank could see the massive patchwork wolfhound sitting on the hardwood floor, its eyes glued to him.

Alone, Frank turned to Nick. "How the hell do you, a twitchy little meatstick, know all those tomatoes?"

Nick hopped up onto the washing machine. "Well, I don't call them tomatoes for one thing."

Frank snorted. "Yeah, yeah."

"Betty works at the Nocturnist," Nick said.

"*She's* a waitress?"

"Sure. Being a back-alley doctor doesn't pay as well as it used to. Once goblins and zombies stopped shooting each other, the work dried up."

"It's a shame whoever pushed the button on the Gobfather never thought of that, huh?"

Nick shifted, staring at the wall behind Frank. "She's good at what she does."

"I'll say," Frank agreed. "Thought I was a goner for sure."

"Frank...what the hell happened?"

It felt strange, unburdening himself to a human, but Nick had earned it. Came when Frank called even when he'd had no reason to. That was the Nick who'd jumped out of a plane over France. Of *that*, Frank was certain. "My captain set me up to be bumped off. I should be thanking my lucky stars zombies can't shoot straight."

"Your captain?"

Frank shook his head as a reel of the last conversation he'd ever had with Talbot spun out on the movie screen in his mind. "The bastard called me into his office and asked my permission."

"He what?"

"Not in so many words, but he did. Asked my damn permission to have me killed. And like a sap I gave it to him." Frank had no illusions. Talbot would have done it regardless, but that one last insult, that Talbot had asked absolution and Frank had given it was almost enough to wake the wounded wolf.

"I didn't think captains were on the take," Nick said.

"Sarah Bellum owns the cops. All of us. Ones who don't do what she wants, well, we get a call. When we show up, the corpses all have guns and bad tempers, if you follow me."

"Right," Nick said, seeing the shape of it. "Couple hours, we'll get you out of town. I could drive you as far as San Diego, Santa Barbara. Las Vegas, if that's your poison."

"You don't have to stick around. You've done enough."

Nick shrugged. "If I was home right now, all I'd be doing is drinking and hoping my neighbors don't wreck too many of my wards before dark."

"Really popular in your neighborhood, huh?"

"Happens when you're a Daaé like me."

"This is because of that..." Frank fumbled for the name, found it. "Jane, right? She was one of the sk...one of the meat golems from the Nocturnist?"

"Yeah," Nick said, and didn't say anything else.

"What happened to her?"

"She left town."

Frank nodded. "Been trying to get my...a certain...there's a lady I'm trying to get to leave town."

Nick looked up. "Yeah?"

"You're looking at me like I'm fit to cut out paper dolls."

"Find the right lady, seems to me you don't try to get her to *leave*."

"Never said she was the right one."

Nick smiled, shaking his head. "Yeah, you did."

"Not much I can do about it. There's still some things I have to finish before I go."

"You finishing them for her?"

"No. Yeah. I don't know. I know it's something I have to do, and if I don't, there's no way I'm who I need to be if I'm with her." Frank looked over at Nick, and saw in the other man's eyes that he was with his Jane. "We try to be worthy of them, but the truth is, we're not worthy of ourselves."

"So you, what, after you settle up with your captain, you'll go with her?" Nick asked.

"Maybe," Frank said. "At the end of this, if Captain Talbot's still breathing, I better not be. You don't get to do what he did without paying. There was a time when the LAPD was honest. You know that? There was a time when we kept order on the streets. We locked up gangsters. We got justice for those who were hurting. We kept people *safe*. We were trusted then. Admired. And it wasn't too long ago, neither. There were a couple bad apples, sure, but most of us were on the up and up.

"Then the Godfather gets the push, and guess who reaps the benefits. Not the boys in blue, no. It was the Gray Matter. Fills her bank account with illicit cash and she uses it to buy up whoever she wants. We think we can't be bought until she asks, and we do it. We think we can keep ourselves intact, stay breathing, maybe even enjoy a little bit of the rewards. No. She's always gonna ask the one thing that breaks you. The one thing that makes you not *you* anymore. After that? Might as well be one of her zombies. Dancing on her puppetstrings, with nothing to say. At least they're honest about it."

Nick stared at him like he couldn't believe what was coming out of Frank's mouth. "You know how much it's changed for us humans since Bellum bought you? Not one little bit. Your clean, trusted force? No different than gangsters. Hell, you were worse. Never heard of one of them roughing up some fella just trying to drive to work. At least now you don't have any illusions."

A meatstick talked like that to him, Frank had always assumed the wolf would slip its chains and go snapping. But the way Nick said it, without even an ounce of malice, just like he was reading facts on the news, nailed Frank in place. Nick wasn't lying. Wasn't in him to lie about this. Frank felt like a beetle drying up in the sun. He couldn't speak to that, so he asked the closest he could get to it.

"Your Jane...she ever make you feel like you were any different from her?" Frank asked.

"Only the last time I saw her," Nick said.

"You got a picture?"

Nick hesitated, then went for his wallet. He handed over a yellow-tinged photo. It was a shot of a meat golem, standing on a lawn as squared away as a sailor's bunk. She was posing, but whoever was taking the picture was making her laugh, and Frank saw that it was all she could do to hold that position: hand on her hip, a grin that was almost a laugh. She wore shorts and a checked shirt, a scarf in her hair. Even without color, Frank could tell her eyes were mismatched, one black, the other white. She wasn't what Frank would call gorgeous, but there was something about her. Maybe it was the way she looked at the camera, because she loved the man behind it.

Frank gave it another glance. She felt familiar; he probably saw her at the Nocturnist. He nodded and handed the picture back.

"How about you? You got a picture?" Nick asked.

"Wish I did."

"Tell me about her."

Frank had never been one to talk like this, but there was something about this situation. Sitting in this street doctor's back room with a man who had saved his life multiple times. It was like being back in the war, when the walls came down just so there was nothing to collapse.

"She's something, I'll tell you that. World wanted her to be one thing, and she listened to it. Only right now, she's waking up to what she wants to do. It's there, in front of her. She just has to reach out and take it, right off the tree. And I tell you, I think she's going to. I *hope* she's going to. If she leaves here and I never see her again, but she gets to go someplace and be a cop? I'm a happy man."

"She wants to be a cop?"

Frank nodded. "Only she's...you know, a dame."

"Dames can want to be anything. We don't always let them go do it."

"Found that out the other day."

"Jane wants to make dresses. Well, clothes. She just likes dresses best. She made me this suit."

"Fits nice."

"Used to fit a little better."

Frank could see the way Nick's eyes and cheeks were a bit sunken, the way the cuffs and collar were loose. He'd missed more than one meal since Jane left. "She's good at it."

"Yeah, she is."

"Take it she's how you know Betty."

Nick nodded. "How are you feeling?"

"Not dying anymore."

"Never seen a wolfman get hit with silver and live."

Moon's autopsy folder flashed in front of Frank's mind. The bullet had gone straight through his heart. He would have been dead before he hit the ground. No chance to get to a surgeon, back alley or otherwise, even if Nick and Garou would have taken him. "It ain't fun, I'll tell you that."

"You'll heal up fine?"

"Maybe. Silver wounds don't heal quick or easy. Or all the way."

"Seen a lot of them?"

"More these days than before."

The two of them talked on and off for the next hour, but soon Frank felt fatigue catching up with him, and he dozed on the metal table. The idea of trusting a silver-armed human was a new one, but he did. And when he opened his eyes one of many times, he saw Nick curled up across the washer and dryer, sawing logs himself.

FORTY-FIVE

Betty was a looker in a bloodstained dressing gown; she was a knockout in the hotpants and halter getup of the Nocturnist. Frank nearly asked her if she'd ever dated Bud, and only then remembered that Bud would only have feigned interest in her. Betty pointed to herself, then to the front door, pointed to them, and to the door leading around the side.

"We got it, Betty. Thanks again," Nick said.

She nodded at him and went to the door, pausing. She looked back, her eyes going the slightest bit soft before turning flinty again. She scratched the head of her wolfhound right behind a line of stitches and left for the Nocturnist. Frank found out later it was only a few blocks away.

It took him an embarrassing amount of time to don his shirt. He moved gingerly with his wounds, and every false twitch sent an aching bolt deep into him from both. As he buttoned the shirt, the fingers of his left hand stung with distant pins and needles. Flexing that hand only moved them around. He was tired in a way that he never even felt in the Day War, like his body wanted to give up for a time.

"We need to get you some fresh clothes," Nick said. They'd run Frank's shirt through he wash, but the bloodstains had stubbornly remained, not to mention the bullet holes.

"We ain't the same size."

"Yeah, I noticed."

Frank had come to the decision while staring at the ceiling. "You're taking me home."

"You don't think that's the first place Bellum and your captain will look for you? I mean, I'm no expert, but that's usually where I start."

"You ever stop talking?"

"When I'm not nervous."

"You can just say 'no' next time."

Nick gathered himself. "Frank, I don't know how straight you're thinking here."

He wanted to snap. Nick might have proven himself to be better than your average meatstick, but he was still human and Frank was still a wolfman. But he needed Nick. As annoying as he could be, he was all Frank had.

"I'm thinking that I lost my gun, which I might need pretty soon. Among other things." He said the words as measured as he could, and though the wolf in him was beaten, he felt the ghost of a snarl in the words.

"Yeah, okay. Let's get going."

They went out the back to the driveway. Nick's backseat looked like King Solomon had sacrificed a goat there. Knowing that much blood had come out of him made Frank queasy. There couldn't be a whole lot left.

"Sorry about your car."

Nick glanced at it. "Don't worry. Been thinking it might be time for a change."

Frank frowned, but he wasn't thinking straight enough to know what the meatstick was talking about. He got into the front, and Nick slid into the driver's side.

They were on the road, driving through Hollywood, when Nick asked, "Where do you live?"

Frank told him. The sigh Nick gave afterwards said it all. It was well past dark when they rolled into the orange groves. Frank could barely smell the citrus over his own blood.

"You live all the way out here," Nick said. Hard to miss the wonder in his voice.

"Yeah. It's not bad."

"No, it's not." Frank looked over at Nick and he could see what was going on behind the other man's eyes. He was thinking about how no one would paint DAAÉ on his house way out here. No one would even know he was out in the middle of the trees and winding dirt roads. Frank directed him down the correct lanes, up the small hill overlooking the groves. "There it is."

Frank's house was completely dark. He leaned out the window and inhaled. He didn't catch any rot, or any heavy perfume. Mostly he smelled oranges, but he wasn't going to trust that alone. Nick pulled the Ford off the road about ten yards from the front door and turned out the lights. They spent a few moments staring at the house like it might light up and yell "Surprise!" at them.

"I think I should mention again that this is a terrible idea," Nick said.

"Noted. Shaddup."

Nick nodded and pulled the Luger from his jacket. It was surreal to see that pistol all the way out here in California, but something about it felt right. Frank wouldn't have wanted to be on the other end of it, but on the same side? Yes. That gun was a dealer of death. Frank could smell it.

They got out of the car, still looking up at the house. It remained defiantly dark.

"Can you change?" Nick muttered.

"Don't think so," Frank said back.

"I was just thinking how the odds weren't stacked against us enough."

Nick hunkered down, and the way he darted from shadow to shadow, Frank got thinking he'd never made it all the way back from the Night War. Maybe none of the humans did. For his part, Frank tried to balance moving quickly and gingerly at the same time, and managed to do both poorly. He felt like he should throw up, but there was nothing in his stomach to do that with. He hadn't eaten since breakfast which might have been yesterday—he wasn't entirely sure—and he was in such pain everywhere else that he hadn't noticed.

Nick made it to the front door and Frank had to jog to make up the time. The door was still busted from when Bellum's gunsels kicked it in, so it was easy for Nick to slip inside, smooth as you please. Frank had the unnerving feeling this was not the first time in the recent past that the private eye had slinked into some monster's house. Maybe Bosch was right and Nick wasn't a gangster, but he was *something*.

Following behind as quietly as he could, Frank paused in the front hall. The house was empty. They'd made it this far, and no lights had boomed on from the groves, no zombies had come shambling out, no wolves had materialized from the trees. Frank sagged against the wall and caught his breath. Hell of a thing. Just moving around was exhausting him like combat.

Nick came out of the back room, the gun by his side. "This place looks empty to me," he said.

"Sure does. Guess I was worried for nothing."

"Guess so," Nick said, moving into the living room. He looked down at the newspapers, reading the headlines. He coughed, and said in a way that was too casual. "They still got that Monster Slayer unit?"

"Yep," Frank growled. "Chasing a fake ghost when there's plenty of real ones need to be caught."

"You think they'll figure that out? That the Monster Slayer isn't real?"

"I think believing lies is all that gets most folks through the day."

Frank went into his bedroom at the back of the house, stripping off his ruined clothes. He briefly considered a shower, but the thought of water against the wounds was too much to countenance for the moment. He peeked under the bandages. Betty knew her work; the stitches were neat and even. He donned a fresh suit, but that was a matter of degrees: nothing he owned was all that fresh. Then he went into his closet and got what he was after. The M1 Garand was wrapped in a blanket on the top shelf like a baby. Frank hadn't fired it in over ten years, but he still maintained it.

Something about the weapon that had gone with him from the boot to Berlin mattered in a way he couldn't quite verbalize. He always treated it like an artifact, but today it was a tool.

He emerged from the bedroom to find Nick by the front window, gazing out over the orange groves.

"Got something for you," Frank said, holding out the gun.

Nick jumped; he'd been completely lost in thought. In love with the view, maybe. Frank couldn't blame him. He'd done the same thing when he and Susan found the place.

Nick took the weapon, turning it over in his hands, checking the chamber and finding it empty. He folded the stock against the gun, then locked it back into place, shaking his head in faintly amused wonder. Frank wrinkled his nose; the carbine had carried over some of the smells of the war, and he was having trouble getting the scent out of his nostrils. Death, sure, but also the gasoline smells of a working Sherman tank. And cigarettes. He and the others had smoked like chimneys back then.

"This could almost be my weapon. Had the folding stock and everything."

"Same rifle for you Airborne boys as us tankers."

"Guess you didn't have much room in those boxes."

Frank snorted. "You got no idea. My knees and my chest are intimately acquainted."

"Haven't touched one of these since the war." Frank didn't ask if Nick meant Day or Night. He wasn't sure he wanted to know.

Nick held the gun easily, stock under one arm, barrel at the floor. Frank knew the posture, and Nick had settled into it without thinking. It was the weary, yet alert mien of a soldier. "A man doesn't hand someone a weapon like this for no reason."

"No, a man doesn't."

Nick nodded. "Don't suppose you have silver bullets for this thing."

"I don't, and I'm gonna pretend you didn't ask."

"Don't need silver to put down zombies. That the take?"

Frank nodded. "That's the take."

"I should tell you to get bent."

"Probably."

Nick nodded. "Okay, what's the plan?"

The smell wasn't going away. Frank coughed in his hand. The smell wasn't from the gun, and Frank put together why it had appeared when it had. Made sense; leave a private eye alone and what was he supposed to do? "Did you *have* to smoke while I was changing?" he growled.

"Smoke? What are you talking about? I don't—" Nick trailed off, his eyes widening. Frank made the same leap a second later. He whirled, sucking in air, trying to find the scent.

Nick's hand went into his jacket. "Where?" he shouted.

A thump sounded from the archway into the dining room, and the wall rattled. Frank pointed, trying to run but the twin aches made him so slow.

Nick was fast—beyond fast. He threw something, shouting, "Close your eyes!"

Frank obeyed, and only opened them when he heard the *whump*. He opened his eyes to see that the border between the living room and dining room was covered in a burst of flour. And in the middle of the flour was the half-revealed shape of an invisible man.

Frank snarled, ignoring the burn of his wounds, lurching forward for the glass man. The flour-covered shape was in the midst of a full-blown panic. He hollered in a smoker's rasp, desperately trying to wipe the stuff off himself and only succeeding in spreading it around. Nick sped by like a bullet, knocking the flour-covered head with the butt of the carbine. Some of the flour turned red, and the invisible man went limp on the floor.

Frank dragged himself up next to Nick. "Well, that answers a few questions."

FORTY-SIX

The rope floated around the dining room chair like an Old West halo. It moved slowly, rhythmically, along with the soft sounds of breath. Glass was under that rope, truly invisible again now that they'd sponged the flour from him. If he woke up and he was still doused, he would have panicked, and wouldn't spill anything other than some more screaming. Frank sat mere inches from him, staring at where Glass should be. Nick stood away, the loaded carbine in his hands.

"There's got to be a better way of keeping track of him," Nick said.

"I think I've got something."

"Good, because the last thing we need is an invisible man running around."

Frank didn't mention that they'd had one running around for a full night and it had cost Bud his life. He went into the kitchen and returned with a gelatinous green lump in a glass tray. When he uncovered it, Nick turned green and took a step back. "Jesus, Frank, what is that?"

"Ham," Frank said. "Well, it *was* ham. Now I don't know what you'd call it."

"I thought you wolfmen had a good sense of smell."

"Gamey meat's good. Gotta let it go off a little before it's worth eatin'."

"That's more than a little off."

"Pipe down. You smelled worse than this."

He pulled it out and began to slather it on the unconscious invisible man.

"You're a mean bastard. Anybody ever tell you that?" Nick said.

"Maybe once or twice." He returned the ham to the tray and the tray to the fridge. When he came back, Nick's face was a mask of frustration.

"Why did you put it back?"

"That's where the food goes."

"When ham looks like that, it's not food anymore, Frank."

Frank grunted. "My house, my icebox."

Nick shook his head, admitting defeat.

A groan sounded from the approximate place of the invisible man's head. Frank lightly slapped where the rotten ham smell told him the face was. As much as it stank, he kind of preferred it to the cloying cigarette smoke that had been dogging him for a significant chunk of his investigation. "Come on now, wake up. Come on, Lieutenant."

"Lieutenant?" Nick moaned.

Frank waved him off. "You heard me, Lieutenant. You don't have to play possum."

"Wolfman," Lieutenant Temple Glass croaked. "Let me out of this chair."

"Sure thing. You want a gun, too? We got one with silver bullets and everything." Frank slapped him, harder this time. "Answer some questions, I'll think about letting you walk out of here."

The invisible man's silence was unnerving. No reading his eyes, or the tiny ripples going over his face. Frank couldn't even smell his fear; there was just the stink of jellied ham and the faintly clinging smoke. He tried to remember every time he'd smelled that, but his memory inserted it everywhere during that long night.

"Detective, you need to look at this rationally." Glass's voice was raspy, and probably an octave deeper than it should be thanks to his habit. "Now, right now, nothing's been done that can't be undone."

"Assaulting a cop is still a crime. For now."

"You didn't assault anybody," Glass said. "*He* did."

Frank didn't have to be able to see the guy to know that the invisible man had just cocked his chin at Nick Moss. "Now wait a minute," Nick started, ready to let the dam loose on the blather that made Frank regret bringing him along. Frank raised his hand, and Nick smartly shut his flycatcher.

"You're actually trying to sell me on that," Frank said. "Incredible."

"I'm not selling you. I'm trying to make you listen to reason. You let me go, we arrest him, and you go back to being a cop. It's your *career* you're playing with."

Frank finally laughed out loud. He turned to Nick, whose face was stamped with a confused expression. "You gettin' a load of this?" He turned back to Glass and looked where his head was. "Stop tryin', Glass. It ain't as charming as you think it is. Talbot set me up to die, and he sent you here to wait for me. I bet you were either gonna call it in if I stuck around, or you were gonna do what you did the other night, and trail me wherever I went."

He could hear the invisible man's breathing: raspy as his voice.

Frank bared his teeth—wasn't a smile, no one could mistake it for one—and said, "You should start talking, Glass. You're not getting out of that chair otherwise."

"That was the plan," Glass admitted.

"Good. I believe you. That's important if we're gonna keep jawing."

"It's not personal, Detective."

"It's financial. I know how the LAPD works, Lieutenant. At least, how it works now. I expect there's a reward out for me."

"A big one," Glass said.

"And Talbot wants it."

"Of course he does."

"And you're helping out of the goodness of your heart." Frank slapped Glass. "What was your cut?"

"A quarter," Glass grumbled.

"A quarter. Willing to sell out a fellow cop for a *quarter* of the take. What would you have done for half?"

The ropes moved a bit, like Glass was shifting uncomfortably in the chair.

"You don't have to answer that," Frank said. "You were shadowing me the other night, weren't you? When Bud was here?"

"Yeah," Glass said.

"When?"

"I tailed you to Garou's flop," Glass said. "Classy what you're getting up to with his missus."

The snarl that tore its way out of Frank's throat came all the way from the Black Forest. The ropes jumped in place. The wounds did the same thing, screaming at him to stop, but he couldn't. When Frank spoke again, his voice had fur on it. "You might want to keep your mouth off that."

"Yeah, of course." Glass sounded rattled. "What...uh...I had plenty of time. Parked down the street, hopped into your trunk."

"Hiding back there the whole time."

"Trick I used back in the Night War. Find a meatstick caravan, let them carry you back to their base. Take you right past the wards if you were quiet enough."

"Got a meatstick right here might have something to say about that," Frank said.

A metallic click, then a catch. A lighter. The quick intake of breath from Glass said it all. Then another click, the lighter shutting. Frank had to admit, he liked the meatstick's style right then.

"You were the one who called the zombies. Wasn't one of them smoking."

"I called Talbot. Talbot called Bellum."

"That supposed to make you sleep better?"

"I didn't call the Gray Matter!" Glass shouted. "I got the orders from Talbot. I got my envelope every month *from Talbot.*"

"You knew where the money in that envelope was coming from."

Glass was silent. Then, quietly: "I knew."

"We all knew," Frank said. "And I bet we all came up with good reasons why it was fine for us to take it. Only the thing is, whatever we came up with was a lie we told ourselves."

"Detective. *Frank.* I don't have anything against you. I don't need to see you get chewed up by the Gray Matter. How about this. How about you and your meatstick just leave? Get in your car and go, and never come back."

"And Talbot?"

"I'll tell him I never saw you. You never came home. You disappear, there's no one to tell him anything different."

It was a hell of an offer. Frank wished he could take it. How much of it was the hex and how much of it was his need, he'd never really know. But he couldn't do what Glass wanted and they both knew it.

"Can I ask you something, Lieutenant?"

"Temple, Frank. Call me Temple."

"You were the reason Bellum's corpses were at the train station, weren't you?"

He heard the click of Glass's throat as he swallowed. "Yeah."

Frank remembered the feeling of stepping over Bud's body as he and Nick fled from the platform. "Sorry, Temple."

"Frank, you can't do this. I'm tied to a chair here. That's not you. That's not what you are."

"Calm down. I ain't gonna kill you. I need you to make a phone call."

"Phone call?"

"Yeah, you're calling Captain Talbot."

FORTY-SEVEN

Frank's front door was wide open, with only the screen between him and the outside. *C'mon in*, the door seemed to say, *we're waiting for you.*

The place in the jamb where the deadbolt had gone in was still shaggy with broken wood. Frank sat in the entryway on a chair he'd dragged in from the dining room. He stared out on the dirt road out in front of his house, silently waiting, his eyes in an approximation of a gunfighter's squint. He hadn't been cut out for the Wolf Pack in the old days, but today an observer would never know it.

Plumes of dust flowered on the horizon, right where paved road gave way to dirt. It'd been maybe an hour since Glass had called the captain, but time had a funny way of stretching and shrinking when death was on either side.

Frank's heart gave a kick, and ice trickled into his veins. The two wounds throbbed, faster and faster. Before this was over, they were going to hurt a lot more. They'd probably have company.

Frank watched the line of cars—four of them—drive along the ridge to his house. He hoped Glass had been convincing. No way they'd get a second chance at any of this.

The cars pulled to a stop in front of the house, brakes emitting short squeals. Frank was already regretting this play but there was no going back now.

Four cars. That was about three cars more than they needed, and about three cars more than Frank could handle.

He sniffed the air, hunting for the scents he wanted, through the rotten ham, old cigarette smoke, and oranges. Decay wafted in on the settling sheets of dust. He tried to pick Aida's smoke or a whiff of *Catacombe*, but couldn't catch any. Nick had been right; the ham was a bit strong.

The passenger door to the third car opened up and Talbot stepped out. He stood in the noontime sun, squinting at Frank, who would appear to be little more than a shadowy lump, in a dark hall and behind a screen. *There's one*, Frank thought.

"That you, Frank?" Talbot called.

"That's me, Captain," Frank said.

"Knew I was coming?"

"Hoping's more like it."

"Why don't you come on out? We can have a little chat."

"I'm pretty comfortable where I am. Besides, I don't think I need to make a bigger target for those stiffs you brought."

Talbot offered an embarrassed smile, but it was impossible to tell if anything real fueled it. Frank wasn't sure if it mattered one way or the other. "Sorry about that, Frank. They insisted."

"I bet they did."

The other car doors opened with heavy clunks like coffin lids. Zombies stepped out into the sun. Frank counted fifteen of them, some with pistols, others with shotguns. More than Frank was hoping for, but fewer than he'd feared. Some of the zombies stared at the doorway; others scanned the horizon, hunting for hills or rooftops where a sharpshooter might perch. They wouldn't find much, just miles of oranges, far as the eye could see. Frank's gaze flicked to Aida Parrish, who had emerged from the backseat of Talbot's ride. He imagined her whispering "Brains," as Bellum rattled off commands in that honey-burned voice of hers.

"Detective Wolfman." The voice was Bellum's, crackling out over the speaker around Parrish's throat. The Brain was sitting comfortably in her Beverly Hills estate, nowhere near the impending carnage. "We seem to have found ourselves in a difficult position. You've been taking my money for a year, but the minute I needed you, you broke our contract."

"Sylvia Screen," Frank said.

Parrish remained unmoved. Bellum said, "Is that name supposed to mean something to me?"

Frank thought about telling her, but it was a waste of time. "No. It isn't."

"So, are you planning to come out?"

Frank snorted. "What, you'll go easy on me if I do?"

"It's not too late," Talbot said, with a nervous glance at Parrish. "We can sort this out. Nobody else has to get hurt."

"You believe that, Captain?" Frank asked. One last lifeline. Maybe the Captain would grab it. Then he could die with a halo.

Talbot looked at his shoes. The choice was made.

"What's it going to be, Detective?" Bellum asked.

Talbot frowned, a thought rippling over his features. "Frank? Where is Lieutenant Glass?"

Frank glanced at where a dark blue bandana was wiggling, apparently floating in thin air in the front doorway. It'd be hard to see through the screen, what with it being so bright outside.

It was time, if ever there was. "Come and get me," Frank said, diving off the chair.

The zombies' guns popped and thundered as Frank cowered behind the built-in shelves dividing living room and den. His wounds woke up with a ragged snarl. Bullets perforated his screen door, making wet sounds apparently without source. A foot back from the entry, jets of blood suddenly streaked the air, painting the entryway. What they couldn't see was where the ropes were secured through holes hastily punched into the walls. Ropes that could quite easily keep a man held fast in front of the door in a kneeling position.

"Hold your fire! Hold your fire!" Talbot was shouting, but it was already too late. The fresh gunshots stopped, the last ones echoing through the trees. "Goddamn it, Frank! What did you do?"

"Not a damn thing, Captain! Glass was perfectly safe until *you* had him shot!" Frank shouted.

He couldn't hear what transpired, not over the tinny whine left by the gunfire, but he figured Talbot would put up a fight with Bellum and get overruled. Next to him, the chair had been shot up pretty badly; wouldn't do any entertaining on it. Other bullets had pockmarked his walls and shattered both front windows. If he lived through this, the house was going to need a lot more work.

Frank reached down inside of him, grabbing the leash from the wolf. He couldn't pull it off entirely. Lose control and they'd fill him with silver and daylight, but without the strength, without the speed, he was dead meat. He stared into the wolf's eyes, trying to make it understand. Trying to get it to move past the pain and the fear of silver. Pure instinct, unleashed by rage and hunger, couldn't understand something like control.

But it could understand justice. Maybe.

A gunshot cracked the day in half, and panicked cries of "Brains!" followed it. Frank crawled over to the window, gingerly avoiding the biggest shards of broken glass now littering the floor and tops of old boxes, and peeked out up over the sill. One zombie had fallen into the dirt, clutching her leg where a hole now went right through her shinbone. Her hat rolled some distance away. A second gunshot cracked, and her head exploded. She thumped to the earth and was still.

"He's shooting! Frank is shooting!" Talbot yelled.

Frank grimaced—he couldn't manage a grin—and hauled himself back to the shelves. A few dusty figurines—pigs, horses, cows—stood by him. Those had been Susan's. She'd left them and he'd never known they were there. He stared at them dumbly, like seeing an old acquaintance he thought he'd never see again. They had nothing to say on the subject.

Another gunshot cracked, and Frank heard it slam into a fender. He silently cursed Nick. *Pick your goddamn shots.*

The front screen door slammed open. Frank pressed his back against the shelves. On his left was the archway into his living room. A few grunts of "Brains" followed, carrying the air of curses. Next, a wet thump—the corpse of an invisible man falling to the floor.

The gunsels were coming in.

He closed his eyes, pleading with the wolf. The burn of silver flared too brightly in its memory. He tried to tell the wolf that it was going to feel some more if it didn't come out right the hell now and give him what he needed.

Outside, one shot echoed through the groves, chased by another.

Come on.

He *felt* the zombies in his house. Maybe it was the whisper of clothes as they hugged a wall too close, or a shoe brushing over his filthy carpet. They were fanning out, hunting deeper into the house for him. He didn't want them out. He wanted them *dead.*

The wolf tugged on its leash, a snarl rippling over its features. The world got a tiny bit hotter, a tiny bit smaller. Frank opened his hands, his nails sharpened, curved. The crescent-shaped cuts where they had bitten into his palms weren't healing.

The crack of the M1 was the heartbeat of the skirmish. One-two, like a good boxer's combination. Other pops, from pistols, joined it. Bullets smacked into the side of the house. However many there still were, Nick seemed to have most of them pinned. He wasn't Bud, but he'd do.

A wingtip scuffed across the carpet, pausing at the entryway to the den. His left ear grabbed a sepulchral whisper of "Brains." His heart wasn't thundering. No, this was what it was supposed to be doing. The zombies out there thought they were the hunters, but they weren't. Frank had the wolf in him, and it wanted blood.

Or whatever a zombie had instead.

The footsteps were almost on top of him.

Frank stood and rounded the corner in a single movement. The zombie in the archway, a half-rotten man with a single mad eye, held his gun around waist level. "Brains!" he protested, and the gun boomed loudly.

Something behind Frank shattered.

Frank snarled, picking the zombie up bodily and slamming him face-first into the wall. With a crunch of bone and wood, the zombie went limp.

Frank's wounds howled at him, but he couldn't stop moving now. The zombies wouldn't be caught off guard again, and their shuffling and moaning was closing in. A shape loomed in the corner of his eye and a gun went off. The bullet went through the side window, and Frank thought that wasn't such a bad idea.

He dove after it. Broken glass traced burning lines over his skin. He barely cared, landing on the hot earth with a *thud*, his breath fleeing as the impact shuddered through his shoulder and his side. The wolf yelped in agony. It was all Frank could do not to curl up right there. The wounds felt horribly *loose*, as though everything that was truly him would begin to fall from them.

On the dirt between the cars and his house, four different zombies lay face down, each with a bullet hole through a leg, then a second through the head. None of them were Aida Parrish. A few shapes crouched behind the cars, and whenever they moved, the M1 gave a crack and a bullet punched into a tire, a hiss of air following the impact as the rubber sagged. Wasn't going to take anybody out, but it would hold them in place.

A gun boomed, and the dust by Frank's hand kicked him in the face. Scrambling to his hands and knees over the objections of his injuries, he bolted down the side of his house, putting his back to the wood. All around him, the orange groves stretched off into the distance. It would have been so peaceful on any other day.

"He's outside!" Bellum shouted.

"Brains!" called one of the zombies from behind the cars. Nick answered him with a shot. He had to be running low on ammo by now.

The front screen door cracked open. "Where's the other one?"

"Brains."

"Under the house!" That was Talbot, somewhere by the cars. Fitting that the captain would be taking cover.

"Is he firing silver?"

"Lead!" Talbot called back.

"Then what are you waiting for?" Bellum demanded.

Frank swore, but it came out more as a growl. The wolf told him to run around to the front, to protect his packmate. He had to remind it that the meatstick wasn't a packmate. Nick might die, but if Frank went on some damn fool charge now, they'd *both* be finished. Best way to protect the weasel was to pull everything he could to him, and trust the guts that had gotten Nick through two wars would see him through the next two minutes.

He loped around to the back. An enclosed porch led into the kitchen, where a small door opened into the crawlspace beneath the house where Nick was presently crouched. If he had a brain in his head, he'd be coming out of that door in seconds. The rear of the house had a single window, this one in Frank's bedroom. It was impossible to see through. Just reflection of the trees, and now of Frank's face: the jutting brow, the undershot jaw, the protruding canines. He was a beast. His eyes held rage, but also the cold wash of fear. The feel of that silver hadn't gone away, maybe never would. And now, it was everywhere.

Frank tried to ease the door open with the doorknob. The wolf didn't let him. Instead, he turned and wrenched it open, and the door clattered as it slammed against the wall. Frank couldn't have ducked back out if he had wanted to. The wolf was going to get what it wanted.

Frank stalked into his kitchen, running directly into a zombie that had either lingered behind or had run to the sound of the door. Frank grabbed his wrist and yanked, relishing the pop that came from the zombie's shoulder, and broke his head on the sink. Frank was moving with easy violence, but every move unzipped his body more. When he dropped the now-still corpse on the floor, his arm throbbed, and when he tried to raise it, found he couldn't. The silver was out of him, but his body was quitting piece by piece.

He poked his head through the doorway into the dining room. Aida

Parrish stood with four zombies at the mouth of the living room. "Brains," Parrish said. They raised their guns, filling the air with silver. Frank ducked back into the kitchen. Three exits here: one back outside, one leading to a short hallway, and one to the dining room itself. He knew Parrish would be sending some of her men through the hall to pen him in, and he had to assume they'd soon be closing in from behind as well. His ears rang with the gunfire and the wolf demanded he go out and show them whose den they had invaded.

"Where is he?" Bellum demanded, her normal icy calm beginning to melt. "Watch yourselves!"

Outside, the M1's beat turned to panic. Then silence. Frank supplied the rest of the information: Talbot, furred and fanged, crawling under the house for Nick. Putting him down there had been a stroke of genius. They had a weasel, might as well use him as one. He'd done all the work he could until a wolf went in to dig him out.

"Quickly now," Bellum ordered. She didn't have to. Frank's breathing was shallow. Panting, really. Anything deeper and the wound in his side stuck a branding iron into his guts. His limbs—the ones he could move, anyway—were made of lead. He wouldn't be racing around the house anymore. For better or worse, this would be his last stand.

Outside, a thundering boom echoed over the groves. Then a second one. Calls of "Brains!" followed it, and the panicked pop of gunfire.

"Find out what the hell that is," Bellum said, and some of the footsteps moved off.

Frank would have known, even if he didn't hear Jack yelling at the top of whatever he had instead of lungs. "The hell are you doing in my grove? Orange thieves!"

The zombies shot back, but they would be rapidly discovering what Frank did the first time he tried to arrest a scarecrow: bullets didn't do much more than air out their clothes. Jack's shotgun sounded again, and for the first time in his life, Frank was glad he'd moved in next to that lunatic.

"G'wan! Git! Git!" Jack yelled in his Okie accent. "I got some for everybody!"

"Give 'em hell," Frank murmured.

The footsteps from the dining room grew closer. He didn't want to die in his kitchen. A silly thing to think, maybe, but it took root in his mind. It was the principle. He'd lasted through two wars, three if you counted the one between Bellum and the Gobfather. Dying now should be against the rules. He grabbed a bag of flour from the cupboard and regarded it with an amused snort. Out of weapons, out of time, out of luck.

He waited until the zombie was right through the door, then threw the contents of the bag over his head and shoulders. "Brains!" the zombie protested, and the gun was a thunderclap. He wasn't an invisible man, but zombies still needed eyes. Frank was on him a second later, and while this zombie probably always looked faintly surprised thanks to not having much in the way of eyelids or cheeks, Frank liked to think he was more surprised than usual when he beat the gunsel's head in with his own hat.

Another gun fired, but the flour hung in the air like snow, and Frank felt the heat of the bullet passing right next to his cheek. That could have been it, had he been a little to the right. Lights out, everything ends. But it missed, and he had another moment on Earth.

He backhanded the gun and lurched to its wielder. It was Aida Parrish, regarding him with faint disappointment from her dead eye. Her pistol hit the wall and clattered away. On a good day, with Frank wearing the wolf on the outside, Parrish would have been too slow, but he was burning now, and breathing flour couldn't have been helping much. She filled her hands with her famous hatchets.

All the while, Bellum was speaking to him calmly. Why shouldn't she be calm, she left the bleeding up to everybody else. "I don't know what you were thinking, Frank. All you had to do was your job and you could have had more money than you would have ever wanted."

Parrish spun the hatchets in her hands once and went to work. They weren't silver, but they still hurt, especially when they bit into the silver wounds. Frank grabbed at her wrist with his good arm, but on the other side she had free rein, and she used it to chop Frank down like a tree. Frank snarled, and twisted the wrist he had ahold of, and was rewarded with the sound of kindling breaking over a knee. The hatchet fell. The other never stopped moving.

The remaining hatchet chopped hard into Frank's bad arm, and the blow set his teeth on edge. When Parrish pulled, the hatchet didn't come free. It was buried into the bone.

The wolf howled. The hex needed blood. Or maybe it was Frank. Aida Parrish had murdered Wyeth Wyrd. Had murdered Sylvia Screen. There were undoubtedly many more whose names Frank would never know. The ones who cared about them wouldn't ever be whole again. Wouldn't know what had happened here. But that didn't stop the need to mete out some kind of justice.

"Brains," Parrish whispered. Maybe she was pleading for her life. Maybe she was telling him to go to hell.

Bellum never begged. "You're a fool, Frank. Nothing you do here will change anything. Best you can do is buy yourself another day."

Frank hooked his claws under Aida's chin, right where the collar started. His fingers sunk into the papery flesh under her jaw. He felt the underside of her tongue writhing against his fingertips. fluttering another "Brains." Then he popped her head like a bottle of beer. Just pulled upward until her head came away from her spine. She collapsed to the floor. Frank knelt, picking up the collar, now free of its owner. Bellum's voice crackled from it, distorted and nearly broken.

"Aida, Aida what's happening?" she asked.

"She's dead."

Bellum was silent for a second, then, "So are you, Frank. You bought yourself a little time is all."

"I know," he growled, hurling it away. The collar hit the wall and the speaker broke.

"Brains," said a zombie.

Frank turned. No part of his body was free of hurt. He was like a hill during fire season, places blazing away, others red with embers, but the smoke told the tale. The zombie stood in the back doorway, a pistol leveled at Frank. A few steps away, but it might as well have been a football field. Frank had done the last he was going to do. That was it. This zombie was the end of the line.

Frank sighed, and waited for the shot.

A furry hand snaked in from behind the zombie and pulled him out into the sunlight. One startled and cut-off cry of "Brai—" later, it was quiet. Frank fell, his back against the wall. Fresh bolts of fire streaked through his body. He couldn't stand even if he'd wanted to. He was done. That much was obvious.

Captain Talbot stepped over the dead zombie's feet and into the room, sunlight leaving him for shadow. The wolf faded, but he was still a giant of a man. His suit was filthy and peppered with fresh buckshot holes, but other than that, he looked all right.

"Jesus, Frank," Talbot said. "You're a mess."

"You should talk," Frank rasped. He looked down and realized the wolf was gone out of him too. Too much pain maybe. He couldn't blame it. He'd like to go somewhere else, but it was a long way until a full moon.

"Crazy scarecrow came in with a shotgun. Had to take care of him."

Frank felt a momentary twinge for Jack. He'd be shooting angels in heaven now. It had been so long since Frank had seen the inside of a church that he wasn't sure if that was something you could get up to in heaven.

"Saved the bacon of your little friend under the house," Talbot chuckled, shaking his head. "Nifty trick. One place zombies don't ever look is down. I'd'a had him if not for that scarecrow. By the time I turned around, the shooter ran. He was no Bud Hound."

Frank wanted to give him a weary nod, but it hurt too much to move his neck. "So what's it gonna be?"

Talbot looked around. Parrish's gun lay on the floor, not too far away. He picked it up with a grunt and checked the chamber. "Sorry, Frank. If I let you go and Bellum finds out, I'm a dead man. Only way this works is if I put you down, too."

Frank chuckled. "That scared of her?"

"That *you're* not is your problem. All you had to do was track those men down."

"Cops, Captain. They were cops."

"They stopped being cops when they became criminals."

"They took money from a criminal. Same as us." Frank's breath rasped. "We can tell whatever lie we want, but it's just that. Just a way where we can sleep at night. And this ain't anything new."

"Goddamn it, Frank. Wish there was another way."

"Sure you do. You wanna pull that trigger? I don't got all day."

"Yeah," Talbot said.

Talbot brought the gun up. Frank stared at him. The gunshots cracked, but they were muffled. Frank hadn't expected to hear them at all. Talbot shuddered, his chest turning crimson. He looked down at himself in mute incomprehension, before dropping to the kitchen floor. His eyes were stuck wide open, shocked the bill finally came due.

"Frank? You in there?" came Nick's reedy voice wafting through the open door. Frank almost chuckled. Saved by a meatstick. Frank was glad he didn't have much longer, because he was *not* going to live that down.

Nick slunk into the house, stepping gingerly over the fallen zombies, the Luger in his hand. His suit was covered in dirt from under the house and sported a few new rips. That dame of his wouldn't be around to fix it. A line of red stretched down his cheek, and his face and collar were covered in blood, but otherwise he looked fine.

"Thought you said you don't kill cops."

"First time for everything," Nick said.

FORTY-EIGHT

The pain in Frank's silver wounds wasn't as searing as it had been when they'd first been made; somehow it had worsened. Now, it felt like a rot, like he'd always imagined gangrene or cancer to feel: a piece of his body turning against the rest with tooth and claw made out of his own tissue. The black came and swallowed him up periodically, and things would be subtly different around him, a shadow in a different spot, a fly where there hadn't been one, the gunpowder or blood scent waxing or waning. The worst was when the hatchet came out of his arm. His stomach lurched, and he was gone, only waking up when Nick tightened a dish towel over the wound.

"Come on, Frank. Hold on. I'll get you to Betty," Nick said, looming large, hands coming away from the towel.

Frank shoved Nick off him. "No. We're not going to Betty."

"She can help." Even Nick didn't sound like he believed it.

"I'm done for and you know it." Frank took a breath. It sounded like wind through rushes. "Go into my closet. You're gonna find a bunch of envelopes. Put them and the suitcase next to them in your car."

"Frank, I don't know if it's time for your mail."

"Do it, or I'm gonna make one more body, got it?"

He didn't see Nick go. The blackness threw a sheet over him. It felt like a blink, but when he opened his eyes, Nick was squatting in front of him. "Thought I'd lost you," the man said, relief in his voice.

"Never been better. It's done?"

"It's done."

"Get me up. You're drivin'."

Nick did as he was asked. Frank leaned on the little man. He bent, but didn't break. On the way through the house, he glanced at the bodies on his floor, only it didn't feel like *his* floor anymore. For no real reason he could name, the house didn't belong to him. The familiarity was distant, unattached. It would be the last time he saw them anyway.

They emerged into the sun. More zombies littered the ground here.

"Hey, Frank? Little help?"

Jack lay scattered over the front, dismembered, beheaded, and his straw shaken out like a busted pillow. His limbs clawed and flopped toward one another.

"Sorry, Jack."

"Say, Frank. You don't look so good."

"Yeah, I know."

"Little guy, you gettin' him to a hospital?"

Nick nodded, loading Frank into the backseat. "You gonna be okay?"

"Oh, I'll be fine." The rolling head stopped, peering up into the trees. "If the goddamn crows don't stay away, so help me, I'll...!"

Frank lay on the bloodstains from the day before. They'd be bigger before the day was out. The bag and suitcase were on the floor back there.

"Where are we going?" Nick said, turning the engine over.

"Burbank."

"Are you gonna make it to Burbank?"

"If you quit jawin'."

Nick sighed and turned around. The car raised dust from the road, eclipsing the house. And just like that, it was gone.

The ride was quickened by the way Frank kept fading in and out. When he got closer to their destination, he gave Nick more detailed directions, and soon they were on Garou's street. "That house," he said, pointing.

"Where are we?"

"Doesn't matter," Frank replied. Nick moved to help him out of the car, but Frank held out a hand. "Stay here."

He grabbed the suitcase and the bag of envelopes and made his way up the walk, moving like an old man. It was the only way he could keep the poisonous ache from biting too deeply into him. When he stood on the doorstep, he looked down at himself. He was a wreck, a pile of mortified tissue. He could try to hide it, but Lulu was a wolf the same as him. She'd smell the blood. Besides, he wasn't going to lie to her now. He could at least be the one person who didn't do that.

She answered the door at his knock, almost like she'd been expecting him. Her face fell in horror as she took him in. "Frank? What happened?"

"Not important," he said. "I just wanted to bring you some things."

"You look like you need a hospital."

He nodded. "My next stop. Just had to get this off my chest first." One lie, but he saw in her eyes that she didn't believe it at least.

She let him in. He hesitated at her couch, but she helped him into it. He could have stayed there for a long while. The black crept in at the edges of his vision; he pushed it back. She sat down opposite, watching him, glancing only once at the bags he'd brought.

"That's your husband's suitcase," Frank said. "He was planning to run after the moonlight special the other night, and was all packed up."

"So he *was* leaving me." Lulu took the information with simple equanimity. She even straightened her posture. "I wish I were surprised. Why did you bring it back?"

"I don't know," Frank said. "I didn't know where else to take it. I thought you deserved some answers."

She nodded, indicating the grocery bag. "And the other?"

"Can you promise me something first?"

"Think I'm done promising men anything for a little while."

In that statement, Frank loved her more than he had ever loved anyone. He wished he could reach for her, but he couldn't. It was too far. "Fair," he said. "I was going to ask you to promise me that you'll leave town. You'll find someplace else, and you'll go be a cop. A real one. A good one."

Her gaze went to the place on his shoulder where he had bled through his shirt. "I think I can promise you that."

"What's in that grocery bag will help out."

She nodded, then went to the suitcase, dragging it back. "Maybe this is petty, but I'm curious."

"About?"

"About what he was going to take to his new life."

"I haven't looked."

"Why not?"

"Didn't feel right."

She unzipped the suitcase, revealing clothes, neatly folded. Sitting on top was a photograph. Lulu picked it up and uttered a rueful chuckle. "Here she is. At least she's pretty. I don't know why that matters. She looks so young, though. Too young for him."

"Hard to tell under the fins and scales," Frank said.

Lulu frowned. "Fins and scales?"

"Yeah, you know sirens," Frank said.

"This isn't a siren." Lulu handed the photograph to Frank. It was of a human girl, standing on top of a hill. She couldn't have been older than twenty. Gorgeous, with her long, black hair waving in the wind. Frank knew her, too. He'd seen her once before, on the hill over Chinatown.

"Lulu, I need to go." He got up with difficulty, noting that he had left small bloodstains on the couch. "I'm sorry," he said.

She waved that away. "Frank, what's wrong?"

"I'm fine. Gonna get to the hospital."

She smiled wearily. "All right. Take care of yourself, Frank."

He limped to the door, clutching the photo. The black was hungry at the edges of his vision, but Frank wouldn't succumb. Not yet.

"Can I ask you one thing?" he said, pausing. "Why do you like me?"

Lulu thought about it. "It's the way you look at me. Like you've never seen a woman before."

"Never seen a woman like you," he told her.

And then he left. Because he knew that if he didn't move then, he never would. He staggered out to the car, climbed in. Lulu Garou stood in the doorway to her house, watching him. She lifted her hand in a wave. He returned it.

"Go," he told Nick.

"Where?"

"Chinatown."

FORTY-NINE

T he black was hungrier now, but Frank had a way to push it back. He had the answer to the question that had started this whole thing. He waited until Bunker Hill was in sight before he spoke.

"You know who she was?" Frank asked.

"Your lady friend?" Nick said. "Looked nice."

"Her name's Lulu Garou."

"Lulu Gar—" Nick coughed violently. "I knew he was married. Never knew to who."

"She told me that before he disappeared, he was obsessed with Phil Moon's autopsy. That's weird, right? After all, he was there when Moon got the bump. We all know the story he told, and I know the story *you* told."

Nick was still driving, but his knuckles had gone white on the wheel. "That's what happened."

"No. No, it ain't. See, Moon was killed with a rifle round to the heart. Not a pistol. Somehow I don't see Garou pulling a rifle on his partner, and I know for damn sure it wasn't you. You said you never killed a cop, and I believe you." Frank coughed, the rot gnawing at him. Wouldn't be too long now. "So that leaves me with one conclusion: there was somebody else on that hill that night."

Frank watched Nick's Adam's apple bob up and down. "Don't pull this thread, Frank. Please. Let me get you to Betty, and we can get you out of town."

"That's what Garou couldn't get out of his head," he said, ignoring Nick. "He had the moonlight special planned. He was going to leave this rotten burg behind, but he couldn't let it go. He even saw her." Frank looked at the photograph in his hand. A splotch of blood now had soaked into the edge. "Her."

Nick glanced over. Recognition rippled over his face. He tried to hide it, but he couldn't. Frank was close, the girl had something to do with it, but she wasn't it. "She didn't touch Garou. I can promise you that. Her name's Sofia. One of Bellum's zombies kidnapped her, wanted to change her. I pulled her out of his house."

It should have been a lie, but Frank recognized the truth there. "After you put a bullet into him."

"Add him to the list."

"There's one more question I have. You found Garou after all. You know what happened to him."

Nick hesitated, but nodded. "We can talk about this after I take you to Betty."

"Take me to the hill. Take me to where Phil Moon died."

"Lou tried to solve a mystery that shouldn't be solved. Come on, let me help you."

"Moon. I gotta see where Moon got the push."

Nick swallowed again, but obeyed, taking the car into the blasted hills between Chavez Ravine and Chinatown. He knew precisely where to go on the winding streets, like he had driven the route again and again. It had called to Nick the same way it called to Garou. Soon, he pulled to a stop.

"Frank, I'm begging you. Only thing out there is an unmarked grave."

"I got a favor to ask." Frank told Moss what he wanted, the one last little bit of good he could do in a bad life. "Can you do that?"

"Sure. I can do that."

Frank stared at him, then nodded. "For a twitchy little meatstick, you're okay. Take care of yourself, Moss."

"Yeah," Nick said. He couldn't look at Frank.

Frank stepped out of the car, still holding the picture. He wasn't sure if it was scent, or if it was Bud or Lou or something guiding him from beyond the grave. His body and mind were shutting down. The silver had done its work; it had just taken a little bit of time to really get going. No reason to keep it waiting. So he walked to it.

He walked along the same track the day he had when he spotted the girl in the snapshot. He passed houses on both sides of him, melted into modern art. He found himself in what had once been a living room, half burned away by a martian death ray. As he stared at the couch, it moved aside as though by magic. A trapdoor opened, and at the bottom was the girl. Some meatsticks had hidey-holes like this one from back in the war, retreating underground when the monsters took the world. She stared up at him in surprise, but only for a moment before she turned and fled out of sight, down the earthen corridor.

Frank followed, brushing past feathers and holy symbols hanging from the ceiling like ornaments. The tunnel terminated in a thick wooden door, now standing open. Frank pushed his way in. He was having a hard time seeing. The black was swallowing him up, like he was at the bottom of a well, and the top was closing.

He barely saw the room beyond. Just the girl, radiant like an angel. Breathing hard, frightened. She was looking at something behind him, pleading. Frank turned.

A woman stood there. She had golden skin, as beautiful as the other. He knew her: her picture had hung on Friday's wall, and he had never seen a woman so graceful. She'd been on the Gobfather's arm, one of his disappeared damsels. He wanted to say something, but their beauty robbed him of speech, or maybe it was the silver's venom. Two angels, underground, ready to take him away. She raised a pistol, and Frank knew exactly what had happened to Garou. He smiled to himself. It was almost funny. Garou thought Moss plugged Moon, but the story didn't fit. He'd come up here to solve it himself, and he did.

Frank never heard the shot.

EPILOGUE

Pearl Friday left the roller rink, another night of sweat and wheels in the rearview. Other monsters fanned out around her, going to their various methods of conveyance. Her normal, everyday car was almost quaint next to the flivvers and tripods and whatnot that now filled the parking lot. Her car waited at the north end of the lot, near a stand of trees. She spotted the shape loitering in the darkness beneath those trees quicker than another monster could. One of the benefits of being a crawling eye.

The silhouette was short and lean, and she caught a pair of bulges—so slight as to be almost unnoticeable—beneath the arms. He looked like a gangster, but heat radiated off him like an aura in the night. He was human. Out. At night.

"Can I help you?" she asked, projecting her voice next to the man.

He jumped. Then, after a moment, stepped into the light of one of the bulbs illuminating the area outside the rink. He wasn't an impressive sight. Maybe a shade over five and a half feet, and made her think of a weasel. He wore a mustache and a thick five o'clock shadow, and his perpetually darting eyes grabbed up all the whereabouts of the monsters in that parking lot. One thing was strange, though, beyond the idea of a human out at night—this one was in a new suit, and one tailored perfectly to his frame. Made him look even more like a gangster.

"Pearl Friday?" he asked.

"Could be. Who's asking?"

"Frank Wolfman sent me."

Friday had to give the man a second look. Frank had disappeared a few weeks ago, around the same time his captain and a handful of others were killed in the line of duty. The same thing that happened to anyone who looked too closely at the levers of power. The funerals had been front page news, and were already being forgotten.

"What did he send you for?"

The man held out a piece of paper. "He had me find somebody for you. Call that number. Quite a story on the other end."

She looked at the paper, and if her eye could widen, it would have. "What did he...?"

"Up to you."

"Nice suit," she said.

"I came into a little money recently."

"Is there a number where I can reach you? If I need to ask some questions?"

"You'll never see me again." The man touched the brim of his hat, and walked back into the dark. "Goodnight."

"Thank you!" Friday called after him. Then she looked at the paper. A phone number, and the name above it: Sylvester Bullet.

She supposed she had a lot of writing to do.

THE END

ACKNOWLEDGMENTS

Frank first appeared as the main character of a short story called "Twice-Dead Man" originally appearing in *Undead Worlds 3: A Post-Apocalyptic Zombie Anthology*. While I never thought of the City of Devils series as post-apocalyptic, Valerie Lioudis, the mastermind of the Reanimated Writers group assured me it is. I've since come around to her way of thinking and wanted to thank her for first requesting, and then publishing Frank's first foray into the world. This book would not exist without her faith in me.

I also need to thank Athena Andreadis of Candlemark & Gleam. She continues to believe in this series and gives me the kind of leeway that any author would kill for. C&G remains the gold standard of small presses under her able leadership.

No book is easy, and this one gave me more trouble than most. Maybe because I wrote it in early/mid-2020 when I wasn't in the most optimistic of places. Kate Sullivan and Julie Hutchings both lent me their editorial skills, helping me craft what ended up being a strong, if extremely dark, entry in my flagship series. Kate and Julie are two of the finest editors in the business and I am lucky to be able to work with them.

Lastly, I want to thank you, the reader. Whether you're picking this up on a lark or you've been with me since the beginning, I am eternally grateful. I couldn't do this without you.

About the Author

Much like film noir, Justin Robinson was born and raised in Los Angeles. He splits his time between writing and taking care of a small human. Degrees in Anthropology and History prepared him for unemployment, but an obsession with horror fiction and a laundry list of phobias provided a more attractive option. He is the author of more than 15 novels in a variety of genres including noir, humor, fantasy, science fiction, and horror. Most of them are pretty good.

Follow the Author Online

Website: https://www.weirdnoirmaster.com
Bluesky, Twitter, Instagram, Patreon: weirdnoirmaster
Facebook: facebook.com/weirdnoirmaster

The ADVENTURE
CONTINUES ONLINE!

Visit the Candlemark & Gleam website to

Find out about new releases

Read free sample chapters

Catch up on the latest news
and author events

Buy books! All purchases on the
Candlemark & Gleam site are DRM-free
and paperbacks come with a free digital version!

Meet flying monkey-creatures
from beyond the stars!*

www.candlemarkandgleam.com

*Space monkeys may not be available in your area. Some restrictions may apply.
This offer is only available for a limited time and is in fact a complete lie.

Milton Keynes UK
Ingram Content Group UK Ltd.
UKHW031045120324
439302UK00006B/581